Zor  .

Mark Tufo

Discover other titles by Mark Tufo

Visit us at marktufo.com

and http://zombiefallout.blogspot.com/ home of future webisodes in addition find me on FACEBOOK

Editing by:

Monique Happy

Editorial Services

mohappy@att.net

Cover Art:

Cover Art by Shaed Studios, shaedstudios.com

Zombie Fallout 3: The End...
Dedication

My wife Tracy, my love, the rock around which my maelstrom revolves, I thank you, I love you and I appreciate you more than I can sometimes tell you. May we always make each other laugh.
My Dad whose unflagging love and belief in my 'What me worry?' attitude is a constant source of inspiration for me.
My Mom who passed in April of 2010, you will always be remembered.
My brother Ron who has devoted countless hours listening to my ideas and cleaning up my words that sometimes seem to be more thrown on the page rather than typed.
My editor Mo Happy, you dusted off this book and brought a high polish to it and in so doing have made a new friend and business partner.
My illustrator Zeilo Vogta, your work is amazing and I will always appreciate you picking up a dropped ball and running with it.
To all on FB who have friended me. Your messages, your reviews, your kind words, I thank each and every one of you. There were some of you that came early and gave me a lift when I was feeling down. There were some of you that have helped me with particular questions or problems I may have had. One of you was the best boss I could have ever asked for, some of you have to work with me now and the even luckier ones are related to me (Sarcasm). But each and every one of you has at some point taken the time out of your busy days to reach out to me and say 'Hi' or 'Love the book' or 'What were you thinking?', to all of you, I would like to express my deepest gratitude.

PROLOGUE 1 - 

War torn Europe in the early 1500's was not a safe place to wander even during high noon. Tomas could not fathom why he was skulking in the shadows on this cold November night. Finding his sister as she passed from cruelty to cruelty had been an all-consuming endeavor. It had been five long years since they had sat together and shared a meal in their father's small one room hut. They had clung to each other like only siblings could in a world so violent.

Tomas had wept for weeks when his father had sold his sister for some corn meal to help them get through the winter. For a year longer Tomas had suffered under his father's severe tutelage in an attempt to beat out the 'insanity' in his own son. Tomas had finally had enough and ran away. Barely into his teens with no apprenticeship and no master, he narrowly scraped an existence. The meager gains he made were used for any information he could garner to find his sister.

Many times he had come close, only to have her whisked away to some distant town. He would doggedly follow but always a moment too late. Finally his break had come. He could see her at the end of the alleyway. He shook not only from the intense cold that blistered through his ragged garments but also for the joy of reuniting with his beloved sister. The dark cloaked figure she was with held Tomas at bay as he sent waves of malice radiating away. Tomas didn't dare move from his concealment behind some crates. Fear jogged through his spine. The fluid that leaked down his leg was most likely the only thing that kept him from freezing where he crouched.

Tomas noticed the man look exactly where he hid, but that was impossible nobody could see him in this darkness. Tomas watched as The Stranger 'kissed' his sister's neck. A flash of anger welled up in him. 'How dare someone do that without a marriage first!' He stood up just in time to see his sister swoon and fall. The Stranger looked back once at Tomas, laughed a small cruel laugh and then seemingly vanished into a darker shadow. All fear vanished with the removal of The Stranger. Tomas ran the length of the alleyway dropping to his knees to cradle his sister's head.

Her eye's fluttered open as he cascaded her face with his tears. "Tomas? Is that really you Tomas?"

"It's me Lizzie, it's me!" He cried. "We're finally together again! How I've missed you! Now we can be together again forever!"

"Tomas." Lizzie said sadly, stroking his face gently. "It's too late for me."

"What are you talking about Lizzie? I'm here you're here, we're together." He wept for joy, but something evil was coming he could feel it. Tomas had always had a highly developed sense of apathy. It had proved an invaluable tool while he lived on the fringes of a distraught society. "What is the matter Lizzie? You are burning up." The heat emanating from her prone form was melting the snow around her.

"You should go Tomas." She said closing her eyes.

"I can't leave you Lizzie. We're all we have, you and me. You told me you would always look out for me. You were the only one that told me I didn't have witches living in my head." It was common in early Europe to convict the mentally challenged of witchcraft. "I love you Lizzie." Even as he said it, he could tell his sister was slipping away.

"I love you too Tomas. And that is why you should go."

"Why won't you open your eyes Lizzie? Please, please look at me."

Tears pushed through her closed lids. "Please Tomas don't look at me this way. I'm not the sister you used to know. Unspeakable things have been done to me and I found a way to right those wrongs and I took it. I will exact my revenge."

"That's not how my Lizzie talks." Tomas said wiping his blurring eyes.

"GO!" She said pushing him away. Her eyes seemed to produce their own light as she looked at him menacingly.

"I will not!" He screamed, even though his inner thoughts revolved around one word 'RUN'.

Lizzie sat up. Factions warred within her. The looks she sent him fluctuated between love, sadness and predatory awareness. Tomas kept backing up even as he shook his head in denial of what was happening right in front of him.

With an ungodly speed Lizzie wrapped her hand around Tomas' neck. He found himself suspended 6 inches off the ground.

"Lizzie, please." He begged.

Lizzie pulled him in close and punched two neat holes into his exposed collar. Tomas screamed in pain.

"Lizzie please, I love you!" his tears splashing down on her upturned face.

Some last remnant of Lizzie rose to the surface. She pulled her extended canines out of his neck. "GO!" She screamed again. "I won't be able to stop next time." She looked defeated, with her head bowed. Tomas dropped to the ground as she released her grip.

He scurried away scarcely believing the turn of events. "I love you Lizzie, I will follow you until I find a way to fix whatever has happened here tonight."

PROLOGUE 2 - 

Eliza's biting of her brother Tomas' neck had profound effects on his physiology. It was not enough to 'turn' him into the monster she was to become but it nearly stopped his pineal gland in its tracks. Tomas would age but at a rate the giant sequoias in Northern California would envy. The link that Tomas shared with his family, not always willingly, intensified.

Over the years Tomas repeatedly sought ways to communicate with his sister, only to have every avenue closed to him. Eliza was stronger than him and would not allow the contact. But still he was aware of her presence and would follow her around the world hoping that one day she would once again sit with him and tell him bedtime stories. As for his clairvoyance? Who knows, maybe he does have 'witches in his head.'

PROLOGUE 3 - 

I swear to God I had better be dead if this, my third journal turns up and I'm nowhere to be found. My first journal sits in my office at whatever remains of my homestead in Denver Colorado. I had no time to save that book as zombies flooded through my master bedroom wall. As it was I lost Bear, the Rottweiler who had saved my life. My second journal, I was to learn, was burned with all the clothes that I had been wearing when that asshole Durgan shot me with a crossbow. Seems I had bled like a stuck pig and they did not want to risk infection from the clothing so they peeled me out of it and tossed it into an incinerator. Most likely the journal would have been unreadable coated in that amount of congealed leakage anyway, but maybe I would have been able to salvage some of it. So my dear fellow survivor IF you find this journal, you will notice I am dead because this thing will be stapled to my forehead and I'm not moving!

CHAPTER ONE - 

"Can you see anything?" Tracy said nervously as she looked out over the expanse of the dead.

Travis stood on top of the truck roof, looking over the same vista as his mother. His grandmother's house stood almost a half-mile away. A citadel under siege, thousands of zombies enshrouded the house. His dad, BT and Jen had made a plan to lure their enemy in and destroy as many as possible, hopefully taking with them their presumed leader Eliza. Travis stood stock-still but rage and anxiety coursed through his body. His father, Michael Talbot, had not figured on this many of the living dead assembling. He was going to need all the help he could get to make it away from that house.

All he could do was stay here with his mother Tracy, his sister Nicole, his brother (who he was convinced was an agent of the enemy) Justin, Henry the wonder bulldog and Tommy, who Travis had no classification system for. Tommy played the part of a smiling simpleton, but that was becoming a cover that was increasingly difficult for him to pull off.

"Can you see anything yet?" Tracy asked for the fifth time.

"I can see that they're going to need help." Travis answered back.

Tracy looked up the truck at her son who at 16 was rapidly and forcibly becoming a man. Tracy had known the moment Mike had made this shitty plan what his true intentions were. He had never been a good card player, his emotions always bled through. When he had held her tight and kissed her tenderly as the rest of the family went to the storm shelter out in the south fields, she'd known his plan was a one-way trip. She should have left an hour ago, like

Mike had told her to, but she'd known that crap about meeting down the road was just that, 'bullshit'. Could she sit here not helping and on top of that watch her beloved die? She felt there had to be something she could do, she saw it in Travis' eyes. He was like a snapping pit bull on a thin leash. He would rush into the fray in seconds if she did anything more than nod at him. His sense of duty to the rest of the family though was what was keeping him in check. Mike fearing that Travis would attempt this rescue had made it abundantly clear that if anything were to happen to him that it fell on Travis' shoulders to keep the family safe. As much as it pained Travis, he would not join the fight.

"The house is on fire." Travis said flatly.

The end game was in play. Tracy knew her window of opportunity to escape was rapidly closing. "Help me up." she told Travis as she climbed into the bed of the truck and onto the roof.

Hundreds of zombies had entered that house and still the brunt of them remained outside. With the house burning, Mike's chance at a viable defense no matter how feeble, was over. There was nowhere for Mike, BT and Jen to go. Tracy wept. The look of pain and anguish on Travis' stoic face ripped her heart. Nicole was in the backseat of the truck sobbing quietly, she couldn't watch. Justin slept the sleep of the drugged. Henry stood guard over his dreams. Tommy had witnessed the assemblage of the abomination and then left to sit in the minivan by himself. Even through the closed windows they could hear him periodically wail to the heavens.

"Mom I can help." Travis said through clenched teeth.

She almost relented. She'd drive. He'd shoot. They could get there. If they didn't? Could she watch her son die? "No, we're leaving, we'll go to the place your dad said we'd meet and we'll wait for an hour like he said."

Travis' eyes blazed. She could see the hurt a thin level below the surface. "What happens after an hour?" He asked her straightly.

"We go on." Tracy said resignedly.

Tracy and Travis turned as they heard the door to the minivan open and slide shut. Tommy's face was puffed up from his excessive crying. "They're out of the house now." He said in a monotone voice.

"How...how could you possibly know?" Tracy asked. "You can't see them from there."

Tracy was still looking at Tommy. Travis knew better than to question his abilities and had swung his vision back to the farm house trying to verify the new information. "I see them! He shouted.

So did Tracy, she didn't know how, they appeared as clearly as if they were being viewed through a good pair of binoculars. Three lost souls in a miasma of death. The house burned so brightly it was difficult to look in its direction. She saw the futility of hope. There was no escape. She had crossed the line. She had stayed long enough to witness Mike's death. A large piece of her would go with him.

"Mom, let me go?" Travis nearly begged.

"For what Travis? So I can watch you die too!" She snapped.

Travis turned away. His gaze fell upon Tommy who was looking off to the east and away from the house. Travis followed his line of sight. On the fringes of his vision he thought he saw something. A trail of whipped up snow made him realize he was not witnessing an illusion. Hope crept dangerously close, but he forced it down, for all he knew this was zombie reinforcements, although he couldn't see the point. They wouldn't even be able to get into the fight before it was over.

The air ripped open as .50 caliber chain gunfire erupted. Zombies fell in sheets. Tracy turned to the din. Three vehicles raced into the coalescent horde of zombies, two military vehicles, one a fortified troop transport and the other a humvee with a white Ford pick-up in between.

"Brendon?" Tracy asked.

Tommy wept silently and nodded.

Three feet of fire spewed from the turret mounted guns on each military vehicle. Zombies couldn't die fast enough as bodies were shredded, decapitated, de-limbed, disemboweled and de-lifed. The carnage was on a scale none of them had seen, even at Little Turtle's final stand, and yet it wouldn't be enough. The zombies didn't turn to face this new threat. They still pressed forward and toward the doomed trio. The staccato burst of Mike's AR had been replaced with the much tamer 9mm, she knew he was running low on ammo. Hope was on the verge of breaking through but was being held back actively by reality.

"Come on Mike, don't die on me now!" Tracy screamed, barely able to hear herself over the ear splitting bursts of large caliber rounds.

"Come on Brendon!" Travis shouted.

Nicole came out of the truck. "Brendon? Did you say Brendon?"

Travis pointed, but his sister at all of 4' 11", who would have a hard time making height at an amusement park to ride the teacups, could not see anything. He extended a hand down and lifted her clean up.

"Oh my God." Nicole whispered.

The hummers were cutting swaths through the zombies. The carnage was beyond comprehension. The small caravan picked up speed as it approached the stranded castaways. The dire straits the trio was, in spurring the usurpers on.

"Are they going to make it mom?" Nicole asked.

Tracy wasn't sure if she meant Mike, BT and Jen or Brendon and the Marines or just plain all of them. The flood of relief Tracy felt as Mike hopped into the back of Brendon's truck nearly made her swoon with relief. Travis gripped her shoulder to keep her from pitching head first off their perch.

"Yeah!" Travis screamed a battle cry.

The caravan was pulling away from the destroyed

house with its precious cargo.

"Someone fell out of the truck!" Nicole screamed.

The flood of relief turned into a dirge of dread for the watchers.

"What's going on? Have they pulled him in yet?" Tracy asked, trying to focus her eyes through the smoke and blood screen.

Nicole turned away from the scene, tortured and twisted by the drama unfolding before her.

"That's Jen." Travis said gravely.

"What is going on?" Tracy cried.

Travis jumped from the truck roof, running full speed towards the battle.

"Travis!" Tracy screamed. She shuddered at his response.

"Dad's been shot!!" He said without turning or slowing down.

"Nicole! Tommy! Get in the truck! Fred, Esther get out of here!" Tracy bellowed as she alit from the truck roof.

Fred didn't hesitate. He had his own family to take care of. Tracy swore though if she lost her family because of his, she would find him and even the score. Tracy had covered half the distance to the melee in the truck before she caught up with Travis.

"Get in!" She yelled into his ear.

He didn't break stride. "I'm going to help!"

"So are we! Get in!"

He glanced over at her making sure this wasn't a ruse, her expression was stone cold. He jumped into the bed of the truck. The fifty cals from this close were making the Ford shake. Tracy's teeth hurt from the percussions. Travis' rifle started to explode rounds. Zombies were caught in a crossfire. If she hadn't hated them so much, Tracy thought, she might actually feel sorry for them.

"Fuck that." She fishtailed the truck into couple of zombies on the fringe of the excitement. Spines shattered as the heavy truck crushed over one of the unlucky ones heads.

She was running parallel to the military convoy, which was fighting desperately to get away from the entanglement. Tracy could barely control her gorge as the trucks began to inch closer and closer.

The bottom of Brendon's truck bed looked like a swimming pool of blood, BT was cradling her husband, the tears streaming down his face matched the crimson flowing freely from Mike's chest.

"Oh my God!" Tracy wailed. Her truck was skimming into the outer ranks of zombies in a desperate bid to be with her husband at the end. For that's what it was, nobody could lose that much blood and survive.

Tracy was alongside Brendon's truck trying desperately to look over Nicole and into the bed of the truck.

Nicole was screaming. She couldn't hear anything over the hell fire from the military guns. A zombie crashed over the hood of the truck, Tracy instinctively hit the brakes as the zombie slid back down. The trailing hummer caught up, the corporal was bellowing at her. She couldn't hear him but his gestures were universal and you didn't have to be a lip reader to understand 'GO, GO GO!'

She wanted to stop she wanted to hold her husband one more time. BT's face was towards the sky, he was yelling something to the heavens.

"NO!!!" Tracy screamed. Tommy had thrown up. A caustic aroma mix of vomit and strawberry Pop-Tart.

"What the fuck is going on!" Nicole screamed. "Pull up mom, pull up!"

Tracy gunned the engine. BT had put Mike's lifeless body down and was reaching through the rear glass. Brendon was slumped over the steering wheel, his foot lodged on the gas pedal. BT had moved his body to the side so that he could steer the truck. The truck had rammed into the rear of the lead truck, the gunner swung around to realize the new threat.

He thumped the roof of the transport letting the driver know about the new development, and then resumed his place as judge, jury and extreme executioner. BT had regained relative control of Brendon's truck. The lead hummer had slowed and allowed itself to be used as a braking mechanism. Speeders were keeping pace as the four trucks raced alongside the mob of dead. The lead driver veered away to make distance.

Tracy could feel the lost seconds as they slid away, like so much sand in an hourglass. Over untended fields the trucks careened as the hounds of hell were chomping at their heels. Mike's hollow body bounced around, more than once he rose as high as the sidewalls and threatened to be tossed into the North Dakota wilderness. Ten minutes later the lead hummer had finally come to a stop. Tracy had nearly dropped the transmission when she shoved the gearbox into park.

His body was so cold as she hopped into the back of the truck and felt for a pulse. There wasn't one. A small blue frozen smile was splashed across his lips. Nicole was torn between her father and her fiancée. One of the Marines had come from the first hummer carrying a medical bag. He stopped briefly to check Brendon, and then slowly shook his head. Nicole fell to her knees. Her keening so high that it was barely audible. BT screamed in rage.

He came over to Mike, Tracy wanted to run away, she couldn't handle that all knowing and death certifying shake of his head. The corpsman was in no apparent rush when he stepped up into the truck. Nobody could be the color of blue that Mike was and be alive.

Tracy pulled Mike away from the corpsman. "NO! You will not tell me he is dead!" Tracy screamed.

"Ma'am let me see if I can help him." The corpsman told her, though even he didn't sound believable to himself.

Tracy relented. The corpsman spent considerably more time than he should have to pronounce someone dead. "Corporal Beckett! Bring the morphine and a blanket! Quickly!" The corpsman shouted.

"He's alive?" Tracy whispered.

"What's going on?" BT asked through the veil of tears.

Tracy hushed him, fearful that his words might break the tenuous grip on life that Mike clung to.

The corpsman had ripped Mike's shirt open. Tracy had momentarily become fearful that Mike would die from the cold although that seemed the least of his problems as she looked at the bolt from the crossbow that had punched a hole damn near straight through. The force of the impact had created a melon sized black and blue mark that radiated broken blood vessels in all directions. She wouldn't swear it on a bible but she thought she saw the arrow rise a fraction of an inch, though she couldn't tell if it was from Mike breathing or the buffeting wind.

The wound had stopped bleeding, congealed blood of the dead or just plain empty neither symptom a good sign. "Corporal NOW! If this man dies, you're next!"

"Sir, yes sir." The corporal shouted from beside the truck he cautiously handed over all the supplies asked for.

"He's alive?" Tracy asked again, still not sure why the corpsman was taking the time to administer pain killer to a corpse.

The truck rocked slightly as BT extracted himself from the scene. BT pulled Brendon out from the truck and laid him gently onto the ground. BT knelt beside Brendon. "Thank you." He said softly as he covered the body up with one of the blankets that the corporal had brought over. BT grabbed Nicole they sat together like that for long minutes. Long after, Mike's IV-laced body was placed onto a stretcher and placed in the lead hummer, even after Brendon's still form was taken and placed in the second hummer, blood dripped in a puddle from the tailgate of Brendon's truck. Tracy was in shock as another Marine placed her into the rear of the hummer with her husband.

"Miss." One of the Marines asked Nicole. "Do you want to ride in the hummer?"

Nicole looked up from the ground, cradled in BT's

arms. She let the Marine take her hand and help her into the military truck.

"Speeders!" Travis yelled.

A wall of zombies was running full tilt across the fields. "Mount up!" A sergeant who had been smoking a cigar said from the driver's side of the lead hummer. "Private how much ammo you got?" The sergeant asked the gunner on the second humvee.

"Couple hundred rounds max." The private shouted back.

"Richmond, you?" The sergeant asked the gunner on his own truck.

"Seven, Sarge." Richmond answered back.

"Seven hundred?" The sergeant asked for clarification.

"Seven." Richmond said. "Just seven." He added for clarification.

"Alright let's get the fuck outta here." The sergeant bellowed. "Big man, you want a ride or do you want to drive that truck?"

BT didn't want to do shit except sit on his ass and wait for the end of the earth, which according to the zombies was roughly four minutes away. BT got up and without answering got behind the wheel of the Ford.

"Guess that answers that." The sergeant said.

Travis and Tommy hopped into the Ford with BT. Henry stayed with Mike and Tracy, Justin was still under the influence of some heavy sedatives and had missed everything. For seemingly endless hours the trucks traveled across a ghost land. Nobody spoke in the Ford as each person was lost in their own thoughts, trying with great difficulty to reconcile the events that had just happened.

"Is this worth it?" Travis asked of BT.

BT looked over, his eyes burning. "Well you are your father's son." And he turned back to the road.

Long minutes passed, the road blurred past. "That didn't really answer my question BT."

"No, it sure didn't. Before today I would have given you a different answer."

"And now?" Travis prodded.

"Now...now I'm not so sure. I just watched two people I care for die and a third who is nowhere near out of the woods. I'm no philosopher, but I am a religious man. I know that eventually every man has to meet his maker in his own way. It's what you do while you're alive that defines how that meeting is gonna go. I cannot imagine that there is a God who wishes for us to merely survive, we would be no better than sheep. We are left behind for a reason, Travis. It is up to us and others like us to right this great wrong. Some will fall along the way. It is the price that must be paid, sacrifice of the ultimate kind. Without the blood of the righteous, the wicked cannot be smote."

"You're not going to go all Reverend Sharpeton on me? Are you?"

BT nearly lost control of the truck his laughs shaking him to the core. "Holy shit if it was ever in doubt whose son you were, you slammed that door shut."

CHAPTER TWO - 

"Yes, they got away."

"How is that possible, you pathetic human?"

Durgan fell to his knees as it felt as if someone had laid his scalp open and was dragging razor blades across his exposed brain. The pain was terrifyingly blinding. He could not even begin to comprehend how to answer his master. Blood began to flow freely from his nose from whatever form of psychic torture was being administered.

"Please." He said weakly. He buried his head into the snow hoping that would diminish the shards of glass rattling around in his brain bucket. It didn't.

Eliza wanted to crush his feeble brain. It would have been no harder than smashing an egg. She hated the fact that she had to rely on a human but she was not yet strong enough to pursue Talbot and The Other. She released her death grip on Durgan and he gasped in great gulps of cold refreshing air.

"That is the last time you will fail me." She said directly into his mind.

Durgan could tell that Eliza had turned her attention away from him. The feeling was both distressingly lonely and agonizingly wonderful. He stood up, wincing, his missing leg still pained him as he gripped the plastic coated prosthetic. His other leg itched uncomfortably from whatever Eliza had done to him to make him heal so rapidly. She had given him power, not enough, but it helped him to walk months ahead of what the most optimistic orthopedic surgeon would have set for a timetable. Blood flowed rapidly from his nose. He absently brushed it away with his cuff. The fat droplets fell to the snow covered ground and were quickly descended upon by the zombies. Durgan was fearful that with so many chomping teeth close by he would be inadvertently bitten. "Vermin, I hate being around these things, just one more reason I'm going to enjoy killing you and your entire family, Talbot!" The zombies eyed Durgan greedily. More than one looked like they were a moment away from taking a bite of his flesh. Only Eliza was keeping them at bay and she was hundreds of miles away. Durgan tried his best to not break out into a run as he pushed past the zombies and stood as close to the burning house as he could to regain some heat. The zombies followed him closely, trying desperately to break through whatever was gripping them and tear the warm meat carrier to bloody, ragged, tasty shreds.

CHAPTER THREE - 

"Clear!" The medic shouted as he applied the defibrillator paddles to Mike for the fifth time. Mike's lifeless form arched 6 inches off the stretcher. The monitor still blazed a bright flat line, the monotonous wail of its siren more piercing than the worst alarm clock.

Tracy and Nicole embraced each other as they watched. "What are you doing?" Tracy asked the medic as he turned the monitor and the paddles off.

"Ma'am it's been seven minutes." He replied as if that explained everything, and ultimately it did.

"You will not give up on me!" Tracy screamed.

The medic didn't know if she was talking to him or her husband. He figured it out though when she slapped him.

"Ma'am!" The medic said. "He's dead!" He yelled hoping the volume would solidify his answer.

"He's fucking dead, when I say he's fucking dead!" She yelled. "Hit him again."

The medic thought she was probably insane, but the best way to prove someone's insanity is to show her the light, so to speak. Against his better judgment he sparked the paddles back up. 'Great' He thought to himself. 'We get to ride the rest of the way back to camp with the smell of burnt flesh, that oughta make the MRE's go down better.

"Clear." The medic said without any sense of urgency.

Mike's body arched up again and struck back down with a solid thud.

"You see? He's dead." The medic said trying to put as much sympathy into his words as he could, but after seeing so much death it was becoming a more difficult emotion to muster.

"Hit him again." Tracy growled through gritted teeth.

The medic couldn't stop himself. "He's going to start to burn."

"So help me you little FUCK, you hit him again now or I'll take those paddles to your balls!"

The sergeant turned from his driving. "You'd better get to it Murphy, I think she'd do just that." He said half laughing.

Murphy was nearly in shock as he said the word "Clear," for the seventh time.

"Seven times a charm." The sergeant said without looking back.

Mike's body didn't so much arch as it did spasm, as if the hand of God himself was thrusting his life back into his disabled and broken body. The medic had never taken his eyes off of Tracy as he had administered the charge, fearful she would grab the paddles and do just as she had threatened. "He's dead." Murphy the medic said with a hint of fear.

"Mike?" Tracy asked as she pushed past Murphy. "Mike?"

The medic looked down to the fluttering eyes of a cadaver. "No fucking way." He said as he turned the monitor back on, fearful that they had brought a zombie into their midst.

The sergeant had an inkling of what might be going on. "Get the fuck away from him!" He shouted as he pulled his 1911 out of his holster. The transport had pitched to the side as the sergeant slammed on the brakes. The sergeant's gun was pressed to Mike's head the trigger half depressed just as the monitor sounded to life with the telltale beating of a human heart. "Well I'll be a monkey's uncle." The sergeant said as he holstered his weapon and got the hummer moving again, no more out of sorts than if he had found some extra change in his pockets.

"He can't be alive." The medic said clearly confused.

"You'd be amazed." Tracy said as she held Mike's head.

"I already am." Murphy said in all honesty.

Murphy muted the volume on the monitor when it appeared that his patient was in no imminent threat of dying again, at least not on his watch. He could however not stop watching the green line as it made its way across the screen, not out of caution but out of awe. "He was dead for seven minutes." He mumbled to himself. "He shouldn't have enough brain function left to beat his heart. Do you mind?" Murphy asked Tracy, as he pulled a penlight out of his pocket.''

Tracy was momentarily fearful of what he might discover and was inclined to say no, but nodded in ascension instead. Murphy reached over and gently pulled an eyelid back, shining the light into first one then the other eye. Both pupils reacted.

"I don't understand." Murphy said to no one.

"What's going on?" The sergeant asked as he pulled a cigar out of his breast pocket. "Anyone mind?" He asked as he showed the cigar to everyone. He bit the end off and lit it before anyone had a chance to respond.

"This motherf…should be dead." Murphy said. "Or at least brain dead. But his heart is beating strong and his pupils are dilating normally. He's lost somewhere in the neighborhood of half his blood. He was clinically dead for damn near ten minutes and for all intents and purposes this guy could be asleep. Everything I've ever learned tells me that this guy should be dead."

"I guess you need to learn some more." The sergeant said as he took a big puff from his cigar. "He must have a lot worth living for," the sergeant said as he looked over to Nicole and then Tracy. The medic shook his head again and not for the last time either.

CHAPTER FOUR -

The hummer rocketed towards its destination. Nicole had long since fallen asleep, her mind's way of coping with her immense grief. Tracy cradled Mike's head. His eyes rapidly moving below the closed eyelids threatened to open on more than one occasion but never did. The arrow bolt stood like a blunted tree branch out of Mike. She had wanted to just rip the vile invader from his body but she knew the futility of that endeavor.

"We have a great surgeon at the base." Murphy told Tracy as he saw her looking at the arrow. "But I bet if we gave Mike another day or two he'd just take it out on his own."

Tracy half laughed half cried at his words. "Sorry about the whole balls thing." She said.

"No, no, you were right." Murphy said.

"How much further?" She asked Murphy.

Sergeant Stanton answered for him. "Another hour at our current speed."

Fifty caliber rounds broke the silence of rubber meeting roadway.

"Bandits," came over scratchily through the MUCS radio receiver. "Seven, no eight cars and trucks bearing down on us. Multiple gun fire, we're taking hits back here."

"Shit they must be desperate if they're attacking military." Sergeant Stanton said as he ground his cigar into the ashtray. "Base Custer, Base Custer, this is Rover seven, can you read?"

"Custer huh." Tracy said. "Couldn't think of anything better?"

"Seemed appropriate at the time." The sergeant said. "And now it just stuck."

"Well I hope for all of our sakes it's not really the last

stand." Tracy finished.

"Rover seven, this is Base Custer, haven't heard from you in a while, what is your status?" Came the even scratchier, static laced voice.

"Had a bit of a detour." The sergeant said summing up the battle of Carol's homestead. "We could use a little assistance Base, we're on route 80 mile marker 94, just outside of town and we've acquired some company. We've got eight militant vehicles chasing us."

"Roger that, Eagle two is in flight, eta 12 minutes."

"Roger that." The sergeant said calmly.

"Twelve minutes?" Murphy said incredulously "We'll never be able to out run them for that long."

Tracy was looking questioningly back and forth at the conversation. "Murphy answered her unasked question. " A hummer could climb a wall if it had too, but as far as speed goes, a not so well trained athlete on a ten speed could go faster than we could."

"Wonderful." Tracy said sarcastically.

"They won't get too close with the fifties going." Sergeant Stanton said.

"How many rounds we have again?" Tracy asked.

"Good point." The sergeant retorted, pushing the gas pedal through the floorboard. The transport surged from fifty-five miles an hour to nearly fifty-eight.

"Sarge, they're peppering the shit out of us back here!" A Marine's voice came over the radio.

"No warning shots, Corporal." The sergeant yelled into the handset to be heard. "Light 'em up, help is on the way."

"Private, light 'em up!" The corporal yelled to his gunner, finger still depressing the send signal, the lead hummer was able to listen in stereo as the blasts came over the airwaves. Mutilated metal screamed in protest as high velocity rounds crucified the lead attackers sheet metal covered car. The dull explosion of the car could barely compete with the expenditure of the machine gun.

"They're pulling back Sarge!" The corporal said excitedly.

"Take out another one before they get courageous." The sergeant said.

The corporal relayed the message. Two rounds later an eerie quiet descended over the travelers.

"Any chance that's a jam?" The sergeant asked the corporal.

"Fuck." Came the corporal's flustered response. Seems we're out of ammo and those crazy sons-of-bitches know it."

The pops and bangs of multiple small arms fire dominated. "Shit they got a tire Sarge!" The corporal shouted.

"You're fine corporal, the 'run flats' run rough but it's drivable."

"Run flats?" Tracy mouthed the question to Murphy.

"Yeah all military vehicles have them, it's a hard rubber insert within the tire. So if the tire is shot out the truck can still move. Kind of a necessity."

"Apparently." Tracy said with concern.

"Eagle two, eagle two this is Rover Seven, can I get an updated eta we seem to be in a little bit of trouble, over." The sergeant spoke into the hand piece.

"Rover seven, this is eagle Two, when aren't you in a little bit of trouble."

"That's what everyone needs, a smart ass." The sergeant said to the occupants of the transport.

The sliced air percussion of the chopper blades was an unmistakable sound as the Apache helicopter closed in. The attackers were either extremely desperate or extremely stupid or both. Three of the attackers peeled off as the helicopter came in. The other six pressed the attack. The Apache hovered in the sky, a lone sentinel dispensing justice one tank-busting round at a time. Thirty seconds later four cars and two trucks were nothing more than twisted, shredded remnants of their former selves. The small military convoy raced away from the scene. The Apache hovered for a few more seconds looking for any signs of life, nothing moved except for the lazily drifting smoke from the wreckage.

"Base Custer, Base Custer this is Eagle two."

"Eagle two this is Base Custer, over."

"Base Custer, six of the attacking vehicles have been disposed of, permission to pursue the three that have fled the scene."

"Eagle two, that is a negative. Repeat that is a negative. The Colonel wants you to watch Rover Seven's back."

"Great babysitting duty."

"Say again Eagle two."

"Roger that Base Custer. Eagle Two out."

CHAPTER 5 - JOURNAL ENTRY 1 -

Holy shit, I'm in Heaven. Any place that smells like fried chicken has got to be heaven. My mouth worked on its own volition as orts of something wondrous crossed my lips. My eyes fluttered open.

"Dad! Dad! He's awake!" The shouting came less than six inches from my face. That was my introduction to 'Porkchop' as he leaned down looking at me, flakes of deep fried goodness spilling down from the chicken leg he held close to his mouth. I was mildly repulsed as his yelling let pre-chewed bits of food fall from his mouth and into mine. I might have pushed him away if I had possessed the strength. The second part of the equation though was the sheer look of exhilaration in his face at my awaking. His sincere visage and husky features completely endeared him to me, and then the cold cruel world shattered the well being that had momentarily enveloped me.

"Brendon?" I asked him. His look of not knowing of whom I was talking about answered my question.

'Dad' came over to my bedside. "Didn't think you were going to make it, Michael."

He looked regular army in his pressed digital battle fatigues and captain bars. He might have been a little on the heavyset side but that was nothing new to the army.

"Hardly seems worth it at this point, Doc." I answered. Abdication was interwoven with my words.

He ignored my self-pity. "You're family has been here for three days straight. I finally had to send them out to get some sleep. I don't think they would have left except the big kid, what is his name?"

"Tommy"

"Yeah Tommy said you were going to be alright. At

that point I wasn't so sure but they deferred to him. Sure is something about him." The Doc said with a faraway look. "Your daughter is a mess. I've been keeping her lightly sedated."

"Oh my God, Coley!" I lamented even harder. I was too mired in my own depression to realize there might be someone else grieving harder than I was.

"She'll eventually be alright Mike." The Doc answered more familiarly.

I braced myself for my next question but it needed answering. "Doc can you give me a list of everyone who did come in with me?"

"You up for this?"

I nodded in ascension, but my heart said abso-fucking-lutely not.

"There was your wife, her mother…" He hesitated. I almost shit myself in panic. "Then your older son Justin who I have on antibiotics, he was in rough shape, some sort of low grade fever was running rampant through his body. I went in…"

"DOC!"

"Sorry, umm okay, and then your younger son, Travis, I believe is his name. This mean tempered giant."

"BT" I answered. He looked at me inquiringly. "Big Tiny or Bad Tempered, take your pick."

"And then of course Tommy."

He stopped. As heart struck as I was that my family had survived, I was still desolate. We had suffered two devastating losses. I turned from the Doctor not willing to cry in front of him. He respectfully walked away. Porkchop, however did not.

"Hey mister what's the matter?" He asked, as chicken still spewed forth from him. I could feel the bits as they clung desperately to my previously fever streaked face. "Why you crying? Do you want some chicken?"

"Porkchop let him be." His dad called from across the room.

"I'll get you some chicken." He stage whispered to me.

A few minutes had passed and the depth of my mourning had somehow deepened. A bottomless chasm of despair, I gained momentum as I sank deeper and deeper.

Porkchop came back, ruddy with exertion. "I would have been here sooner, but Buddha knocked me down and then Henry took the piece of chicken I had got for you so I had to go back and get another piece."

A brilliant beam of light pierced the darkness. I wouldn't believe it, not just yet. False hope is worse than no hope at all. I looked piercingly at Porkchop. My red-rimmed eyes making me look a little more unstable than usual. "Who's Henry? Porkchop."

"He's Buddha's newest best friend." Porkchop answered back innocently.

"What is it with you and your dad? Why do you guys keep circumventing answers?"

"Huh?" Porkchop answered as he tilted his head.

"Dad, I think this guy needs some more medicine or something." He said as he absently took a bite of the chicken that he had promised for me.

I wanted to grab the boy's shoulder and shake the answer out of him, but it became unnecessary as a large brown bundle of fat and slobber walked through the door, most likely after the piece of chicken that got away. I bawled like I was 3 and my favorite balloon had loosed from my wrist and was now halfway to the stars.

"See dad. I told you he needed more medicine." as he took another bite.

Henry didn't hesitate. He somehow launched himself onto my bed, the pain as he stirred my injury was nothing in comparison to the relief that flooded through me as he licked my face. Now I'm not ignorant, I know a large part of the licking had to do with Porkchop's chicken, but not all of it. His stubby tail spoke volumes as it shuffled from side to side. Within moments a brindle colored bulldog of roughly the same size of Henry sauntered in.

"That's Buddha." Porkchop filled in.

Buddha looked to his partner in crime. I watched as the dog looked at the floor and then at the bed trying to figure out how Henry had got that high. He also smelled the chicken. His great head swiveled towards Porkchop.

"Dad?!" Porkchop yelled, looking for backup.

"Both you mutts out of here." The Doc ordered them.

True to their breed, neither moved. Oh it wasn't that they didn't understand. They just weren't given the proper motivation. The Doc reached into a drawer he had filled with biscuits just for these occasions. Both dogs were 'rewarded' with a cookie for doing what they had been asked to do, leave the room. A tear fell from my eye as I watched his ass waddle out. A quick smile came to my lips as I wondered if we had the dogs trained or they had us trained.

"Fuck can't a guy get any sleep around here?" BT bellowed as he pulled his privacy curtain open. BT's massive body was laid out in an undersized bed. His leg suspended in some sort of medieval torture device was wrapped in a blue cast. "Good to see you Talbot." He said with a broad smile across his features. Puffiness around his eyes threatened to limit his vision. The pain of losing Jen and Brendon was still a fresh oozing wound upon us all.

"Good to see you too BT." I said honestly. Neither of us commented on the others wet eyes. We bonded like all men, silently and in pain.

"Lawrence why are you awake?" The Doc asked.

"Who the hell is Lawrence?" I asked of the only other two occupants in the room. BT directed a stare at the Doc that should have stopped him in his tracks. The vapid gaze did not go unnoticed by me. "Lawrence? Your name is Lawrence?" I asked BT.

"I'll wring your scrawny little neck Talbot if you let anybody know!" BT threatened.

"It's not like you're going to be able to catch me in that get up." I answered him.

If the human body contained gaskets, BT would have blown one. He shifted around on his bed looking for a way to get out of his traction. BT grabbed the stand that was holding up his IV bag and started to use it like an Italian gondolier, pushing his bed closer and closer to mine, which in itself was pretty impressive, considering the rubber wheels were locked in place.

"Doc!" I yelled in near panic as BT inched nearer. "Doc!" I yelled again as I tried to sit up.

"Hold on you two!" The Doc yelled. "This isn't a frat house! This is a fucking hospital!"

"Sorry Doc." BT said as he lifted up his IV pole and swung it towards me, narrowly missing my leg.

"Do you want me to put restraints on you, Lawrence?" The Doc yelled.

"No Doc." BT answered, bowing his head.

"He called you Lawrence." I taunted. "Ow!" I yelled as something pricked my arm.

"Nightie-night Talbot." BT said smiling. "It'd be a damn shame if something happened to you while you were sleeping."

I turned to my left. Doc Baker was just pulling out a needle roughly the size of a turkey baster.

"You're next Lawrence." The Doc said.

"Aw come on Doc. I just woke up." BT Pleaded.

"He said Lawrence." I mumbled right before sleep dragged me down into the twilight.

CHAPTER 6 - JOURNAL ENTRY 2 - 

To say my dream was vivid would be an understatement. I don't know if it was due to the drugs the Doc had used, my battered consciousness or a message from a higher entity. I found myself in a small valley, surrounded on all sides by majestic peaks. Fields of bright orange poppies were all around me. Don't think for a second that the irony of that wasn't lost on me as I walked around in this preternatural world. Hummingbirds flitted from plant to plant, a cool breeze caressed my face, a bumblebee nearly the size of the hummingbirds drifted by, slowing slightly to look at me as it passed. Is that possible?

I walked a few steps reveling in the world I found myself in. It had much the same feel as Tommy's playground, but I could not sense the kid's hand in any of this.

"Where am I?" I asked aloud.

"You're in between." A familiar voice answered.

"Brendon? You're alive?" I asked incredulously. I wanted to cry with relief.

"Not quite Mike." Came the measured response. There was a sadness intermingled with expectancy. Sadness for what was lost, expectancy for what was to come.

"Are you...dead?" I choked out.

"I guess by the standards of the living Mike, I am. But I have never felt more alive in my life." He laughed. "Will you tell Nicole that I love her?"

"Of course Brendon, and thank you. But why, why did you come back?"

Brendon sighed, the echo of it reverberated throughout the valley. "I should have never left you guys, Mike. I let pride and ego get the best of me. Those petty human qualities mean so little here, Mike."

"Is Jen with you Brendon?"

"She was for a while. But the pull from the other side was too great. Jo kept calling for Jen to join her. She did want me to pass a message on to you though. She wanted to thank you."

"For what, I got her killed," I sobbed.

"For giving her a reason to keep living."

I dropped to my knees, the weight of the message driving me to the ground. Brendon appeared in front of me. He bent over, extending a hand to me. "Take hope away from here, Mike." He said as he pulled me up. "That's why you've been allowed to come. If not for yourself, then for your family." He paused. "For your grandson."

"I don't have a grandson." I answered him, the dawn of the realization slow to shine on me.

Brendon smiled as he slowly faded away. "Tell Nicole I love her and Chase is a fine name."

I shook violently awake. BT was softly snoring off to my side. Henry had at some point in the night snuck back into the hospital, and was crowding in on my bed. A small light had been left on in the far corner. Night had fully descended on this place. Shit, I didn't even know where I was. That hadn't happened to me since my college days, and that usually involved copious amounts of alcohol.

"Hi Talbot." For the minutest of seconds I thought Henry had spoken. His head still rested comfortably on my thigh.

"Hi hon." I answered, as my drug addled brain began to put the pieces back together.

"How you feeling?" My wonderful wife asked.

"Like a truck ran me over, then backed up to hit me again, then put ice chains on and then..."

"Enough!" She said exasperated. "I get the picture. There's something I need to tell you."

"Nicole's pregnant." I said.

I could hear the sharp intake of breath as Tracy tried to understand how I got that information. "There's more."

"Brendon's dead."

"How do you know all this? You've been unconscious for over three days."

"Brendon told me."

Tracy just about cried. "How Mike? Brendon died in that damned truck and Nicole herself didn't know she was pregnant until this morning."

I shrugged my shoulders, which in light of my present condition might just have been one of the singularly most stupid things I have ever attempted. Blood ruptured from an opening that by all accounts shouldn't have been there. A distant klaxon sounded, the night darkened around me, blackness tunneled my vision into twin pinpricks.

"Mike!" Tracy screamed.

I heard some panicked voices and then I found myself back in the safe, warm valley. This time I was alone. "Brendon? Jen?" I yelled. It wasn't that I was scared I was alone, it just would have been nice to share the experience. When I had first arrived in the valley the colors had all seemed muted. Everything from the smallest speck of dust now all shone with their own brilliance, so much so that I found myself squinting. The sun, which had seemed no bigger than a marble in the sky earlier, now threatened to overtake my entire field of vision. I found myself once again drawn to the light like a kid to a Toys R Us.

"Mike, not yet." An agitated voice said. "How many times do I have to send you back?"

"God?" Oh shit, I think I've annoyed God, that can't look good on your personal resume.

"It's not yet your time, Mike. Soon but not yet."

"Mom? Is that you? Mom, I'm tired. I don’t know how much longer I can do this."

I was full out sobbing now, my feet shuffling ever forward. As I write these words I find myself ashamed. I had given up. I wanted to crawl onto my mom's lap like I was five and she would tell me the Indians were coming to get me.

Ever forward I moved; the light didn't diminish this time. I was being repelled and accepted at the same time.

"Mike." A voice said forcibly from behind me.

I paid it as little attention as I could, left foot forward, right foot forward. The sweet summer grass I glided across became six-inch thick heavy mud. My feet became mired. Forward progress was slowed to a crawl. Still I pressed. If nothing else, I'm a stubborn son of a bitch.

"Mike!" The behind voice yelled. "A few more steps and it'll be too late."

"Don't you think I know that!" I screamed with everything I had. The rawness of my rage scraping against the linings of my throat.

The six-inch thick mud, turned into some sort of twelve-inch thick tar and mud mixture. I pushed forward straining with all my being to push through this obstacle. I could feel my essence being sucked up and into the light, like I was made of dust and the light was a giant Dyson. I was close! I pulled my left leg up out of the soup to rest it on the once again soft summer grass. I knew instinctually that once I pulled my right leg up and placed it onto the grass I would have passed a barrier from which there was no return.

"Mike." The behind voice cried once more. "We need you here."

I pulled my right leg up. It released with an audible pop from the ground. How long it hovered I don't know, not sure that time is relevant in purgatory. I looked upon the faces of my mother, of Brendon, Jen, Jo, Jed and dozens if not hundreds of relatives, this I knew not from sight but by the feelings of warmth and love that emanated from them. They all stared at me expectantly, waiting to embrace me within their collective grasps. I screwed up, I turned to look and see my pursuer. Tommy stood no more than ten feet away, tears streamed down his face. His body shook violently.

"Mr. T, it's not your time yet."

"Are you sure Tommy, because it really seems like it

is."

"Have I ever lied to you Mr. T?"

"Tommy I don't know if you've ever lied to anybody." And still my right foot hovered a foot from the ground. I was twelve olde English inches from literally meeting my maker. Maybe not the closest call ever, but then again not everyone truly knows HOW close they are to death.

"Think about your family, Mr. T."

"I have Tommy, but what's the point? Won't they all end up here eventually and then we'll all be together again."

"Don't you want your grandson to grow up, Mr. T? To have a life and a love of his own?"

That hurt more than I care to admit.

"If he dies before he's born Mr. T, he doesn't come here."

"That's a lie!" I screamed.

Tommy's features didn't change.

"Eliza knows about this place, she can keep your family away from here, forever." He added.

I wanted to scream at him, to throw him to the ground, to tell him that God would make him burn for telling those untruths. The problem was it was all true, instinctively I knew he was speaking the truth.

"I hate that bitch." I swore under my breath. What circle of hell do they reserve for people that swear on Heaven's doorstep? I nearly and literally almost fell over into the great abyss, only Tommy's steadying hand on my shoulder kept me from going over the edge. "Nice grab." I told him.

"You ready to go home?" He asked.

"I thought I was." I answered truthfully. I turned back. "Bye mom, I miss you."

"I'll see you soon." She said softly, with a ghost of a sad smile on her lips.

Now that I had made up my mind to stay on this side of the death divide, I hoped she didn't mean too soon or else this was going to be a short novella punctuated by my untimely demise.

"Thank you Tommy, you've saved me again."

"Want a Pop-Tart?" He asked as he pulled me close.

CHAPTER 7 - JOURNAL ENTRY 3 - 

As the emergency room lights grew brighter, the field I was in grew dimmer. Like the Cheshire cat, Tommy's grin was the last thing to fade.

My eyes fluttered open, bright light pierced into my soul.

"We have brain function." I think a nurse might have said.

"Blood pressure is 70 over 20 and climbing Doctor. Another 20 cc's of epy?"

"No we've already pumped him with more than I feel comfortable putting in a rhino. Mike can you hear me?"

"Get…damn…light…out…of…my…eyes." I rasped.

"Good to have you back."

I wasn't quite as sure.

"You've lost a lot of blood again Mike. You're making me doubt my expertise. Nearly everything I did on your shoulder came unglued all at once. You were clinically dead for twelve minutes. If I hadn't seen it with my own eyes I wouldn't have believed it."

Tracy was squeezing the shit out of my right hand.

"Hurts.." I muttered.

"I bet it does Mike." The Doc continued. "We had to go in…"

"No…" I took a breath. "Hand."

"No we didn't have to do anything with your hand we…"

"Oh I think he means me Doctor." Tracy said releasing her death grip on my hand. She began to rub blood back into my purpling appendage.

My head ached as I scanned the room. Travis' red-rimmed eyes were what I caught first. He turned away when

he noticed me staring at him. "Not...quite...dead...yet." I said in my best Monty Python English accent.
"I…think…I'm…getting…better." He turned quickly to leave the room, his shoulders bobbed up and down in heavy sobs. I knew what it was like to be a teen, all those hormones surging to the fore and there was always the constant cool that had to be maintained under any and all circumstances. It was nice to see that I had broken through to his humanity, something which I think had been slipping from him, minute degrees at a time.

Justin was next, his eyes were red-rimmed also but they were more the result from whatever poison surged through his body. His words froze me. "She knows we're here."

"Justin!" Tracy screamed.

Justin's face fell. "Mom." He began.

"You tell that bitch!" Tracy yelled. "That she can go to hell, and if she comes here I'll send her there personally. Why don't you and your girlfriend go for a walk!" Tracy sobbed.

"Hon…" I said almost grabbing her with my damaged arm. The Doc must have known I wasn't the brightest bulb on the string. This time he made sure that I would not be able to make any sudden movements. My arm, no scratch that, my entire upper half of my body, was immobilized. Tracy stopped her tirade to look at me, the pain and the hurt was etched in her eyes.

"I don't think he was taunting, I think he was just telling us."

"I don't care Talbot, I just don't." Tracy stormed out, her shoulders doing a fair impression of Travis' from a few moments earlier.

"Do…do you want me to leave Dad?" Justin asked, his eyes never picking up off of the floor.

I didn't want him to leave. I did however want Eliza to piss off. Was pretty sure she wasn't going to listen though. "No it's fine." I said through gritted teeth. The lingering effects of being dead were beginning to wear off and the pain of life was rearing its ugly head.

Next in line was Nicole. She looked worse than Justin. She wore the affliction of loss heavily.

"Hey Peanut. How you doing?"

Porkchop pushed past Nicole. "I'm doing good Mr. Talbot. Thanks for asking. Wanna see my transformers?"

"Porkchop!" Doc Baker called over from the corner, doing his best to be discreet while also actually monitoring my progress. "I'm pretty sure he's not talking to you."

"Dad yeah he is. You heard him right?" Porkchop asked Nicole.

"Well actually…" I began.

"So see this one is Bumble Bee. He goes from this guy into a yellow Camaro." Porkchop said as he hastily began to do the magical folding and bending of plastic to make the action figure turn into a sports car. Sweat began to bead on his brow as the arm assembly was not being very cooperative. "Almost got it." Porkchop said in deep concentration. I would have laughed a little when Porkchop's tongue came out while he was in deep concentration but I knew the pain that would have ensued was not worth the expenditure.

Doc Baker had to physically remove Porkchop from the vicinity. Porkchop was entirely too wrapped up in the transmorphing of his toy to realize that he had actually been moved.

"Dad I've got something to tell you." Nicole said, her eyes as downcast as her brother's.

"It's alright honey Br…" Holy crap I was half a sentence away from telling my grieving daughter that her dead boyfriend had already told me that she was pregnant. That wouldn't have gone over too well. Nicole picked her eyes up to meet mine. A questioning look fleeted across her features.

"Brendon's dead." Nicole sobbed flatly. The shock of those words spoken aloud stunned her. Up to this point I don't think it had been vocalized. Obviously she knew but the spoken word carried its own weight, a finality, a punctuation to an ending.

A new fear wormed into my heart. Would my daughter begin to look at me as the person for whom her fiancée had died. Being Catholic meant I already carried an immeasurable amount of guilt around with me. I didn't want to add to the load. I wanted to reach out and comfort my daughter; the cloth strap bound tightly across my chest thought otherwise.

Nicole moved in for a hug, oblivious to the myriad of machinery and tubes hooked up to me. I wished that an EKG machine was also hooked up to Doc Baker at that point. He looked on the verge of a cardiac infarction, I knew because I watched ER.

Nicole wept as she gripped me tight, the deep sobs reverberated throughout both our bodies. The movement was causing me quite a bit of pain, which I was doing my best to squash down. Out of the corner of my eye I could see the Doc unobtrusively working his way closer and closer to my bedside. Nicole kept her final secret to herself. That was fine with me. We all carry certain things we don't want the rest of the world to know, problem was hers was going to reveal itself no matter what she did or did not say.

She pulled herself up so we could see eye to eye, which was still difficult due to the copious amounts of tears being spilled. The big bad ass Marine side of me would like to say they were all hers or even mostly hers but this water works display was a joint effort.

"Nicole I know this won't help now and most likely won't make any sense, but in The End we WILL be all together." I told her. I wanted to finish with. 'Once I take Eliza's head and slowly feed it through a wood chipper.' Sounded good in my head, got the feeling Nicole wouldn't appreciate it nearly as much.

"I love you Dad." She said squeezing me tighter.

The Doc couldn't take it anymore. He gently placed

his hands on her shoulders. "Miss, we really need to let your dad rest. If anything else happens to him, I don't know that there will be enough left to sew back together."

Justin led his sister out and I would imagine to their quarters. Nicole had always been a very petite girl. Somehow she looked even more diminished, like her soul was wrung out. I know mine was.

"Mike you should get some sleep." The Doc told me.

"Doc I'm sick of sleeping."

"I can see your point, but the more rest you have the quicker your body will heal."

"First things first Doc."

He stopped what he was doing to look at me.

"Where am I and what is going on?" I asked him.

"Well I guess a few more minutes won't make a difference," as he pulled up a chair. "Where would you like me to start?"

"I was thinking maybe the Mesozoic era." I said smart-assedly.

"The beginning it is." The Doc said immediately picking up on my sarcasm. "First off you are on an impromptu military base called Camp Custer in Indiana that abuts up against the great lakes, Lake Michigan to be specific."

It was nice to have someone recognize my acrimony.

"The newscasters had one thing right, it did start with a flu shot. When the vice president died from complications arising from the H1N1 Influenza strain, the administration, in an effort to squash public panic, pushed researchers and vaccine developers past their breaking point. Safety measures were cut or completely ignored. Tests on the vaccine's effectiveness were never validated. Most likely the tests weren't even conducted. I'm not going to go into what specifically went wrong, microbiology is not my area, suffice it to say that something went completely awry."

"You think." I grunted. "Did you say Custer?"

He nodded with a weak smile. "The vaccine they

were inoculating everyone with was a live strain, something they haven't done in over thirty years because of the inherent danger this type of dose can cause. Obviously nothing on this level, but the live strains of vaccines used to cause upwards of a 7% infection rate. Meaning..."

"Meaning that out of every 100 people given the shot to prevent the flu, seven actually got the flu."

"Exactly." The Doc nodded. "Those were great odds back in the day, but as we learned more about how to combat the influenza virus, it was discovered that the success rate with 'dead' vaccines was much larger. Odds of actually getting the flu from a flu shot were infinitesimally small. So much so it was widely believed that the people who actually got sick already had the virus within them."

"Why the live vaccine then Doc?"

"Time, Mike. It would have taken another 3 to 4 weeks to adapt the 'dead' viral agent. The country was already on the verge of a pandemic. Thousands were getting sick daily. Hundreds, if not thousands of deaths were imminent. Schools, businesses, hell even government buildings were shutting down to prevent the spread of the virus. All of the president's admonishments that the flu was not as bad as the media was making it seem went down the drain the very minute the VP died. Vaccination producing facilities began to work around the clock to get enough doses out there, and even with those extraordinary measures it wasn't going to be nearly enough."

I could not get the image of small vials of zombieism heading down an assembly line. An innocuous clear liquid in a small bottle with a cap especially designed for the insertion of a needle. If I had not been laid off my family and I would have been first in line to accept the deadly shot. "There were no tests?" I asked angrily.

"Well maybe I spoke too soon. In a gesture of 'Goodwill," the Doctor said with air quotes. "The good old US government sent crates and crates of the newly fashioned immunization to third world countries around the globe."

"Bastards. They might as well have been giving smallpox laced blankets to the Yup'ik."

The Doc looked at me a little funny. "I knew you were a smart man Mike, I didn't know that you were educated also."

"There are a lot of things about me Doc that might confound you but my knowledge of that has more to do with my fear of conspiracies than book learning."

"I see." The Doc said looking off into the distance as he assimilated this new information.

"So didn't the scientists get a clue that maybe the vaccination wasn't so good when Peruvians began to walk around eating their relatives?"

"They would have, had they waited. Within a day or two of shipping out the crates they began the roll out the first shots to area hospitals."

"Are you kidding me? So being the assholes that we are, we use whole nations as our guinea pigs and then don't even have the follow through to see the results?"

"It gets worse Mike."

"How is that even possible?"

"I could probably get shot just for telling you, but it's not like you're going to be able to go to the media with this information." The Doc looked back to the door as if expecting Big Brother to be standing there, they weren't, so he continued. "There is every indication that the higher ups within the government knew the shots were tainted."

The look of shock nearly froze my features into place.

"No, no wait. It's not that they were trying to take down civilization as we knew it. I guess it was more of inaction that may have doomed our species. Just as the first few people in the states were coming down with the infection, the boxes of shots began to make their way ashore all around the globe. In typical government fashion, this new development of death and reanimation was immediately covered up. In its defense the government tried their best to quickly and quietly retrieve the shots. But with vague directions, hospitals and caregivers were reluctant to give their hard won shots back. They immediately began to dose as many people as was possible before government representatives could get there to retrieve the stock. What's infinitely worse is that once the U.S. realized it could not contain the shots within their own borders they didn't act to save any other country."

"They figured if we were going down then we were taking as many people with us as possible."

"Quite." The Doctor said resignedly.

"But you said third world countries, Doc. Is there anywhere that is zombie free?" I asked hopefully.

"We have satellite communication with most countries that are still people populated." He pulled his hand across his face. "It seems we lose contact with a handful every week as they go dark."

Going dark could mean a lot of things. Possibly running out of power, burnt out diodes, laryngitis, bad case of the hiccups might keep someone from broadcasting.

"Australia seems to be the least infected, but it really is only a matter of time."

"An exponential disaster, one becomes two, two becomes four, and so on."

"And so on." The Doc repeated sadly.

"How much of humanity is left Doc?" Where do you go, what do you do, when hope is gone?

"In the states, maybe 5% aren't zombies yet. The rest of the world, well they're lagging behind like usual but are coming on fast, they may have upwards of 15% of their populations still alive."

"Is there any way to stop them?" 'Them,' being our neighbors, our friends, our families.

"We've been working on a vaccination."

I must have looked at him funny.

"I know, it seems a little late in the game for that. Haven't had much success anyway, volunteers have been scarce." He said weakly. "The new agent might counteract the flu immunization if someone were to immediately seek out help. But at this point I can barely give someone a saline solution intravenously. If we have generations left it will take that long for the fear of needles to subside."

"What if someone is bitten?" I asked hopefully.

"Maybe in the beginning a stronger vaccination could have helped, but the disease has mutated. The pathogen that floods the body in a bite now is much too virulent. It overwhelms the body's defenses in a matter of hours, what used to take a day or more now happens in half that time. Individuals don't even have the capacity to die in the traditional manner before they are re-animated."

"The speeders." I said aloud.

"Speeders?" The Doc questioned.

I related our experience with this new breed of death dealing machines.

"With the original 'zombies,' I'll use that term because it seems to be the current vernacular to call them but not completely true. Anyway, the older agent could take up to 24 hours to overwhelm its victims. The patient's body temperature could swell well above the 107 degree threshold before the brain literally began to cook. Once the infected 'died' the microorganisms or parasites really began to go to work."

"How is that possible? Doesn't the parasite die when the host does? How can it keep going without that symbiotic relationship?"

"And that's the difference. Our little carnivorous sycophant values its existence above all others. Sort of like man itself." The Doc said wonderingly.

"Doc, come back."

"Right. So I can't even begin to go into depth about how, but apparently when the leech realized that its very life was on the line, it developed a way to reroute the functions of its host. It took control much like a marionette. Unfortunately, this type of hostile take-over requires copious amounts of proteins to sustain."

"Meat." I said softly.

"Precisely."

"What happens when their food supply runs dry?" I asked knowing full well I was talking about people.

"You may or may not have noticed that they will eat just about anything they can catch. Funny though they will have nothing whatsoever to do with high protein bars which would sustain them just as easily as meat based proteins."

I knew the answer but I asked anyway. "How do you know all this Doc?"

He didn't hesitate with his response. "We've got ten of them on base for studying."

"What the fuck?" BT yelled. "You've got those things on site? Are you fucking crazy?"

"Strange." The Doc said as he stood up and walked over to BT's bedside. He tapped on BT's intravenous bag. "I gave him enough sedative to keep him asleep for another eight hours."

"You know those things can talk to each other right?" BT said panicked. "Tell him Talbot."

"Lawrence, they can do no such thing." The Doc said as he plunged another hypodermic into BT's IV line. "The virus burns so hot in humans that it virtually wipes clear all higher brain functioning, like a magnet to a hard drive."

"Talbot!?" BT pleaded.

"Doc, they aren't hard drives." I said. "I'm not saying that they have conversations, but they have the ability to communicate somehow. They know when prey is available and they have a pack mentality. They know when to converge or even to diverge if a more readily available food source comes into play."

"These are all interesting theories, Mike," the Doc said with a small slice of condescension on top.

I could tell he was about to start rambling on with a myriad of explanations and reasons why this couldn't be true. I didn't give him the chance.

"How many battles you been in Doc?"

"That's not the point."

"The hell it isn't Doc. How much about a wolf's behavior could you learn from him if all you knew was from a caged specimen."

"I understand the analogy Mike, I really do. But I am telling you that the host brain is quite literally liquefied from the experience."

"You said the host brain."

The Doc paused.

"Good one Talbot!" BT said barely able to muster a thumbs-up under the assault of the newly added sedative.

CHAPTER 8 - JOURNAL ENTRY 4 - 

I don't know if the Doc didn't like my answer or was just done talking, he plunged a sedative into my IV line. Unlike BT, I was out in seconds. I slept wonderfully. No visions of Heaven or Tommy's playland. I think I dreamt something about the New York Giants playing the Red Sox in the World Bowl and somehow the Boston Bruins came out on top. Don't judge me, you know you've had weirder dreams. I was graciously accepting Lord Stanley's Turkey Platter when I was rudely shoved awake.

"Michael B. Talbot, are you awake?"

"Fucking am, now." I don't wake up very well. I wanted to sit up a little straighter when I noticed who had pulled me out of dreamland. This guy had more ribbons and shiny shit on his uniform than I had ever seen.

"Michael B. Talbot, I am Lt. Colonel Byron Fox, 1st Marine Corps Air Station."

"Little far from home Colonel?" I asked. First MCAS was at one time stationed in Hawaii, probably not anymore.

The Colonel did not even acknowledge my comment as he threw out his own question. "Doctor Baker came to see me a few hours ago with some disturbing new details about our enemy. What can you tell me?"

"How much time you got?" I asked him.

"I have to be in a briefing with the base commander at 1830, so about an hour."

Great, this guy was about as dry as toast. He grilled me for the entire hour, ringing out every iota of minutiae he could garner. He must have been a supply commander. I glossed over Eliza for the time being. I don't know why, maybe I was afraid that he would kick my family and me out if he knew we were being targeted. The Marine Corps is all about the greater good, sacrifice of the one for the many. I just wanted to make sure that my family was not the 'ONE.'

He knew I wasn't giving him everything but not from lack of trying. He would ask the same questions just with different wordings. More than once I had to stop and sort through all the 'half-truths' I had told him and make sure that I was consistent. I was exhausted after our verbal sparring, another half hour and I might have admitted to creating the tainted shots.

"We'll talk more." The colonel said as he abruptly rose and walked out of the room.

"Why didn't you tell him Mike?" BT asked.

BT startled the crap out of me. I had to remember that I did not have this room to myself.

"Shit, BT don't you sleep?"

"Only when I want to. Something about this place has me on edge. Obviously you feel the same or you would have told him."

"I don't know what it is BT. We are on a military base with more guns and trained personnel that we could ever hope for and I felt safer in Little Turtle. I think most of it has to do with the fact that we're pretty much stuck in these beds. Part of it could be that I just don't think he'd believe me."

BT nodded in agreement.

"I mean we're living through it man, and still I am harboring doubts."

"It all seems pretty improbable. I always thought the downfall of civilization would be a socio-economic collapse. I fully expected China to demand all of our debt to her in one fell swoop. They would have won the war without firing one shot."

I looked over at BT. I must have had a confused look on my face because he asked me what the hell I was looking at. I could not reconcile the size of the man with the obvious amount of smarts he possessed.

"How in the hell do you have enough time outside of the gym to learn all this stuff?"

"Blow me, Talbot."

"Ah there's the BT I know and love."

"So what do you want to do about this place?" He asked more seriously.

"I want to leave. But not yet, I want us to be as close to 100% functional as is possible. This place has…something."

"A feeling of expectancy."

"That'll work. Calm before the storm and all that shit. There is just way too much food here for the zombies to pass on by. I don't give a shit how many bullets and grenades and claymore mines they have here, it isn't enough. They will either come on their own or Eliza will bring them. Either way I really don't want to be here when it happens."

"How long you figure, Mike?"

"It's never good when you use my first name BT."

He cocked a half smile at me.

"Well, provided I don't find some new and unusual way to reinjure my shoulder, which may be difficult. I should be semi-functional in a few weeks. You on the other hand are probably looking at a good 3 or 4 months before you are even close to approximating something close to normal."

BT laughed before he asked his question. "So again Mike, how long?"

"Do I look like CNN?" BT's gaze withered me. "Fine, I've got to figure that the bitch is even now amassing an army. It'll take her a while to get anything together that can take on this base. I can only hope that the majority of zombies out there are still of the slower variety. I figure if everything goes our way we have a max of a month."

BT breathed heavily through closed lips. "When you feel better Mike you could leave."

"Yup sure could."

"But you won't." BT said resignedly.

"Yeah not really a chance of that BT, I've come to grow fond of you and the constant threat of getting my ass kicked by you."

"Mike, you've got your family to think of."

"BT you are part of my family now. I mean we might not be able to pass as twins and all, but we are brothers."

"Brothers in arms."

"I've been to war BT. There are not many stronger bonds that can be created than with your fellow soldier. When the world disintegrates around you and all you have is your buddy next to you watching your back and to rely on, well hell man, what more do you need? Don't sweat it for now, we'll see how we're doing in three weeks and we'll go from there. If we're up for it and these Army guys can see it out of the kindness of their hearts to give us a hummer, we'll just go."

"What if they don't have any kindness?"

"Eh, won't be the first time I stole a military vehicle."

"You scare me Talbot."

"Those are the same words my parole officer said."

"What'd the Doc say about your leg?"

"He said I should have got a second opinion before I let you operate."

I laughed, even though the movement caused extreme pain through my shoulder. "Asshole." I mumbled.

"Hey I'm just telling you what he told me."

"Seriously, BT."

"Well my pole vaulting days are over." He said with some serious lament in his voice.

He sounded so pathetic I was half tempted to believe him, but the guy would have had to use an oak tree to vault over a pole.

"BT, shit. You know it hurts me when I laugh." I said gripping my shoulder.

"It'll heal, in fact it's done remarkably well in this short time span. I'll probably always have a limp, but that just works in my favor."

When he didn't answer I asked. "How so?" Knowing full well that I was walking into a set up trap.

BT flashed a smile. "Now I won't have to work so

hard on my pimp walk."

I sighed in feigned disgust. It hurt less than laughing. For long moments there was a calm silence between us. BT broke it.

"I miss Jen, Talbot." BT said.

I thought he might have wiped a tear away but I couldn't be sure and either way I wasn't going to call him on it.

"I miss her too, BT. She saved my skin a couple of times. Did you know we were neighbors before?" No need to explain before what.

"I think I remember her saying something about that. How the hell did she put up with you?"

"Back when civilization ruled the world, I reined myself in a lot better. I guess now there's nothing left to hold the crazy back."

With no small measure of difficulty BT sat up so that he could get a better look at me. "Talbot you're hilarious." BT guffawed for a few long seconds.

"I was being serious." I said to him. His laughing, which had been ebbing began to flow full throttle again.

For forty-five minutes we reminisced about Brendon and Jen, sometimes laughing, sometimes crying, more times than not it was a combination of the two.

"BT I haven't had the chance to ask anyone, but what happened to Brendon?"

"He shot himself."

I couldn't think of anything to say. There were reasons why in these times someone might decide to off themselves, but why then?

"He was bitten?" It was half statement half question.

"He must have been there was a bandage on his hand and when they laid him down I saw one on his leg, I don't know how he even managed to get to Carol's."

I missed the kid, allies were falling fast and replacements were slow to come forward.

BRENDON'S STORY - CHAPTER 9 -

Brendon could never remember being able to change a tire that fast. Lug nuts that should have literally been frozen on, seemed hardly finger tightened as he used the tire iron to unscrew them. Adrenaline, fear and anger seethed through his system. He had no direction to focus his turmoil on. Justin was a spy, he was also his friend and the brother of his fiancée. Mike could just about be considered his dad and he knew what was up with Justin but did nothing. Realistically, what could he do.

Brendon felt justified and cowardly as he sped away from the Talbots'. They would never be able to survive without him.

"Oh who the hell am I kidding." He said to the steering wheel. "I won't survive without them." His gut wrenched from the inner conflict. He was thirty miles down the roadway before he finally pulled over to reevaluate his situation. "How could I leave her?" He wailed. Pride is listed as one of the seven deadly sins for a reason. Brendon knew his life was almost forfeit but he'd be damned if he would grovel back to the all-knowing Michael R. Talbot.

He drove another five miles before he once again pulled over to rethink this course. He knew to within a few miles where they were going. He could just meet them there, all would be forgiven. "No!" He yelled. "Mike will have some smart ass comment about, I knew you'd be back. Or couldn't stay away could you?" Brendon punched the accelerator, gravel spun out from the back of his truck. A lone crow perched on a non-functioning phone line watched his departure.

Brendon spent his first night alone in a mini-mall parking lot. He slept in fitful starts, always fearful that something would go bump in the night. The truck windows kept completely fogging over, so even when he did thrash to full alertness he could not tell if something was out there or an overactive imagination was to blame. Brendon quickly sat up. Wiping his sleeve across the wet glass, images of yellowing chipped, meat encrusted teeth pressed against the windshield jump-started his heart. "This sucks." He repeated for at least the twenty-second time. A little ribbing from Mike was a small price to pay.

Brendon spent the majority of the next morning sitting in his truck, constantly shifting his decision to keep on driving away from or toward the Talbots'. He dozed in and out of sleep, his legs cramped under the dashboard. It was sometime past noon when his knee slammed up into the steering column, his eyes were drawn to the far side of the parking lot as a young woman of nearly the same age as Nicole walked steadily in his direction. Age was the only thing his former fiancée and this interloper had in common. His heart snagged on a barb of realism as he realized that his engagement was now terminated.

The woman that was headed his way was dead and just didn't know it. Her gore-streaked hair covered most of her visage but yet she did not once reach up and brush it away. Ripped lips revealed blackened teeth and a cavernous throat. She looked something between a sea gull and a shark with her black eyes. Her once white sweat pants were completely ripped up the right side revealing purple-bluish flesh that had torn in more than one spot. Oval mouthfuls of muscle and tendon were neatly removed. Brendon fumbled with his gun as his pulse quickened and his pupils dilated. He debated whether to leave, get out of the truck and kill it or shoot from where he sat.

He decided he would get a cleaner shot if he got out of the truck. He was completely unprepared for what happened as his foot hit the pavement. The zombie shifted from the typical side-to-side ambling and started a full on sprint towards him. The buffeting wind pushed her hair back to reveal red-rimmed black eyes. Saliva spewed forth from her mouth and ran parallel to the ground on her cheeks as she picked up speed. Brendon’s shot went wide right, nicking the girl's ear. She would never wear hoop earrings again. Her pace never wavered as she kept locked on like a meat seeking missile. Brendon’s next shot shattered the right side of her head. Head plate flew into the air, gray brown brain was clearly visible and still she came. Brendon's third and final shot dropped the zombie a mere 10 feet from him, the push of the bullet forced the majority of her brain out of the exposed hole. His heart nearly cramped from the encounter.

"One zombie." He said shaking his head. "Just one more and I'd be dead." He didn't know it on an intellectual level yet but his instinctual side had clearly made up its mind. If he wanted to survive, which he did, he needed to get back with the Talbots. He pulled out of the parking lot, passing seven zombies who started their relentless pursuit.

He got a few miles away from his close encounter, his breathing finally under control. He stopped this time on the roadway with a 360 degree view all around him, with at least 100 yards or more of clear sight. Nothing or nobody was going to be able to sneak up on him, at least not until night. His fuel tank and his stomach were both running on empty; he would need to rectify those situations soon.

Brendon looked at the flat black matte finish of his 9mm pistol, one pull of the trigger could end all of his doubts and misgivings. “Would it hurt?” He asked no one. A response was not forth coming. He smacked his gun-laden hand against the steering wheel. The bullet pierced the cab roof, a brilliant beam of light struck him in the eye. “Holy shit!” He said sticking a finger through the new exit point. “Great that ought to make it a little cooler in here tonight and let anybody in the general vicinity know I’m around.” His ears stung from the noise in such a confined space, his mood souring by the moment.

There was a Wendy’s up ahead, but unless he wanted to eat frozen ketchup packets he didn’t see the point. In a few more hours though, those would probably sound good.

Brendon started the truck and drove slowly up the roadway looking for a place to grab some food and to keep a look out for any signs of the dead. A mini-mart that had seen better days came up on his right hand side. Both front doors were smashed and an F3 tornado seemed to have swept through the inner aisles but there still seemed to be plenty of food available, or at least food-like products, this was a mini-mart after all.

Brendon pulled up close to the front doors and then reversed a few feet just in case he needed the extra space to get away from something. He hesitated in the cab whether or not to leave it running or take the keys with him. "At this rate I'll just end up pissing my pants where I sit so I won't have to get out." He smiled at his own grim realization that paranoia was taking more than a foothold. He opted to shut the truck off. The idling diesel engine was loud enough to sufficiently hide the dragging foot falls of zombies. His only middle ground was to leave the keys in the ignition so that there was no chance he'd drop them and not be able to find them.

The popping of the door as it opened startled him more than the earlier gunshot. His breath lingered in front of his face causing a momentary smoke screen. The morning was quiet, there was no traffic, no bustle of everyday life. Just the occasional 'caw' of a distant crow and the more unsettling barking of dogs that were increasingly becoming feral without ownership. Brendon laughed as he thought of a snarling mad Henry, but then immediately chilled when he thought the same thing about Bear, the Rottweiler. A bunch of poodles and a Chihuahua might not be so bad but throw in a Doberman Pinscher or a German shepherd and things could really start to get ugly.

Brendon had his gun drawn as he stepped onto the broken glass. He noted that more than one person had been here just for the fact that most of the glass had been ground down to almost a fine powder. The thought that live humans were in the vicinity was of no comfort. People could be just as deadly as zombies and you had the added bonus of not knowing which side of that line they were on. At least the zombie didn't try to pretend. As if to confirm his worst fear there were at least six or possibly seven scattered dead people, it was tough to tell because the aforementioned wild dogs had ripped them apart. They were nearly stripped clean and the bones that remained shone a bright white. Even the skulls had been crushed and the contents muzzled out.

"They had to have been humans, the dogs wouldn't have touched zombies. Right? Who am I asking?" Dogs hadn't done the initial killing though, various caliber brass littered the floor, and there were no guns around. The empty shells sounded like broken rain as he kicked through it. "It was bound to happen sooner or later." He thought. "Dwindling resources bring out the worst in folks." Brendon shivered as he saw the outline where the previous blood spills were. Tongue marks criss-crossed the floor, leaving red smears behind. His hunger, which had seemed such a pressing need only moments earlier, was rapidly losing its appeal. "You've seen worse." He said aloud trying to bolster his nerve.

He nearly cried when he passed a smashed box of pop-tarts on the floor. "Maybe I should grab them and I can use them as an excuse to go back. You know Mike, I was heading to Mexico and I came across these cherry pop-tarts and I turned around because I figured that Tommy would want them. No." He said shaking his head. "Tommy hated the cherry ones, are there any strawberry?" Brendon was so intent on looking for a different flavor he did not realize when visitors came to join him.

The deep bass growl was his first inkling that all might not be right in his world. He looked up at not the largest dog he had ever seen but clearly the most ferocious. A Siberian Husky stared back at Brendon, no wagging tail on its emaciated frame. "That's a good fella." Brendon said. "Want a pop-tart?" The dog's growling increased. "I don't blame you, the cherry ones suck." The dog warily moved forward never taking its eyes off him. Patches of fur were missing from its black and silver coat. Dried blood had solidified on its right side, half of his left ear was torn. Brendon at first thought that possibly the virus had gone cross-species. Except for the eyes, they were a deep blue, he might have kept on thinking that.

Brendon held up his gun, the dog paused. “You know what this is don’t you!” Brendon said forcibly. The dog hesitated but only long enough to wait for three of his friends to join him in the hunt. A Golden Retriever, a Black Lab and a Dachshund joined the fray. The retriever and the lab could be trouble because of their size, but Brendon could not wrap his head around a violent dachshund. That was of course until the Dachshund seized the initiative and charged head long down the aisle at him.

“Oh come on.” Brendon pleaded. “A freaking wiener dog?” All the same, he scrambled up on the shelving, pushing some boxes of half eaten Cheerios out of the way. The Dachshund stopped below him, yipping up a storm. If not for his larger and fiercer friends this would be comical. The Lab and the Retriever slowly approached coming down the same aisle as the smaller dog. The Husky came down the aisle to Brendon’s rear. ‘Great, they know how to hunt.’ He thought.

The Lab looked ready to spring. Brendon placed a well-aimed shot in its chest, the dog skidded backwards and slumped against some Angel Soft bathroom tissue. The softest final resting place anybody could ask for. The dogs had backed up a bit but they weren’t leaving quite yet. Brendon turned to get a better shot at the husky, figuring if he took out their leader the rest of the pack might lose heart. Seemed like a great idea until the pack began to swell, Brendon stopped counting when the tenth dog came through.

“Three shots at the zombie, one at the Labrador. That gives me six, and there’s at least 13 of you.” He looked to his truck. The husky followed his line of sight. Backing it up earlier which seemed such a great idea now might end up being the last great blunder in a long string of them. Cognitively he knew the husky wasn't smiling at him but it sure did look like a shit-eating grin from where he sat. Two more dogs jumped up at him only to be met with varying degrees of fatality. The one that was shot in the throat would die much sooner than the one that had its paw blown off, but it was still only a matter of time.

A few of the dogs were paying no heed whatsoever to the melodrama playing out, too busy foraging for scraps that previous hunting parties might have missed. A particularly vicious fight broke out between an Australian cattle dog and a Boxer over what looked like a bloody hairpiece but was in fact some poor soul's scalp. Brendon absently touched the top of his head. A good portion of the dogs began to rip pieces out of their fallen brethren. "Glad to see that cannibalism isn't just a human trait." Brendon said darkly. No matter what else was happening in the store the husky never took his eyes off of Brendon. It was unnerving and to make matters worse the dog had pulled back far enough to make any type of shot difficult. "Does he know how much ammo I have left." Brendon didn't voice his thought for fear that the hound might understand what he was saying. It wouldn't be the strangest thing that had happened to him in the last few weeks.

Brendon pulled his gun up again. The husky retreated even further, placing himself squarely behind an unsuspecting poodle. Brendon shot. "Fuck it, I hate poodles anyway." Two rounds later the white poodle lay on its side and other dogs began to jockey for position to get some of the tastier morsels on the cadaver. The husky had circled back around. "You are starting to piss me off!" Brendon yelled. The dog curled its lips up, exposing blood stained teeth. "Come here good boy." Brendon said in a cajoling voice. "I've got something for you." A cur from the back came up. Its tail tucked firmly between its legs, the sound of a human promising treats sparked a fading memory in its rudimentary ken. The husky bit its hindquarters for its disloyalty. The cur yelped its way back to the back of the pack. “Well it’s not like I didn’t know who the alpha dog was anyway.”

The dogs dispatched quickly of their former mates. The meal did little to stave off the effects of starvation that the majority of them were feeling. Most would die by the end of the month, but that would do little for Brendon’s present situation. “Three rounds left, do I kill two dogs and then myself?” It sounded like a decent plan. He just couldn’t reconcile being eaten by animals. There was some base part of him that this thought repulsed to the core. Must have been a hold-over from the early hominids. It kept them from letting a saber tooth tiger eat them.

Brendon didn’t think matters could get much worse. He chastised himself for his lack of imagination when three zombies ambled down the street and into the store. At least one good thing came of it, the dogs having realized that they were also on the zombies’ menu moved out of the way as the new hunters joined the mix. Two of the zombies started to go after the dogs, a young man somewhere in his early twenties, however, locked on Brendon. The dogs moved as the zombie approached. Always staying out of arm’s reach but close enough that they could grab scraps once the dominant hunter had taken down its prey. Like hyenas they cackled around the lion.

Two shots and one broken open brain bucket later the zombie man was on the ground. The dogs avoided the carcass like the plague-infested carrier that it was. The commotion did not go unnoticed by one of the other zombies, who had peeled off from trying to catch the dachshund and instead focused on the non-moving prey, Brendon. The third zombie had somehow managed to corner one of the dogs and was tearing through it. The blood strangled barks of pain were ignored by the pack. "Survival of the fittest." Brendon said, as he stood on the shelving almost falling over when his left foot came down awkwardly on a can of Spam.

The zombie that was coming for Brendon was also in

his mid-twenties or so and dressed as if he had at one time been going to a dance club, a tattered black silk shirt and a thick gold chain still clung to his grimy neck. No shoes to speak of but his pants were still in pretty good shape, considering. Brendon couldn't help but wonder if the three amigos had all been together when they changed over, did their friendship transcend the change? That question got resolved fairly quickly as zombie number two stepped on zombie number one's family jewels; the egg cracking sound of bursting genitalia got Brendon moving.

The zombie was within arm's length. Brendon ran down the top of the shelf, gauging where a good jump would take him and then how long it would take him to get to the truck. The husky paced him on the floor. The zombie wasn't going to be a problem unless he jumped too far and knocked himself out on the top of the doorframe. The husky was the issue. He might have, against all odds, made it to the truck unscathed if his jump hadn't landed him squarely in spilled dish detergent. His left leg shot out at an unnatural angle, the pain in his groin letting him know that if he survived it was going to throb for weeks. Brendon went down on all fours, traction was measured in inches when it needed to be feet. The clubbing zombie was closing in as was his friend that decided human tasted better than collie.

Brendon looked like an extra on Avatar with blue goo covering everything that made contact with the floor. The husky was able to avoid the spillage as it sank its fangs deep into Brendon's calf. He screamed as he rolled over to kick at the dog. The husky, like a professional wrestler, matched him move for move. The dog started to shake its head back and forth causing Brendon to nearly pass out from the pain. Red flowed freely into blue. Sparks danced in Brendon's field of vision. He didn't remember doing it, if someone had asked him later on he would have thought that someone else had taken the shot. The husky jumped away, a deep crimson gash perforated its side, rib bone protruded through the injury. Brendon turned back over to begin his crab walk out of the store. The clubber might have caught him if not for the same trap that had temporarily snared Brendon. The zombie went head first into a display of pickles, shards of vinegar laced glass peppered his face. Brendon stared in horror as the zombie tried to right itself, a jagged piece of glass sticking out of its now empty eye socket.

As it got free from the La Brea Dawn Pits, Brendon got to his one good leg and half hopped, half jumped his way to the truck. Blood followed him. He pulled himself into the cab and immediately shut the door. Some of the hungrier and more dominant dogs began to assert themselves, within seconds the truck was surrounded. The circle was only broken to allow the Clubber and the dog muncher entry. Brendon nearly broke the key in the ignition when the zombies smacked up into the side of the truck. The truck started immediately. He ran over at least one of the zombie's feet and had possibly hit one or maybe two of the dogs. Brendon had a mild sense of satisfaction when he left and saw three big dogs closing in on their former leader. "That's what you get!" He shouted, spittle flying on the inside of the windshield.

He could not, for the life of him, remember why he had stopped at that little shit-hole, that was of course until the blinding yellow light warning of eminent fuel depletion started to blink. His leg hurt so bad he could barely think, he feared pulling his pants up to look at it, thinking that his calf muscle might only be secured to his leg by a severely chewed through tendon. Droplets of blood began to merge on the rubber floor mat, an ant might not yet be able to drown in the burgeoning puddle but it sure could go for a nice swim. Brendon's head began to swoon. The previous bright sparks of pain began to darken and become blotched and that was making vision increasingly difficult.

He drove until the tank gave out, which was fortuitous considering he passed out at roughly the same time. The truck came to an unaided gliding stop on a snow covered embankment. There he would have stayed until time eternal if not for a long range military patrol on a search and rescue mission.

"Is he dead?" Murphy asked his sergeant. As he looked through the windshield, his M-16 pointed directly at the occupant's skull.

"Why don't you get your stethoscope and see if he has a heartbeat." The sergeant said as he lit a cigar up.

"Shit he just moved!" Murphy yelled.

"Shoot him so we can get out of here." The gunner on the second vehicle shouted. "It's as cold as my first wife's tits out here." The gunner thought about his statement for a second. "And probably my second too."

"How many times you been married?" The gunner on the tracked vehicle asked.

"Guys, this thing is moving." Murphy shouted above them all.

The sergeant came up to the side window. "Looks pretty pale and there's blood on the floor. He's a gomer, hurry up and shoot it, Dickens is right, it is as cold as his second wife's titties."

That got a good round of laughter from everyone, even Dickens.

Brendon's eyes fluttered open. His throat was closed and as arid as the Sahara in high summer. He somehow croaked out. "Help me."

Murphy immediately went into medic mode, shouldering his rifle and opening the door to the truck. He handed Brendon a half full canteen.

Brendon drank greedily, half convinced that he already had early onset rabies. He snorted some of the water back up after trying to gulp it down too quickly.

"Take it easy bud." Murphy said. "What happened to you?"

"Bit." Brendon said as quickly as he could so he could get back to the canteen.

Murphy jumped back, and raised his gun half way up.

"Dog." Brendon clarified bringing the canteen down

quickly.

"You sure?" Murphy asked not wanting to get too close.

Brendon gingerly pulled up the bottom of his pants, wincing as the denim fabric snagged on a jagged piece of rended flesh.

"Yup definitely dog. Let me get my med bag."

Brendon nodded going full tilt back on the canteen.

"What are you doing out here alone?" Murphy asked, trying to distract Brendon from the unpleasant sensation he was about to administer to his leg.

Brendon braced against the slapping sting sensation the disinfectant had on his wound. "I messed up." Brendon said between clenched lips.

"How so?" Murphy asked rubbing the wound out with what felt like steel wool but was actually a sterile pad of cotton.

"How bad is my leg?" Brendon asked afraid to look down and only see bone.

"Eh ten, twelve stitches max, you won't be dancing anytime soon. But you'll live." Murphy said as he reached into his bag for a suture needle. "So you were saying?"

"I got into a fight with my fiancée's dad and we parted ways."

"Before or after the end of the world?"

"After." Brendon said resignedly.

"Must have been a hell of a fight, that you'd leave your fiancée and travel companions in this shit." Murphy said as he snugged tight the second stitch. "Is that how all this happened?"

Brendon couldn't blame him for his supposition. His leg was shredded from a dog bite. He was covered in blood and dish detergent and his face was all puffy from pain, tears and lack of sleep. "No I walked away from them in perfectly fine condition, the rest of this I blame on myself."

"Seems like you should have made nice and stayed with them."

"You think?" Brendon said sarcastically.

Murphy made sure to pull the fourth stitch a little extra tight, happy when Brendon jumped in response. "Did anyone die because of the fight you had?"

Brendon shook his head in the negative.

"Can't you go back?"

"They're on the road."

Murphy stopped his suturing to look at Brendon squarely. "These aren't the best of times to be out and about."

"We had no choice, our home was overrun."

Murphy nodded. He had seen many a home, town and even cities completely wiped out.

"Where were you going?" Murphy said tying up the last of his sutures.

"North Dakota first to get my girl's grandmother and then ultimately back east to see if her dad's family was still alive."

Murphy kept quiet. The odds that either of those destinations were going to be fruitful ones were dismally low.

"I thought the same thing." Brendon said picking up on Murphy's lack of comment.

"Is that what you were fighting about?" Murphy asked as he began to bandage up the wound.

"Yeah something like that." Brendon had not even the slightest desire to go into the true reasons, and Murphy didn't look like the type that would believe anyway.

"How many were in your group?"

The word 'were' hurt Brendon more than the dog bite. He sincerely hoped that wasn't the case. "Nine including Henry, he's a bulldog."

"English?" When Brendon nodded, Murphy added. "No shit! I love those dogs, couldn't really afford one on military pay but I was saving up. But by the time this crap is over I don't think there will be any left."

Brendon nodded. Dogs like the Husky and hardy

breeds like German Shepherds will have significant die off from not having human intervention, but they will eventually adapt to their new surroundings and most likely eventually survive. Specialty breeds like Henry or those stupid rat dogs won't make it. They are entirely too dependent on their human masters.

"What are you going to do now?" Murphy asked after taping the bandage off and standing back up.

"Probably try and find them."

"You can come with us, we've got another week or so on patrol and then we head back to what some might construe as civilization."

"There's some place to go to?" Brendon asked hopefully.

"Sure as shit, mankind's last stand, Camp Custer." Murphy said laughing.

Brendon could not even begin to pick up on the humor, but he saw hope if he could find the Talbots again he could bring them back to this camp. "Could I get a map of where this place is?"

"I think I know where you're going with this and I can probably do you one better. Hey Sarge!" Murphy shouted to the man behind the first vehicle who looked somewhere between asleep and smoking a cigar.

"Yeah?" The sergeant said through clenched teeth, tilting his cover back up.

"This guy was with eight civvies and an English Bulldog."

"No shit?" The sergeant yelled back.

Brendon was completely convinced the sergeant's interest was piqued way more by Henry than any of the 'civvies'.

"This guy." Murphy started.

"Brendon."

"Brendon." Murphy began again. "Says he knows where they are going."

"How much time they have on us son?" The sergeant

asked Brendon.

Brendon knew his answer was critical but he knew the sergeant would pick up on a lie. “About a day and a half.”

“I’m sorry son.” And Brendon thought he was. “But we’ll never catch them, not in these.” He said, slapping the side of his armored troop transport.

Brendon saw one chance to convince the sergeant. “My girlfriend's father was a Marine.”

The sergeant stared hard into Brendon’s eyes. “You wouldn’t be shitting me son? Would you? I really hate being shit on, makes everything smelly. And then I’d be really pissed off. You understand where I’m going with this son?”

“Completely.” Brendon nodded. “He was stationed in Kaneohe Marine Corps Air Station, Hawaii.”

“Air wing, huh.” The sergeant said derisively. “Still one of us though. Mount up everyone. We never leave a Marine behind.”

BRENDON'S STORY-CHAPTER 10 -

Murphy got one of the privates to put a few gallons of gas into the Ford while he fished out a couple of Motrin for Brendon. "Wish I could give you something a little stronger for the pain but Motrin is the medicine of the Marine Corps. You sure you don't just want to ride with us."

"Naw." Brendon said for the second time. "I've always wanted a truck and I've grown kind of fond of this one.

Murphy shook his head, there were car lots full of trucks that would never be driven again, but who was he to say. The Marines' pace pushed Brendon to his extreme. They most likely wouldn't have stopped that first night if Brendon hadn't nearly skidded off the road.

The sergeant got out of the lead truck and walked over to Brendon who was leaning over his steering wheel, a fresh bead of sweat on his forehead. "You ready for a break son?"

"About three hours ago." Brendon answered honestly.

"Well why didn't you say something?" The sergeant asked walking away.

"Dickens, get the radar array up. Ramirez you have first watch."

"It's because I'm Mexican isn't it?" Ramirez yelled.

The sergeant stopped. "No, we go to your room on Wednesdays for Mexican food because you're Mexican and you cook like a Latin God, now shut the hell up and do your watch."

The men smiled, this seemed to be part of a ritual the tight knit unit had.

Brendon pointed to the dish Dickens was setting up. "What's that thing?"

"This?" Dickens said, smacking a large plastic case.

"Is our HAZARD."

"Your HAZARD?"

"Yeah Have Any Zombies Arrived Radar Detector, HAZARD."

"Don't mind him." Murphy said. "Marines are really into their acronyms, otherwise they can't remember anything. That thing is pretty sweet though. Originally, it was used to track tanks but they dialed up the sensitivity and it can detect kid sized objects up to a mile away."

"It's saved our asses more than once." Dickens said, as he attached the second pole for added length. "Man this one time we were in a valley and it was so foggy you couldn't see your dick when you took a piss."

"Real eloquent." Murphy said to Dickens. "But you should tell our new guest that you can barely see your dick when the sun is shining."

"Real funny Murphy." Dickens replied.

Murphy hand motioned to Brendon as if to say 'See what I deal with.'

Brendon laughed, but he was wondering how he could come across his own HAZARD.

Dickens started up anew. "So we were taking a break figuring that driving was more dangerous than just sitting tight until the fog blew over. I had no sooner flipped on the power and we had multiple bogies converging on us."

"You sure they were zombies?" Brendon asked.

"They weren't deer. Plus most of them were up ahead almost like they were lying in wait for us to get there. I know that sounds crazy though. No such thing as smart zombies right?" Dickens looked to Brendon for confirmation on this crazy idea. Brendon merely shrugged. Zombies might not be smart but their leader sure as hell is. "I took down the HAZARD real quick like and we buttoned down into the trucks not twenty seconds 'fore they started running into us. It really wasn't much of a fight but without the radar they would have been on us 'fore we knew what do to. The fog really has a way of deadening sound, never even heard them coming. Fog scares the hell out of me now."

Zombies were bad enough. Zombies silently appearing out of the mist were the stuff of acid infused nightmares.

"We decided to stay somewhere else that night." Dickens added needlessly. Dickens finished setting up the array. The other Marines were still on alert, tense even. They didn't visibly relax until the green control panel lit up and the small eight by eight screen began to light up bogeys.

Brendon was alarmed when at least 4 different 'bleeps' showed themselves on the screen. "What are those?" He asked.

"Deer." Dickens said matter-of-factly.

"How do you know?" Brendon asked not entirely ready to trust Dickens expertise.

"Well size for one thing and secondly cuz they aren't headed this way."

Brendon couldn't argue with that. Zombies had an uncanny ability to detect fresh meat from long distances and some of the blips weren't more than 500 yards out according to the screen. "Why post a guard then?"

The sergeant joined the conversation. "I can answer that question. You see this here, is Marine Corps equipment. Which means it is probably in excess of twenty years old and the army most likely had it first. They only give their stuff up when it doesn't work so well anymore."

"Comforting isn't it?" Murphy said. Brendon could only nod. "Sleep with your windows up, I'll get you some blankets."

That first night went virtually trouble free. The second night more than made up for it.

The drive was mind-numbingly boring, a white world of desolation, and still Brendon's heart continuously slammed in his chest. He knew they were too late. "I should have never left her." He berated himself to the empty cab for the umpteenth time. Each time they stopped for fuel or food he became increasingly agitated to the point where Murphy had somehow scrounged a Valium and damn near threatened Brendon with his life if he didn't take it.

Brendon had swallowed it, but it had done painfully little to ease his feelings of dread. When the small convoy had stopped for the fifth time for the day Brendon nearly ripped his door off the hinge trying to ascertain 'why in the hell they were once again stopping, maybe Dickens should just piss in his pants for once! That is if he could find his dick.'

Dickens true to the nature of his miniature bladder was first out of the hummer but it was not for relief, he looked scared and with good reason. "Whaddaya make of that?" He asked Brendon.

Brendon was too hot to think of anything other than 'let's get going already!' But that changed in an instant when he looked out across the expanse and saw what could only be described as a horde. The zombies were traveling at varying speeds and having different degrees of success navigating over the frozen ground. Speeders were well out in front, sometimes trampling over their slower companions. Many slipped and fell, got up and just started running full tilt again. The eerie quiet of so many zombies so close, traveling with what appeared to be a purpose only increased the tension Brendon was feeling. He knew where they were going.

"Well, will you look at that." The sergeant said, lighting up one of his signature cigars that smelled suspiciously like chamomile. "They sure look like they're in a real hurry to get somewhere. You ever seen anything like this?" The sergeant asked Brendon.

Brendon shook his head no, but somehow he got the distinct feeling the sergeant didn't believe him. "Nope, never." He said with a waver in his voice. 'Great, that oughta really convince him now,' he thought to himself.

"Sarge they aren't even looking at us. They can't be more than a couple of hundred yards away and they're not even looking at us." Dickens noted.

Murphy's hand shook as he lit a cigarette. "Never did

smoke before them." He said motioning out into the field and he left it at that.

"I don't like this at all." The sergeant said.

"I do." Dickens replied. "They ain't coming after us."

"Yeah there's something to be said for that." The sergeant said pausing to ponder the situation. "But they do seem to be traveling in the direction we're going." He made sure to lean forward and look directly at Brendon. Dickens and Murphy also looked but were not connecting the dots at all.

The heat of so many gazes, flustered Brendon. "We sightseeing or are we going?"

"Oh we're going, if for nothing more than to see how this pans out." The sergeant said.

"How what pans out?" Dickens asked. But no one was listening; they were all getting back in their prospective rides. Dickens watched as a lone zombie peeled off from the rest and began its pursuit of him. "Fucking Gomer." He said, placing a round in the zombie's shoulder, spinning it around and to the ground. Dickens was back in his truck before the zombie had regained its feet and started back after them.

The line of zombies was at least a couple of miles long and stayed parallel with the Marines until the highway made a sharp easterly turn and the zombies faded from view. Even the sergeant felt better when they were no longer in sight. For another fifteen miles they traveled, finally gaining entry into North Dakota. Night had descended quickly and the sergeant was hesitant to keep moving with that many zombies around.

"Dickens, I want you to set a land speed record for getting the HAZARD up and running. Ramirez, Henderson, dual watches tonight."

The most ominous thing Brendon noticed was that there was not the usual banter or complaining. The Marines went about their business professionally, their training kicking in to help usher out the welling panic that threatened to overtake them all. The HAZARD kicked on, the green display completely devoid of life or death. Almost as one the Marines tensed up.

"That's a good thing right?" Brendon said looking at the monitor and not able to discern the current mood from what he was seeing.

"Not really." Dickens said tensely. "There's usually something on the screen, even if it's only a raccoon."

Brendon got it now. "Nothing living likes to be around when the zombies are."

"You nailed it." Dickens said, holding tight to his rifle.

"How far out can that thing see?"

"When it was used just for tanks and vehicles it was specced at almost 4 miles. When they dialed the sensitivity up it lost distance."

"So?"

"Supposedly 1000 yards, maybe more maybe less, depending on the surrounding landscape."

Brendon instantly began to do the math of how fast the average man can run 1000 yards full tilt. "What's that give us, a couple of minutes warning time?"

"At the most." Dickens said straining to see into the murkiness of the darkening night.

"That's plenty of time right?"

"Depends on how many of them there are."

The world is full of seemingly unrelated random events that have profound impacts, sometimes for the positive, sometimes for the negative. Tonight was of the latter.

A rogue wave in Taipei, which coincidentally had wiped one of the few remaining human strongholds off the face of the planet had also caused water vapor to go high into the atmosphere. The result was a thick cloud cover that slipped into the El Nino slipstream that was four months early due to the global fires that still raged in most countries. The cloud cover raced across the United States and right across the dividing line between North and South Dakota.

The last Farmer's Almanac that would ever be printed had called for clear skies but how could they have known. The moon which was three quarters full, should have supplied ample light; unfortunately it was veiled.

Ramirez and Henderson were three hours into their four hour shift. The nerve racking silence was grating on Henderson. A pack of howling wolves would have been more comforting. Henderson purposefully sought out Ramirez just to break the oblivion.

"Psst, Ramirez." Henderson whispered. It sounded preternaturally loud with nothing to diffuse the sound.

"Scared the shit out of me." Ramirez said, appearing out of the gloom. "What are you doing here, you know we're supposed to be on opposite ends. The Sarge finds out you abandoned your post he'll shoot you."

Henderson shivered, that was not an idle threat. "I know man, I'm just going crazy. I needed to know somebody else was alive out here."

"I hear you man, been seeing ghosts my damn self." 'Ghosts referring to phantom images brought on under duress.'

"You want some chocolate?"

"Do Mexicans hate fences?"

"Huh?"

"Shit yeah, I want some chocolate."

"Fences?" Henderson asked.

"Poor humor, give me some of that."

Henderson handed over half of a Hershey's chocolate bar, which Ramirez promptly dropped. And to compound his error he booted the chocolate away, it skidded a good ten feet before it came to rest on the base of the HAZARD.

"Hell man, if you didn't want it I would have eaten it."

"Real funny and keep your voice down." Ramirez' footfalls echoed off the stillness in the air. A cold wind blew through. Ramirez bent to pick up the fallen prize, the muzzle of his M-16 caught on the base of the HAZARD and as he stood the array came crashing down. One missed audible blip pinged the radar display before the whole assembly came crashing to the ground. “Shit.”

Henderson took off, not wanting to get caught this close to Ramirez’ post. Within seconds, Marines that had been slumbering heavily but uneasily were out and ready to face whatever threat had befallen them.

“It’s alright!” Ramirez shouted over the din. “I just knocked over the HAZARD.”

“Dickens!” The sergeant yelled.

“On it Sarge,” came Dickens voice from somewhere off to the left.

Brendon was beside his truck, his breath coming raggedly. Not from the commotion in the makeshift campsite but rather from the nightmare world from which he had just emerged. Nicole had been screaming in pain of his betrayal. 'Why did you leave me like this?' She had asked. It wasn’t so much the question as it was the condition of his fiancée. She had been completely skinned alive. Nothing remained of her to allow identification except for her diminutive size and her hair. Her fleshless lips had screamed his name, her bleeding arms had struck out seeking to cling to him. Her ravaged legs walked ever in circles as her sightless eyes moved rapidly looking for something that wasn’t there.

When the sergeant was convinced everything was in order he came over to see how Dickens and Ramirez were faring with the array. He could smell the chocolate on their breaths from two paces away. “I thought Henderson was the one with the sweet tooth.” Ramirez’ look of guilt was all the information he needed. Nobody was dead but this breach of protocol would not go unpunished. “If this thing doesn’t work Ramirez, you and Henderson are going to be on patrol every night until we get back. Get back to your post. How’s it looking?” He asked Dickens.

“Couple more dents than before but it should be fine. I think it was built with its users in mind.” Dickens replied. The sergeant trained his flashlight on the wingnut the

Corporal was tightening.

Brendon walked up just as Dickens was getting ready to cycle the machine back up. Then hell broke through the flimsy film between normalcy and the abyss. The sergeant's flashlight was punched out of his arm as the zombie ran full tilt into his side. The scene was surreally lit as the flashlight did cartwheels in the air. For one horrible flash, Brendon watched as the zombie bit deeply into the neck of Dickens. With the light removed, chaos ensued. As the light did one last arc a blaze of iridescence was tinged with the red of Dickens blood as it cascaded out of the gaping wound in the side of his neck.

Brendon's first and fatal reaction was to push the zombie away from Dickens. The zombie latched on heavily to the webbing that separated Brendon's thumb from his forefinger. The pain was excruciating as the zombie tore free. Brendon rolled off to the side, wrapping his damaged hand in his shirt. Three quick rounds later from the Sergeant's 1911 .45, and the zombie and Dickens lay forever still.

"Someone get some light over here quick!" The sergeant yelled a little louder than normal, the only clue that he was flustered in any way.

Brendon knew time was short, if the Sergeant saw his wound he would kill him as fast as he had taken out Dickens. At least three different flashlights were bobbing in from around the camp. Brendon stood up forcing the gorge in his throat down. All the lights were thankfully trained on the horrid scene before them. Brendon feigned sickness at the sight. It wasn't too much of a stretch. The congealed brain matter of the zombie was intermingled with the pinker healthier looking brain matter of the friendly Marine tech Dickens.

"You alright Brendon?" The sergeant asked as Brendon moved away.

Blood flowed freely from his left hand, he had to make distance before it soaked through his shirt and onto the snow covered ground where it would stick out like a sore thumb. ‘Not funny’ he thought to himself. “Fine.” He grunted out, it sounded more like a retch but that was still fitting to the circumstances.

Brendon got back to the truck fairly convinced that he had staunched the flow, although his shirt told a different story. The dome light in the truck was equipped with a dimmer switch for which Brendon was thankful. Mostly because it would bring less attention to himself and also it would be more difficult to see the damage done. He took two quick breaths before he could muster the courage to look. He gazed long and hard at the death sentence that awaited him. It didn’t look particularly life threatening. A half inch thick jagged semi circle of skin and muscle was ripped free. That it was a bite was not in doubt. If he so desired, he could have marked out each individual tooth groove as it had sunk deep into his hand; he chose not to.

Brendon shut the light off. He sat there for long minutes staring out of the windshield. He was looking in the direction where the Marines were taking care of their fallen comrade and getting the HAZARD back up. His eyes saw it all. His brain registered none of it. The pain he felt at the loss of never seeing Nicole again far outweighed his life, which was now forfeit. After he had inwardly cursed out every known deity, he silently sobbed for each loss and made peace with himself. He had resolved to show the sergeant the wound. Would you feel the bullet as it punched through your skull? Or did it happen too fast? Would you be able to register the damage as the bone shards and lead projectile tore through the mind? More importantly would the Marines continue on this quest without him there? They had already lost one of their own and might be close to calling it quits especially if their guide was gone. No that was unacceptable! “I’m not a zombie yet!”

The sergeant startled the hell out of him as he came up to the window. “You alright?”

He could only wonder how close to the truck the sergeant was when Brendon had made his statement. “Fine.”

He reiterated, doing his best to cover his hand and shirt up even though it was now pitch dark in the cab, guilt has a habit of shining bright.

"You sure?"

"Yep right as rain." Brendon strained. 'Right as rain? Who says that? If he was suspicious before you just gave him more to think about.' The sergeant walked away, he had more concerns at the moment. Sweat broke out spontaneously almost completely over his entire body. 'Is this how it starts?' He wanted to cry again but that would accomplish nothing, and he still had one thing left in this life to do before he died.

Brendon got out of the truck. He was looking for Murphy. He found him by the back of the troop transport smoking a cigarette next to the now body bagged Dickens. Dark circles and a drawn look punctuated his usually affable features.

"Hey Murph." The medic nodded. "Hey are you bound by the Hippocratic oath or anything like that?" Brendon asked.

"I'm a corpsman not a Doctor." The cherry of the cigarette lit up Brendon's features. Murphy could tell Brendon was weighing the merits of telling him something or keeping it quiet. "You got the clap or something?" Murphy's attempt at humor fell flat for both of them. It would be a while before things looked funny again.

Brendon had made up his mind. He pulled his rag wrapped hand out of his pocket and showed Murphy.

"Oh shit, when did that happen?" Murphy said taking a huge drag out of the cigarette.

"I was trying to help Dickens, it didn't go so well."

"Does the Sarge know?"

"I'm still alive, what do you think?"

"Shit." Murphy said pulling his cap off to rub his hand through his hair. He grabbed Brendon's hand and poured the remains of his canteen over it, washing some of the detritus away. He started rooting around in his medical emergency kit grabbing disinfectant, gauze, a needle and some thread.

"How much time do I have?" Brendon asked as steadily as he could.

Murphy never looked up as he kept working on the wound. "Uh cleaning out the wound and putting disinfectant on it helps."

"Listen Murphy I know I'm a dead man walking, I just need to know if I'm going to have enough time to help my fiancée and her family."

"If we get there tomorrow, yes."

"Is there a changeover period, will I be able to tell what's going on?"

Murphy finally looked up meeting him eye to eye. "You'll know, there's about a three to five minute window where the person can feel themselves slipping and then...you know what happens. What are you going to do?"

"I'm not going to become a zombie, that's for sure. I'm not a religious man Murphy, but do you think God will make an exception for me if I take myself out before it happens?"

"I think he will be able to find it in his heart to absolve you of that sin. The true sin would lie in you allowing yourself to become a zombie. That is not the work of God. I am truly sorry Brendon."

"Yeah me too. Got an extra cigarette?" They sat in silence. Words carried no weight now.

The sun couldn't come up fast enough. Brendon did not sleep at all. It was to be his last sunrise and he did not want to miss it. The air had a sweetness he could not bring himself to identify. "Almost like poppies." He said as he stretched.

"Incoming!" Ramirez shouted from his perch atop the troop transport. "Henderson anything showing on the HAZARD?"

"Nope, wait there it is, holy shit! Sergeant, multiple gomers heading this way."

"Alright vacation is over. Pack up and let's get the hell out of here." The sergeant yelled. His command was obeyed before it was finished being given.

During the drive to Carol's, Brendon fluctuated between peculiar calmness, flushed sweating and searing pain. 'This must be what menopause feels like.' He mused.

Brendon's truck shook as heavy armament was expended by the troop transport in front of him. Four zombies were reduced to ribbons of flesh on the side of the road. Brendon had a momentary pang of compassion for them and then quickly tore asunder the stray thought. He couldn't help but wonder if that was to be his fate.

Three hours later they were in the center of Carol's home town, if you can call a gas station, Post Office and a Piggly Wiggly grocery store a town center. From here Brendon's recollection of exactly where Carol's farmstead was became increasingly foggy. This would have been an issue if not for the near continuous line of zombies that cut across the town in a northeasterly route. A few zombies turned to appraise the new 'eats' but none strayed from their vector.

The sergeant halted the caravan and walked over to Brendon who had also exited his truck. "What are the odds they're going to where we need to be?" The sergeant asked appraising Brendon. "You don't look so good."

"Nerves."

"Oh that's right, you have some pride swallowing to take care of."

'I hope I get the chance,' he thought. He, however, answered the sergeant with a mere nod.

"Is there something I need to know here son? I've never seen zombies act like this. They look driven. The fact that they aren't paying us any attention at all has me flummoxed."

"Would you rather they were?" Brendon asked impatiently wanting this conversation to be over. The sand granules that measured his time remaining were running dangerously close to single digits in the hourglass of his life.

"Now that's not really the point, is it? Something is not adding up, not at all, when this is all over you and I are going to have a long talk."

'Doubt it.' Brendon thought. Brendon thanked God that Marines are more men of action than thought. The sergeant strode away, got back into the troop transport and took a right turn no more than 15 feet in front of the traveling zombies. It was another three miles before a left turn presented itself. Because of the zombies angling away, they had been lost from the line of sight for a few minutes. Another mile in a northerly route and the stain of them once again became visible.

It was another right and then left before the sergeant once again pulled over to a stop. The zombies' final destination was now clearly in view even though it lay a full mile away.

Henderson checked his ammo on the turret of the troop transport. Ramirez opened up the hatch on the hummer, readying his weapon also. "We can't be going in there Sarge?" Ramirez asked bewildered at the sheer number of undead that surrounded the house. "We're going in there." He answered himself impassively. "I hate it sometimes when I'm right."

"You done jawing over there Ramirez?" The sergeant asked him.

Ramirez rattled off a string of what can only be construed as eloquent foreign cuss words.

"That doesn't look like a Country Buffet on kids eat free Wednesdays son. Any chance you could be a little more forth coming on any information?"

"I really wish I knew." Brendon had no sooner finished the sentence and he bent over from crippling cramps. His stomach muscles nearly ripped under the strain.

"Murphy!" The sergeant yelled in alarm.

"Fine, I'm fine." Brendon whistled through his teeth. Placing his hand on the sergeant's arm to stop him from summoning help.

It was then the sergeant noted the bandage. "What's this?" He asked suspiciously. "You didn't have this yesterday." The sergeant stepped back, fingering his holster.

Murphy rushed up and quickly accessed the situation that was quickly turning from bad to worse. Murphy had seen enough victims turn to zombies to realize that Brendon was close to joining the ranks of the enemy. His skin was taking on a gray pallor. Severe stomach cramping would immediately be followed by whole body spasms and then death. The body's last gasp so to speak.

Brendon was able to get himself under control and stand without a noticeable stoop. "I'm fine." He slurred. "Let's go." Claws of stinging stitches tore out from his stomach and spread throughout his body. It took every fiber of his being to stand and endure under the scrutinous stare of the sergeant. Murphy placed himself between the sergeant and Brendon. Somewhat to hide the pain the kid was going through but mostly to keep the sergeant from just outright shooting him. "We've got to go now." Brendon whispered. The strain of the words clearly evident.

"I think it's rabies." Murphy told the sergeant. "The sooner we can get him back to base the sooner I can get him treatment," although that was a lie. Once symptoms of rabies showed, treating it was far too late. Murphy could only hope that the sergeant didn't know this.

The sergeant thankfully stopped touching the hilt of his gun. "You stay here kid, we'll get your future in-laws and then we'll get you all back to Custer."

"I'm going." Brendon said defiantly.

"Don't push it." Murphy whispered.

"This is it for me Murph, I just want one more chance to see her."

"Sarge, I can give him a heavy dose of antibiotics right now, it will get him through the next few hours." Also a lie.

"Have it your way kid." The sergeant got back in the

transport and strapped himself in.

Murphy proceeded to give Brendon a mild sedative. “This will help a little with the cramping.”

“Thank you for everything Murphy. I’ll put a good word in for you when I get to where I’m going.”

“I’d appreciate that.” Murphy replied, and that was not a lie.

“What’s the plan?” Henderson asked leaning down from his gunner’s position.

“Guns blazing, I suppose.” The sergeant answered.

‘I was hoping for something a little more concrete.’ Henderson mumbled to himself once again checking that his weapon was fully ready to fire.

Murphy got into the passenger seat.

“Rabies my ass, Murphy. That kid’s dying." The sergeant said. "We all watched what happened to Greenfield after he was bit.”

“I know Sarge, he just wants to see his girl one more time.”

“Well let’s not disappoint him.”

Henderson cussed as his head smacked against the machine gun's breech due to the unprepared for acceleration.

“The house is on fire!” Henderson yelled down.

“Do you think I’m driving blind.” The sergeant replied. “You’d better start cutting us a path or this is gonna be a bumpy ride.”

The Browning M2 .50 Caliber roared to life as it dealt ever-lasting death. The full-throated scream of the bullets as they emerged from the barrel brought a certain sense of satisfaction to the Sergeant as he slammed the troop transport into the outskirts of the zombies.

“Fucking gomers.” He said grimly.

Murphy had grabbed every available handhold as the transport lurched from side to side under the assault, his ears almost bleeding from the noise of the small cannon above him. “Should have joined the Air Force.” He said, not for the first time nor the last.

Various pieces of zombie appendages slammed against the reinforced battle windshield. “Hope you topped off the windshield wiper fluid.” The sergeant needled a green tinged Murphy.

Time had slowed for Murphy. He watched a piece of hot brass as it lazily floated down and stuck to an eyeball of a middle aged zombie woman. The contact of the hot metal made her eye explode sending viscous fluid shooting out dislodging the offending ejecta. Murphy could not figure out how the sergeant even knew where he was going. Gore and blood covered every available port. It was like they were traveling within the innards of some giant beast of mythical proportions.

The smell of fire began to overtake the smell of zombies. ‘Must be getting close.’ Murphy thought. He felt the lunge of the transport as the sergeant decided that more speed was needed.

Brendon was having severe difficulty controlling his extremities. Tremors coursed through him; compounding the difficulty was the uneven ground caused by zombie bodies that he was traversing over. “Too late, too late, too late,” became his mantra. His legs were spasming just as the truck ahead of him sped up. Brendon had to will his leg to his bidding before he fell behind and without the grace of a machine gun hacking a trail he would be cut off quickly.

He scooted down on the seat, the movement forcing his leg down onto the accelerator. Control came back slowly and with difficulty. He was able to press the brake on his own as he pulled up to what little remained of Carol’s house.

“All aboard!” He said as he spotted, Mike, BT and Jen. His heart lifted at the sight of them.

“Glad to see you boy!” BT shouted from the truck bed. Brendon agreed.

Brendon heard some commotion in the back, but cognitive functioning was becoming increasingly hard to do. “I’m me!” He yelled.

“Yes and soon you will be mine.” A cold voice

burrowed out of the depths of his mind.

"NICOLE!" He screamed, his second to last sane thought. The last being when he shoved the Walther 9mm under his jaw and double tapped his disease addled brain.

CHAPTER 11 - JOURNAL ENTRY 5 -

"You're Catholic right?" BT asked me.

I was hesitant to answer, religious conversations rarely go well, most in fact end in Holy Wars. Don't believe me? If there are still any left, find a Muslim and ask him or her what they think of Christianity. That will be a short conversation revolving around the blade of a knife being inserted into various parts of your being.

"Yeah why?" I answered reluctantly.

"That's the religion where you go up to the Priest and get wine and bread right?"

"Where are you going with this?"

"Just answer the question."

"Yes, the congregation receives the Eucharist, the representation of the Body and Blood of Christ."

"That's what I thought."

"You just needed a semantics lesson then?"

"Not really, but I did wonder something." He paused. I didn't prod he was up to something I could tell by the way he was smiling at me, like a jungle cat getting ready to pounce. He was looking at me waiting for a reply. Apparently it would be funnier if I prompted him.

"Fine BT, what are you wondering?" The words practically oozed scorn, he didn't care.

"How did you do it?"

I instantly knew what he was talking about, but I'd be damned if I was going to let him corner me that quick. "BT I'm tired and I'm in pain, I just want to go to sleep."

"Bullshit!" He said sitting up. "You know what I'm talking about, spill it."

"Is this really necessary?"

"I don't have anything better going on right now. Not

unless they're hiding Naomi Campbell somewhere on this base."

"I figured you for more of a Halle Berry type."

"Don't change the subject, but yeah she's third."

"Who the hell is second?"

"Man, don't laugh, I've got this thing for…oh, you sneaky bastard you almost got me."

"I tried. Alright if you must know I bought a carton of Eucharist wafers and had them blessed. I used to bring my own to church along with a thermos of grape juice, I hate wine."

BT would have rolled out of his bed if his leg wasn't in suspension.

"Have you ever been to a Catholic mass? Its friggen disgusting." I said starting my defense. "First they make you shake hands with all your neighbors. There's Kenny, the eleven year old that has had his finger shoved up his nose the entire time. There's old man Baker, who smells like 4 day old meatloaf left on the curb during a heat wave. Then there's Mrs. Porter with her infant and she just changed a dirty diaper without using wipes. Yeah real effen sanitary!" My voice was rising with the increase of potential germs. "So then we get through that particularly nasty infectious test tube archaic trait and move right along to sipping wine out of a golden chalice that the entire mass has put their cracked, canker laced lips on not to mention those with cold sores." I was shuddering. "Then the priest hands you a wafer that he had clutched between his thumb and forefinger, but what's worse than that is he's been doing that to everyone else also and they have had the chance to breathe all their germs on those two fingers as he placed the wafer on their tongues."

"Oh man, I needed that!" BT said holding his gut he was laughing so hard.

"Ass." Was all I could muster.

After a significant lull, I realized that BT had drifted off into slumber. I was close too, when distant gunshots rang out. Fully alert now, I realized my dilemma. Here I was with a damaged arm tied to a bed without a weapon, I was sort of like a human kabob without the marinade or the accompanying vegetables or wooden skewer or…OH STOP TALBOT. Great just great, I was pissing the other half of me off.

"BT you awake?"

"Yup I heard it too." BT said with his eyes still closed. "Relax Talbot."

"Not really in my nature."

"We're in a military base, I'm sure they can take care of whatever is going on."

"Yeah you're probably right, I just hate being this helpless. Bambi could come in here right now and kick both of our asses."

"Now are you talking about a zombie Bambi or just a regular type Bambi?" BT asked in earnest. "Cause I'm going to freak out a little if you're thinking that there could be some zombie animals. Can you imagine nests of zombie rats coming after us, with that little hairless tail, or what about zombie pigeons? They're already the rat of the sky. Or maybe cockroach zombies."

"Stop already. I thought I was bad."

"I think maybe we have too much time on our hands." BT said. "But you don't think there are animal zombies do you?"

"Fuck no." I said much too quickly, more to defer my unbounded imagination than to qualm BT's fears. Could the disease pass the species line? Why not, other diseases did. Super, nothing like a 600-pound silverback gorilla wanting to munch on your head. "Oh no."

"What Talbot?" BT asked alarmed. Looking wildly about the room for this new threat.

"I was just thinking about a zombified Big Foot."

BT was a half second away from calling me crazy, before he really let the thought of that set in. "Oh man, that would be really bad." BT said and he meant it.

"Big Foot as a zombie?" Tracy asked from the

doorway. “What are you doing Talbot? Didn’t I tell you not to infect others with your touched thoughts?”

“It could happen.” I said, defending my position.

BT nodded in agreement.

“The Doctor either needs to up both of your meds or halve them. I don’t know which.” Tracy laughed.

“So what gives?” I asked, nodding my head to the doorway.

“I figured the gunshots would get you thinking, I just didn’t know how far and fast you’d go down the rabbit hole.”

“What? BT thinks that there are zombie cockroaches.” I said deflecting the conversation.

“He’s a pretty big guy Talbot. Are you in such a rush to throw him under the bus?” I noticed that she did look down around her legs as she asked the question, a small shudder of revulsion coursed through her.

It’s funny how thoughts, even inane (or insane) ones, have a habit of wriggling their way through your psychoses. That’s why therapists are (were) some of the most screwed up people on the planet. It’s impossible to listen to that many people with that many problems and not begin to inherit more than your fair share of them. Just think about it. What if I were to tell you that before you sat on that public toilet a grotesquely dirty male/female had just sat there and they had crusty sores that leaked a viscous oozing liquid that slightly resembled phlegm from a person suffering from bronchitis. You know what I’m talking about, that thick green/brown lung cookie. And that these seeping pustules carried small microscopic teethy worms that will burrow into your soft exposed flesh spreading their infection throughout your body. Will you ever be able to look at a toilet ring the same again? Or will you picture miniature monsters awaiting their chance to do you harm.

“Talbot, you’re doing it to me again!” Tracy yelled.

“What I didn’t say it.” I said surprised.

“Did BT think about zombie cockroaches on his own?” Tracy asked.

"Well yeah, he did." I answered her honestly. "I mean I might have brought up something about Bambi."

"Bambi? Really Talbot?"

"He did say something about nothing being left to rein the crazy in." BT threw in for good measure.

"Thanks man." I said to BT

"Anytime, there's enough room under this bus for the both of us."

"Is it a double-decker? Although that wouldn't really mean any more room underneath it." I said as I started to wonder if there would be more room or not. I felt the heat of two sets of eyes on me.

"Talbot sometimes I wonder how you got us this far." Tracy said.

"What?"

"The shots. Remember those?"

"I was getting to it." I said, but in fact I wasn't. I had completely forgotten about them, so intent was I on flesh eating rabbits.

"Zombies came ashore." She answered.

"Ashore, what the hell does that mean?" BT asked

"Ashore like in landing craft?" I asked

I got the look that was becoming all too common. The, 'are you crazy glare.'

"No boats then?" I added.

"Yeah no boats." She shook her head and continued. "Dozens of them just started walking up the beach. Caught an older couple that was getting a little randy behind some dunes."

"At least they went out happy." I said. The words were out of my mouth long before I realized how tasteless a statement that was.

Tracy thought it. BT said it. "Fuck Talbot what is your problem?"

"What?" the dawn of recognition coming slowly. "Oh sorry, I wasn't even thinking."

"I wouldn't mind so much but it seems to happen

more and more." Tracy said.

"I'm sorry let's get past this." Of course I wanted to, it was my shattered reputation on the line. Tracy reluctantly let it go. "Was this the first time?"

"The first time you've inserted your foot in your mouth or the first time the zombies have come up the beach?"

BT pointed at Tracy and nodded. "Good one."

"Funny, but deserved." I said. "Let's go with the beaching."

"I'll tell you what, the Army guys were running around like chickens without heads and the Marines looked pretty concerned."

"So I'm going to go with a yes on that then."

"What do you think it means Talbot?" BT asked me.

"I've got a couple of ideas BT, and none of them are good. You still want to hear them?"

"No." BT answered truthfully. "Well get on with it."

"Well first off it could mean that some zombies fell into the water sometime in the last few weeks, maybe off of some transport ship and just finally made it ashore here."

"Eh, maybe." BT said shaking his head in the negative. "Next."

"Some local zombies have figured out a more viable option of how to get into the gated buffet."

"Possible." BT said. "Or?"

"Or Eliza sent some forward troops in the hopes of finding some weaknesses to this base's defenses."

BT eased his back down towards the pillow. "Shit."

"Eliza? Already?" Tracy asked, hoping against hope that I was wrong.

"It feels like something she would do. I know the zombies have some rudimentary intelligence. I just can't imagine that they'd be able to pass tactics to each other. Possibly one might figure out that he could walk into the water and bypass all the fences and guns but not dozens at least not all at once."

"Okay though Mike." BT said. "If this is Eliza in all of this, why tip her hand now? She had to know that a few dozen zombies weren't going to breach this place. She could have waited until she had a few thousand zombies. That would have really thrown this place into mass chaos. These military guys aren't dummies. Now they're going to set up defenses and patrols."

I pondered BT's question. Eliza's actions made absolutely no sense. Unless. "It's a feint."

"What?" BT and Tracy asked simultaneously.

"Jinx!" I yelled. "Now you guys have to get me a coke! Man, what I wouldn't do for that carbonated drink of pure refreshment right now."

"Are we on hidden cameras? Are you getting sponsorship money for your product endorsements? Can you get back to the 'feint' thing."

"Sorry that just sounds so good, in a tall glass with lots of ice and the huge condensation droplets sweating on the outside of the glass."

"Talbot." Tracy and BT once again said in synch.

"Again! Huh! This gets better and better."

Tracy glared at me.

"Sorry, sorry." I reiterated. "It's just that my mouth is so dry right now."

"Talbot!" BT shouted. "If my leg wasn't busted I would run all around this base to find you that damn Coke just so I could bust it over your head. Now what are you talking about? Although that does sound really good, maybe with a little vanilla in it."

"I'm leaving." Tracy said.

"Hold on hon." I said coming back to a Cokeless reality. "Eliza has something else planned, she has to know that this place only has so many resources to combat a threat and she is going to stretch those resources as thin as she can. I don't have a clue as to what she's thinking but it's obviously better than having a water assault."

"Seemed like a pretty good plan to me." BT said

"Yeah me too, so whatever she's thinking must be even better."

The room must have dropped twenty degrees because we all shuddered in unison. I don't think there is a 'jinx' rule for that.

"How's your leg feeling now?" I asked BT in all seriousness.

"Better by the minute." He answered.

Tracy garnered what we were talking about. "Neither of you two is in any sort of condition to go back on the road. Mike you have literally died twice in the span of five days. And don't even say it! Three is not the charm."

"How'd she know I was going to say that?" I asked BT.

BT shrugged his shoulders, and then miraculously hit his power down button.

"How does he do that?" I now asked the slumbering giant.

"Mike?"

"I know Tracy, we can't leave. I'm not sure I could get out of this bed and make it into the head to take a piss without passing out. Eliza just keeps forcing our hand. There's still time but the meter is definitely running.

CHAPTER 12 - JOURNAL ENTRY 6 -

"Mike you awake?"

"What is it with hospitals?" I asked with my eyes closed. "You keep giving me sedatives to sleep and tell me I need rest so that I can recuperate and then you wake me up every half hour to see how I'm doing."

"Mike." The Doc said calmly. "You've been asleep for nearly 36 hours."

"Holy shit, no wonder why I kept having dreams about pissing. In one of them I was at an old abandoned town pool. It was empty when I got to it but I started to take a leak and it was filling at this really alarming rate, and I was like 'Holy crap this had better stop soon or its going to over flow and I'm going to be really embarrassed when my piss starts flowing down the streets and into storm drains The whole time I'm taking this piss I don't feel any relief. I am never getting that satisfactory release of pressure from my bladder. You know what I mean Doc?"

"Mike to be honest I've given up a long time ago trying to figure out what you are talking about."

"So you've never had the 'piss dream'"?

"Can we perhaps move on to another subject?"

"Oh I get it Doc, did you have some bed wetting issues as a child?" The Doc's face was beginning to look a little indignant. "Do you still have some issues? I mean cause it's alright with me. I mean we all have our own skeletons in the closet so to speak. I mean I don't personally wet the bed but…"

"Oh for the love of God Mike, I really have no desire to discuss my fictional bodily function problems. I came here with a serious problem and a potential solution."

"Alright, alright but I still think I'm going to bust at

the seams."

"Fine!" The Doc said handing me a bedpan.

"This might go a little smoother if you weren't looking at me like you wanted to punch me."

"Let me know when you're done." The Doc said as he went back over to a small table that contained a rather large syringe. I was hoping the needle looked so big because the table was so small and if that wasn't the case, I hoped the needle was for BT. Hell he was still asleep. It wouldn't hurt him until he was awake. "You done yet?" The Doc called over his shoulder.

"You're really ruining the mood over here, Doc. I haven't pissed in 36 hours I would really like to enjoy this."

"The elimination of waste should not…"

"Doc! You're killing me over here."

"Shoe doesn't fit quite so right when it's on the other foot, does it?"

"Point taken, I think." After a couple of more minutes I took probably the best non-beer induced piss of my entire life. I bet I lost 3.5 pounds in 2 minutes. I was going to market this new diet sensation. 'Piss Away the Pounds'. Might be tough to get a sponsor though. Oh well, I had time to work on a new name.

I sheepishly handed over the near brimming bed pan to the Doc, I don't know which of us was more disgusted and embarrassed when some sloshed out and onto his arm and chest. "Sucks for you." I said under my breath.

"What?" The Doc asked, completely mortified with this new development.

"Nothing, I didn't say anything."

The Doc looked at me suspiciously. This was not a good position for me to be in. I had one arm tied down and he had a nearly full bedpan of hot steamy piss. I'd probably die from shock if he threw it at me. The last time I had been this scared I was in my living room with Henry in my arms and a small contingent of zombies were trying to make me their breakfast. Doc Baker walked over and put the bed pan in the industrial sized sink, and then proceeded to take off his now urine infused scrubs. His vigorous washing had turned his skin into a cherry pink version of its former self. He was muttering something way over there. Every once in a while I would catch single words like 'asshole' or 'nutsack'. He could call me whatever he wanted as long as he didn't pick that bedpan back up.

Doc Baker came back his left arm considerably redder than his right.

"You know." I said. "That pee is sterile."

"Don't!" He said pointing an angry red digit at me.

"Fine, fine." I said holding up my one good arm.

"Can we get on with what I wanted to talk to you about?"

"Does it involve that needle?" I said pointing past him.

"It does."

I felt like I had already been pricked, deflated. "And me?"

"Not directly."

"BT then? He's a big guy he won't even feel it." That actually elicited a small laugh from the Doc.

"No I was thinking of your son Justin."

"What's going on Doc?" I asked, all triviality discarded.

"If I had a team of virologists and biologists and a couple of dozen other ologists I might be able to use his blood to produce some sort of vaccine against this scourge."

"You're throwing a lot of hope out there with a significant amount of negative tone to it Doc."

"Well there's hope Mike, but not on as broad a scope as I was hoping for. I've been studying Justin's blood since the day he got here. There's a key there, of that I'm sure it just so happens to be locked in a world class bank vault and I'm trying to safe-crack it with a sparkler."

"That bad?"

"The sparkler might be an overstatement, more like a

wet match."

"Ouch."

"Don't get me wrong, I'm taking vials of his blood in the hopes that an epidemiologist somehow stumbles into camp. But until then I might have an answer or at least a way to treat what afflicts him."

"I'm listening." Hell he could have been talking about the Baroque movement and I would be listening, couldn't really go anywhere in the state I was in.

"I am going to put this in as easily explainable layman terms as I can, not because I think you're an idiot."

"Thanks."

"But because my grasp on the concept is tenuous at best. In a normal human when they receive a bite from a zombie, their immune system is completely destroyed by the parasite. The system doesn't even have time to offer a viable defense. The saliva of the infected appears to be the most optimum way to spread the contagion, unfortunately not the only way. But in Justin's case he received such a small influx of the bug his body was able to rally and offer something almost as good as a victory."

I was remembering that night not so long ago when I had sat over my son's bed dreading the fact that in all likelihood I was going to have to put a bullet in him. One does not easily get over one of the darkest days in their existence. "What's that Doc? What's almost as good as a victory?"

"A sliding stalemate, the parasites have been stalled, somewhat."

"I don't much care for 'sliding' and 'somewhat', there's more Doc, I can see it in your face."

"It's a war that Justin can't win. He might be able to hold them off for weeks, months maybe even a year or two but eventually they will overwhelm him. If he catches a cold or gets bronchitis and his body has to start spreading white blood cells around he won't be able to produce them quick enough. The antibiotics I'm giving him are helping but it's more like giving Percocets to a man with a dislocated shoulder. It dulls the pain but doesn't fix the root of the problem."

The Doctor seemed hesitant to continue, I prodded him on. "And?"

"And, I've got an idea."

"The needle?"

"The needle."

"What's in the needle Doc?"

"It's what the CDC was developing when this whole thing started."

"You told me yourself it didn't work Doc."

"It didn't work because it just wasn't strong enough. But it might be enough to tip the scales with your son."

"Last time I checked Doc, scales can tip both ways."

"And that's the problem."

"You can't be asking me this Doc."

"Mike he is fighting a battle with a predetermined ending. This might be his only chance."

"What if it doesn't work?"

Doctor Baker sat back in his chair pinching the bridge of his nose in his thumb and forefinger. "Then the inevitable happens a lot sooner."

"If we, and by we I mean Tracy myself and Justin agree to this will he be cured? Will the virus be destroyed?"

"No this is a symptomatic treatment, it is much like giving insulin to a person suffering from diabetes. It will keep the parasite in check. It will allow his body to recover an equilibrium; it can stop the war that is raging within him."

"An armistice?"

"Armistice, détente, stasis, whatever you want to call it, your son will be back."

"Where is Justin now?" I asked a cold chill sweeping through my soul.

"He's in our isolation ward."

"Doc, I can't do it again." Doc Baker remained silent. "The night he was injured I stayed with him. I had a loaded gun with the hammer pulled back in my lap. I talked to him the entire night about every good and not so good thing we had done in our lives together. I fully expected to end his life that night." An unforced sob issued forth from the depths of my being. The Doc placed his hand on my good shoulder. "Can you know what it's like to take a piece of you, something that contains all your hopes, your dreams, your love and just destroy it? CAN YOU!?" I yelled.

I was sobbing nearly inconsolably. BT faked sleep. I owed him big for that. Tracy, true to her nature, was Johnny on the spot. She had somewhere along the line honed the skill of always being at the right spot at the right time to a science.

"What's going on Mike? Doctor?" She asked with concern. I was thinking that she thought I had received bad news about myself. Trust me I wouldn't have taken that news half as bad as what the Doctor was proposing. "You alright Mike?"

I wiped my eyes. "You know how I feel about you seeing me cry."

"I know, I know, you're Ironman. That's what has me concerned Mike, in twenty years of marriage I've seen you with more punctures, burns and body parts hanging on by a thread where you've just grunted about going back to the emergency room. The two times I've seen you cry, one involved the death of my dad and the other was your mom. So what's going on?"

The Doc took about ten minutes to lay out everything to her like he had to me.

"To quote my husband! Abso-fucking-lutely not!" She shouted.

"Go to him then." The Doc started.

"I do! Every day." She retorted.

"You didn't let me finish, Tracy."

In my head I couldn't believe he had pulled out the condescending card. BAD, BAD move.

"You've got about ten seconds Doctor, to explain yourself before I turn and walk out of here. I'd rather kick your ass right now. The only thing that's keeping me at bay is the gratitude I have for you saving my husband, but that will only get you so far." Her finger of doom was in full thrust mode. A diamond tipped jackhammer would be less lethal.

I could tell the Doctor was especially appreciative of the fact that his chair had wheels and he was on a tile floor, but he would run out of running room long before she ran out of fuel.

"Tracy go to your son, ask him how he's doing." Tracy looked about to respond. "No really, ask him how he is doing. I've had long talks with him. He's told me that he feels like he slips a little deeper every day. That a little more of who he is gets dragged away and discarded like so much trash. Sometimes he just feels like giving up." Tracy sobbed much like I had. "He's tired of fighting both inside of himself and against the outside world. He knows what kind of threat he poses to all of you. He can't bear the thought that his mere existence could bring harm to any of you. He has lost hope. He's asked me more than once to give him enough pills or a lethal injection to end it all."

Tracy came over to me crying. She was careful to avoid my wound. She didn't do such a good job. I did my best to bite back my tears of pain.

"I don't bring this to either of you lightly."

Tracy held her hand up.

"It's just that…"

"Doc, stop talking now." I told him.

"Right, I'm going to check on my other patients."

"Thanks Doc." I wrapped my good arm around my wife. Her racking sobs jostled me, but that was a kind of pain I was familiar with. It was the kind that I could cope with. It was like a bad friend who you knew was going to borrow money that he had no intentions of paying back. He was the friend that would turn over your couch cushions after he burned them accidently with a cigarette after you specifically told him that nobody smokes in the house. He was an asshole, but he was YOUR asshole. That other pain? Well let's just say that pain was like a lawyer who just so happened to be a Yankees fan after they just bought their 26th championship. Yeah, he's that asshole.

Tracy and I did about another hour's worth of mutual consolation. We had a way of taking the little bit of strength we possessed and bouncing it back and forth between the two of us, adding to it at each and every toss. Do all married couples possess this super power? Probably not or there would have been fewer divorces.

"What do you think Talbot?" Tracy asked, lifting her tear soaked face off my tear soaked chest.

"I think I need a new shirt." Tracy made as if she was going to punch me. "I think we have the Doctor lay everything out there for him, the pros and the cons and we let him decide."

"Okay."

"Okay, that's it? No expletives about how crazy I am? Or how nuts this situation is? I was expecting more."

"There is no other answer Mike, you heard the Doctor. Our baby is ready to give up."

"I know." I said stroking her hair, which also happened to be wet. "You'd better wait before you go back out."

She looked at me funny. Ah, the Tracy I know and love.

"Your hair is soaked, you go out now and you're going to get an ice helmet. Although I really kind of dig chicks in uniform."

"Well maybe if you weren't in that hospital bed."

"That is not right. Not right at all." I lamented.

"I'm going to see Justin."

"Tell him I love him."

"Do I look like I've been crying?"

"Besides the running mascara, red eyes and Rudolph nose? No, you look fine."

"I'll tell him you love him. I'll see you tonight."

"Bye love."

"Bye Talbot."

Tracy walked out of the room. I turned to adjust myself. I had only been awake for a couple of hours and I was exhausted. BT's blanket was up over his head. I could see his whole bed shaking.

"You crying?" I asked him.

"I'm sleeping, leave me alone." He sniffed.

CHAPTER 13 - JOURNAL ENTRY 7 - 

Justin was in a small room maybe ten by ten feet with a heavy lockable oak door. He was usually able to walk around his room but for this experiment he was fully restrained to his bed with cloth straps. I involuntarily got the heebie-jeebies thinking about being completely tied down and then getting an itch on my nose. I was convinced that would drive me insane. The room was cramped with myself in a wheelchair, Tracy behind me, Doc Baker, a fully armed guard and the center of attention, Justin in his bed.

"For the fourth time, Mom, I want to do this." Justin said looking up as high as he could with the strap across his forehead.

Tracy reached down and grabbed my hand out of my lap. "Is the guard necessary?" Tracy asked.

Nobody responded. He was necessary in case the unspeakable happened.

"Justin, I am going to put this mask on you for our protection, okay?" The doc asked him. Justin nodded his head, his eyes locked on a fixed location on the ceiling. The 'mask' was nothing more than a leather strap with a wide piece that fit securely over the most dangerous part of a zombie, the mouth. Images of Hannibal Lecter streamed through my head as the mask was placed into position. To say my stomach was in knots would be an understatement. I could barely pull in air. Even the guard who had zero vested interest was uptight, but then he'd be the trigger man if this went bad and killing any defenseless enemy strapped to a bed would not ever sit well.

Without another word spoken in the room the doctor administered the shot to Justin's arm.

"How long Doc?" I asked quietly. The doctor didn't

even have time to respond as Justin's body struggled against the bonds. He thrashed so violently against them I thought they would start to saw through his skin. Tracy's grip on my hand was excruciating. She had my first and forth knuckles nearly touching. Saliva ran down the side of Justin's face in amounts I wouldn't think a human would be able to produce. Henry yes, Justin not so much. The doctor was checking Justin's pulse when he jumped back. The guard tensed up, undoing the snap on his holster. Tracy might have broken my hand. Justin's scream was muffled from the leather.

I won't swear to it. I can't. My mind just can't wrap around it securely enough to give a definitive answer but when Justin looked over to me and Tracy his eyes looked unbelievably black and flat. They reflected perfectly the soul of a black, dead heart. And just as quickly they returned back to their normal state. I hoped this wheelchair wasn't dry clean only.

"Oh my God." Tracy said under her breath. Apparently she had seen what I had, it was good to at least know that all those years of tripping on acid hadn't finally caught up to me.

Justin arched one more time and relaxed, his eyes were closed. Doc Baker hesitantly walked closer to check his vital signs.

"Doctor." The guard said. "Maybe you should step back." It was looking more and more like Justin's transformation was not such a secret.

"Nonsense." The doctor said without much conviction. "Can't you see his chest rising and falling? He's breathing."

I don't know why these thoughts run through my head, they just do. Maybe it has more to do with the aforementioned acid trips from my college days than I would like to believe. What if the doctor had just created the first hybrid human-zombie? A living zombie? Would he be able to reproduce? Talk about unruly grandchildren.

Justin opened his eyes. "Did it work?" He asked. The

flood of carbon dioxide that was released into the room as everyone let go of the breath they were holding was nearly intoxicating, possibly suffocating, no wonder why Vegas used to flood their casinos with oxygen.

"It'll be a few days until we can be sure but this is a great start," Doc Baker said. "I'm going to need some more blood Justin," he added apologetically.

"You sound like Eliza." Justin said jokingly.

"Poor taste son. We'll have to work on your material. Tracy could you wheel me up to him. If I try to do it I'll end up doing donuts."

"That wasn't much better than Justin's attempt at humor." Tracy said.

The doc got his measure of blood and left, giddy as a schoolboy that got to touch his first female breast. The guard also left the room but was in arm's distance of the door in case his services were still required. Tracy and I stayed with Justin a few more hours before my reserves started to give out. It was great to see our kid come more into his own with each passing minute. He looked happy, he smiled, and more importantly those flat black eyes never returned.

CHAPTER 14 - JOURNAL ENTRY 8 - 

I don't know what I had done in a former life to deserve this (although I had some guesses). Porkchop and I had become fast friends. Not sure what he saw in me, maybe it was my captive audience to his incessant questioning. I didn't begrudge the kid, like so many others his road up to this point had been extremely difficult. I was to learn that Doc Baker was not his biological father but rather a much needed stepdad. Generally, Porkchop wore me out like no tranquilizer could. Where was he when I used to suffer through bouts of insomnia? This next story had me riveted though. I am going to attempt to translate it as best I can, right from Porkchop's mouth to this journal.

PORKCHOP'S PAGES

"It was an awesome night. I had just made Major General on Halo ODST. I had killed like thirty-two guys and only died twice." (Tommy was here this time. The big kid usually came to see me right after lunch. He also held up two fingers to mimic Porkchop's hand signals but I think it had more to do with licking off some errant jelly.)

"The night it all started, my dad had come home from the bar early. Said he had got into a fight and didn't feel so good. Which was kind of a bummer 'cause when he goes out drinking he always comes home late and doesn't bother me when I'm playing my 360. He just walked into the living room, grunted at me and walked into his bedroom. I was pretty psyched, it was a school night and I'm not even supposed to be watching TV, although mom didn't care. Dad used to always say it rotted your brain, but what about booze?" Porkchop stopped his narrative and was actually asking, looking at me to answer his question.

I'm not one to rain on another's libations, I've enjoyed the devil's brew entirely too much to call someone else on it but Porkchop was fairly demanding an answer. "Um well, shit…sorry."

"Oh its fine my dad used to say motherfucker all the time."

"Porkchop!" Doc Baker admonished from across the room.

It was funny to see someone so innocent looking use one of the higher echelon cuss words, but I didn't let on to either Porkchop or the doc.

"Sorry." Porkchop said without a hint of truth, he was looking right at me with a smile in his eyes.

"No big deal." I said smiling right back at him.

"So?" Porkchop prompted.

"Right, well it's like anything Porkchop, if you do it in moderation."

He was looking at me with the glazed over stare of a lost teenager.

"If you don't do it too much."

"Oh." He answered. I had got him back. "My dad used to go to the bar every night after work and on Saturdays too, sometimes on Sunday but not all the time. He used to like to say that if God could rest on the seventh day so could his liver. What does that mean?"

"Um, I'm really tired Porkchop." I was shooting for evasiveness. There was no way I was going to start dragging his dad through the mud. I didn't even know the guy.

"My mom says he was an assaholic."

I think I ripped a hole in my intestinal wall trying to stifle a laugh.

"That's enough swearing Porkchop." Doc said absently as he was prepping what looked like a surgical tray.

"It was getting late and I had finished playing Halo and had moved on to Rockband."

It took me a moment to realize Porkchop had started

his story back up. No matter how funny the kid was I had to remember this was the night he had become an orphan. He had lost a mom who most assuredly loved him more than the air she breathed and the food she ate and a father who might not be the best role model in the world but he was a provider. That was the best I could offer his memory.

"Smashing Pumpkins was on, do you know the song 1979?"

He didn't stop for my answer. He needed to tell the story and if he stopped he might not get the nerve to start it up again.

"I was halfway through on expert!" He said proudly. "I hadn't missed more than 3 or 4 notes."

I knew this was impressive, I had never even graduated to the 'hard' level. 'Medium' was all the coordination I could muster when I played.

"My dad comes into the room and just walks right in front of the television. I couldn't see shit." He added softly looking over in the Doc's direction. "I wanted to yell at him to get out of the way, but that's not a good idea, ever." He stressed. "The crowd on the game starts booing at me 'cause I'm missing so many notes. My dad turns away from the screen, it was then I noticed he had blood all over his face." A tear streamed down Porkchop's face. I wanted to take the kid in my arms and hug the bad thoughts right out of him. "So I asked him if he was alright. He looked back at me like he just realized I was there. He…he lifted his arms up and started walking towards me. He was holding a hand. I knew it was my mom's 'cause of the wedding band."

That was something that no kid should ever have to see.

"He dropped the hand on the floor. I…I couldn't do anything Mr. Talbot. I just kept looking at my mom's hand on the floor. I was wondering why she wasn't screaming, why wasn't she coming out of the bedroom to get it. I mean maybe it wasn't too late to sew it back on. I wanted to get some ice but then my dad stepped on it and I heard her hand bones crack. All I could think, Mr. Talbot, was that my assaholic dad had just ruined my mom's perfect hand and now it could never be put back on. I got so mad I stood up on the couch and just started swinging my guitar controller. The first swing caught him square on the side of the face. I thought he was going to get so mad but he didn't say anything, it was almost like he didn't even know I had done it. So I did it again thinking that maybe that would get his attention. And then I did it again and again. Something snapped I didn't know if it was my controller or my dad's head. I was bummed about the controller. I had saved up all my allowance for 5 months to get it."

Porkchop was full on crying now. But he marshaled on. There was a strength to the kid that you might not account for upon first glance, but the fact that he was alive was testament to that.

"I don't know how many times I hit him but my arms were tired by the time he went to his knees and then he kinda fell over. My controller went with him. It flew right out of my hands cuz it was stuck in his head. His arms and legs were twitching and I could hear him moaning a little bit, but I didn't care, I needed to go check on my mom."

If this was a movie, this is where I would start yelling at the person on the screen to 'RUN, just get out of the house, LEAVE NOW!' "Oh Porkchop. I'm so sorry." I knew what was coming long before he could begin to tell me about it.

"The bedroom door was open, but it was super dark in there. I couldn't see anything. So I called out to my mom." He wiped his nose, rivulets of snot running into his mouth. "She didn't say anything, she wasn't moaning or anything. So I started to think that maybe she had gone to the hospital. Then I thought that she might need some stuff while she's there. I needed to turn on a light so I could get her a bag packed. I turned on that light Mr. Talbot. I didn't even think it was mom. How could anybody be in so many pieces?"

The doctor had come over and was fiercely hugging Porkchop. I had a lump in my throat that could have been used for ski jumps. "It'll be alright." The doc said, slightly swaying to Porkchop's full-throated cries.

After a few minutes, Porkchop had got himself in a near semblance of control. "I went over to Doc Baker's house."

"We were neighbors in our condo units." Doc elaborated.

"I thought maybe he might be able to fix my mom up." Porkchop said biting on his lower lip in an effort to stifle anymore crying.

"When Porkchop had come to my door, he was covered in blood. I thought that he had been involved in some sort of accident. He told me that something was wrong with his parents. I walked into that apartment completely unprepared for what I saw. I honestly thought it was a domestic dispute turned horribly wrong. I told Porkchop here to take a shower while I called the police. Well by then it was too late, most if not all of the cops were either out on other wild calls or had abandoned ship altogether having realized that the world had indeed shit the bed."

"Doc." Porkchop said.

"Sorry, can't tell you not to do it and then turn around and do it myself, not much leadership by example."

"I'll let it slide this time, if you let it slide the next time I do it?"

"One, I'll give you one. But don't tell Mrs. Baker and it can't be a really bad one."

"Deal." Porkchop said through blurry tear stained eyes.

"We heard sirens and gunshots all night. The news talked about a virus running rampant but I just couldn't believe there was something out there that could make people eat other people, much less re-animate the dead. I mean medically there is nothing more preposterous. Porkchop wasn't in much of a condition to answer any questions but I had seen his apartment. Something terribly wrong had happened, but I could not reconcile it. That night as the sirens and the gunshots grew louder and more drawn out, my family, Porkchop and myself crammed onto my couch. I don't know why I did it but I had turned out the lights. We sat there the whole night like that. By the time the morning came at least three quarters of my body had fallen asleep, I had pins and needles nearly everywhere."

"That's a lot of sharpened steel." I said absently.

The doc eyed me sharply. I hadn't meant anything by the words just an observation. Forty-four years old and I still hadn't figured out how to disengage the thought from speech button in my brain. There were seven year olds that had this simple basic function mastered.

"The scene outside my window was horrific. It was equally as bad as the scene in Porkchop's own abode. There were dead and dying people everywhere. What I would come to know as zombies weren't yet out in great numbers but there were still plenty afoot. The real problem was that Gary, Indiana was on fire. Mike, we were four stories up in a condominium. I figured we'd be able to wait this whole thing out and let the government deal with it. I had done an inventory the previous night and figured between my house and Porkchop's we had at least a week to ten days worth of food, surely by then order would be restored."

"Wouldn't that have been nice," I threw in for good measure.

"Quite. I wanted to wait. That seemed the most logical course of action. I'm a doctor. I don't know how to kill, unless its malpractice." The doc paused for dramatic effect.

"Really Doc? That's your attempt at humor?"

"That was a secret passion of mine, to become a stand-up comedian."

"Well lucky for us all you settled your sights lower and became a doctor."

The Doc looked at me. "See now, THAT'S funny, do you mind if I use that?"

"Knock yourself out Doc."

"They do shows every week and I've been gathering enough material and…well forget about that. Needless to say those fires saved my life. If the city hadn't been burning I would have never left. The most dangerous thing I had ever done in my life up to that point was work at a strip club."

Doc didn't elaborate at this point, so when someone tells you that they worked at a strip club, you tell me what you assumed he did. All I could think was that I hoped that establishment had an 11-drink minimum. That might be the only way you could get through his routine.

"I worked my way through college as a disc jockey there."

"Whew." I blurted out. Luckily the Doc didn't make the connection.

"There were fights almost nightly at the club but we had 5 or 6 bouncers who did all the heavy work. All I had to do was play music, announce the dancers and crack a joke or two."

"I heard your jokes Doc, good thing there were breasts involved."

"I guess I always thought the cheers were for my witticisms."

"Oh yeah definitely not for Miss Double D's tatas."

"I gather you don't have many friends Mr. Talbot."

"Ouch, that hurts, but you're more right than you know. I apparently was born without the gift of a thought filter."

"And yet that lovely lady Tracy still married you?"

"That's probably got more to do with my prowess, if you know what I mean?" I said with as much leering as I could muster without letting Porkchop in on my meaning.

"Oh I'm sure that was it." The Doc said condescendingly.

"Can we get back to your story?" I asked a little snappishly.

The doc laughed and then just as quickly turned serious. "I was scared Mike. I mean I was frozen from indecision. Do we all go out as a group and get the car? Do I get the car and then have everybody come out then? Do we bring all the food? Do we need supplies? Formulating a plan was beyond me. My entire life revolved around order, things that involved stepping out of bounds were dealt with by my staff or my wife. I mean my wife is as smart as she is beautiful but this wasn't a soccer practice running late or a skinned knee, this was Armageddon. Not many people have a plan for that sort of thing."

I meekly held my hand up.

"Well of course except for you, Mike." I nodded, and he continued. "But the rest of us like to think our ordinary lives are going to continue on as planned, two week's vacation in France, dinner every Thursday at Chez Palace, building my practice up to the point that I can finally sell it and retire to Arizona, just normal stuff."

I wanted to tell him that wasn't normal for 98% of the American population. Most of us would have been happy with a 4 day weekend at Six Flags, a Wednesday night run to Wendy's, and hopefully making enough money so that we wouldn't have to hand out stickers at Wal-Mart when we had retired. No offense Tommy. If nothing else the zombies had leveled the playing field. We all were equally mired in the shit of existence now. I just nodded. I saw no sense or purpose in kicking the man while he was down.

"It was my middle kid Blake that finally got me going. He's asthmatic and the smoke from the fires was really starting to affect him. Waiting it out was rapidly losing any appeal it may have contained. We grabbed everything we could carry, blankets, food, Xbox 360."

"What?"

Doc shrugged his shoulders. "My oldest son Jesse said he wasn't leaving without it. I figured what the hell, I couldn't ever picture a time when the world would return to a state of normalcy again but for him I think it was more of a security blanket."

"To each his own." I personally however like the

security that a Mossberg 12 gauge shotgun provides over that of a wireless game controller, but who I am to judge. Porkchop for one would see the validity of a game controller turned defender.

"We ran out to my car. Mike, if just one zombie had got in our way I think we would have been finished. All of our hands were full. I hadn't even thought to grab a weapon. Looking back the best I would have had to offer was a steak knife or a golf club and I don't think I could use either one except for its intended purpose. It was a tight fit with the six of us and Buddha but we made it. We weren't 5 miles out of Gary when we ran into a military convoy. When they found out I was a doctor, I was instantly drafted. I tried to explain that I was a General Practitioner and not a surgeon but when you're in a desert and somebody offers you something wet to drink you don't stop to question what it is."

"Well you did right by me, Doc." I said, alluding to my shoulder surgery.

"So that's my story. We've been here ever since. I've done more surgeries in the last few weeks than I care to count and not all have been as successful as yours. So I would greatly appreciate it if you take care of that shoulder so it heals properly."

Porkchop had for the most part recovered from his remembrance of his parents' demise. The runny nose and bloodshot eyes, the tell tale signs of getting a good cry-on would however take a good fifteen minutes or so more to diminish.

The doc turned to Porkchop who had just finished wiping his nose on a rapidly snot-hardening sleeve. "Porkchop, could you please track down Rachael? I've got some work for her to do? Thank you." Porkchop headed out the door, his normal cheery self rapidly coming to the fore.

We said nothing for long moments after the door closed.

"You did good Doc. You did right by Porkchop and by your own family."

"Taking Porkchop in was as natural as if he was my own. He spent more time at my house than his own. I just feel like I should have done more."

"How many kids do you have Doc?"

"Huh?" The Doc asked pulling back to the present from his own thoughts. "Uh three, well four now."

"They're all here right?"

"Well not right here, but yes on this base."

"And your wife?"

"I see your point."

"That's all I'm saying Doc. You kept your family safe. There's nothing more you could have done." I was getting the distinct impression the doc wasn't fully convinced. "How old are they?"

"Well I can't tell you my wife's age."

"Wasn't asking."

" Jesse is my oldest son, he's 15. He's kind of quiet around strangers but warms up like vinyl seats in July when he's around friends and family. He's got a little bit of a mouth on him and is definitely the family's prankster. He's addicted to video games."

"Yeah I got that when he took his 360 with him." We both shared a laugh over that.

" Call of Duty Modern Warfare 2 is his poison and he can tell you the stats on every gun available in the game. He despises his younger brother and sister but doesn't tolerate ANYONE screwing with them (except for Porkchop). He's kind of wise beyond his years in his ability to understand the human condition even if he can be a bit emotional himself. He's a big kid and loves guns. He spends most of his spare time training with some of the other kids. The military has set up an ROTC type program. They get the kids some combat training in fire arms safety and marksmanship skills. It worries me Mike."

"Those aren't bad skills to have right now, Doc."

"I just had so much more planned for him in life than one the military has to offer."

The doc was a good man, and saved my life at least twice that I knew of so far, but he was definitely more of the small picture ilk. The world had dramatically shifted on its axis and he had not yet caught up. "Doc, learning those skills now might be his best chance to stay alive and have a different life!"

"I…I guess I hadn't thought of it that way."

That seemed to perk him up marginally.

"Next is my middle child Blake, he's 13. Unlike his older brother, he's very outgoing and has an IQ that puts the rest of us to shame. He's not as physically intimidating as Jesse but he can make you look like a fool if you want to argue with him."

I figured that had something to do with the limiting factors associated with being an asthmatic.

"Where Jesse is more of a warrior, Blake is the thinker, the artist, his obsession is books. Being the artistic middle child and kind of a mama's boy, he takes a lot of crap from the rest of the guys in the family. I figure he's the one who will be able to pay for my nursing home should I make it that far so I've decided I'd better be nice to him. Rachael is 10 and she is my only daughter."

"Be thankful for that."

The doc wouldn't understand the backhanded compliment at least not for another two and a half years when his daughter turned from a sweet daddy's little princess into a multi-headed demon from hell, as all teenage girls must.

"She is without a shadow of a doubt, the strongest personality in our house. She is the most wonderfully devious of children. If there is trouble to find, she's not only in it but in it to win it."

I had learned the hard way after punishing my own boys way too much, that my daughter not only sought out trouble but was usually the root cause of it.

"Rachael's very smart but loves to tell you that she's not (the better to get away with things). She is a mini version of her mom, entirely too cute to be as cunning as she is. She scares the hell out of me because she is going to need to be locked in a closet VERY soon."

Maybe that secret desire of all fathers to be able to lock their daughters away from testosterone infused boys could now be realized. So maybe a zombie invasion wasn't all bad.

"Doc you did good. Now if you could up my Demerol, I'm in pain and really tired."

"Thank you Mike, I take my quip about you being friendless away."

"Don't be so hasty Doc, wait until you really get to know me." My eyelids began to slide shut as the Doc pumped some pain killing juice into my IV line. "One more thing Doc."

He was checking my pulse. "What is it?"

"Don't let her out of that closet until she's about 18, the demon spawn in her will almost be gone." And with that came blissful pain free sleep.

CHAPTER 15 - JOURNAL ENTRY 9 - 

I had been in a hospital bed for nearly two weeks before Doc Baker thought I'd most likely be alright to stay in my own bed in the quarters assigned to myself and my family. The quarters were nice enough. They harkened me back to my Marine Corps fleet days. The barracks were basically a no frills apartment complex. Square non-descript buildings with a square non-descript room, with an off-shoot bathroom in each apartment. In my Marine Corps days we had been stuffed 4 jarheads at a time into a 15 by 15 foot room. Honestly didn't care about it at the time, pretty sure I'd go nuts if that was the case now. Turns out there weren't enough survivors to merit any sort of over-crowding. Tracy, myself, and the ever stinky Henry had our own room. Nicole had the apartment next to us by herself, and Justin (when he was released from the hospital) had a room with Travis, on the other side of our room. Carol was actually down the hall, by request, go figure. It was my first night back and I couldn't sleep to save my life. The kindly doctor had begun to wean me off the pain meds I was on. I might add that I thought it was entirely too early in the healing process to be put on aspirin. Oh what I wouldn't do for a nice Percocet.

Tracy rested lightly next to me. Between the throbbing in my shoulder and Henry's outbursts from his butt and mouth (farts and snores), I was getting exactly zero amount of sleep. Me and the doc were going to have a good old conversation in the morning. If that didn't work, this was a military base, there had to be a decent black market trade going on. I got up for the fifth time. Henry raised his massive head up off the floor. I swear if he could talk, he'd be saying something like 'Don't blame me for not being able to sleep. My gas smells like cherry blossoms on a warm spring day.' I patted his head, and he lay back down contentedly. I wanted to look out the window just for something to do, but the base was lit up like a Christmas tree on crack. If I had moved the blackout blinds even a fraction of an inch the room would have been flooded in light as if it was high noon and not 4 a.m.

When the throbbing in my shoulder had subsided into something less than a thundering rhino charge, I figured I might be able to give elusive sleep another chance. My ass was just about to make contact with the bed when I heard a small thud followed immediately by a muffled yelp coming through the wall, which just so happened to be the wall that we shared with my daughter. I still almost went through with the whole bed thing. The noise was that slight and unmenacing sounding. I hesitated, the burn in my thighs making itself known as I hung in that unnatural in between pose of standing or sitting.

"Effen paranoia." I lamented. I quietly padded across the room and out the door, I didn't even bother completely shutting the door. I didn't want the latching mechanism to wake my wife when it closed. The four-foot walk to my daughter's door did nothing to instill any sort of fear into me. I felt foolish. I almost turned around. "In for a penny, in for a dementia." Wasn't that how the saying went? I was at her door, what was I going to do? Knock at 4 in the morning and see how she was doing? Hell, she was probably just having a bad dream, weren't we all? And that decided it. Maybe I'd be doing her a favor if I woke her up.

I knocked lightly, and waited. Nothing happened. I knocked maybe just a little bit louder. I waited, still nothing. Dammit, she's probably sleeping pretty good. 'Talbot get your ass in bed and leave everyone alone,' my inner psyche spewed. I'm sure you've noticed by now, I rarely listen to my higher consciousness. I turned her knob. The door was unlocked. Now I was pissed, hadn't I taught that girl anything! This was going to suck for her. I was about to wake her from a nightmare only to scold the hell out of her. I opened the door. I was immediately struck with the oddity of the scene that was laid out in front of me. The light was on in her bathroom, which shed enough light to let me see that Nicole was nearly naked on her bed. 'Oh fuck! A dad's worst nightmare. That's what I get for not minding my own business.'

"I'm so sorry." I said aloud.

Things at this point happened rapidly. Her head whipped up, I couldn't help but notice the gag in her mouth. I moved forward. "What the hell?" Then I smelled burning flesh (my own) as my body collapsed to the floor. I twitched like a bass out of water. The stun gun had sent upwards of 50,000 volts of charged electricity through my body. The arc and contraction of my muscles nearly made me bite my tongue off. My teeth chattered under the assault. I had 100 charley horses happening concurrently across my body and there wasn't a thing I could do to ease the pain.

"Bet that fucking hurts!" A tobacco teeth stained mullet wearing cracker said in my face. Redneck Number One was back. "After you kilt my friends, I swore I'd get me revenge on you all. It was just a stroke of pure luck that brought me here. Old Vern froze out in that field that night when you took our trucks. I stumbled back to the road and the next morning these military trucks picked me up. They says I was a referee."

Through my muscle clenched teeth I was able to muscle out "Refugee, douchebag."

That got me another charge of electricity into my rib cage. It felt like muscle was tearing away from tendon, the pain was that intense.

"So's, I was already here by the time you's got here but 'course I didn't know that. I just happened to come across your little flower of a daughter just this morning."

I strained against the paralysis.

"Don't waste yer time, you piece of shit. I shot you with 'nough 'lectricity to keep you from moving for the next fifteen minutes. Oh, I couldn't have planned this any better iffen I had tried. You're going to get a front row seat, well so to speak, front row floor maybe. As I do all sorts of things to your daughter. Then I'm going to slit her throat and I'm going to make sure you'll be in position to have her blood flow over your face. This is going to be so much fun!"

Nicole's face was strained with terror. My body was immobile,. I was impotent. A ten-ton elephant sitting on me couldn't have had the same effect the stun gun did. Redneck number one stood up and began to walk over towards the bed. He produced a foot long bowie knife from under his jacket. Nicole looked over to me, pleading for her life with her eyes. I did not even have the coward's option of closing my eyes. They were frozen in the open position. Tears formed. The room before me got blurry but it would not be enough to spare me from the horrors that were mere moments away.

I could feel a small pressure on my foot, I didn't know it then but it was the apartment door being forced open. Henry came up beside me, he licked my forehead. I wanted to tell him to leave. There was no sense in two of us witnessing this atrocity.

Redneck Number One turned to look at the new intruder who had entered into his sick fantasy. "What the fuck is that ugly thing? Looks like he was runnen' too close to a truck that stopped short." He snorted at his own joke. Redneck Number One came back towards me. "Whassa matter ugly?" Redneck asked Henry. You gonna be sad to see your master dead? That's okay, I'll kill you too just to make it an even three." Then Redneck did something that I think saved mine, Nicole's and Henry's lives that night. He walked back towards me, I strained against my invisible bonds and was rewarded with a kick square in the ribs.

Henry then did the unthinkable, at least as far as anyone who knew that dog was concerned. He attacked. This was no play attack. His deep grumble alerted the Redneck that something had changed. Redneck had no sooner turned than Henry had latched onto the dirty bastard's shin. I don't know what clicked in the dog's head. Lord knows he'd seen Tracy whack the crap out of the back of my head enough to not be too distraught when I was under attack. Henry must have known this was different but it still did not completely explain his behavior.

I'm not sure what you may or may not know about English Bulldogs, so I'll give you the 101 version. There is no more passive breed of dog on the planet, unless of course you're trying to hide food from them. Most Bullies have what you might consider scraggly teeth. They don't so much bite as they do crush. Their jaws are massively powerful and extraordinarily large. I can attest to that fact from the numerous times Henry and I have played and he will put my entire forearm in his mouth. He'd break my bones long before he'd be able to break my skin. That being said Henry would much rather sleep than play. They know true affection and they love to be the center of attention. I once did a test with Henry to prove to my wife how loving of a dog he was. This is no lie or exaggeration. One night I was cooking steaks on the grill and I might have had a few too many beers as I was cooking. Well lo and behold one of the steaks I cooked fell off the plate when I hit the tray with the screen door. There was no chance on God's green earth I was going to eat this thing now, so I dusted it off, cut it up and placed it on a platter for Henry. 'Watch this.' I told my wife. She asked me what the hell I was doing as I got down on my haunches next to my furry friend. She placed one hand on the phone a heartbeat away from dialing 911. I literally got down on all fours, head to head with Henry, and made like I was going to eat his food. Now this is steak mind you, not kibbles and bits. You know what that dog did? He moved over so I could get a better angle on the dish. That's Henry, not a mean bone in his body.

So when Henry's giant maw literally wrapped around Redneck's lower leg, I was just as surprised as Redneck was. The pain must have been intense, I watched as Redneck's eyes began to bulge out. Dirt bag or not, he still had a knife and now realized he was going to need it for defense instead of fun. Henry snapped that man's tibia and fibula, the cracking of bones was as loud as a percussion grenade in the small room. Redneck's knife came down, his aim blinded by the pain. I watched in helplessness as the knife arced down, Henry's yelp of pain was all the proof I needed that Redneck had struck home.

"Gotcha fucker!" Redneck yelled as he fell over, the pain in his broken leg making standing a losing venture. Henry was bleeding profusely from a wound to his side. The redneck was slumped against the wall, knife still in hand. His outstretched arm would still be plenty close enough to finish the job. "Fucking ugly motherfucker! I'm gonna kill you now!"

'Oh no, Henry'. I could accept a lot of things that a hard life had to offer. This was not going to be one of them.

Those were the last words Redneck Number One ever uttered. Not because he died, but because Henry ripped his jaw off. If that SOUNDS gross you should have been there to witness it. The splintering of bone and muscle as Henry tore into the soft flesh of the redneck's face was gruesome. Teeth popped out of the redneck's jaw as Henry applied more pressure. When Henry shook his head, the bottom half of the redneck's jaw just came unhinged. Gristle, blood, teeth, and jawbone fragments flew around the room. A smear of blood landed on my right eye. Half the room became bathed in red as I desperately tried to blink, to no avail.

Two MP's and my wife simultaneously made it to the doorway. To my wife's credit she only retched half as hard as one of the guards.

CHAPTER 16 - JOURNAL ENTRY 10 -

A half hour later we were all in Doc Baker's house.

"How is he Doc?" I asked nervously.

"Mike you know that's the fifth time you've asked me that question right?" The Doc answered.

I looked longingly at him.

He sighed loudly. "He's fine Mike, and he'd be a lot finer if you'd stop bugging me and let me finish sewing these stitches."

Henry hadn't even required any sort of numbing agent so intent was he with the frozen hot dogs he was sharing with Tommy, I'm not even sure he knew somebody was working on his side. Nicole in between sobs couldn't contain herself from wrapping her arms around the lovable mutt.

"See I told you it was worth saving him back at the house in Little Turtle." I said to Tracy smugly. (Note to all men, wrong fucking time to prove a point!)

"Talbot, are you kidding me?" My wife shot back. "You and your daughter almost died tonight and you want to throw an 'I told you so' in my face?"

"Well I uh… had thought so. Not really so much anymore."

Tracy glared at me.

"So are those hot dogs really frozen?" I asked Tommy in a vain attempt to thwart the hostility. Tommy ignored me like only someone who valued their own existence could. "Could use a little help here Tommy?" I begged

"Wanff a hoff doff?" He answered.

Henry took that as his queue and wolfed down the proffered frozen meat snack.

I turned my attention back towards Henry. The laceration looked nasty. Fourteen stitches later he was as good as new.

"Alright." Doc said as he snipped the excess thread away. "I recommend as little movement for Henry for the next three days as possible."

"I don't think that's going to be a problem Doc." I said. Henry had fallen asleep on the operating table with half of a frozen hot dog sticking out of his mouth.

We went back to the barracks. I had rounded up an old musty cot to sleep on, while Nicole got into the bed with her mother. Henry had never woke back up as Tommy had carried him back up to our room. I waited until I was sure everyone was asleep and then I sobbed silently. There were just so much pent up emotions looking for an escape. A big chunk was relief, relief that my daughter was physically ok. Emotionally, that might take a while. Relief that Henry was ok. I was going to buy that dog a cow tomorrow. Out of us all he seemed the least affected. If I'm being honest, I think a big part of my tears were of frustration. I had walked into a trap. I had almost gotten my daughter and my best furry friend killed. That was a tough thing for me to reconcile. The cot swayed under the assault of my cries. I was being as quiet as was possible under the circumstances. It wasn't enough.

From the shadows came my wife's voice. "It wasn't your fault Talbot."

I wanted to answer her. It's just that my throat was closed off.

"Get some sleep Marine, we've all lived to fight another day."

She was right, of course she was right, she's always right. Now if I could just heed her words I'd be all set. Three minutes later I stumbled into slumber.

CHAPTER 17 - JOURNAL ENTRY 11 -

It was sometime way after noon when I finally dragged my ass out of bed. Any movement more involved than scratching my nose sent excruciating bolts of pain radiating at the speed of fire from my shoulder outwards. If not for the fact that my bladder was sending an 'imminent release' warning to my head, I would have stayed in bed even longer. I might have cried a little (definitely some heavy moaning) when I reached over and grabbed my pain meds, Doc had hooked me up at his house last night when he had seen how bad I looked. I dry swallowed two but was not going to be able to wait the twenty or so minutes before they kicked in. I briefly wondered how ticked off Tracy might be if I just went where I lay.

Yeah, that wasn't going to work, for two or three good minutes I rolled around trying to find the least pain inducing method to get up. None were significantly better than any other. I went with the band-aid removal method. Bad, bad idea. Isn't it always? I sat straight up and fluidly stood as quickly as I could in a vain attempt at daring the pain to keep up. The pain had no problem doing that and nearly sent me to my knees. I fought to keep my vision from reducing to a pin point. I steadied myself on the steel headboard, thankful for the cool touch of it. When the spears of pain subsided to small knives, I shuffled my way to the bathroom. Two minutes later I stood in the bathroom, bladder completely pressure free and bathed in a fresh coat of sweat. This simple bodily function had nearly wiped me out and yet as my first day out of the hospital it was world's better than pissing in a bedpan. Not much is more degrading than having someone remove your waste and then make comments about it as they do so. 'Oh someone's not drinking enough water' or my personal favorite 'You had corn last night?'

Either I had been in the bathroom longer than I had thought or the pills were working faster than expected. The dull pleasantness of the buzz did its best to help me forget that my shoulder was knitting itself back into place. I longed to go back to bed but the mere thought of getting back out prevented me from doing that. I figured I'd go in the living room and sit in a chair and maybe pretend to read as the Percocets really went about their business. Let's not kid ourselves, I was soon going to be high enough to watch a candle melt and enjoy the hell out of it.

Tracy and Henry were nowhere to be found. My olfactory senses were thankful for the latter although that dog always managed to put a smile on my face even if it was hidden under my pulled up shirt, the better to hide my nose. The timing was impeccable. My ass had just made contact with the cushion when a knock came at the door.

"You had better be a pizza or a candle delivery service." I yelled.

Tommy walked in thinking that was his invitation. "Hey Mr. T, how you feeling?"

"Hurting a bit buddy. What's up?"

"Mrs. T thought I should hang out with you because I'm feeling a little purple." He said with a long face.

Even on pain pills it was not difficult to realize his meaning. "Blue, Tommy? You're feeling blue?"

"Isn't that what I said?" He asked truly puzzled.

"Hell you might have. What's the matter? Why are you under the weather?"

"We're all under the weather Mr. T, of course, unless we're in a plane really high."

I laughed, and that hurt like shit. So I was somewhere in the midst of a 'Ha – ha and ooh – ooh.'

Tommy looked ultra-concerned. "Don't worry about it." I said patting him on the leg. "Could you get us both some water and then come sit down?" The majority of my pain had eased as he sat down handing over a tall glass of

Coke. I didn't think we had any Coke but I wasn't going to turn it down plus there was no piss Nazi to tell me I wasn't drinking enough of the right kinds of fluids. "Thanks." I said raising my glass.

Tommy stared diligently at a condensation droplet.

"Alright Tommy, out with it. I can't stand anything but an extra wide on you." (And by that I meant smile).

He looked up at me with tears in his eyes, my heart was breaking. "I miss my parents Mr. T." He said looking back down at that droplet, trying his best to not cry. Screw it, I did. I mean not your full out bawling, but between the pain and the pain meds I was already raking the coals of my emotions.

My tears sent Tommy over the edge. He let go. I don't know how long he had been holding onto his grief but if the pure pain that poured forth from him now was a hint then this was the first time. I got up and used my arm to hug him as tight as I could. His heaving body sent shock waves through my injury. That pain, however, was preferential to what he was doing to my soul. After a half hour or so and a small puddle on the floor later, Tommy had finally got to the bottom of his reserves. There was the occasional sob and I'm sure that he had a sinus headache that would rival any migraine. Images of Porkchop began to pop into my head. It took me many clouded moments later to put the puzzle pieces together.

"Tommy." I said as I stepped back a pace.

The bleary teary-eyed face that stared back at me had absolutely nothing in common with the boy I had come to know and love.

"Yeah Mr. T?" He said using his sleeve to wipe his dripping nose.

"Why don't you start calling me Dad?"

"What?" Tommy asked as he snorted.

"Let me run it by Mrs. T, Tommy but if you'll have us I would love to adopt you."

I don't know how it happened but Tommy's face fell

even further. A heretofore unknown untapped reservoir of water sprang a leak. 'Stupid Talbot, always know how to say the wrong thing at the right time.' I was only beginning to berate myself when Tommy took a momentary respite.

"You would really do that? You would really become my dad?"

Holy shit, now it was my turn to spring a leak. At first I thought he was crying because I had been so presumptuous as to think I could possibly be a stand-in for his real father when all along he was crying because of his thankfulness. I should have known better, Tommy is a better person than I could ever hope to be.

Tracy came in at some point. "What's going on?" She asked as she pulled the leash off of Henry.

"I want to adopt Tommy." I told her amidst my blubberings.

"I was wondering when you were going to get around to that." She said nonchalantly as she hung the leash up on a peg. "I was going to suggest it once you got better." She added coming over to us.

Tommy beamed as he hugged us both. "I love you both, Mom and Dad." Henry broke up the party as he began to lick the salty tears off of the floor.

One thing that's nice about the end of the world, it really cuts through the old administrative red tape. The next day we were able to make the adoption official in the eyes of the tattered government and hopefully some other higher power. The Talbots, plus BT (maybe I should adopt him too) and the Bakers attended the small ceremony. Next came the Feast of the Cakes, as Tommy liked to call it. It was his party and therefore his request had been granted.

As the soiree was coming to a close I pulled him aside . "Hey Tommy."

"Hey Mr. Dad."

"Maybe we should just stick with Dad." He smiled sheepishly. Chocolate cake and strawberry frosting lined his chin like a beard. "Listen Tommy, I just want you to know,

I'll never be your father." His brow furrowed. "But I'll always be your Dad." His cheesecake lined smile was all the confirmation I needed that I had made the right decision. The hug he administered was just the cherry on the top.

CHAPTER 18 - JOURNAL ENTRY 12 -

I was itching in a couple or three different ways. I had an itch to get back on the road and away from sanctuary, call me crazy. Maybe I was becoming an adrenaline junky, I needed the drama of action in my life. No, that was crap, the simple fact of knowing that my family was safer now than at any time since the zombies came, was comforting. I had massive itching going on around my shoulder, but this was a deep tissue itching. No matter how desperately I tried to rake through the top layers of my skin, I was not going to get that satisfying sweet spot. You know, that point when you finally get at a difficult location on your body and just scratch that itch into oblivion. Oh, it is such sweet, sweet delight.

That wasn't to be my lot. I had flakes of epidermis piling up under my fingernails. It was actually kind of gross. Doc Baker had become so concerned he had even placed me back on my blessed pain meds. Hey, I'm not an addict, but I like a good high as much as the next guy. I had another itch too, well maybe more like a tickle, a psychic tickle. It was way back in my head but it was ominous and it kept telling me to get long gone. I would have heeded it too, no matter what my wife said, but every extra day I could give BT and myself to heal up improved all of our chances of survival. Besides my true life 'shit' forecaster (Tommy) didn't seem in any rush to leave. Of course that might have more to do with the 24-hour chow hall and the truly unbelievably delicious apple turnover they made here, than with any inherent danger that may or may not be coming.

When I got up for the 47th time and jammed my shoulder into the corner of the door using it like a large scratching post, Tracy had had enough.

"Get your jacket." Tracy said.

"But it's freezing out." I replied lamely.

"Hence the jacket." She retorted.

I was moments away from a not so manly whining. Tracy could sense it coming and was having none of it.

"Now, Talbot."

"Fine." I answered like a petulant 8-year old. Again not a finer moment for me, but even the Percocets were doing little to eradicate the discomfort of my healing shoulder, and Tracy will attest to the fact that I am a horrible 'sick' person.

"Where are we going?" I asked, resigned to the fact that we were going out no matter what.

"The beach."

"The beach? You say that like this is Hawaii. It's gotta be 10 degrees out there with a wind chill of something like 10 below."

"Yeah, I know that." She answered flatly.

"You hate the cold." I was trying desperately to get out of this field trip.

"I hate you getting up a couple of hundred times every hour, more."

"Forty-seven."

"Forty-seven what?"

"I got up forty-seven times."

She looked at me incredulously. "You counted?" She shook her head. "Forget it, you need this diversion as much as I do. Maybe you'll be too cold to want to scratch."

"Yeah, probably because my blood will congeal."

"Ha ha, we're still going. Get your jacket."

I turned to grab my jacket off the peg, stopping only once to rub up against the hook.

"Talbot!"

"Fine! But if you weren't my wife I'd tell you a thing or two." My voice had been trailing off since the first word, so that I had ended on a mumble.

"What was that?" Tracy asked.

"Yes dear."

"I thought that's what you said."

The short walk to the shoreline was actually invigorating. The cold air was refreshing. The monster irritation in my shoulder was tamed to a minor troll. I felt slightly naked not carrying my AR but base rules prohibited the carrying of rifles. Pistols were alright and actively encouraged. I carried both my Glock 9mm and my Smith and Wesson .357. Tracy was actually carrying a Walther 9mm. She made me so proud, had I not been on a military base with so many military personnel around I might have shed a tear of pride.

We walked completely ignored by the myriad of soldiers that passed us. We were just a couple of refugees in an ever-growing community. I wondered how long the resources on hand would be able to sustain this impromptu base, and then as quickly as the thought popped up it blew away. I planned on being long gone before that ever became an issue.

We reached the shoreline. A few miserable looking guards patrolled the beach looking for any wayward zombies. I didn't see how that was going to happen though. The bay had frozen solid since the last time zombies had come ashore. There were a bunch of kids actually playing hockey a hundred or so yards off shore. The scene was serene, almost idyllic, Norman Rockwell-ish.

"Travis should be out there." Tracy said pointing to the 20 or so kids skating around in the semblance of a game.

My nerves pulled tight. I don't know why but the Hershey squirts would have been denied passage, my sphincter had slammed so tightly shut. I go over these things again and again, not even sure if I should keep flagging my 'not so proud' moments. Did I fear he would fall through the ice? That seemed unfounded, considering that there were at least ten or more hummers driving near the ice water freeze line. The ice had to be at least 18 inches to support that weight and the vehicles were at least another hundred or so yards past the kids.

"Why are they so far from shore?" I fairly begged of

Tracy.

"Relax, Talbot. Travis told me that the ice was a lot smoother out there."

"You knew?" I nearly yelled.

"What's the matter with you?" She asked.

"I don't fucking know!" I said as I started to speed walk nearly busting out into a sprint.

"Talbot don't you go out there all willy-nilly, you'll embarrass him."

"Fine." I said, doing everything in my power to keep my muscles from firing at full tilt.

We were half way to the kids when I felt a tremor.

"Did you feel that?" I said as I stopped and turned to Tracy who was hastening to catch up.

"Feel what?" Tracy said catching her breath as she pulled up alongside. "I thought I told you no running."

"That." I said as another minor quake erupted under our feet.

"That's probably just the humvees." Tracy said. I don't think she even believed the words as she spoke them.

The roar as ice began to crack was unnerving. Brontosaurus leg bones snapping under sound amplification could not have competed with the blistering reverberation. Everything and everybody became as frozen as the landscape around us. That false harmony ended quickly and badly as first one and then another hummer sank into the fracturing ice. Kids, hyper aware of danger, were not slow to react. The majority of them had already closed half the distance to Tracy and I as the second hummer finished its icy descent into hell. Tracy started running out towards Travis. I got up to her and grabbed her arm.

"Forget him!" I yelled.

"Are you out of your mind?!" She screamed trying to tug her arm away.

"Shit I didn't mean it like that, he's on skates, he's going to pass us by in a few seconds. Us on the other hand, need to start running back NOW!" I yelled as I pulled her towards shore. She didn't need any more prodding as the ice behind us literally began to explode under an as yet undetermined assault.

"Mom? Dad?" Travis asked as he skated next to us. "What's going on?"

"Go!" I yelled to him. "Get to shore and get your boots on as fast as possible, we'll be there in a minute."

"Mom?" He asked.

Tracy nodded, holding on to the terror that was building up within in her. Not wanting her son to see it.

Travis had made it to shore and was nearly done putting his boots on when we finally huffed and puffed our way to shore. Walking on ice is already a slippery proposition, pun intended. But when you're running because your life depends on it, it becomes infuriatingly difficult to gain any sort of momentum.

We turned to watch as one more hummer became forever locked in a watery graveyard. One of the two occupants barely escaped only to succumb moments later when another fissure opened up in front of him. I wanted to help but there wasn't anything to be done. The remaining hummers pulled onto shore. They must have felt what I did because each passenger manned the mounted .50 cal submachinegun. Tense glances were passed around as we all wondered what in the hell was going on.

"Dad." Travis said grabbing my arm and pointing off into the distance.

I could barely make out a glint of reflective light. I walked up to the closest hummer.

"Could I see your glasses?" I asked a tense looking Lance Corporal seated behind the wheel. I hoped my use of combat vernacular would aid in my question.

"Sure, whatever." He said never taking his eyes off of the water line. He pointed into the back storage compartment.

"Thanks." I said as I grabbed the binoculars. "Sweet Jesus!" I said as I pulled the binoculars down from my eyes and handed them to Trav. "Sorry God." I mumbled. It was something I did every time I took the Lord's name in vain, old Catholic habits die hard. "Time to go." As I grabbed the binoculars back and threw them back into the hummer. "Lance Corporal." He didn't move.

"Yeah, yeah." He said thinking I was going to thank him for the binoculars.

"Lance Corporal!" I yelled.

He finally spared me a glance.

"Close to the shoreline on your left, use the binoculars."

He held the binoculars up. "Sweet Jesus."

"Yeah I thought the same thing, you Catholic?"

"What? You need to get out of here. Lutheran by the way" he said, getting out of the hummer to warn his fellow Marines.

"Yup, thought the same thing about getting out of here. Wouldn't have taken you for a Lutheran."

"Mike, what the hell is that thing?" Tracy asked, squinting her eyes and shielding them from the majority of snow blindness to see.

"Not a hundred percent sure, mind you, but Terex 5500 comes to mind." I said grabbing her arm and rushing her back towards our barracks.

"A what?" She said turning back to get a better view of a rapidly approaching monstrosity.

"Oh just one of the largest dump trucks ever created on the good old planet Earth."

"A dump truck? Big deal." Tracy said digging her heels in and stopping our forward momentum.

""I really don't think you're getting it. That thing is probably 30 feet tall and 50 feet long and can haul 100's of tons of dirt. But I've got a pretty bad feeling that thing's payload doesn't involve dirt, only things that should be buried in it."

Tracy was a little slow on the uptake, but quick to realize the horror. "There's zombies in that thing?" She asked.

"That would be my guess."

"Who the hell is driving it? Not the zombies right?"

Now at this point did it really matter who was driving? I guess there would be a higher threshold of fear if zombies had learned how to drive. The only thing that could be potentially worse would be a drunk Asian woman on her cell phone. The most likely answer though to this equation involved an old friend, and I had a significant throbbing in my shoulder to prove it.

"Durgan." I said. The name came out flat, but it was charged with emotion. He had a lot to atone for and I was feeling in a judicial mood.

Tracy nearly pulled me over as she grabbed my arm and started to run back to grab everything we could and get out while the getting was possible. I had my doubts we'd be in time. Those trucks could travel somewhere in the 40 mph range, granted not on ice. But that thing was still moving at a good clip. We were just getting to the front door of our quarters when I realized a significant problem.

"Hon, you go on up and get everything ready. I will be right back."

"Mike what are you doing?" Tracy asked with concern.

"I have to get something."

"Could you be a little more vague?"

"I could but I don't have time. Trust me I'll be back in about twenty minutes, just have everything we can carry ready to go."

"Mike I hate when you do this shit." Tracy said. I thought she might put up more of a fight but was super-thankful she didn't.

I kissed her before she wheeled away and up to our temporary home.

I was headed to the base commissary, which is basically just a stripped down super market. I was halfway through my ten minute run there when the battle for Camp Custer began. I hadn't heard this much munitions being expended since my days in Iraq. No scratch that, this was worse, in Iraq there was a controlled rate of fire. Acquire target, fire, reacquire, fire. This was frenetic, panicked, blind dispensing of lead hoping to seek a target. I know I was placing human emotions where they didn't belong but I would swear there was almost an anguish to this blitzkrieg. Mankind was desperately trying to keep a toehold here in an increasingly difficult world. Someone or something was doing its best to terminate that germ of humanity before it could put down roots.

Helicopters whipped past me heading towards the front of the base, not the back. Shit, apparently there was more than just the attack at the beach.

The ground under my feet was rumbling like the world had just eaten the largest burrito ever produced and now a killer case of indigestion was setting in. M1A1 Abrams tanks rambled past me going close to 50 miles an hour. God save anyone that got in their way. Nope I take that back, FUCK whoever gets in their way.

"GO!" I screamed. "Get those bastards!" Patriotic pride swelled up in me. If I thought I could have jumped on one of those tanks without getting my arm ripped off I might have done it. A young gunner, couldn't have been more than 19, spared me a glance, the fear in his eyes brought me back to center. 'Relax Talbot get what you need and get to where you need to be.' The distinctive sound of missiles being fired and exploding gave me hope. Not much on this planet can survive the hell fire that is an Apache attack helicopter, but then again this wasn't a conventional enemy.

As I approached the store I could feel what hearing I had left begin to slide further down the scale. I'd never be able to hear those stupid tones again at my next hearing test. The gunfire had increased, how that was possible was beyond my scope. I immediately found what I was looking for and just as quickly regretted my decision. Whatever was happening outside was coming to a crescendo and I was still a good 15 minutes from where I needed to be. 'Stupid,

stupid, stupid.'

Too late to question myself now. I grabbed what I needed and hoped that it was fully charged. Outside the store the Gods deigned to shine down on me. A lone hummer stood sentinel in the parking lot. I figured whoever owned it was busy elsewhere. I opened up the rear hatch and with a concerted effort and some help from an elderly man who was stocking up on Similac, no clue why, we placed my ill-gotten booty into my ill-gotten booty. I remembered the last time I had 'borrowed' a military vehicle. Damn near got me a prison sentence. I was pretty certain that wasn't going to be the case this time.

I shut the hatch and turned back to the store; the earth was still rumbling like Godzilla was laying waste to the Japanese countryside. I had to know, I had to look back at Sodom and Gomorrah, it's who I am. I walked to the far corner of the parking lot so that I could look past the store and get a decent view of the front of the base. It was singularly one of the worst decisions I had made thus far in my life that was rapidly losing precious moments of existence as I stood there. Godzilla and King Kong side by side would have been less frightening (not really, just using that for dramatic effect) but I was pretty petrified.

Not one, not two, but three Terex 5500's had already crashed through what little fortification the base had offered. Sure one was completely ablaze but that wasn't stopping its progress. Multiple rocket launchers fired from different locations on the trucks. This I could tell by the telltale smoke trail. 'Humans? Why?' Then the second wave of despair crashed into me. The putrefied, pustulant smell of the dead. I tracked my visage lower, thousands of zombies were rambling into the base. 'Humans and zombies? Why?' I asked again. Only one thing in the world could have pulled this off, Eliza, the bitch that had planted the tree that had the evil roots.

I stood a few moments longer watching as the two trucks that were seemingly still fully functional raised their dumps up to discharge their payloads. Hundreds, maybe thousands of zombies spilled onto the ground, many became damaged or even crushed from the not so fragile dismounting, but true to their kind, they didn't seem to mind all that much. The trucks looked like they were taking huge shits, the sight and smell confirmed my thoughts. Time to get moving.

Escape from this base was impossible. Eliza had pulled it off. I could have and I should have ended this all months ago, if I had just let Justin take that original shot back when we first came across Eliza. I felt weak. I had let my humanity rule back then and now Eliza was going to make me pay for it, in spades, some diamonds and maybe even with a heart or two. I ran back to the hummer, the glow plugs seeming to take hours to ignite, giving me ample time to lament my decision for this detour. It wasn't that the time lost would have spared me the coming fate. It's just that I would have been able to have a few more moments of life with my family. The hummer started. I put it into drive and slammed my foot down on the accelerator. I rolled out of the parking lot at a whopping 10 mph.

My next stop was the base hospital. Thankfully it was back towards the barracks. If I had to go forward I wouldn't have made it. I wasn't being pessimistic, just realistic. I would have tried because I had to, but I wouldn't have made it. I grabbed my precious cargo that I had liberated from the commissary and headed into the hospital.

Doctors, nurses and patients were running around trying for an orderly mass evacuation. Where the hell they were going to go was beyond me. I heard one voice above all others.

"Someone had better tell me what the fuck is going on!!" The voice boomed from Room 312.

"Oh what is it Lawrence?" I said as I ran into his room.

"Oh fucking Talbot, man, I am so glad to see you. And if you ever call me Lawrence again I'm going to rip your head off and shove it up a zombie's ass. What's going on? Forget that, get me out of this contraption."

I got over to the side of his bed and began to undo the traction sling that had his leg suspended.

"Seriously though Talbot, what is going on?"

"Pretty much the end game BT. Eliza somehow got people to work with the zombies. They got these huge trucks and just stormed the gates. At least a couple of thousand of the rotten meat bags have breached the gates." I helped BT into a sitting position.

"How much time do we have?" He asked.

"None."

"Say again. Because it sounded like you said none."

"There's no way off this base bud."

"Than what are you doing here?"

"Personal reasons BT, I was afraid that if the zombies got to you and turned you, the first person you'd come and try to eat would be me. And you already scare the shit out of me without being a monster too."

"Fucken hilarious."

"My wife tells me that too. Let's go."

"Mike I'm just going to slow you down. Go spend these last few minutes with your family."

"See I knew you were going to say that. So I got you a present." I ran out to the hallway and grabbed my 'gift' and drove it in.

"A scooter? You got me a scooter? Do I look like I should be collecting social security benefits?"

He was giving me shit the whole time, but he was still shuffling his ass over and onto his cherry red ride.

The scooter sagged under the assault of his weight. Such an inappropriate time, but I couldn't help it, laughter started slowly in my gut and frothed out my mouth.

"What are you laughing at Talbot?"

It took me a bit before I could get it out. The effect of my words on BT made me break out into a fresh chortle. "You look like a Russian bear on a tricycle." I told him. It wasn't nearly as funny when he ran over my toes.

"Yeah not so hilarious now is it?" He said as he drove out into the hall.

"It sort of is."

"This thing has reverse Talbot, don't make me use it. Where we going?"

"Ambulance exit, hope my ride is still there."

CHAPTER 19 - JOURNAL ENTRY 13 - 

Tracy was at the entrance to our building, her demeanor shifted from 'worried sick' to 'where has your ass been' as I pulled up.

"Talbot, everything's packed. We're ready. Are we all going to fit in that thing?"

"Get the shit and get back upstairs."

Tracy seemed to misinterpret my message. She looked relieved.

"They've been stopped?" She asked.

"Not so much, this is Camp Custer after all."

"What's going on Mike?"

"Trace get the boys, grab the stuff and head back upstairs, I'll tell you when we get there."

She was definitely not appreciating my curt manner.

"Hon, remember that huge truck?"

She nodded.

"There's three more coming and they're full of zombies, there's zombies everywhere. There is no way to get off this base."

I watched as the light of hope in her eyes flickered and then went out.

"So this is it then?" She asked looking straight into my eyes.

"Oh come on, you know me better than that." I said. Not really a lie, I never said we'd get out.

BT pulled his bulk out of the hummer. Tracy was relieved to see him. She ran over to help support him, as much as a 110 pound woman can support a 300-pound man. But it was the thought that counts.

I could tell BT was really laying it on thick with Tracy. "Mike." He said through gritted teeth and a false pained expression. "Could you get my ride?"

"That thing is heavier than hell, you get it out of the trunk." I said.

"Mike!" Tracy shot back.

"Fine." I answered.

As they headed into the building, BT turned over his shoulder and threw me a wink. He mouthed the words, 'That's for calling me Lawrence, asswipe.'

"Real nice, real nice. That's the last time I risk Armageddon to come get your over sized ass."

"Mike!" Tracy yelled from within the foyer.

"Fine! But if I get a hernia lifting this thing out, you're the one that's going to have to push my intestines back in."

"Uh huh." I heard from her as she headed upstairs, BT daintily leaning on her shoulder.

Gunfire had diminished significantly. I didn't take that as a good sign. The earth was still trembling under my feet, which meant at least one and probably more of those behemoths were operational. I stowed BT's new ride under the stairwell. I don't know why. I honestly didn't think that he'd ever get the opportunity to use it again.

Travis was looking out the window when I got up to the room.

"Would you shut the curtains, please?" I asked him.

He turned to me; this was the first time in weeks he looked more like the boy I knew than the man he was becoming.

"What now Dad?" He asked.

I was out of answers. I sure as shit wasn't going to tell my youngest that we were waiting for death. I turned to Tommy who had somehow got a hold of Tonka truck that looked suspiciously like the rolling death machines outside. He was peering into the plastic windshield in an attempt to get a closer look at the figurine driving the truck.

"What's going on Tommy?" I asked him. Something had fastened itself to his attention and I wanted to be there for the reveal.

"Ryan keeps telling me to look closely at the synthesizers." Tommy answered, his tongue nestled securely between his upper and lower jaw. Henry had come over to sniff at the purple goo covered appendage.

I couldn't have been any more confused if I had just tuned into an English Cricket match. Flat bat, bouncing pitches -- it's madness!

"Did he mean 'sympathizers'?" BT asked.

"Well that makes a shitload more sense." I answered.

"Talbot." Tracy said.

Damn cursing. "Tommy, what are you looking for?" If Ryan thought it was important enough to share with Tommy, than it was.

"I don't know, it's really fuzzy. It looks a lot like the old cable boxes TV picture when you would try and watch the scrambled adult channels."

"Hey wait now, I was just a kid."

Tommy looked at me funny.

"Okay so you weren't talking about me personally then, I take it?"

"Talbot what is wrong with you?" Tracy asked?

"Come on BT, help me out every kid did that."

BT looked away. "I don't know what you're talking about, we couldn't afford cable when I was growing up." He winked at me again over Tracy's head.

I flipped him off.

Tracy thought I had done it to her and reciprocated the gesture.

"No wait, honey it wasn't for you it was for that effen big jerk behind you." BT winked again. "You're lucky you're that huge."

Tommy spoke up, the room instantly quieted down. "Ryan keeps saying we have to go look at the humans. Like now."

BT made as if he was going to get up.

"Not this time BT." I said. He looked hurt. "BT, I

can't think of a better friend I would want to stay here and defend everything that is sacred to me." Now he looked honestly touched, I couldn't leave it like that. "And besides I think your cherry red scooter might draw us some unwanted attention."

"I know where you live Talbot." BT rumbled.

"What are you going to do Mike?" Tracy asked.

"Most likely the stupidest thing possible. Justin, grab your stuff." Travis made to get his gear too. "I put my hand on his shoulder. "Not this time. I want as few of us out there as possible." I thought he might be hurt from my decision and maybe he was and wasn't showing it. But not having to go out into a deadly nightmare has its pluses. Justin's health was vastly improved from when we had arrived on base, but he still harbored the virus within him. I was hoping that this would somehow benefit us while we looked for some answers to Ryan's questions. Uncertainty mounted upon ambiguity, sounded like a crappy foundation from which to launch an escape.

I hesitated in the stairwell. Sure, part of it was because who willingly wants to go into battle. What really had me stopped in my tracks was how were we going to blend in, and a lot of that had to do with how the battle outside was going. If we ran out there in civvies (civilian clothing), it was damn sure guaranteed the army and Marines weren't going to ask whether we were refugees or invaders before they shot at us. If we went and changed into camos and the attackers were winning we pretty much were going to suffer the same fate. Dead is dead, doesn't really matter how you get there.

"I think we need to cover both bases." I said to Justin. Not being privy to my inner dialog he was now thoroughly confused.

I ran back into the apartment; not much had changed in the 15 seconds I had been gone. "Trav, get away from the window." The fighting had not yet reached this far into the base but it was only a matter of time and an eighth of an inch thick pane of glass would do little to stop a bullet.

"What are you doing Mike?" Tracy asked looking up from the couch. Stress was etched into her features. The small reprieve from a world gone mad had done us all some good, but that plush rug had been violently pulled from beneath us and we were going to have some serious difficulty righting our collective equilibriums.

"Blending in." I told her.

There were many reasons why our marriage had survived and she continually never ceased to amaze me. Her insight into my mind could at times be frightening, but not this time.

"You know, Mike, that we don't all reside in that head of yours right? We are not figments of your imagination. Unless you tell us what is going on we don't just know."

I've referenced it before but I'll give you some more clarification. The male mind is truly only designed for the task at hand. If we were an operating system and you were to take a look at the resources being used for the job we were working on (whether it was sex or watching a football game or just eating a sandwich) we would be pinned at around 98%, the other 2% would be available for possibly looking for dangers that threaten like a rabid polar bear crashing through your front door during the third quarter. We would have just enough system resources left to recognize that and then shift over into survival mode.)

And being prior military that 98% might actually get ratcheted up to 99ish percent, when there is a military operation running through my grape, I am constantly thinking through contingency plans and odds of success and failure. Banalities and frivolities are things of a peaceful civilized society, they have no place in conflict.

So when I answered Tracy with "Huh?" it really shouldn't have been a surprise to anyone.

Seeing the stonewalled face I portrayed, she turned to Justin.

He shrugged his shoulders. "He didn't tell me anything either." Justin told his mother.

I ran into my bedroom and into the closet rooted around for a few seconds and was rewarded for my trouble. I came out and threw a pile at Justin. "Put these on."

He started to take his jacket off. "No, put the cammies on over your other clothes. I think we're going to need to have both teams' uniforms on for this."

Tracy placed her face in her hands. Nicole emerged from the bathroom, morning, afternoon and evening sickness had settled in for the long haul with her. The road was no place for anybody, much less someone in her condition.

"Hi Dad." She said, her pale green color nearly matching the décor of the room.

"What's the matter 'Oley, I don't smell any buns?" Tommy said with a sorrowful look on his face. The room turned to look at him. "Are they hot cross buns?" Tommy asked. "Cinnamon buns? Because that would be awesome, but that doesn't make sense because those would be rolls. Corn muffins?" Tommy asked expectantly.

All this talk of food was not having an agreeable turn with Nicole's fragile stomach so she launched herself back into the bathroom, the door barely closing as the first of the retches racked through her.

"What'd I say?" Tommy asked nervously.

"Tommy what are you talking about?" Travis asked him.

"Ryan says Nicole has a bun in the oven. Is it a big bun? I mean because how is everyone going to be able to eat it, are we only going to get one bite to eat each, because I really like hot buns. Do we have butter? I don't really like margarine, I could put some peanut butter on my bite though, that would be pretty good."

I was tense because there was still some serious danger in my immediate future but Tommy's words always had a way to warm my heart. I could tell that BT was near to out loud laughing. The embarrassment he would cause

Tommy was the only thing keeping that in check.

"I'll tell him what's going on Mike." Tracy said with a soft almost ghost of a smile. "Just hurry up and get back here, both of you." I gave her a small kiss. She gripped my hand before I could turn to leave. "I'm not kidding Mike, get your's and Justin's asses back here soon."

I nodded. I was not going to verbally promise something that I wasn't sure we could deliver on.

"Not even a false promise Mike?" Tracy asked.

"Get your shit Justin, let's go." I didn't turn back to face her, I might not have left. Inaction can be as deadly as a poorly executed action.

CHAPTER 20 - JOURNAL ENTRY 14 -

Outside of the barracks it was eerily quiet, like we were in the eye of a hurricane. The housing area was located nearly dead center in the camp. Fierce fighting was still raging to the front of camp and sporadic fighting was coming from the rear but for the time being nothing was blessedly happening here. Some people milled about, lost in confusion, indecision; some just plain scared out of their minds.

"Sir, sir." An older balding man came huffing and puffing up to me. When he got closer I realized he might actually be younger than me, he had just led a soft life and his unconditioned body showed it. How had he made it this long? "Sir, what is going on, what should we do?"

Up close, how the hell he figured me for military I don't know. First off I had a very unstandard goatee and my cammies which weren't meant to be worn over my civvies, couldn't have been any more ill fitting if I had tried. My drill instructor would have beat me into the dirt if I had ever showed up to revelry looking like this. That got me smiling. I think it might have looked more like a sneer though the way the roly-poly man backed up a step.

That didn't stop him completely from marshaling himself. He grabbed my cuff as I began to walk off. "Sir, what should we do?" He said pointing back to the small throng of people looking nervously around.

"Fine, you want to know what I think you should do?" I said addressing the crowd. I got some nods and a general consensus of 'Yes's' "This is for ALL of you. I don't care if you're Catholic, Protestant, Lutheran, or into Buddhism, Hinduism, a Jehovah's Witness or better yet an atheist or agnostic. First thing you should do is pray, because even if you don't believe in a God or a higher power, what do you have to lose? If I'm wrong and there is no God you only lost a few seconds comforting yourselves and each other, but if I'm right?" I left that one unanswered. It was self-explanatory.

"The second thing all of you should do is get indoors and arm yourselves." Roly looked like he might protest. "There are no pacifists or atheists in a fox hole. We are all about to be in a fight for our very lives, do you want to meet your maker knowing you went down meekly or you did everything in your power to eradicate all evil on this planet?" Most took the majority of my words to heart and would at least go down swinging after their one sided correspondence with a higher entity. Others, like Roly, still wandered around aimlessly looking for someone or something to get them out of this jam. They would be among the first to be ground to dust under the wheels of the war machine.

"Justin you stay behind me, anything happens, you head back. Got it?"

"Sure something happens to you, I go back alone and tell mom I left you behind. Got it."

"That's not what I meant smart ass."

"I've got your genes."

"Lucky you." I said, not as a compliment.

After a moment's thought, I headed towards the rear of the base and Lake Michigan. More enemy humans to scope out towards the front but that also meant more fighting. More fighting meant more bullets and more explosions, more of an opportunity to get killed. I had checked my itinerary earlier in the day. Nowhere on it did it say anything about dying. We hadn't gone more than a block when we began to run into wounded soldiers who were being medevacked out of the hot areas. The shell shocked look of defeat shone through their eyes. Hastily made bandages were soaked through with blood. More than one unlucky soul screamed for their mother, most gripping what remained of a slightly tethered leg or arm. One poor bastard's entire lower half had been compressed to a third of its former size, how he was still alive was proof to me that God had turned a blind eye towards his children. His glassy shock-tainted stare was having an unnerving effect on Justin. To be fair, Justin's illness had kept him largely out of all the battles we had thus far been in. Unfortunately for him, he'd be able to get some much needed experience today.

Justin was having a difficult time compartmentalizing the sights all around him. He kept stumbling into me, so intent was he on looking around at the human carnage and subsequent debris. I'd seen it before, happens all the time in combat. Some guys, no matter how much training they've received, can't cope with the sensory overload. We used to call them 'freezers', more times than not these 'freezers' would get their buddies killed because the friend would go out to save them and usually take the bullet.

"Justin, you have got to stop walking up my heels."

"Sorry Dad, I've just never seen so much…"

"Death."

"I was gonna say blood, but whatever."

"I know, but you've got to move on. We've got to concentrate on what we need to do. These men and women were brave. They died for us and have given us this chance to save ourselves. The best way we can remember and honor them is to succeed."

My words seemed to have the desired effect. Justin stopped ramming into my back and his gazed stayed to the front. More likely his stomach was right now rivaling his sister's and he didn't need any more fodder for his stomach canon. The barrage of injured began to slough off to a trickle and then to nothing. As good as that was visually, it was that bad in terms of the direction the battle had taken. No more casualties being taken off the field of battle meant that there weren't enough healthy soldiers to do the task. That fact was punctuated when at the very next block we began to encounter soldiers in full on retreat. As if they were dragging it behind them, came the pustulous smell of the dead. Justin volleyed forth a greenish-yellow bile that seemed nearly incandescent in its hue.

"Feeling better?" I asked him without turning around.

"Worlds."

"That sarcasm?" I asked.

"What do you think?"

"You really are going to need to get away from me when you get your first chance. A few years more with me, you'll be my clone," I said swatting his shoulder, his hunched over form getting a closer look at his refuse from the impact.

He stood straight up, eyes wide with fear. "She's here." He whispered.

"Like here, here?" I asked pointing to our general vicinity. "Or here in the camp?" I asked. I wanted to push him away from what was looking like a good place to dispose of any undigested food and maybe some twice churned stomach soup, I might possess.

"Close but not here."

The worst passed, it was looking more and more like I might get to finish the processing of the omelet I had eaten earlier in the day.

"Can she tell that you're here?" I asked concerned. She could have us rounded up and served on a platter in under twenty minutes if she could locate us.

Justin was concentrating hard, a thick vein stood out on his forehead. Was he fighting for control of his mind, or was he trying to break through Doc's vaccine and back into the cold embrace of his dark mistress? Both were disturbing thoughts and I was getting nervous just standing here. If an errant patrol were to come around the corner of the building and they were of the ilk to shoot first and kick our bodies second, well that would just be shitty.

"Justin we gotta go." I said shaking his shoulder, I could hear movement and it was getting closer. It wasn't the haphazard flight of the retreating either. This was the stealthy approach of the nearly victorious. Justin was coming back from whatever depths he had ventured but as a snail's pace. If he hadn't been joined to my side for the last 20 minutes I would have sworn he had just got stoned, and then I'd really be pissed because he hadn't shared. No matter how much I wanted it to be, we were not on a movie set as extras for some Alfred Hitchcock horror flick. This was proved to me when I looked up and down the side of the building and there was no super convenient place to hide. If this was a movie we could just press flat against the building and miraculously the enemy would fail to turn in our direction. Yup, good chance that wasn't going to work.

I half-dragged Justin away from our tentative last resting spot, the cries of screaming men and women masking our move. We hid behind a deuce (that's a two ton truck to all you non-military folk, although if you're still alive you must have had some sort of training and would have known that.) I started taking Justin's camo pants off, that seemed to bring him all the way to his wits.

"Dad? Wait, where are we? What the hell are you doing?"

"Good to see your back. Now get your cammies off, we're playing for the other team now."

"What?" He asked still dazed.

"The camp's overrun, I want to look more like the enemy right now. You know, the whole hiding in plain sight."

"Dad that's not really going to work so much." Justin said flatly.

"Sure it is, it's a great plan, thought it out all by myself."

"Maybe that's the problem."

I stopped in mid-motion taking my blouse off (that's a camouflage top to all you non-military types, must I keep explaining myself?) and looked him square in the eye. "It's good to have Justin back." His wit and sarcasm had been severely lacking during Eliza's hostile takeover bid.

"It's good to be mostly back." He said, stressing 'mostly.' "Look through the windows, Dad."

We were on the driver's side of the truck. I looked

through and past the passenger window; the two thick panes of glass did very little to hide the nightmare that stumbled our way. "Oh fuck." I said without much emotion. What is the best way to meet your end? Angry defiance? Resignation? 'Oh fuck' seemed an appropriate blend of the two. "You ready to run?"

"Too late, speeders have already passed us."

"Well aren't you just full of good news. Wish I had a grenade, I really saw myself going out in a big movie ending explosion."

"Dad, get behind me!" Justin whispered urgently. I checked my safety off. Zombies were within feet of us. Justin pushed the barrel of my gun down. "Dad, please get behind me." He beseeched.

"Justin, this isn't how I want to go out, it's the whole machismo thing. You know the guns a'blazing and all that." It's funny the words that were coming out of my mouth had nothing to do with how I really felt. I pretty much wanted to piss myself. Who the hell would know the difference? The zombies wouldn't give a shit if I self basted.

Justin pulled me behind him and pressed the both of us uncomfortably hard up against the body of the truck.

"What the hell are you doing? Even if I piss myself I'll be damned if I watch you die first."

"What?"

"Did I say that out loud?"

"Just shut up." Justin whispered. A few speeders had come around the back of the truck. I wriggled to break free of Justin's pinning. "Stop, this might work." He said out the corner of his mouth.

"Might?" I hate 'might'.

Two speeders ran right up to us, every fiber of my being fought for action a war raged in my skull, run! Fight! Puke! Sex! (oops, my bad, errant thought).

The nearest zombie sniffed around Justin, its eyes opaque and its mouth hanging open, small maggots wriggling in the meat-infested mouth. This one looked like he liked to gnaw on bones, its teeth were all jagged and in some serious need of dental care. The smell that emanated from his mouth was death incarnate. I can't even begin to describe that odor. If you found my first journal, I talked about carrying fresh Henry shit in a plastic bag around your nose, that would now be what you used to try and diffuse halitosis Hal's breath.

Justin flinched as the zombie licked up the side of his face. What would I do once that lick turned to a bite? Justin's screams would cripple me. The zombie kept licking though, up the side of his face and over to his left ear, where I was now eye to eye with this thing. It paused hesitantly, still licking Justin, but now its nose went into hyper action. He was sniffing around like Henry would be when I'm hiding a peanut butter treat in my fist. Henry knows it's there because he can smell it, he just can't see it. Then it dawned on me what was going on, Justin was somehow hiding us 'in plain sight'! See, this still could be a movie set! I'm holding onto that.

The confusion was evident, the zombie wanted to do what zombies do, 'eat' but Eliza held sway and by default Justin was able to bend a piece of that to his will. Rivulets of sweat were pouring down Justin's face. The exertion he was spending was burning through him like a wildfire. Halitosis Hal greedily licked up the fluids like it was the fountain of youth. Justin was burning like a furnace. I was soaked through and through and 'no' it wasn't because I had let my bladder get the better of me.

Distant screams off to our right perked Hal's interest. He took one long soul searching look into my eyes and ran to his dinner bell. Like that, the spell was over. The other zombies completely lost interest in us, as if Hal was their leader and if he didn't think we were worth eating than neither did they. Justin collapsed, the only reason I was able to keep him from hitting the deck was that I was almost meshed completely with him.

"Holy shit Justin, what just happened?" I asked him as I gently helped him to the ground. Zombies streamed past us, paying us no more attention than if we were a plate of brussel sprouts at a chocolate bar.

"I…I'm not a hundred percent sure, I sort of told the zombie that we worked for Eliza."

"Not that I'm complaining but why didn't Hal…"

"Hal?"

"That zombie, why didn't he eat me?" Ideas were popping up in my head.

"I was screaming in my head to him that you didn't exist."

"He bought that?"

"Well he is a zombie, Dad, I don't think he could even get a job at the post office."

"Again back to the whole this is awesome 'but' part."

"Why aren't we still under attack?" Justin asked.

"Sure, I mean maybe we weren't on Hal's fine dining experience."

"Hal?" Justin shook his head.

"Forget him." It was surreal to be having this conversation, actually any conversation, as hundreds, maybe thousands of zombies ambled on past us.

"Dad, best I can tell you is that they have an almost herd mentality. Where the leader goes the rest follow."

Idea number one popped in my head. "Can you do this thing." I asked pointing to his head. "Again, and get the whole family out?"

"I don't think so." He said dejectedly. "If that zombie had stayed a few seconds longer I wouldn't have been able to hold him off."

I shivered knowing I had been that close to having my eyeball eaten out, or possibly my nose removed in a teeth-filled vise.

"I'd never be able to hide you all." A small tear of frustration coursed down his face.

"Justin, you just saved our ass, you did great. Can you get up?"

"You there! What are you two doing?" An

authoritative voice shouted.

I had been so intent on using Justin's newfound powers I failed to realize that the zombies had gone on by. (Please don't ask for a clearer explanation than that. I know it's difficult to believe that I could somehow miss the small fact that dead people who loved to feast on the living who were within biting distance had gone by without my noticing.) My first priority was to the collective safety of the Talbots and Company, all else was secondary. Still survival relies heavily on quick thinking.

"He's been shot!" I shouted.

"Leave him." The voice shouted, sounding impatient that someone had had the audacity to get wounded.

"He's my brother, I can't just leave him." I shouted back.

"Dad, what are you doing?" Justin whispered.

"Fake that you're wounded. I'll tell you what I'm doing after it's over."

"Ow, ooh, ah this hurts so much!" Justin moaned.

"Tone it down a bit, not looking for an Emmy." I slowly reached my right hand down to my ankle.

"Fine!" The insurgent said, clearly getting closer. I didn't look up to watch his approach. I was fearful that he would suspect my ruse and shoot us both where we were, me down on my haunches and Justin half sitting up and in my arms. Out of the corner of my eye I could see our discarded cammies, could he? The sun was blocked as the man came in to get a closer look. "Where's he shot? I don't see any blood."

"Funny thing." I said as I launched up from my kneeling position. My K-Bar slid effortlessly into his Adam's apple. The angle of the blade pierced his jugular and went up and through his tongue. There was some small resistance as it burst through his upper palate and then into his brain. A look of shock and betrayal was lined on the man's features as I helped him down much as I had Justin only moments earlier. The man had expired long before I was able to pull my blade out. A strong suction was followed by an audible pop. Only Justin's retching disturbed the quiet morning.

"You going to be alright?" I asked Justin, looking around to see if anyone had witnessed this event. I wiped my blade on the man's jacket. A glint off his chest brought my attention to center, a tickle in my head fused into thought. A tiny vial no bigger than a push tack was attached to a thin chain that hung from the man's neck. A pin-prick amount of red fluid swam lazily within. "What do you think that is?" I asked Justin. He still appeared to be varying between a yellow and greenish hue.

"Please tell me you're not into trophies, Dad?"

Justin couldn't bring himself to look at the dead man. Killing the dead is one thing. We're just finishing what nature had intended all along. Killing a living breathing man, that was an unnatural act. It violated all that should be sacred. I wouldn't lose much sleep, if any, over this piece of shit. He had chosen his fate the moment he hooked up with Eliza. Who in their right mind aligns with the living dead and the undead and doesn't expect a bad ending? That's just piss poor planning on his part if you ask me.

I ripped the chain off the guy and held it in front of Justin's eyes. Probably should have wiped some of the guy's blood off first though. The quickly thickening blood hung in long dangles before releasing from the chain links and striking softly into the not so pristine snow. Justin was rapidly going for a complete disgorging.

"Blood." Justin said breathlessly as he heaved what little remained inside of him.

I looked to his puddle of vomit, alarmed. Blood is never a good thing to discard. I was relieved when I didn’t see any. I looked at him questioningly.

"Blood, it looks like blood." He said pointing weakly to the vial in my hand.

"I think you’re right." I said looking more closely at it.

"Why?" He asked.

"I think we need six more."

Justin lurched a little with the thought of killing six more 'live' men. "Why?" He asked even more weakly.

"I think I'm holding zombie repellant here."

CHAPTER 21 - JOURNAL ENTRY 15 -

I removed the charm from the chain and placed it in my pocket. "You up for this?" I asked Justin.

He gave a thumbs-up and a greasy smile. It wasn't the 'Ooh Rah' war cry of the Marines but it was going to have to do.

"Dad, you sure that thing is going to work?" Justin asked alluding to my new favorite piece of jewelry. Mind you it's not that I have other jewelry that I'm fond of, it's just that this piece could potentially save my family's collective asses. "I don't think I've got enough energy left to mask you again."

Now he had me thinking. What if this thing was useless, no more than a trinket fished out of a gumball machine. Death by rended flesh was not my ideal way to go. I was really looking for a massive coronary during mind blowing sex as my opt out. "Maybe you're right. Let's do a test. Let's make this quick though, time is definitely getting short."

Some of the slower ambling zombies were no more than 100 feet ahead of us. I was figuring better to let one of the deaders realize I was food than a pack of speeders. We approached some of the zombies who looked like they had gone through in an industrial washing machine full of glass. They were torn to shreds, shards of skin hanging askew. Occasionally birds would swoop down and feast on the proffered meat. To say it was disgusting would be like saying Henry's farts smelled like sweet ambrosia. I was willfully getting as close to them as I could; the repulsion I felt nearly rivaled the fear. My blood was blistering through my veins. The flight mechanism in me was in hyper drive. I could just turn around and…do what? The zombies were heading in the direction I needed to be in. Whether I blended in or fought my way through I had to get to where they were going before they got there, and I had to do it fast. The speeders up front were still meeting some resistance but it wasn't the resistance of a dug in enemy, it was the sporadic firing of an opponent during controlled retreat. The Marines were giving up territory in an attempt to save lives.

My concern for my family spurred me on. Justin fought to keep up, his reserves nearly depleted from his magic act. I was within 15 feet of the first zombie when he turned to look at me. One eye had completely rolled back up and into its head, his nose had been stripped clean of all edible pieces as had half his lip. The exposed brown teeth were forever frozen in a sinister looking stare.

"Shithead, should have used a whitening agent in your toothpaste." It was my way of dealing with the horror within. "I bet you've got the breath to match that smile."

The zombie had stopped its forward momentum to get a better look at us with its one good eye. His tongue flapped independent of any conscious thought. A seagull took that opportune time to swoop in and latch onto the lolling appendage. I nearly vomited when the bird used every ounce of its wing strength to rip the tongue from the zombie's mouth. The zombie paid it no attention whatsoever as his tongue first stretched to unimaginable lengths and then like an over taut rubber band just snapped free. Viscous black liquid oozed forth from the wound. The zombie smacked its lips around the new au jus.

"Oh Dad, what the fuck?" Justin cried.

My sentiments exactly, but if I had voiced my thoughts it would not have been the only thing to spew forth and with the human enemy behind us I could not give them any reason to suspect that we weren't part of their group.

"What do we do if he tries to eat you?" Justin asked realizing we couldn't kill it without exposing ourselves to some serious issues, flying lead being among them.

"Well he's a deader and he looks like he's been

through the ringer. We should be able to outpace him without drawing too much attention." I was however intentionally leaving out the thousand or so zombies to our forefront.

The zombie wavered a few more seconds as we got closer, like he was deciding if we were tasty enough to eat.

"Come on, come on." I said softly. "Make up your mind, it's not like you're doing trigonometry." Then I laughed.

"Dad, is this really a laugh worthy moment?"

"It is if you're wondering can a zombie do trig, when even I can't."

"Real hilarious Dad."

"You had to be there."

The zombie made one whistle snort sound through his completely open sinus passage and turned. I would swear that he looked a little bummed that we weren't on the menu but it's difficult to tell these things on a person who has had most of their facial tissues destroyed.

"I think this vial is our golden ticket out of here, Justin." I said excitedly.

"How are you planning on getting more?" Justin asked. We knew how I had to get it. The question was HOW was I going to get it.

I started to slow up a bit, letting the zombies get ahead and the human attackers from the rear catch up. The first opportunity presented itself almost immediately and it almost ended up being our last. I was thankful that the usurpers did not appear to have prior military training. They were basically broken up into independent units. There were no fire teams or squads, just loose bands of traitors, traitors to all of mankind. The zombies were mortal enemies, of that there was no doubt, but they did not choose their fate. These humans were tantamount to a tic latched onto a parasite. They were living off of a scourge. I would be glad to rid the world of as many of them as I could.

Nobody even looked at us twice as we meshed back into a group of them. Apparently leeches don't communicate.

A couple of guys that bore a family resemblance and a third headed off to check out one of the base houses.

"Hey, do you mind if we come?" I asked the person that I assumed to be the leader of the trio.

The guy spit out a wad of tobacco, turned to look at us both. "You don't get all weak in the knees with killing do you?"

I shook my head in the negative.

"What if its women or kids?"

I shook my head again and even added in a lip scrunching to get my point across.

"What about him? He already looks a little queasy." The guy asked pointing to Justin.

"Naw, he's fine." I said. "He just had a bad can of Spam for breakfast." I proxied.

"I hate that shit. Either of you get in my way, I'll kill you." And with that he turned back around and headed towards the house.

The third man of the trio brazenly walked up to the front door and kicked it in. I more than half expected a shotgun blast to send him reeling back down the steps. I was more concerned the vial around his neck would get broken than the douchebag's neck getting busted. When nothing happened we all walked in. The first man walked straight down the hallway like he had just come home from work. The leader quickly followed but got halfway down the hallway and took a left into the kitchen. His brother would have followed except for the seven-inch blade I stuck in his rib cage and through his lungs. You could barely hear the small 'thud' as he slipped out of my arms on the way to the floor or you might have never known about his passing.

"Bollie! Get in here man, they have your favorite." The leader shouted from around the corner.

I never did learn what his favorite was.

"What the fuck man!?" The first guy through the door had made a circuitous route and was now coming in from the living room. Tough not to figure out what was going on considering I was standing over the dead body of his friend with a bloody knife in my hand.

"Earl!" He yelled. "Get in here, these fuckers killed Bollie."

Justin's MP4 jumped in his hands as he fired a burst at close range into the man. The first round caught him square in the chest. Subsequent rounds neatly climbed up his body as the gun recoiled. The second bullet ripped out his carotid artery and the third would have made any Mohawk Indian proud as the top of the man's skull plate was neatly sheared off. Zombie pate.

And yes that did go through my mind. My errant thought nearly got me killed as Earl had come around the corner, his AK-47 ripping through the siding next to me. I pushed Justin into the living room. We toppled over his fresh kill. We would never be in a position to defend ourselves in time. Divine intervention, sheer luck, fate, I don't know. I don't have the answers. Bigger things than my mere life were going on. I sometimes felt like we were on a cosmic chessboard and far superior beings than myself were playing a game for our survival. Who knows, maybe it was nothing more than 'Trading Places' and the whole screwed up thing was based on a wager of a Narflack, which basically translates to one American dollar. The distinctive chatter of the 7.62 lead shedding dispenser was cut off by a much smaller almost fire cracker sounding weapon.

"That a .22?" Justin asked me. We both scrambled as far away from the doorway as possible. A loud thud, presumably Earl, hit the floor. We were safe for the moment.

"You in there." A voice trying to be bigger and bolder than it really was, rang out. "Your friend is dead and you're next if I don't see your guns and then your hands."

"Jesse?" I asked.

"Who is it?" His voice cracked and he immediately attempted to recover thinking this might be a ruse. In a much deeper tone he said, "You should get out of my house before I do to you what I did to your friend."

"You keep saying that but I can assure you that he was far from my friend. Jesse, its Mike Talbot and Justin."

He wasn't prepared to give in quite so quickly. "Why are you with these guys?"

"Jesse we weren't. We took out two of them before you got the third. Is your dad around, I might have found a way to get off this base?"

"No it's just me, Blake, Porkchop and Rachael."

"What are you doing Jesse, what did you tell him that for?" Blake admonished his older brother.

"Jess, it's me Justin." All the boys had become fast friends during my days of rehabilitation. If anyone could break through this détente my money was on Justin. "I'm gonna slide my gun out and then come through, don't shoot me," he threw in for good measure.

The relief on Jesse's face as we all made our impromptu reunion was evident. His dad and mom were getting some supplies when the invasion had happened. Jesse was assigned with babysitting duties. He was under the distinct impression that it wasn't going to involve gun play though.

"You did good." I told him as he did his best to avoid looking at the man he had shot. Blood was beginning to pool in the foyer.

"Eww, gross." Rachael said as she stepped into the hallway.

"Cool." Porkchop said. "Hey Mr. Talbot, Justin, did Dad send you guys?"

"Someone did, Porkchop, but I don't know who." I told him cryptically.

He understood about as much of that sentence as was possible, so basically none.

"Holy shit!" Porkchop yelled.

"Dad says you're not supposed to swear." Rachael told him.

"Sorry." He said absently, but he wasn't. His vision was fixed squarely on the gun by Earl's head. "Can I have that?"

My first inclination was to say absolutely not. But more guns meant more chances of freedom. Actually, wasn't really my call, I wasn't in charge here. I deferred to Jesse, after all he was watching them and had already proved adept at the task.

"What do you think Jesse?" I asked him.

I'll give him this, he thought about it for a few seconds, then he handed Porkchop the .22 and grabbed the AK for himself. Porkchop couldn't have been any more pleased. Blake grabbed the hunting rifle off of Earl's brother. Rachael started to head for the man in the living room. Jesse, Blake and Porkchop in unison, told her 'no way' in three different manners. She stomped her foot and turned away. I could guarantee if we got through the next week together she was going to make their lives a living hell.

I was happy we had saved the Doc's kids and they had saved us but not at all thrilled this now meant we had to kill another nine humans. As any soldier can attest, man is the most cunning, devious prey out there. Zombies were a mindless killing machine. They wouldn't be doing any trigonometry, ok scratch that, bad analogy, I wouldn't be doing any trig either. You get the point though, killing something that has an equal chance of killing you, that's hunting. It's not like a white tail deer is going to hide behind a tree waiting for you and then clobber you on the head with its hoof. I guarantee a lot less people would be trying to get a license come hunting season, although redneck population growth might be kept in check if deer could even the odds.

Alright, I'm off course, I had a major dilemma. If no one got too close I could pull off the illusion that Jesse and Porkchop were fellow fighters. Blake, because of his size would be stretching plausibility, but no way was I going to be able to pull off that a 10 year old girl would be in this fight. Our chances of success depended wholly on being able to blend in. I couldn't leave them here though. Sooner rather than later somebody else was going to come into this house and with the dead bodies and blood everywhere they would not be caught unawares.

"Dad, we should get moving." Justin said as he peered out the window.

"Tie her up." I said without any further clarification.

"Tie who up?" Rachael asked indignantly. "Me?" She asked pointing to herself. "Nobody is tying me up, I'm a woman!" She roared.

"Mr. Talbot?" Porkchop asked querulously.

"Cool. Been wanting to do that since they brought her home from the hospital." Blake said. Rachael looked as if she was going to explode.

"Probably you too." I said pointing to Blake. Rachael smiled, sticking her tongue out at her middle brother.

"What's going on Mr. Talbot?" Jesse asked moving closer and closer to a defensive posture.

"Jesse, we'll never be able to convince those guys out there that these kids are combatants."

"I'm not a kid!" Blake said, his lip trembling.

"You look like you're about to cry." Rachael laughed pointing her finger at her brother.

"I'm sorry Blake, but we have to make it look like you and your sister are our prisoners."

"Dad, it looks like we might be getting some company." Justin said stepping away from the window.

"Alive or dead?" I asked.

"Both."

"Shit, drag Bollie further down the hallway get the pendants and hand them out."

"What are you going to do?"

"Welcome our guests."

Two zombies were halfway up the steps when I opened the front door. Two men trailed a few steps behind, guns at the ready when they saw me.

"Don't shoot." I said holding up my hands.

"What are you doing in there?" The guy on the left asked.

"Getting some food and a little on the side." I laughed. "There's a feisty one in here."

The zombies approached the front door. It was all I could do to not slam the door in their decaying faces and blow large holes through the faux oak paneling. The two paid me no attention as they bumped up against me trying to get through.

"Can you call off your dogs, I'd like to finish up in here and then they can have the scraps."

The guy on the right licked his lips. "How old?" He fairly drooled.

God forgive me. "Ten," I leered. Inwardly I was repulsed.

"Mind if I watch, maybe get a piece when you're through?" He asked. He was already coming forward. I would spare the lives of these zombies before I would spare his worthless existence.

"We don't have time for this, Rax. There'll be plenty of that shit when it's over." The smaller guy on the right said.

"Oh hell Haggart, this shit's over 'cept for the fat lady singing. And I want some now." Rax said grabbing his crotch.

The zombies were still pushing up against me, fluids of varying viscosity and color where being transferred from them to me but still Rax was making me sicker.

"Seriously Haggart, nobody's getting anything if these two dip shits get in here." I said pushing one of the zombies back. My hand went nearly four inches into a corroded chest cavity. I did vomit a little in my mouth. Haggart walked up the steps, got to the side of the two zombies, pulled out a colt .45 and took out both zombies with one shot.

I was in shock and doing my best to disguise it, which is nearly useless considering I can't even play poker because I'm so readable.

"What?" Haggart said putting his gun back in its holster. "It's not like they obey commands. 'Sides, we have thousands more," he said laughing. "Anything in there a little older? I mean in a pinch I'll fuck anything." And I believed him. "But them kids can be a little unaccommodating when you're carrying something as big as I am." He leered.

What the fuck is wrong with these people???!! "Yeah there's a 15 year old too." I didn't tell him what sex, by his not asking I took that as a sign that he was an equal opportunity rapist. I backed up into the hallway, making myself appear as large as possible to hide any incriminating evidence. Rax nearly bowled Haggart over trying to get in.

Rax was busy fumbling with his pants when I shut the door. Haggart was first to notice the blood trail.

"The dad." I told him when he looked at me. "Knife through the ribs."

"Hardcore man." Haggart said clapping my shoulder while making himself at home.

Rax was almost finished undoing his belt buckle. I wanted to slice his throat open but Haggart wouldn't put his damn rifle down. I was hoping to avoid a gun battle as the enemy soldiers were entirely too close and would most assuredly investigate.

Haggart was about five feet in front of me, with Rax in between the two of us, when Rachael stepped into the hallway from the far end.

"Please make them stop." She cried. Tears flowed freely down her cheeks.

"Oh she's hot!" Rax said as his pants fell to the floor. I thanked all that was holy that he had underwear on even if there was more brown than white to them. All's fair in rape and pillage I suppose, as Rax pushed the smaller man out of his way. Rachael cowered as the man headed down the hallway. My chance had come. I grabbed the K-Bar out of my leg sheath and dragged the honed bladed across Haggart's neck. I barely felt any resistance as his skin parted under the pressure. Blood shot out like a fountain. I sliced across the width of his neck cutting deeper than was necessary. I just wanted to hasten his journey to hell. Rax, who was breathing entirely too heavy to hear the final gurgles of his friend, lurched on.

I let Haggart hit the ground. I was in no mood to make his final moments on the planet any more pleasant than they had to be.

Rax turned when the floor under his feet jumped. "What the fuck is going on?" He said angrily.

"You want to mess with my sister? You sick fuck!" Jesse said coming out from the kitchen. "Nobody messes with my sister except for me!" He screamed.

Rax turned from imminent death into the waiting arms of demise as Jesse plunged a butcher knife hilt deep into his stomach. Rax roared from the pain. A back hand sent Jesse skidding across the kitchen linoleum. Rax placed both hands on the hilt and screamed as he pulled it free. I hammered my K-Bar home through the right side of the neck, the point of the blade emerging an inch past the left side of his neck. Blood flowed into his mouth and onto the floor as he fell to his knees, dropping the knife. I pulled my knife free just as he fell face forward. By the sound of the crunching noise his last few moments on this plane of existence were with a broken nose.

"What the hell are you two doing?" I said trying to yell at both kids simultaneously.

"My mom always said I was a good actress. I wanted to see if she was right." Rachael said. She tried for a smile, but even as good an actress as she was she couldn't pull it off with such a gruesome scene in front of her.

"Piece of shit wanted to rape my sister." Jesse said standing up, rubbing his rapidly reddening jaw line.

"You alright?" I asked as I pulled his hand down to get a better look. He nodded.

Blake came in behind his sister. "Don't blame her, Mr. Talbot. It was my idea. I figured you were going to need a distraction."

"It's okay, nobody's hurt," I said. "Just one bruise and 47 accumulated years of therapy and everyone should be fine."

"Dad, we have to get out of here. We're running out of hallway space." Justin said.

"That's funny." I told him. "Sick but funny."

"Got it from you."

"Might have to include you on that therapy time scale." I was worried about Rachael. Sure, she appeared tough and she probably was, with three older brothers, she had to be. But she was still only ten. As a ten year old if this had all unfolded in front of me I probably would have pulled a 'Tommy,' and not our kindly other-worldly Wal-Mart greeter. I'm talking about The Who's rock opera "Tommy." I'd be catatonic.

"You alright Rachael?" I asked. My heart bled for her. I'll give her this, she was pretty upset, but extremely resistant to letting her brothers know.

"I would like to see my mom now," she said, while coming through the rooms to my right to completely avoid the hallway altogether.

"What if Dad tries to come back here?" Blake asked.

My honest answer was that he'd die trying. There was no way he'd be able to get through. I was happy that I was able to give a more politically correct version of that response though. "We're not going to give him the chance. It'll be easier for us to get to him." That might not be completely true. If he did try and succeed, what then? He'd find a blood bath in his house and his kids missing. I know that would drive me over the edge. I had to hope that Doc was lying low, looking for a chance to come back. There should still be time to get to him before he did anything truly foolish.

"Okay, original plan. Get some rope, we'll tie you and your sister up and we'll go get your dad, my family and get the hell out of here."

A couple of minutes later and we were ready to go.

"Geez we got it, Mr. Talbot, these are slip knots. If we run into any problems we pull on the piece of rope in our hand and the knot will fall away." Rachael said with the disdain that only a pre-teen girl can pull off.

"And then what?" I'd been drilling them the whole time I had been tying them up. It was bad enough when I had my own kids to protect. This was brutal.

"Then we run." Blake said nervously.

"That's the plan, Mr. Talbot?" Jesse asked.

A little thin on the meat side. In fact, 'the plan' was mostly filler, McDonald's would be proud. I shrugged. "It's all I've got."

"Eh, okay." Jesse said stamping his approval on the whole venture.

"Dad, we should get going, the last of the enemy is coming and then it's the giant truck and I'm pretty sure she's on it." Justin said as he visibly paled.

"Who's she?" Rachael asked.

"The bogeywoman." I said stepping up to the door.

"There's no such thing." She shot back.

"I wish you were right sweetie. Justin, Jesse you two out first, then Blake and Rachael, I'll bring up the rear."

"Dad, aren't they going to wonder why the zombies aren't attacking our prisoners?" Justin asked.

We were actually plus one in the 'Zombie Off' department. "Let's just hope the zombies are far enough ahead that's not going to be a problem." A heavy vibration began at my feet and worked its way up. The Terex was getting close. "Let's go, and stay close."

There was a time when the world was still 'normal.' I had been driving with Tracy to check out a Black Friday sale. I was going 60 miles per hour in the fast lane and still a black Hearse was crawling up my ass. I immediately moved over two lanes because it felt like death was fast approaching, that was how I felt right now. That same unsettling churn of bile in your guts, the kind that threatens to make hot butt mud. Sorry about the graphic nature, the truth is gross sometimes. There was, however, no way to change lanes this time. We were on a one lane highway and it seemed like this one had two way traffic.

I took a deep breath before I stepped out the door and carefully shut it behind me. I hoped no one else would go in or we might become immediate suspects in the death of those five soldiers. I use the term 'soldier' loosely. Maybe I should call them combatants, or traitorous scum, that seems to fit better, but uses more of my pencil lead. Pieces of shit it is then.

I was happy and dismayed at the same time to realize we were not the only hunting party that had acquired prisoners, although ours seemed to be in the best condition. More than one had been bloodied and beaten by their captors. Some had that glazed-over look of the defeated, and then there were those that were suffering from shock who had just witnessed or been party to some form of atrocity that only the cruelest animal on the planet can bring to its own kind. Man was a plague upon itself.

I have first-hand experience knowing that war brings out the absolute worst in the two opposing sides. Even that can't hold a candle to what happens to the human mentality of the victor over the conquered. It is something about having absolute power over another being that drives men to incomprehensible acts of cruelty. People who would normally avoid stepping on an ant hill for fear of killing some of the creatures will rape a screaming woman merely for the fact that they can. It has absolutely nothing to do with lust and everything to do with control. I don't know what evolutionary purpose this depravity serves but it has existed in the human genome from the beginning. Maybe it would have been better if the Neanderthals had won out. They seemed a much more 'civilized' people, except for that one asshole in Clan of the Cave Bear. What was his name? Glar? Blug? Dammit. Broud! Yeah that's it!

Most of the combatants seemed content to stay where they were in relation to the zombies. There might be a truce between the two but that didn't make them friends. We, however, had an agenda laced with time constraints. We looked a little out of place outdistancing the others but nobody questioned us. Rachael did vomit as we got closer to the zombies and their odiferous ways. This brought on some cheering from those behind us. Rachael did her best to flip them off with her hands tied behind her back. Luckily, this act of defiance was shielded by my body.

"You trying to get us killed?" I asked her.

"No, I figured that's what you were doing." She shot back.

"You're good." I said with newfound amazement for the kid's wit.

I was not comfortable walking among the dead, even with the Zombie Off. Hell, anything less than being surrounded by the four-inch thick steel metal of a tank wasn't going to make me feel secure. One overly hungry zombie could ruin our day. I know it made absolutely no difference but I made sure that we stayed away from the fatter zombies. I figured if any of them might be a little hungrier than the rest it would be them. I guess I was being a sort of zombieist. I had always prided myself on not being any sort of racist bigot. I figured I should be able to gain absolution for this transgression though.

The zombies paid us no attention. We might as well have been white trash entering a Neiman Marcus and the zombies were salespeople. If anything, they unconsciously avoided us which made sliding through them a near effortless proposition. If not for the smell, this would nearly be pleasant. Well not really, but you know what I mean, at least we weren't cutting, slashing, shooting and just generally blowing stuff up in our way to get out, this was vaguely acceptable.

"The hospital's coming up, Mr. Talbot!" Porkchop nearly shouted.

Now I'm not so vain as to think that every zombie and bad guy in the region has reason to look out for me, but at the same time I don't see any reason to take any more undue chances than I already do. "Hey, Porkchop, for now just call me Mike, and are you sure that's where they went?"

"That's what they said. Dad wanted to get some antibiotics for mom. She said she wasn't sick, that she only had allergies, but my dad said she always got bronchitis this time of the year and he wanted to be prepared especially since supplies were so low."

"Alright, let's get there."

"Dad, do you want me to go and check on Mom?" Justin asked.

With all my heart I wanted to go, and if not me I wanted to send Justin, but splitting up was never a good idea and it was something I was already guilty of. I thought with dread of everything that was important to me still a half mile away and in enemy occupied territory.

"No, we finish this and then we all go."

Justin looked dismayed but he did not question my decision.

Within minutes we were at the front entrance to the hospital. By the strewn wheelchairs and gurneys, it was easy to see that we were not the first to get here. A blood trail led behind the nurse's station where a zombie merrily chewed on the lower calf of a nurse that I had come to think of as Nurse Ratchet. It wasn't that she was mean. On the contrary, it was just that she had her hair up in the style that reminded me of One Flew Over the Cuckoo's Nest. I did not blow the zombie's head off like I wanted to, some things in life have to wait.

"Alright Blake, Rachael take your ropes off. Let's find your mom and dad and get the hell out of here." I said.

"Are they alright?" Rachael asked. I didn't answer.

Blood was everywhere but not in vast quantities. It was almost as if someone had a small paintbrush dipped in blood and kept continuously shaking it over their head. It glistened dully in the fluorescent lighting. Blood was dripping down from the ceiling like a soft violent rain. The kids looked to me as I looked to the tiles above us coated in potential disaster. Was the blood that of the infected? Probably not, but when the ante to play is your life it takes a lot more thought before you go 'all in.' A blood-curdling scream ended my inner hesitation.

"That's my mother!" Blake said as he charged down the hallway.

We all followed. I cringed when I felt a warm patter strike the top of my ear and splash down the side of my face. I was doing the calculations of when I had last shaved and if I had any open wounds on that side. By my reckoning it had been three days since I last dragged the medieval torture device across my face, so all should be well.

I caught up to Blake and grabbed his shoulder just before he busted through the operating doors and into the unknown. From the sounds of it there was a struggle going on and someone definitely needed our help, but the enemy location and strength were still unknown and except for Justin, I only had three kids with me. The advantage of our surprise could be turned on us really quick. A loud slap was punctuated by the throaty laughing of at least three men, possibly four.

"Hold on buddy." I whispered to Blake. I could feel the rage quaking throughout his body.

"But!" he yelled.

I clamped my hand over his mouth. "Quietly Blake." I whispered.

"That's my mom." He said as tears of rage, pain and heartache ran down his face. "She needs my help."

"Yes she does, and we're going to give it to her. But if you go in there without knowing what you're getting into you're not going to help. You'll only make it worse and your mom will be heartbroken if anything happens to you."

"Listen to him Blake." Jesse said. "He's got us this far."

"You cool?" I asked letting his shoulder go.

"I'm fine." He sniffed. "But we need to hurry."

"Oh she's a feisty one!" Someone yelled from the other side of the doors, this also was followed with what sounded like a heavy-handed backhand. Someone hit the floor. It wasn't difficult to figure out whom. Rachael was nearly beside herself with fear. She looked like she was hugging the stuffing out of an imaginary teddy bear.

There were two sets of swinging doors, the set we were up against now, then a five foot air lock followed by the second set and then our ultimate goal. I grabbed Jesse. "Alright Jess, you've got to listen to me, this is a military mission so I need you to understand my orders and obey them. Do you got that?" I asked, as he looked over my shoulder and to the doors. He nodded. "Alright, Justin and I are going through this first set of doors and we are going to try and acquire our targets. You with me?"

"What about me?" he asked, realizing what I was asking.

"You, Porkchop and Blake are first and foremost going to protect your sister. Secondly you are going to protect our escape if it's needed. If you hear me or Justin yell 'Bug Out,' that means we're going to be coming out that door in a hurry and you need to shoot anybody that comes out after us. If you don't hear any yelling, you shoot whoever comes out that door. Got it?"

"Shoot the bad guys," he replied.

"That's about it in a nutshell. Protect your sister. We'll get your mom and dad." I hope.

The telltale sound of ripping material made further explanation an unworthy waste of time. Justin and I eased through the first set of doors hopeful that whoever was on the other side was too busy with what they were doing to notice. I stood up, quickly peeking through the observation window in the door.

"There are two to our left, neither is holding their rifles. One is almost immediately in front of us. The only thing he has in his hand is his dick. The fourth is the ringleader and he's just off to the right. Mrs. Baker is right behind him, Doc is tied up almost against the far wall. Now remember like I taught you. There are combatants and friendlies in this room, acquire your target before you shoot.

You take the two on the left, I've got the other two."

I blew out three quick breaths. On one, we each pushed through our respective door. In three shots Justin had dispatched of his targets. I was not nearly as lucky, Dickhand had moved to get a better view of the ensuing rape. My door had slammed into his back, slowing my progress. When Justin had begun to open fire, the ringleader had pulled out a knife and true to any piece of shit had used Mrs. Baker as a human shield. Dickhand had fallen completely over when I finally shoved him out of the way.

I had my AR up and pointed at the leader's head but he made sure to make as little of a target of himself as possible as he hunkered behind the much smaller woman. Dickhand thought this was an opportune time to try and stand. A solid kick from my combat boots to his rapidly diminishing hard-on gave him pause to reconsider his efforts.

"Oh, oh fuck. Sam he kicked my junk," Dickhand moaned.

"Listen," Sam said. "We can share, I mean she's a fine piece."

I pulled my gun tighter to my shoulder.

"Fuck, fine!" he yelled. "You can have her, there's plenty more meat here. You…you just put that gun down and tell your friend to do the same and I'll just get out of here."

Dickhand was still on the ground writhing and moaning.

"You let her go and I promise you I won't shoot you."

"Oh I know that trick, you won't shoot me but he will." He said gesturing over to Justin.

"I swear to you as a man of honor neither of us will shoot you or harm you in any way."

"What about Drew there?"

"You mean Dickhand, sure, take his ass with you."

"Can I grab my guns?"

"What do you think?" I said sarcastically.

Sam didn't like the odds. He didn't know that we had a vested interest in Mrs. Baker. To him she was just a war prize. We'd kill her as fast as we had killed his other two buddies. To him there was very little stopping us from wasting everyone in the room.

"You won't kill us, you swear?"

"I already told you, take this piece of shit," which I prodded with my foot sending him into a fresh set of wailings "and get the fuck out. You're trying my patience."

"Fine, you fucking assholes, but she would have been so sweet!" he said. As he pushed Mrs. Baker to the side, he held up both his arms.

"Drop the knife." I told him. "Fuck you" was his not so pleasant response.

I shot him in the elbow. His shattered joint flopped down uselessly and the knife clattered to the floor.

"You fucking promised!" He screamed, clutching his shattered arm. "You fucker!"

During the ensuing exchange Dickhand had managed to crabwalk past me and was halfway through the first set of doors.

"Dad." Justin said motioning to the nearly prone man making a not so hasty retreat.

I was tempted to let him go and let Jesse and the boys exact their own fair share of revenge, but I did not want to burden them with that. Besides Dickhand was naked from the waist down and nobody, especially a ten year old girl, should be exposed to that. I pulled out my .357 and put one straight through his spine. He collapsed heavily to the floor under the crushing weight of the magnum round, dead.

"You fucking promised."

"Yeah about that, I'd like to say I'm sorry but I'm really not." Two rounds to Sam's chest sent him skidding across the floor and nearly into Doc Baker's lap. It would be weeks before I could shake the nightmares from this encounter, even if a greater good had been obtained. The end did justify the means. But is using a bad method to get to a good end, good in and of itself? How was this one going to end up on the ledger of my life, in the win or loss column?

"Mike!" Jesse yelled during the lull. "Can we come in?"

"No!" Justin and I yelled in unison.

“And why are you yelling in here? How do you know we’re even alive?” I yelled.

“Well, because you’re answering me.” Jesse said without any hesitation.

“Pragmatist, we’ll be out soon, you guard our withdrawal.”

Doc's wife, Elizabeth sobbed in the corner as she did her best to repair her torn garments. Justin had untied Doc’s restraints and the doc was busy administering much needed care and attention to his wife.

“You guys alright, Doc?” I asked softly.

The Doc looked over at me, his wife’s face buried into his shoulder. “You came just in time Mike, I don’t know how I’ll ever be able to repay you, and you brought my kids, all of them?” He nearly sobbed.

“All of them.” The relief in his face was palpable. “Doc, you saved my life and gave me my son back. I’d say we are fairly close to even. Justin can you check the cabinets and see if you can get Mrs. Baker a robe or something. We’ve got to get out of here.”

“Is your family here too, Mike?”

“Not yet Doc.”

Doc understood the implications of my actions. I had forsaken my family’s safety for his.

“Justin.” The Doc said. “In my office, I have some scrubs and a long jacket. Buddha's in there too, grab a cookie out of my desk and he'll follow you to the ends of the earth for it. There's also half a case of your shots. You’ll want to grab those. I’m sorry Mike.” The Doc said turning to me. “I didn’t have enough time to make more.”

“How many are there?”

“About sixty-four.” He said.

Shit, Justin's dose was one a day, two months was better than no months, although six months would have been better.

Justin was back in minutes. He had grabbed extra scrubs and was making a makeshift backpack to carry his much-needed viral disease management syringes.

"Mr. … Mr. Talbot. I mean Mike." Porkchop yelled. "We've got some squishies." That was Porkchop's name for the deaders.

I had grabbed the pendants off of the dead and gave one to Doc and Elizabeth and kept the extras. Elizabeth seemed hesitant to accept anything from her would-be attackers.

"Zombie repellant." I told them. "I strongly encourage everyone who values their flesh intact to hold onto it."

Doc seemed suspicious at best, but as for obtaining visual proof of its effectiveness, his kids rushed in to see their parents. The reunion was powerful, tearful, joyful and for necessity was exceedingly short.

I went through the doors first. A wall of zombies was coming down the hallway. It looked like the last day of school and everyone was trying to be the first one out for the summer. They were shoulder-to-shoulder width wise across the hallway and asses to elbows deep for the entire length.

I ducked my head back in. "Any other way out?"

"That bad?" Doc asked.

"Bad seems like such a lackadaisical verbiage to use right now. I might go with something more along the lines..."

"Dad." Justin said pointing to the kids.

"Everyone have their vial on them?" I asked.

Head nods dominated the room. I took that as an affirmative.

"What about my patients?" Doc asked.

I looked at him and threw as much compassion into the gesture as I possibly could. They were dead. A battalion of zombies were sweeping down the hallways. Even with our immunity we could not use that as a shield for others. I felt sorry for them, I truly did. I hoped each and every one of them was hooked up to a personal pain dispenser so they could load up before the attack. We could stand and fight and take down a fair number of those approaching but it wouldn't be enough, and in the end the only thing I would have gained would be the death of my family. I had already risked enough. A loving God would see that, a vengeful one would not.

Elizabeth had Rachael smothered in her arms. Porkchop and Blake looked envious. Hell I think we all were, who doesn't want to be wrapped tight in their mother's arms when danger is near. Walking amongst the dead in such tight quarters was soul-rendingly difficult. The ripped open flesh of the dead exposed torn muscle and sinew. Broken arteries and veins stood out at odd angles on some of the more damaged. Occasionally intestines and bowels were dragged and trampled behind the unlucky soul. I wondered if Elizabeth would notice if I scootched Rachael over and sought my own piece of solace in her bosom. Anything resembling breathable air had been completely pushed out of the hallway. Chunks of smell assaulted our nasal cavities. Breathing through one's mouth was equally as bad. It's one thing to smell the dead, it's another to taste them. Blake or Porkchop, it may have been both, sprayed vomit freely, the acidic bile smell was comparatively welcome. Like an island of normalcy, we wove through the sea of zombies, unscathed physically. Mentally, well this was the stuff that a life time worth of nightmares are made of.

When we finally managed to emerge into the daylight, it only improved our vision of hell on earth. We were firmly entrenched within the innards of the dead. Heavy gunfire was coming from the area we needed to get to. The good fight was still being waged but the outcome had been decided the moment someone thought to use 600 ton trucks to attack the camp. Doc was garbed in cammies. The dim watted light of an idea came to mind.

"Doc, sorry but you need to take point. And put your pistol away."

"Mike, I don't like being left in the dark. I'll defer to you because you have military training, but it seems to me we could use all the fire power we can muster right now."

"Doc we've got to time this right, for now, you are our prisoner. In another half mile or so we are going to have to play it the other way."

"Makes sense, but I don't like it."

"That's about the way of most of my plans."

I was thankful that the zombies were heading in the same direction as we were. It made getting to our destination worlds easier. Within ten minutes we were just outside the kill zone. The Marines had set up a final perimeter around the base housing and were not planning on taking any extra ammunition into the afterlife. Zombies were piled six or seven feet high in a miasma of parts, some were still moving but most weren't. We were going to have to find another egress. Even if we thought (which I wasn't) about scaling that assemblage of strewn bodies, there was no guarantee we wouldn't meet the same fate of those we had scaled. We would just be another throng of attackers to a machine gun emplacement.

The zombies had been temporarily thwarted by their extra-dead comrades. It would only be a small lull. Already, the wall of decaying flesh jiggled like an over-tall Jenga tower with two of its base beams removed. I was stuck. This was not how I had envisioned our return, held at bay by our own while completely ignored by the zombies.

"Mike?" Doc asked nervously.

"Thinking, Doc."

"Anything yet?"

"You'll be the second to know."

"No plan then?" he asked.

I knew he was nervous and so was I, but he wasn't helping.

'Hey Mr. ... Dad,' ran through my head so clearly I turned a complete 360 looking for Tommy.

"Tommy, you shouldn't be out here." I yelled. I was

concerned for his safety and I thought he might be doing another Rambo stunt like he had back at Little Turtle with the kids' bow and arrow set.

'I'm not out there, I'm in here.'

"Where's here Tommy? I'm going to need a little more information than that."

'In the apartment, where are you?'

"Tommy, you're right here, I can hear you, how is this happening?" I was more than a little confused. Which in itself isn't all that difficult a thing to do.

'We're family now Mr. Dad.'

"Holy crap! You can talk to me in my head? How long have you known?" I asked in amazement.

'As soon as you adopted me, geez don't you know anything?'

I wanted to ask him how in the hell would I know. This kind of thing usually didn't happen to me or any other person for that matter. Sarcasm aside, I asked him if I actually needed to speak or could I think the thoughts. My next concern was how much into my rancid mind could he read. I sometimes didn't like the things that popped in occasionally for an extended visit. I really didn't need anyone else privy to that. I'd check that out later if there was a time in the future.

I screamed in my head, I didn't really know what constituted a conversational tone when communicating telepathically

'TOMMY!!!' I waited as patiently as I could, nothing happened. I barely believed in the paranormal and now I was trying to use it for my own devices. *'TOMMY!!!'* I screamed again. My brain hurt from the pressure I was exerting on it as I attempted to project my thoughts outward. Do you remember when you were a kid and had seen Star Wars for the first time? Then you went home after the movie and tried to move everything in sight with the Force? Please tell me I'm not the only one. This was like that, I had no real clue as to what I was trying, I was just trying.

'TOMM..'

'There you are Mr. Dad, why you shouting?'

'I'VE BEEN TRYING TO GET A HOLD OF YOU,' I said excitedly with my thoughts.

'Use your inside brain voice Mr. Dad.'

'SORry IS ThiS BETter?'

'Sort of, sorry it took so long to respond. I was eating a Pop-Tart.'

Now granted this was all new to me, but it seems like you should still be able to mind-speak with someone while you were eating. I don't know, maybe this was as natural to him as normal talking and he just applied the same rules. Don't talk with your mouth full. Wrong time for a tangent thought.

'NEEd a little HELP TommY. JUstIN and I are outside the perimeter.'

'Wow you guys are close. Mrs. T's… Mom's been worried sick.' Tommy's mind-voice got significantly lower in volume. I thought something might be interfering with our signal until I realized he was whispering to me. *'She said if anything happened to Justin or you she was going to go back and smash your Jeep up with a baseball bat.'*

I knew it was an idle threat but it still struck deep. *'Woo, she's pissed huh?'*

'Not anymore, I just told her that you guys were safe.'

'That's the problem Tommy.' I was getting better with my volume control. *'We can't get back into the barracks without risking getting shot from the Marines. We're outside by the south entrance.'*

I could hear Tommy huffing and puffing. How was that possible?

'Okay Mr. Dad, me and Travis are going up to the Marines by where you are at now, and are going to tell them you are out there.'

'Awesome, thanks Tommy, so now what?'

'He says if you really are out there.' His brain voice lowered again. *'I don't think he believes me.'* And then came

back to normal. *'He says you have about two minutes before the zombies break through again and then all bets are off. What does that mean Dad T?'*

'It means we have to climb over this barricade, shit! Sorry.'

'S'okay.'

'Tommy, you tell him that I'm coming over first and then Justin, we are in normal clothes, then we'll be followed by Doc Baker and his family, you got it?'

'All set, he said he'll believe it when he sees it.'

'Thanks kid, save me a Pop-Tart.'

'Ham or meatball?'

Neither sounded appetizing if I ever got hungry again and that didn't look like it was going to happen anytime soon. I peered at the macabre fence in front of me.

"Alright we're set." I said to the group forgetting to realize that they had not been privy to one iota of my previous conversation.

"Set for what, Mike?" Doc asked.

"We're going over." I told him.

"Over the smooshies?" Rachael asked alarmingly, using Porkchop's descriptor.

That all too apt name rang clearly in my mind as I nearly fell over as my foot slid out from under me. I had stepped on a head that had received its fair share of lead. It completely crushed in on itself as I used it for a stepping stone. Only Justin's quick reflexes kept me from going face first in what appeared to be the eviscerated mid-section of a seventy year old man.

Justin grimaced as he pulled me back. "That was close."

I had a smart assed comment lined up, something about 'your mom's meatloaf' but just the thought of opening my mouth to utter words was not a good idea. Jets of saliva were shooting up from the back of my throat, better to coat the walls of my esophagus as I trained to be a super-model.

Gore covered my boots and I wasn't six inches off the

ground yet, becoming a zombie was looking better and better. "Come on Talbot." I yelled, mostly to psyche myself up. It didn't work so well. Every time I stepped up a foot, I sank half that distance down into a stew of human parts. At this current rate I would be up to my eyeballs in shit. Wow, now there's a cliché I never thought I'd actually experience.

"Dad."

I was halfway up the pile. "I know, clocks ticking. Tick fucking tock!" I scrambled the remainder of the way up, thankful that my earlier prediction did not come true. I was only about shin level sunk in. Tommy was about a hundred yards away, waving. I returned the gesture. Even from this far away I could see the 'Well I'll be damned' expression on the Marines' faces within the machine gun nest. The gunner waved a more exaggerated 'Hurry your ass up' gesture.

"Let's go." I said turning back to our small party. The only one who had a more difficult time scaling the dead than me was Elizabeth and that was mainly due to the fact that she had carried Rachael up. Self-esteem took a minor hit. I was going to try and not beat myself up over it.

We had covered about half the distance to a zone of relative safety when the zombies began to breach the wall made of their own. Guns blazed on full auto. A car could have been made every minute with all the brass that was hitting the ground. Yes I know there are no brass cars, and that it wouldn't have any tires and seats. I was just trying to give you an idea of how many bullets were being fired.

Doc's kids were almost as thrilled to see Tommy as I was. He hugged them all and ushered them upstairs. I leaned against the wall of a home that I would be leaving soon. Even through all the gunfire I was able to finally catch a breath and relax. It was a momentary respite to be sure but as any military person can attest, you take five whenever and wherever you can.

"I'm going up to see Mom." Justin yelled, he was a foot away and I almost didn't hear him.

"I'll be up in a minute, I just need a moment." I told

him.

"You did good, Dad." his throat probably flaying from the volume he had to use to make himself heard.

"You too." I mouthed, and patted him on the shoulder.

I watched as a few speeders halved the distance, but for the most part this was a stalemate. That would change. I'd witnessed that fact first hand. Ammo would run low, guns would jam and misfire, soldiers would fatigue, zombies would break through and eat everything. I'd seen this movie and the sequel, both sucked. I was still a few vials of zombie repellant short, and I was damned well positive that no humans were going to yet try and circumvent this perimeter, not when your ally was a zombie. I couldn't very well ask Doc for the ones I had given him.

The foray had been mostly victorious but I had also come up short. I was still alive to fight another day which counts for something. I tapped on the ammo-feeder's shoulder until he finally looked up. I made the universal sign for 'have a smoke?' You know the two finger 'v' shape up to your mouth and then away. He must have talked to my wife, because he gave me the 'You're fucking nuts' eye roll but then he looked down to his breast pocket where I saw the tell tale bulge of a cigarette box. I reached over, careful to stay out of his line of sight. I was thankful that the lighter was in the pack because I don't think he would have looked up again. I was bummed that they were menthols. I hate menthols. Gotta tell you though, that might have been the best cigarette I ever had in my entire life. I finished it up. Placed the pack back in his pocket and whistled my way up the stairs. I figured at this point and at this pace I had an hour or so left of functioning sanity.

Tracy looked relieved to see me mostly intact, although something in my gaze gave her pause to reconsider just how well I was. True to his word, Tommy handed me a meatball and raspberry Pop-Tart. Climbing the zombie wall again was looking better and better.

Normally this would be about the time Tracy would give me shit about risking my life and the life of her son. But we had saved the Bakers, so that was something on the plus side and she could sense that my soul was pulled as taut as it was going to go before it snapped. What happens at that point? Can one soldier on with a broken soul? What would be the point? I was wrung out, like a dishtowel that had seen better days. The dead were winning. Shit, they had damn near won already.

"Want a beer?" BT asked.

Like a finger to a soap bubble my pessimism popped. Guys sometimes know how to get right to the heart of the matter and skirt around all the bullshit.

"Is it cold?"

"Does it matter?" He threw a can of Pabst Blue Ribbon my way. Damn near dropped it.

Normally I wouldn't touch PBR with zombie-encrusted fingers, but this one beer must have been poured from the kegs of the gods. It was a sweet nectar which quenched more than just the dismalness of this existence. Three large gulps later, I was the proud owner of a mild pleasant buzz. I'm a cheap date, so sue me.

"So what's the plan?" BT asked drinking his own beer. I noticed it was a Molson Canadian.

"Fork it over." I said motioning with my hand.

"What are you talking about?" He replied innocently.

"You get a Molson and I get a PBR? I was the one out there running around like an idiot. I think I deserve something a little better than this." I said tossing the can lightly at him.

"I just figured that was the beer you drank. I mean you seem so 'low rent.'" He laughed, finishing off his own beer in case I came over to get it. "Sorry man that was the last one." He said swishing the bottle around to show me.

"No it's not, BT. You have a whole 6 pack in a cooler behind the couch, did you forget already?" Tommy asked him.

BT gave the meanest look he could muster towards Tommy and then smiled. "Must have slipped my mind."

"Must have." Tommy echoed.

"Yeah must have." I repeated. "Now give me one."

I sat on the couch; this one I was going to savor.

"What now Mike?" Doc asked nervously as he paced the room.

"We wait." I said as I wrapped my lips around the neck of the bottle.

Much fidgeting ensued. I was curious to see who would W.T.F. me first. Tracy edged out the Doc, BT knew better than to waste the effort.

"Mike?" She said questioningly.

"It's the end game." I started. "We're in check. Eliza has us pinned and she has all the powerful pieces left on the board. We can't leave. First off the Marines aren't going to stop shooting until they are out of bullets and once that happens that means that the zombies will be coming."

"What about the pendants the doctor was talking about?" Tracy asked.

"Don't have enough." I said taking another drink off a rapidly draining bottle. Doc looked slightly guilty that his entire family possessed this treasure and mine didn't, especially since I was the one who outfitted them all. "Don't worry Doc, I'm not going to ask for them back."

Tracy looked pissed that I wasn't going to do just that. "So we're just waiting here to die. I just can't accept that!" She yelled.

"Want a beer?" Tommy asked her.

She was going to flip out or calm down. We all watched as she teetered on top of that fence. I was thankful that she toppled to the calmer side, no sense in leaving the planet all in a huff.

"We're not dead yet." As I held up the beer to see if there was anything left in there worth drinking, I commented with "another dead soldier" and threw the empty away in the trash. One of these days I'd think before I spoke.

The zombies advanced very little over the course of the day as the brave Marines threw everything they had at them. I didn't even want to know what kind of damage a Mach-19 (fully automatic grenade launcher) was doing to the enemy. Bugs and birds would feast here for generations. Their kind would sing songs and create poems about 'The Time of Plenty'. Gettysburg was a mild skirmish compared to what raged outside.

I walked to the window when I could tell that the time of Eliza was fast approaching. "She must be getting impatient." I said aloud.

Doc had not sat down since we got here. Now he joined Travis and me as we gazed out the window at a yet unseen enemy. "How can you tell?" he asked.

"Feel the ground vibrating?"

"Yes I just thought it was Henry and Buddha trading off."

Even the twin devastations of Henry's and Buddha's flatulence could not compete with what was coming. By the feel of it at least two, maybe three of the Terexes were heading this way.

"Oh Dad." Justin said lamentedly as he grabbed his head.

Tommy had gone over to rub his back. He was performing the motion but his hand was a good 3 inches away from making contact.

"Shit, have you had your shot today?" I asked him.

"Completely spaced it out." he said miserably.

Doc went to the pack and gave him the shot. Within seconds Justin's demeanor changed.

"Any chance you have one of those for me?" Tommy asked.

Doc was unaware of the bipolar connection that Eliza and Tommy shared and answered in that manner.

"Afraid not Tommy, I don't think that you would like the side effects if this was administered to someone without the infection."

Tommy dejectedly sat back down. If the pain and pressure of Eliza's coming was affecting him, he was doing his best not to show it. Within a couple of minutes two of the formidable Terexes came into view. Whoever was driving them was oblivious to the fact that they were crushing zombies by the score. Mind you, I was in no rush to warn them of the harm they were doing but it was still only akin to scraping shit out of a port-a-pottie with a toothpick.

They were sitting about a half mile away and even at this distance they looked huge.

"What are they doing Dad?" Travis asked.

"She's sucking the spirit out of the Marines." Tommy said in an uncharacteristically sad tone.

CHAPTER 22 - JOURNAL ENTRY 16 -

It was an hour after dusk when the heavier of the ammunition dried up. There was the chatter of small arms fire and some pistols but anything resembling a stalwart defense had finally given way. Zombies mindlessly poured over their own dead. I'll give them this, not a one of those Marines ran. They stood their ground and fixed bayonets or pulled out their K-Bar knives. I thought just the spirit of those men as they fought to defend us and themselves could stem the tide. For a few minutes it did. But then one by one they fell to overwhelming odds. A knife can only go so far. I turned away as the sergeant below our window was torn limb from limb as hungry zombies devoured every morsel of him.

The screams of the mortals were quickly drowned out by the feasting of the dead. The zombies began to enter the other two housing quarters. The screams began anew. Our housing quarters stayed relatively quiet. None of the zombies were coming in.

"Well I guess she knows where we live. Had I known we were having company I might have cleaned up." It was said sarcastically and everyone was entirely too wrapped up in their own final thoughts to pay me much attention. The only noise besides me was Nicole's retching as she suffered through another bout of morning sickness. Weird, because it was six at night. I'm still so grateful to all who will listen that I pee standing up. "Travis, can you get me the 30 aught 6 please?" I asked never taking my eyes off the Terexes as they began their approach.

I heard him get up and then heard him pull the charging lever back to make sure it was loaded. Then he handed me the gun.

"Thanks, is the safety off?"

I heard the click. "Is now. Need a spotter?"

"Sure." I told him as I opened the window; frigid air blew in warming my frozen heart.

The trucks came in slowly, I would swear almost sauntering and swaggering in their victory. Unlucky zombies merged with the earth as the giant tires smashed them into various fat content ground meat. When the trucks were within two hundred yards I began to hunt for my prize. I placed the gun up on the windowsill and adjusted the scope to allow any and all ambient light into the aperture.

Travis had pulled out a pair of pocket binoculars and was scouring the cabs of the two trucks. "Got her!" He said triumphantly.

"Are you shitting me?"

"Far truck, she's sitting next to some ass…I mean guy that just broke the cardinal rule."

"Cardinal rule?" I asked aiming my rifle over.

"He just lit a cigarette."

"He's probably nervous sitting that close to the bitch…I mean lady."

"Where in relation to the steering wheel?" Which was the only thing I could see due to the illumination of the dashboard.

"About two or three feet over."

I took my eye up off the scope and looked at him.

"Okay closer to three feet." He said adjusting his guess.

I could faintly pick up the smoker as he inhaled. The cherry of the butt silhouetted him perfectly and if that was my target he was a dead man. The small amount of light did nothing however to reveal the rest of that giant cab. I had one shot. I waited patiently, wishing fervently that I had gone to sniper school when I had the opportunity. I had proved an accurate enough shot to be considered but all those hours of waiting without moving while you lined up your target was a concept I could not grasp as a hot-blooded youth.

"Please be a chain smoker." I repeated over and over

as my personal mantra.

Travis and I were fixated on a spot in space roughly the size of a basketball. The room was quiet. No lights were on. Even Henry and Buddha's gas wars had subsided, that more than anything gave me hope.

True to his word, the Marlboro man lit up another cigarette, and the cruel ethereal face of Eliza lit up. The warm colors of the small fire did nothing to sway the evil that she exuded; her white skin shone brilliantly. Sweat poured down my face as I squeezed the trigger ever so gently so that when the gun did go off it was a surprise to me. The smoke and the recoil of the discharge knocked me off target and screened me from the knowledge if I had made an impact on my desired target.

Tommy screamed.

"Holy shit." Travis murmured still looking at the truck. I had turned to see what was wrong with Tommy. "Dad, I can't be completely sure but I think you got her."

My heart soared, only to come crashing down with his next words.

"But I don't think she's dead. She's so fast I think she pulled the smoking guy in front of her. I saw him take the impact but the bullet went through and I think got her. By then though she had pushed his body away and had moved." The Terex veered off at an alarming angle. Any chance of getting another shot off was impossible as I was now viewing the dump portion of the truck.

The air went out of the room. Whatever small hope we had harbored was now extinguished.

"Dammit. Tommy, you alright?" I asked him.

"She's really mad," was all he could manage to say.

"Isn't she always?" BT asked seriously.

"True." I said shrugging my shoulders. "How does one know if a rabid wolf is mad or not?"

"Mike, will you get serious!" Doc fairly shouted.

"I'm deadly serious Doc, it's just that my thoughts tend to trend to the juvenile; doesn't mean I don't care."

"Wonderful." he said sarcastically.

"Alright, whoever wants to get in on the shooting start getting your stuff ready." I told the room.

BT came over. "Plan yet?"

"Still blank slating buddy. But I figure we can still exact some measure of revenge."

"Do tell," he said as he started loading magazines.

"Well I figure that she really wants Tommy...alive." I clarified. "The rest of us are just the wrapping paper on the gift."

"Sounds grand." BT said never looking up from his task.

"You giving me shit?"

"Whaddaya you think, you basically just said she couldn't care less if the rest of us were alive or dead."

"Oh I think she'd prefer us dead."

"Perfect."

"Well, yes and no. I mean I have no desire to die tonight, but on the flip side Eliza won't do anything yet to endanger the kid."

"I get it." BT said now slamming rounds into his magazines. "She's going to let us have our last hurrah so that she can get the kid intact, so what's your thought?"

"I'm thinking we wait for the piece of shit traitors to come in closer. I'd almost feel like I was wasting rounds at this point if I shot zombies."

Travis was standing at the window and looking straight down. "Dad, the zombies are coming in the building."

"I thought you said she wanted us alive?" BT asked filling his spare magazines quicker.

"What am I, the vampire whisperer?" I said, mimicking his faster reloading speed.

Doc looked like he was ready to gather his family and bolt. "Bad thought pattern Doc." I told him without looking up.

"How can you know what I'm thinking? With these

pendants we can stroll right out of here!" he shouted.

"That may be true, but she's forming ranks of humans past the perimeter of zombies. I don't think that pendant will work so well then." I replied.

Doc looked out the window to verify if what I was telling him was the truth. Why I'd lie was a mystery to me. Within moments zombies began shuffling outside of our doorway; each time they bumped up against it everyone in the room jolted. There was screaming from various parts of the building but none relatively close.

"She must be pulling on that leash pretty hard." I said to BT referring to the fact that the zombies weren't trying to get in, only keeping us contained.

"Yeah but for how long?" He asked as he eyed the door nervously.

The first Terex had pulled up to within a hundred yards, basically a chip shot for a former Marine with an expert class shooting badge. I peppered the shit out of that cab. Men started spilling out of the doors trying to get away from my hell fire. The ones I didn't shoot immediately upon their escape from the cab usually injured themselves as they fell a good thirty feet onto the frozen ground. Someone, however, had managed to survive in the death cage as the Terex started to back up in a hasty retreat.

Travis had started shooting at the ranks of soldiers as they began to form their encapsulating circle around our perimeter. Within moments BT had joined the turkey shoot along with Jesse and Blake. It was somewhat unfair because they weren't shooting back, Eliza must have expressly forbade it. I just saw it as my unfair advantage. They finally saw the wisdom of pulling back out of effective rifle range but the thousands of zombies still had us locked up tight.

"Any chance they'll give up?" BT asked, drawing away from the window.

Travis and Jesse were actively still seeking targets and occasionally taking a shot. I had also withdrawn from the shooting gallery to sit next to Tracy. Eliza wasn't known for her patience. Something was going to happen and I was pretty much assured it wasn't going to be beneficial to anyone in this room. Tommy and Justin were pale as sheets and were actually together trying to prop themselves up against a common enemy.

After another fifteen minutes or so, Travis and Jesse pulled back when it became entirely to dark to see anything past 50 feet or so. I had dozed off, it might have been an hour or so later when the rumble of an approaching Terex informed me that Round 2 was about to begin. The Terex was close and I could tell from which direction it was coming but the 'new' darkness that had descended on the base was preventing me from seeing it. There was no ambient light coming from anyplace on the base. So when the Terex turned on all her headlights, running lights, flood lights and searchlights I was blinded. I was thankful I hadn't been looking through a night vision scope. The image would have burnt through the back of my head to be displayed on the blank wall behind me. It was long moments before I could see anything other than giant blobs of gray in my field of vision.

BT beat me to the punch, having shielded his vision from the light assault. "Talbot, you seeing this?"

"Not so much." I told him honestly. I was rapidly blinking my eyes in the hopes that I could push force the blinding blue spots away.

"They've got people and soldiers tied all over that truck."

"What? Like a shield?"

"That's exactly it." He said putting his rifle down.

The truck idled menacingly 50 or so yards away. I could shoot a beer out of someone's hand at this distance. I mean I wouldn't, that's a waste of a good beer, but I could. My field of vision was returning. I almost wished it hadn't. Men, women and children were strategically placed all over that truck. An errant shot would easily take out an innocent. Some of the unlucky individuals were tied at odd angles or even upside down, I knew this was intentional; it was to cause us as much angst and trepidation as possible. Some of those poor souls looked like they would welcome a bullet from us.

"Hi Mike!" A familiar voice shouted.

"Durgan." BT said flatly.

"Anyone see him?" I asked raising my rifle up looking for a target.

"You should put that gun down, Mike!" His voice boomed.

I hadn't even thought of it, of course, we were lit up like Christmas trees. "Everyone down!" I shouted pulling Travis down with me.

We could hear Durgan's laugh. "If I'd wanted you dead," he elaborated, "you would be dead. My master would like to have all of you come out."

Without poking my head up I shouted, "We're pretty tired right now. Any chance she could come back next week?"

"What is wrong with you Mike?" Tracy asked.

"Worth a shot." I said

Durgan wasn't expecting that, it took him a bit before he was able to recover.

"Fucking Talbot, that isn't a request, it's a demand. And to prove she's serious... Saunders!" Durgan said.

I had a feeling what 'Saunders' was doing long before I heard someone screaming for mercy.

"What is going on?" BT asked.

I looked down at the floor. "They're killing hostages."

"We gotta go man, we gotta go help them." BT said, shaking.

"BT, they're already dead." Not literally but that was just a matter of degrees in time.

"Then what? We stay here and listen to them slaughter those people?" BT asked.

"No, we're going out, I can't stand it anymore than you BT, I just wish that it hadn't come to this."

"You can't be serious?" Tracy asked, her voice full of concern.

"They'll kill us too." Doc said.

"Doc. stay here, they don't know you're even here, you have the pendants. When Eliza is done they'll move on in search of more fertile grounds to eat."

Doc was stuck in a quandary, the safety of his family versus solidarity.

"Doc", I said, scooting away from the window first and then standing up by him."Listen Doc, you've been a good friend and I've come to love you and your family. You have a real chance to get away from all this. I won't begrudge you that. She knows everyone else in this room and won't stop until she gets us." I didn't say it, how could I tell my family that we were dead men walking.

Doc hugged me. We all made our tearful goodbyes. It sucked being on our side for obvious reasons. Our goodbyes were of the permanent kind. "Doc, just stay low, do not poke your heads up at that window no matter what you hear. Understand?" I asked. He nodded, tears threatening. I was going to miss the Doc he was one of the good guys.

Justin awkwardly picked up his backpack, spilling the contents on the floor. I was going to tell him to leave it, he wasn't going to need it where we were going, but the finality of the thought was entirely too final. Instead I got on the ground with him and started putting the contents back in.

"Talbot, NOW!" Durgan shouted.

The shout had caught me off guard and I had nearly dropped what I had in my hands. Justin stood bolt upright and put the pack on. I didn't want to give Durgan any more reason to come crashing into this apartment. I placed what I had in my hands into the pockets of my jacket and started to head to the door.

"What about the zombies?" Tracy asked.

"Durgan, what about the zombies?" I shouted out through the window.

"Oh, they're harmless for now," he laughed. "Oh and

one more thing Mike, no guns."

CHAPTER 23 - JOURNAL ENTRY 17 -

Possibly the ugliest zombie I had seen since the start greeted me at the doorway. He was a little taller than me but didn't possess the healthy vigor that I did. Half of his forehead from the top of his scalp was exposed, and one cheek had been neatly removed. His top lip was gone along with a fair portion of his nose. Slimy gray cartilage had almost eroded away due to predators and the elements. His breath was going to make halitosis a term of the past. His clothes were in tatters, but I guess the thing that struck me the most for some strange reason was that 'Bob' (as I was going to come to call him) only had one shoe. Why this was the point I fixated on was beyond me. It just seemed to be the crux upon which this jacked-up world now spun. Rational thought was quickly taking a back seat. This wasn't a matter of just going to meet my fate. I was taking the whole family, even Henry, and that saddened me the most, for he didn't even know it. Maybe that was for the best.

Bob moved aside as did his brethren as we entered into the hallway. BT shut the door behind him. I hoped the Bakers would make it out, I really did, but my first concerns lay elsewhere as we descended the stairs. Zombies moved away from us like WE were the plague carriers as we entered into the courtyard. Men, of the living variety, began to fill in the vacated spots.

"You pieces of shit!" I yelled trying my best to shield my family from the predatory gazes of the vermin around me. At least a hundred rifles and pistols were pointed at us. I was maybe a bit flattered that they thought us that dangerous but to say 'overkill' would be an understatement. Henry summed everything up perfectly when he walked up into the open middle ground and took a world class shit. I hoped it was on purpose.

Durgan broke through the ranks with the widest shit-eating grin he could display. So intent was he on making a show to the assemblage he narrowly missed stepping in Henry's excrement. As it was I laughed when he stumbled to avoid it. The insanity within him flared as he turned on me.

"You did this!" he screamed.

'Yeah that's it,' I thought to myself. 'I dropped my trousers in front of God and everyone and took a steaming shit. You dumbass.' I wanted to say it out loud but I was afraid he would take it out on Henry so I kept quiet, letting him think it was mine.

He was huge as he purposefully strode over to me. In a previous life I would have paid big bucks to watch a cage match between BT and Durgan. When he sucker punched me in the stomach it wasn't by complete surprise, but there was no way I could have prepared for the devastating blow. I absorbed the impact and went instantly to my knees. I didn't think I would ever be able to catch a breath again as I rolled to my side. I heard a bunch of gun safeties clicking off in what I could only imagine was some of my family members making a move to come to my aid.

"Who's the piece of shit now, Talbot!" He screamed into my face, spittle coating my pained grimace. I still don't know how getting slugged in the stomach made *me* the piece of shit, and I would have voiced the question if I could only suck enough sweet oxygen back into my system.

"YOU'RE the piece of shit Durgan," BT thundered. "Why don't you try that weak ass shit on me. I'll kick your spindly ass."

'Spindly?' Durgan was a lot of things. Spindly wasn't on that list. I hoped that one day I'd have the opportunity to ask BT about his word choice. I was finally able to take in my first quarter-breath of air since I had gone down, now it only hurt because I was still alive.

Durgan got back in my face. "I lost all respect for you Talbot when you started hanging around with that colored."

"Who, BT?" I croaked. "Is he really? I hadn't noticed."

I was rewarded with a boot to the solar plexus region, which was largely deflected by my arms. They were already wrapped around my tender belly. He was lining up for another go when Eliza's cold voice stopped him in mid kick.

"He is mine to do with as I please," she said savagely.

"Yes my mistress," Durgan said, bowing obsequiously as he stepped back.

"Pussy." I said it just loud enough for the two of us to hear. Devil be damned, I thought he was going to come back and finish what he'd started.

Eliza walked closer. From my vantage point I couldn't see much more than her black boots. "You should have left when I gave you the chance," she said, finally stepping into my line of sight. Her tone carried no good grace, no sadness, no yearning for a different outcome.

"What, and miss all this?" I said, still clutching my mid-section.

Striking cobra fast, she reached down and grabbed my face in her cold hand, lifting me off the earth and into the air as if I weighed no more than a cat. Her fingers dug into my cheeks. Tracy cried out behind me. Now I was afraid, afraid to a depth I hadn't even known existed up to this point in my life. Hope was extinguished, valor and courage were merely sounds made from the mouths of fools. Salvation was unobtainable. She was a chasm from which nothing escaped, a black hole unto herself. She dropped me to the ground. My unsteady legs gave way. I found myself on my knees to the enemy. I had sworn I'd eat a bullet before it got to this point. I had compromised my purpose, my beliefs and everyone dear to me would pay for it. Tommy's sobs were the only thing that could be heard in this circle of hell.

"You shot me Michael," Eliza said. Pointing to a bullet hole in her black leather jacket. "I had thought I might just kill you slowly. Now, however, I have decided you will have the pleasure of living as I slowly kill your entire family." Eliza turned from me, her gaze now on Tommy. "We are going to have such wonderful talks."

Something was poking my already tender stomach. If I was going out it might as well be as comfortably as possible. I reached into my jacket pocket and wrapped my hand around the offending object. It was one of Justin's syringes that had fallen out of his pack. The cap must have come off as I was being so tenderly cared for and now the point was a good three or four layers deep in my epidermis. I gently pulled it out. *'USE IT'* shot through my head. The message was from Tommy but he didn't clarify his thought and I couldn't think to ask him as Eliza turned back to me.

"Use what?" she asked me, one might almost think gently.

Then it hit me what I should use, and as God is my witness I wanted to tell her and I would have if not for Tommy.

"*Deus has relinquo vos*!" he shouted in Latin (God has forsaken you).

She laughed as she replied back to him. "*Ut ego have relinquo him.*" (As I have forsaken him.) "Your God is dead."

My chance was here, I was of no concern to her as I pulled the syringe out and drove it up to the barrel into her calf. Her backhanded blow sent me rolling twenty feet. If my jaw wasn't shattered, I had at least lost some teeth but the pain was too intense to tell exactly what was busted.

"What have you done?" she questioned calmly as she pulled the needle out of her leg.

'I don't know,' I would have told her but the mere thought of moving my jaw stopped that response in its tracks. The zombies that had been generally milling about paying this little drama not a notice, seemed to awaken as if from a dream. I mean as much as a zombie can seem to 'come awake'. I had an inkling of a feeling what was about to happen as zombies began to close in around the circle. I forced myself to stand as waves of pain cascaded down from the top of my head to the bottom of my spinal column.

"You rise when I tell you to," Eliza said evenly. There was no anger in her voice, only a conveyance of truth. She was used to always being obeyed.

I staggered a few steps, moving away from the perimeter guards. All eyes were on me as I drunkenly made my way back to my family. Tracy looked as if she was going to come to my aid. Eliza interjected herself by quickly moving towards me. It is a strange sensation to find yourself hovering in the air, suspended only by your neck. Eliza, was not much bigger than my daughter, so to look down and see those slender arms have enough power to raise me up like a beer for a toast was strange to say the least.

The pain of my nearly shattered jaw warred with the affliction of having my neck compressed to half its diameter.

"Do you find this as fulfilling as I do?" Eliza asked me.

This chick was psycho, first off between my neck and my jaw I couldn't answer her even if I wanted to. And then what the hell kind of question is that? Sure, sure I always wanted to have the life crushed out of me by a character in a horror movie, it was a lifelong dream of mine. Eliza looked over my shoulder as the first of her human guards let out an ear-piercing shriek. Looks like the zombie menu just grew exponentially.

I could see some strain in Eliza's eyes as she attempted to regain control of the zombies. The shot obviously worked. It had interrupted her communication/control over them. I hoped it was a permanent fix, but temporary at this point was alright too. Still though, she could dispose of my entire family in less than a minute, long before her wall of human sympathizers crumbled. Would zombies eat a vampire? Was she in any danger? I hoped so, but at the same time I wondered whether the living dead eating the undead might be taboo.

Several more humans went down before it began to dawn on them that they had better start defending themselves. The circle we were in nearly halved as they pulled in closer to each other and attempted to gain separation from their allies-turned-enemies.

"Clever Michael," Eliza said as she placed me down on legs that I did not think could support a stork. "Too bad it wasn't your idea but my brother's."

"Who?" My voice came out barely above a whisper. Even with that small amount of movement my jaw felt as if it had come unhinged. The croaking sound that came out could never be construed as a word, but Eliza understood my expression of amazement.

Her pitiless laugh grated through my nerves. "He didn't tell you? You are just the latest failed attempt in a long line of pathetic humans who have tried to stop me. I have killed each and every one of them, some in more creative ways than others perhaps. But in the end and in his own way, Tomas has brought all of those people to their untimely oblivion."

"Not true." I coughed out, clutching my throat and shaking my head. I looked over towards Tommy, whose head was bowed in guilt or angst. It was tough to tell from this distance.

"Ask him yourself."

Did that mean she was going to let me live, for now?

She turned from me. I felt like a mouse and the hawk had moved her gaze to other prey. The relief was that intense.

"This is my time, Tomas, all of mankind will bow before me." She thundered without raising her voice. Gunfire that had moments earlier seemed muted, raised to full volume like a crappy neighbor's stereo at midnight on a Tuesday. The cordon that protected us was rapidly breaking down. Death by zombie all of a sudden seemed an attractive proposition, although in retrospect, neither being eaten nor bled dry has much appeal.

The hairs on the back of my neck and arms began to rise as waves of power sizzled off of Eliza. Some zombies stopped in mid-chew, while others happily feasted on. She was fighting through the vaccination. Should I take a chance and try to deliver some form of death to her in this semi-incapacitated state? If I did and I succeeded that meant the zombie leash would come completely off. If I tried and failed, I might actually get to experience the sensation of being skinned alive. I imagine that she would start from my feet up thereby ensuring I stayed alive the longest while this torture was administered.

Third choice it was then, escape. That in itself was going to be a risky proposition. Eliza's guards had been halved by the zombies, but half of a shit load still left a crap load and I didn't think they'd just let us strut on out. I more or less made a beeline for my family who was huddled on a curb at the edge of the parking lot.

I looked to Tommy. "Is it true?" His silence spoke volumes. "We'll make time to talk about this later." Maybe.

"I've got a plan, Talbot." BT said softly, although why he was whispering was a mystery considering WWIII was happening all around us.

"Is it better than mine usually are?"

"Me going up to Eliza and asking her nicely if we could leave would be better than most of yours." BT retorted. He then glanced down quickly; he was standing on a storm drain.

"Are you kidding me?" I stage whispered.

"Tommy made sure that we would be in this general vicinity." Tracy said. She had heard the entire conversation between Eliza and myself and wanted to make sure that I remembered where my allegiances were.

"Can you get that thing up?" I asked BT.

"My leg is busted, not my arms. Close in around me."

We gathered into a tight group, which wasn't difficult considering we were almost in a Rugby scrum as it was.

No bad guys noticed, they were too busy elsewhere, as BT clanged the cover off to the side.

"In, in, in." BT said, grabbing Travis and dropping him down the hole.

Next, Justin handed Henry down to Travis, then

helped his grandmother and Nicole down. He himself then followed, with Tommy clambering down after him.

"Tracy, go." I said as I saw her indecision.

"You're not going to do anything foolish are you?"

"Me?" I said innocently shaking my head. "Get in. You too, BT."

"Talbot?" BT asked skeptically.

"It's cool, get in, we're running out of time." The battle would end sooner rather than later, and whichever side won, the Talbots & Co. would still lose. I had no intention of doing anything. This was one situation I wanted to be as far removed from as possible. I waited impatiently as BT wriggled his way through the narrow opening. I nearly stepped on his head in my haste to leave this place. I was halfway in the hole when Eliza's eyes locked onto mine. The pull of her was hypnotic. I wanted to be with her, to die miserably by her hand. My left foot came up a rung.

Distantly below me I heard BT exclaim, "What the hell are you doing Tommy, there's not enough room on this ladder for the both of us."

And then a moment later I felt Tommy's hand on my calf, warmth spreading from his touch. Eliza's hold was shattered. I flipped her the bird, and ducked out of sight. Her screech of rage could have broken glass.

CHAPTER 24 - JOURNAL ENTRY 18 -

We were in the sewers for fifteen minutes before the sound of gunfire finally and mercifully stopped. But that wasn't technically a good thing. Either Eliza had wrested control over the zombies and now her minions were in hot pursuit, or the zombies had won out and they were in cold blooded pursuit.

"Wish I had my scooter," BT complained.

"Oh, you like it now," I puffed behind him. We had been keeping a pretty steady pace and it was wearing us all down.

"Not now, Talbot," BT said through clenched teeth. I could tell he was in immense pain and still I struggled to keep up with him.

"This reminds me of Bilbo."

"I KNOW you didn't just call me a dildo." BT said, pausing to look back over his shoulder.

"Do I look insane? Don't answer that. I meant Bilbo Baggins when he was under that Orc mountain to get that one ring. He thought he was going to be lost forever in those caverns."

"Comforting thought, Talbot. Any chance you could keep it to yourself?" my wife said from further up.

Justin's lighter was barely a flicker against the pressing darkness but when it flittered out the darkness became complete. I could almost imagine an army of orcs creeping up behind us. Was that worse than the alternative?

"Sorry." Justin said. "Burning the hell out of my fingers." We could hear him sucking on his burnt digits in an attempt to take the heat away. I kept thinking about where his fingers had been before he put them in his mouth. Old habits die hard.

"You better be careful with that lighter," BT said. Justin looked back questioningly. "That dog of yours has some super heated ass air and I've got a feeling its combustible."

"That's pretty funny BT, but all the same Justin you should heed his words. Alright let's take five. Everyone get as comfortable as you can, let's just catch our breaths." Superfluous words to say the least. Panting made conversation impossible. I walked back ten or so paces from the pack to get away from the extraneous noise and truly try to hear if anything besides sewer rats were behind us, although that kind of scared the shit out of me too.

I took deep breaths, waiting long pauses in between exhales, to have as little ambient noise around me as possible. What happened next was not something any of us were expecting. The ground began to vibrate. First it was as soft as a cat jumping off a chair and then it began to shake as violently as an elephant taking a spin on a trampoline.

"Talbot?" BT yelled out questioningly.

"Sounds like Eliza." I replied.

"What is she doing?" Carol asked. The break neck pace was having the most effect on her, she had been game so far but she wouldn't be able to do this much longer. Even the fear in her voice was muted.

"Sounds like she's leaving." Travis said with hope.

"It does at that." I added, not so hopefully.

"Mike." Carol started her question. "Why did the zombies attack those men? Shouldn't the pendants have prevented that?"

"Normally yeah, but I think it's clear now whose blood is in those vials, and when the shot interrupted her control, the pendants became decorative jewelry."

Carol absently fingered the pendant she wore, wondering if wearing the blood of one's enemy around her neck was even worth it now.

We rested a minute or two more before the slow, steady stench of zombies caught up to me. I looked back in the direction we had come. I couldn't see anything, but one doesn't need the sense of sight to know when zombies are getting too close. "Time to go," I said, catching back up to the group.

"Mike, we just sat down and my mother is exhausted," Tracy said irritably.

I didn't say anything. I didn't have to. The smell passed me on by and traveled up to the rest of the suddenly not-so-weary travelers.

"Are they under the control of Eliza?" Nicole asked.

"Does it matter?" Justin replied.

BT helped Carol up. "I'll help her BT, you get in the middle." Justin's lighter lit back up just in time for me to see the questioning glance on BT's face. "I don't trust you." I told him.

"What are you talking about, man?" BT asked.

"Oh I can see you doing some stupid heroic thing because you can't keep up and you're going to sacrifice yourself for the good of the many or some such crap."

"What? Do you think you have the market cornered on stupid heroic crap? I can pull off my own stupid moves you know."

"Can both of you please get your big inflated diva egos in gear?" Tracy said.

"She called you a diva." I said pointing to BT.

"Now I know why Paul and Alex went their own way." BT mumbled. "Who knew? I should have joined them." His muttered comments kept going long after we started anew.

Our pace had taken a significant downturn. The five minutes of rest had done us more harm than good. Lactic acid had enough time to build up in the dormant muscles. Carol and BT were both struggling. Carol, I could assist. Helping BT with anything short of a tow truck wasn't going to work.

Something was getting close. There was the occasional clatter of a bottle being kicked or the sound of a foot splashing into a puddle. There were no arcs of light from flashlights cutting through the tunnel. That was of small solace though. A bullet might be a kinder way to go. It was damn near impossible to tell how far we had come underground. Justin had kept us on a fairly straight course, just as I had told him to, but the disorienting combination of the darkness and the pressing walls made gauging distance difficult. Our direction had mostly been a southeastern route away from Lake Michigan. I figured we had to be nearing the outer edges of Camp Custer and that could possibly mean a dead end. I couldn't imagine any Commander worth his weight in salt allowing an open passage right under his feet. There would be bars across the tunnel soon and once we got to them it would be too late; we would have to backtrack to an alternate exit while hopefully avoiding our pursuers. With nothing more than our bare hands against an enemy that loved to bite, I was looking for an egress now.

"Justin, next junction we go up." I yelled.

"We out of the base?" He asked.

"Doubt it seriously, but close. We need a truck, guns, rest, food, shelter and maybe four or five other things."

"Got it."

CHAPTER 25 - JOURNAL ENTRY 19 -

Within five minutes we were on terra firma as opposed to under it. There would eventually be eternity for that, just not yet. Camp Custer was in ruins. It looked like a set from a 1960's Godzilla movie. Buildings were smashed to rubble, fires blazed, cars and trucks were strewn about. You know the idiom: History always repeats itself. Camp Custer fell just like the legendary General. Who was the idiot that named this place? His first choice was probably Camp Alamo or Camp Pearl Harbor, maybe even Camp Waterloo. I would have gone with a name that didn't ultimately spell doom and destruction, but that's just me.

Sadness threatened to completely overwhelm our beleaguered band of travelers. We were all tired. Add in a heavy dose of depression, stir in a dash of death and you get a recipe that nobody wants to choke down. I had to keep telling myself this wasn't home, this had been merely a brief respite, a healing way station until we were able to get back on our feet both physically and mentally. Another two months or even a year or so here would have been perfection but Tommy's sister had other ideas. That was another wrinkle I would have to deal with eventually; 'all good things to those who wait,' I thought sarcastically.

We hadn't moved very far at all from the manhole cover we had come up from when the stench of death wafted up; it wasn't too difficult to figure out what was down there. For the first time I was thankful it was zombies and not humans. Unless we had moved on to Zombies Version 3.0 they would not possess the motor skills necessary to climb the ladder, but it still made my skin crawl that they were that close. Apparently I wasn't the only one that shared that sentiment, as we all collectively and subconsciously moved farther away from our escape hole.

"Alright, we've got to find some wheels," I said, more to break the painful silence that had settled on us all than to relate any new information on our plan.

"Mike." Carol said as she sat down on some cinder blocks that had once held up a wall on what used to be a nail salon. "I need to rest."

I looked hard at her, not out of anger but only for concentration purposes. I was adverse to splitting up.

"I'll stay with her," BT said. It was part altruism and part necessity for BT. He wasn't in much better shape than Carol was. Pain exuded from every motion as he plopped down on his own makeshift resting spot.

This was sucking more and more. Those two couldn't outrun a crawling zombie and I was about to leave them to their own devices without any protection whatsoever. Their decisions were made. The best thing I could do for them was hurry up. Their concealment in this destroyed stretch of roadway was not by the book battle tactics but it would have to do.

"Go man, go." BT said. "I'll keep an eye on her," as he bowed his head nearly into his lap.

It was looking more like Carol was the one that was going to be keeping an eye on him.

The rest of us moved off, keeping close to the rubble line. Tommy never spoke and barely took his eyes from the road six inches in front of his feet. I was feeling bad for the kid but he had a lot of explaining to do even if Eliza had only spoken 25% of the truth. My gut told me that nothing she said was a lie. She was the essence of pure evil and nothing cuts deeper than unvarnished truth.

The farther we moved away from Carol and BT, the more nervous I became. This was looking more and more like a fruitless effort. What wasn't burning outright had fallen victim to the Terexes' crushing power.

"Mike?" Tracy asked with concern.

"I know, I know." I wiped my forehead free from

perspiration that should have not been able to form in this hostilely cold weather. "We have got to find a way off this base, Hon. There is no other option. Zombies will sniff us out eventually. Walking isn't even an option and not because of BT and your mom either, we're all wiped out."

Travis had gone up to the next corner scouting the way ahead. When he signaled I couldn't tell if it was good or bad. It ended up being a mixture of the two. He had found transportation. It just so happened to be surrounded by a cluster of zombies that were fighting over the remaining scraps of an unlucky soul who had also been looking for a way off the base and had been fractions of a second on the "too late" side. His crappy fortune was to our benefit.

"I've got an idea, Dad," Travis said as he pulled back from his vantage point.

He never gave me the opportunity to dispute the validity of his plan as he quickly crossed the street unseen and then shouted to the zombies, "Here I am!"

I wanted to throttle him. That really wasn't much of a plan. If there were speeders in the mix he didn't have much of a head start on them. Too late now, the play was in motion. I turned, gesturing to everyone to get down. Travis made sure that the zombies had taken an unhealthy interest in him and then he bolted down the trash-scattered roadway. I was going to kick his ass when I got back to him. We hadn't even figured out a rendezvous point and I had to hope that he was smart enough not to bring them back to our original starting point where Carol and BT were.

"Damn him," I muttered as two speeders raced by, followed by four ragged deaders and one crawler that looked as if she had fallen victim to the Terex. From about midway down what remained of her ass was flattened to pulp. The pressure from the tire grounding her into the pavement had caused one eye to completely rupture out and it was now dragging on the path alongside her, leaving a trail of slime much like a slug would. That grossed me out more than the shattered bone fragments that protruded at odd angles through her tattered blue jeans.

Travis and the speeders were long gone. The deaders were far enough away that even if they noticed us we still had plenty of an escape cushion. That left the crawler. She turned her head in our direction as we stood back up and headed to the humvee. Her voided socket stared at us as intensely as her good eye. For someone with so many damaged parts she made short work of turning back around and pulling herself towards us. Tracy and Nicole were nearly riveted in place. I'm not sure Tommy even noticed her, so intent was he on some flattened gum on the sidewalk. As Justin and I headed for the hummer, the movement drew the zombie's attention away from the women, not that they were in any imminent danger anyway.

The small bits of flesh that clung to the remains of the unlucky individual inside the hummer made any sort of identification impossible. The skeletal size suggested a small woman or a kid. I opted for small woman. Neither was a great choice, one just happened to be less crappy than the other.

"I'm so sorry," I said as I dragged the exceptionally light carcass out of the front seat. I laid her down as gently as time would allow, did a short 'Our Father.' Then I sat down in a medley of hair, blood, bone bits, possibly some jewelry and whatever other disgusting remnants come off someone that has just been eaten.

"You alright Dad?" Justin asked as he climbed into the passenger seat.

My frozen features displayed pure disgust. This above everything else was going to cause me many sleepless nights going forward. Blood and gore were seeping through my clothes. If Travis weren't running for his life I might have just completely seized up. I was making inroads into my germaphobe psychoses but I hadn't gone this far.

"Help me" may or may not have weakly made it out of my lips. Luckily, it was masked by Tracy, Nicole and Tommy's entry into the rear.

"Mike, is something wrong with this truck? Won't it start?" Tracy asked leaning forward through the gap in the front bucket seats.

"Uh sorry, waiting for the glow plugs to heat," I told her as I clicked the ignition.

Tracy could see the human goulash dripping from my seat and the perspiration dripping from my head, but with her baby outside she would not suffer my neuroses.

"Let's go Talbot, next Wal-Mart we see I'll get you some Clorox wipes and a new set of jeans, but right now you have to get our son."

"Yup." It was all I could muster without taking the chance of adding my own vomit to the mix.

"You know your son is out there right?" Tracy added.

I thought I might be stuttering at this point but I'm pretty sure it was only in my head.

"And my mom and our friend BT. They are all out there waiting for us Mike," she threw in for good measure.

"Um...the... what now?" I may have muttered. Higher functioning had completely seized up. I was being steeped in human goo and I couldn't move. Ever since this whole Armageddon thing started, I had shot hundreds of zombies, K-Barred a few humans and had been covered in gore. None of it had affected me like this. There was just something about having my genitalia simmering in the blood of another human being that was shutting me down.

"Justin, we've got to get him out of the seat. You're going to have to drive," Tracy said as she moved to the door.

Justin blanched. You may or may not recall, but in my first journal I spoke of how Justin had not deemed driving a priority in his life and had thus far found ways to escape that mundane task. "I'd…I'd rather not," he said, looking down at the cauldron of caustic bile I was in.

"Talbot!" Tracy screamed smacking me upside the head. "Get over it!"

Like shoving a sticky transmission into gear, I moved. It might have been the yelling but more than likely it was the physical force she had put behind that blow. Three older brothers and the Marine Corps had trained me to move into action by physical contact, and not of the tender variety.

In hindsight, my immobility may have saved my son's life. His original plan, unbeknownst to any of us, was to lead the zombies away and then circle back to the original place where the hummer sat. I was going to try and track him down which would have proved disastrous when he came around only to discover that his ride was gone. The speeders hadn't gained any ground on him, but they had the advantage of being tireless. When Travis hopped into the back he was bathed in sweat much like I was, and was dragging in huge gasps of breath.

The hummer jerked forward as I released the hand brake. Speeders smacked into the hood as I moved away.

Tracy turned the ire I had stirred towards her son. "What the hell were you thinking? What kind of plan was that?"

"I got the idea from Brendon," Travis said with a ghost of a smile on his face.

"I thought I recognized that," Justin said, smiling as well.

"This is your fault Talbot!" Tracy said swiveling her beacon of ire back my way.

I may or may not have released a wan smile. I was entirely too busy trying not to vomit, hit zombies or freeze up again. My internal operating system was running at 98% and was threatening to have a fatal error.

Within a minute or so we came upon BT and Carol who were on full alert but seemed no worse for wear as we pulled up. In fact, Carol actually had some color to her and BT looked like he was finally managing the extreme pain he was in.

"Couldn't get anything bigger?" BT joked as he hopped over.

"You might want to hurry," Tommy said from the back seat, his first words in over an hour.

BT's expression changed quickly and dramatically when he heard Tommy's words and saw the lack of expression and color on my face. It doesn't take a zombie apocalypse to realize when something is wrong, but it sure helps. Travis, Tommy and Henry moved into the plastic shell covered trunk to make room as BT and Carol got in. The relief in Tracy's face as she smacked me upside the head again was clearly evident.

"What's that all about?" Carol asked Tracy.

"It's the only way I can get him moving," she answered.

Carol had a look of consternation on her face but did not bother to ask for a clearer explanation.

"Kind of like a slap stick," BT exclaimed, alluding to a popular brand of transmissions during the muscle car years of the early 1970's.

"Hilarious," I mumbled. But I had to admit it was effective.

We were all caught up in our own silent reflections as we left the base behind. Except for Travis and Henry who slept, deeply I hoped.

Tracy thought about the safety of our family and how close to the edge of peril we were again. The base had been a chance to recharge the batteries, a place where normalcy had reinstituted itself. It wasn't home, but maybe it could have been.

Justin was thinking about what was going to happen to him when his two month supply of shots ran out; would he once again fall under the spell of Eliza? That was something he could not go through again.

Carol regretted leaving her life-long home. She had spent a lot of sweat and tears working that land and it seemed only right that she should have shed her life's blood there as well.

Tommy was fearful of what this revelation meant to his new family. Would they abandon him? He didn't really think they would, but that thought above all others scared him.

Nicole still grieved heavily for Brendon and could not fathom raising a child in this monstrosity of a world.

BT hoped that he would have the strength when the time came to defend his friends. He could not shake the feeling that he was somehow responsible for Jen's and Brendon's deaths. The emotional pains of those two losses far outweighed his broken leg.

My thoughts, well they were something along the lines of...disgusting, repulsive, filled with loathing, nauseating, skuzzy. Do you want me to keep going on? Remember I'm a germaphobe so I have an extended thesaurus when it comes to words revolving around 'repugnant'.

I had never before felt so alone, as if on an island than I did that night. The shielded headlights barely pierced the obsidian of the night as we drove eastward. No weapons, no food, no hope, no sani-wipes. It seemed like a good time to stop and make a permanent snow angel. I've learned a lot in these 'end of days' times. Mostly, that when it gets to the darkest point there's always something that manages to drag you just a little farther into the gloom.

CHAPTER 26 - JOURNAL ENTRY 20 - 

I lost myself in the humming of the tires on the roadway. My mind drifted inwards to Tommy and ultimately to Eliza. I had been so enamored with the boy I didn't think to look any deeper than what I saw on the surface. I mean, I knew that he was operating on a different plane than the rest of us mere mortals, but I was figuring that he was some sort of divine intervention into a world that was rapidly spiraling down into oblivion.

The question now was whether he was placed here for the Talbots or was the Talbot family merely a means to an end for him. I couldn't imagine the boy having ulterior motives, especially malevolent ones, but that was before I realized who his sister was. And speaking of Eliza, how did that happen? She was a vampire, a beast who until very recently I didn't think existed in anything other than the over imaginative minds of movie makers. But Tommy was no vampire, at least by any traditional standard, although I'd yet to see a master copy of "Mythical Monster Properties and Powers."

I would have looked in the rearview mirror if the hummer possessed one if only to prove what I already knew. Tommy was eyeing the back of my head. What earlier I would have thought of as comforting was now disconcerting. Now there was no doubt in my mind who Eliza was really after. Would Tommy resist if I made him get out of the hummer? Could I? True hell had begun for the Talbots the moment Tommy came off that roof. Sure, it wasn't peaches and cream beforehand, but wandering mindless ravenous zombies were still worlds better than diligent, relentless, controlled ones. I never thought to question why such a cataclysmic evil presence was in such close proximity to a shining beacon of righteousness. Now that gap in thought could potentially be our undoing.

I could feel Tommy's presence lurking around the psychic connection we shared. He was antsy to 'talk.' I opened up the connection although I'm fairly certain Tommy could come waltzing in no matter what I did to prevent him.

'Hi Mr. Dad. Are you mad?'

'Tommy, I'm going to hold off making any rash comment or decision while you completely explain what is going on,' I said tight-lipped, at least as tight-lipped as one can while they're thinking the words instead of saying them. I could tell my tone was conveyed by the way Tommy's mood changed. Now don't go getting all judgmental on me. I hadn't yet said anything cross to Tommy. You have to remember that Tommy's mere presence was endangering my entire family. What an egotist I was to believe that I was anything other than a plaything for Eliza. She cared less for me than the dirt she carried under her fingernails.

'She's my sister, Mr. T.'

The reversal back to 'Mr. T' and not 'Dad' did not go unnoticed by me. We might be 'family' but Eliza and Tommy were true family. Tommy related the story of his cruel upbringing in 1500's Germany and how his sister 'Lizzie' ('how fucking cute' I thought) was the only person that stood up for him. She would chase away the town boys that would throw rocks at the 'possessed boy.' She would step in front of her father's heavy hand whenever he felt the need to take out his own insecurities on his 'ruined' son.

I got the picture, Lizzie was the world upon which he revolved. I could feel the pain Tomas had suffered as his sister was dragged away and sold into slavery. Tommy was trying to accentuate his story by letting me in on his own emotional distress. It was a low but effective strategy. The linked empathy had me nearly on the verge of tears. I was thankful the interior of the hummer was not lit very well by the dash lights.

'When I finally caught up to her, the devil had already

marked her soul.'

That would imply that she still had one. I was fairly certain that ship had sailed and much like the Titanic had met a watery grave.

'I can fix her though, Mr. T. I know I can.'

'How long have you been trying Tommy? How many others' lives, hopes and dreams have you ruined in an attempt to fix what may be broken beyond repair?' I answered him.

His refusal to reply to my barb, infuriated me. *'Now you dare to take my family down that same path!'* I was screaming in my head, my fingers clenched the steering wheel, knuckles turning white under the strain.

Tommy, who had been leaning slightly forward with his head in his hands, fell back against the seat as if he was physically pushed. *'I never meant it to be like this Mr. T,'* his words soaked in tears.

I honestly didn't care at this point whether he meant it or not, my BS meter was pegged in the red. Everything he said from this point forward was going to be tainted. *'Are you a vampire?'* I asked him.

He mentally shook his head in the negative.

'How then?' I asked as in 'How are you still alive after 500 plus years?'

'After she was bitten, she bit me but she didn't drink. Because she remembered me and she loved me and she couldn't. But something still happened because here I am. I have followed her ever since.'

'So what's happened differently? Why is she now following YOU?' I asked, emphasizing the 'you'.

'She's dying, Mr. T.'

'What's the down side?' The words shot across my brain before I had even a moment to reflect on the pain they would administer.

Tommy began to openly weep. Tracy wrapped her arm around him. "It's okay, we're safe now," she said, words she had no faith in.

We could be, I thought to myself as I closed the door to mine and Tommy's dialog.

CHAPTER 27 - JOURNAL ENTRY 21 -

The hummer's gas gauge was rapidly approaching 'E', and there were no all night service stations open, at least not in this part of Pennsylvania. Sometimes it sucked being human. We needed food but even more importantly we needed rest, especially me. Most everyone in the hummer at some point had dozed on and off during our escape except for me. Scratch that, I caught a few Road Z's too. Damn near scared the crap out of myself when I jerked awake; the flood of adrenaline sending needle daggers through my arms and the back of my head.

The boost had juiced me for another half hour or so but I was tapped physically and mentally. The main question now became where do we stop? We couldn't defend ourselves against rabid woodchucks right now. Luck that had seemingly been in inexhaustible supply was now looking as barren as the gas tank.

"Talbot, we're still moving?" Tracy asked rubbing the sleep out of her eyes.

I got a little piqued. I think it had more to do with the sleep deprivation. But yeah I was still effen driving. Nobody else wanted to sit in the meat pie I found myself adhered to. I was able to pull most of the discontent out of my reply. "Not for much longer though."

"Where are we?" She continued.

(Thought reply – *bad*) 'Well, maybe if you had stayed awake and kept me company you'd know!' (Actual reply – *good*) "Somewhere just inside Pennsylvania, a place called Clarion."

"It's starting to get light out."

(Thought reply – *bad*) 'Yeah, amazing what happens when you drive for 8 hours straight.' (Actual reply – *good*)

Didn't have one, decided to keep my mouth shut.

"You need to rest," she said matter-of-factly.

"You think?" Here came my dumb-ass, dripping with sarcasm reply. Time to back-peddle before she could call me on it. "Sorry, I'm wiped."

She gave me the 'You're lucky you saved our lives last night or you'd be suffering my wrath' look.

BT sat bolt upright and yelled, "what the hell is that!?"

I nearly drove the hummer off the roadway. "What!! What do you see?" I yelled in reply.

Everyone was now wide-awake looking out the windows trying to see what new and unusual death deliverer was heading our way.

"Oh my God!" Travis yelled. "Henry crapped back here. Dad, you need to pull over quick, I can't breathe!"

The entire hummer took on the smell of Henry's offal. What could he have possibly eaten that could come out on the other end that bad? A moldy rat-meat burrito perhaps, or maybe a liverwurst stuffed crepe. Who knows, but it was the first time since I got in this hummer that I had completely forgotten about what I was sitting in. I somehow managed to make anti-lock brakes skid down I-80. I set records for the distance it took to stop that truck. Doors nearly came unhinged as everyone struggled to make a mass exodus at the same time. It didn't work so well, something about quantum physics and how two different masses of matter (meaning passengers) cannot occupy the same space at the same time (meaning the exits).

Gore clung to the seat and sides of my legs and thighs. I didn't even notice as I kept exhaling quickly out of my nose in the hopes I could push out the molecules of shit adhered to the lining in my nostrils. Henry sauntered out a minute or so later, most likely reveling in his delivery.

"Talbot, where did you get the dog? The city dump?" BT asked, pinching his nostrils shut in the hopes that he would not breathe in any more tainted air. "I hope you got half off, because he's defective!"

Henry had no clue that he was the center of all this attention. He pissed on the tire, a look of contentment across his wide maw. Something that strongly resembled a liver plopped to the ground from the back of my shirt. The seriousness of our predicament seemed to be heralded with that one small transaction. It was morning, of that I was grateful. I looked around to check out our surroundings. Rural pretty much summed it up. There was a farmhouse within view, although from this distance it was impossible to tell if it was occupied. No smoke was coming from the chimney, if that meant anything or not.

Travis had opened up the trunk and found an old rag in the back. He was treating the offending pile as if it were nuclear waste, which seemed about right. He heaved the rag and its contents as far as was possible and was about to shut the trunk when Nicole stopped him.

"Yeah, probably should let it air out." He said as he grabbed a handful of snow and washed his hands.

After five minutes the general consensus seemed to be that the majority of the odor should have dissipated.

Justin took it upon himself to check this hypothesis, his partially wrinkled nose let us know that while not exactly pleasant it should be safe enough for human inhalation.

"What do you think, Talbot?" Tracy asked, following my line of sight.

"I think we go up there and check their hospitality. Been on empty for the last ten miles, I can't imagine we've got another ten miles left in her," I said as I thumped the hood. "And who knows what the hell is up the road. I'd rather we have a little bit of cushion gas-wise if we need to run." I started to get back into the car.

"I'd rather walk, if it's all the same to you," Tracy said.

Justin, Nicole, Travis and Tommy all chimed in about how they would like to stretch their legs or get some air or enjoy the weather.

"Awesome," I said as I squished back down into my mélange a la gore.

BT got into the front seat, Carol into the rear. Henry looked from me to the hummer and over to the four who opted to walk. Back and forth he swung trying to figure out what was going on here. Whatever it was, he wanted a window seat as he hopped up into the hummer. I drove slowly, staying next to Tracy and the kids. I was not going to leave them alone and I was still hesitant about approaching the farmhouse, especially since we were unarmed.

The snow on the roadway had melted to a thin skin of ice. That was to change however when we reached the edge of the farmhouse driveway. The small band of travelers moved behind the hummer as I easily cut a swath through the 10-inch thick crusty snow. No champagne powder here, I was east of the Mississippi. Did that matter? Really didn't see myself strapping on a set of skis anytime soon. Another quiver to the heart of loved things lost, along with Monday night football, the Red Sox and my beleaguered Bruins. A random thought permeated my thinking as I crunched up noisily into the front yard. If I came across Kevin Youkilis as a zombie would I be able to kill him? That question got infinitely harder to answer as I pondered whether he would have his uniform on.

I would have to dwell on that later, as I neared the front door and still could not see any signs of life or death. The snow around the house was pristine, marred only by the occasional deer or rabbit track. As long as they weren't rabid we were in pretty good shape.

Tracy came up to my window as I rolled to a stop. "Don't get in if you don't have to but stay near here," I told her as I stepped out from the hummer.

She looked down at my pants and at the seat, obviously hoping that there wouldn't be any sort of problems where we would need to make a fast get away. "Is that a tooth?" She asked.

"Don't," I admonished her. "I don't want to know."

"Do you think you're the best representative to go up there?" Carol asked from the back seat.

I stooped down so that I could make eye contact with her. "Carol, you should know better by now. In the *best* of times I should never be the front man, this is just by default."

She gave me a grim smile. These weren't times for jokes and she had yet to warm up to my 'what, me worry?' attitude, even if it was all a farce. I now worried every minute of every day.

"Dad, you want us to come with you?" Justin asked, as he gestured to Travis and himself.

Normally there is safety in numbers, but if anyone was here they were watching us right now and I didn't want to give them any extra reason to be spooked. This was rural Pennsylvania and we were at a farmhouse. Odds were exceedingly high that at the minimum they possessed a shotgun. If the owner was a little skittish, which he had every right to be, I didn't want my boys anywhere near the door. What would be the point? So we could all be lead catchers?

"No, stay with your mom. Both of you," I clarified as Travis came up beside me.

"We mean no harm!" I yelled, placing my hands in the air. I tried to put myself in the house occupant's point of view. Would I believe me? I answered honestly, no. Even bad guys would start out by saying something along those lines. Here I was covered in what they would think was my last victim's blood. No they wouldn't trust me, the stakes were too high. This wasn't getting ripped off on a Craigslist deal. This was the whole bag of marbles, so to speak.

The house was an old style Victorian, smack dab between dilapidated and brand spanking new. If it was abandoned it hadn't been for long. It looked to be the domicile of aging occupants, ones that could not keep up with the maintenance such a home demanded. The steps creaked eerily as I ascended the stairs. I kept my hands in the air. I got the distinct impression I was being watched and then it hit me like a bolt, 'duh' there were at least eight sets of eyes on me from behind and maybe Henry's too. So much for the spook radar.

I knocked loudly on the door. "Please, we mean no harm. We just need a place to stay for a day or two." I waited for a response; none was forth coming, I did notice though when I knocked that I did not get that hollow echo that accompanies an empty house. A spark of hope ignited in my gut. We might have the chance to get some supplies and not make idle chit chat with residents who were no longer in attendance. You may have read my other two journals. Nowhere in them does it say I'm a people person.

I knocked again and gave the standard time for a response. I checked the doorknob. It was locked. "Who the hell locks their door in the country?" I asked the wind.

"What?" Tracy asked. "Are you talking to someone? Is there someone in there?"

"Just talking to myself," I told her over my shoulder.

"Well that doesn't count, you always have a crowd inside that head of yours," she said with a slight grin.

"Is this really the time for that?" Carol asked her daughter with concern. This non-confrontation I was not having on the porch was starting to rattle her a bit.

"This really is their basic form of communication," BT told Carol.

"You're in on this too?" She asked BT.

He smiled and shrugged his shoulders.

Nice verbal detour, but time to get back to the task at hand. "Please just let me know if you're in there. If you want us to go, we will. But if I don't get a response I am going to kick this door in!" I yelled. I wasn't too particularly scared of the 'Make My Day' law. That was a thing of the past. The owners of this house could have just as easily shot me on the porch and wouldn't even have to worry about cleaning up the blood trails as they dragged me inside to make it look like I had gained entry.

No one responded. I thought I might have heard a distant shuffle but I chalked it up to an overactive imagination. I got into my best Chuck Norris impersonation stance and lashed out heavily at the door with the heel of my foot. The heavy stout wooden door cracked a bit but did not give. I rebounded off, the reverberation from the contact causing increasing concentric rings of pain within my body as it radiated away from my foot. I staggered and nearly fell right off the porch.

I could hear BT laughing his ass off in the back of the hummer.

"Yeah!" I yelled. "Why don't you get your gimpy ass over here and give it a try?"

His chortling came to a quick and satisfying halt.

"The door must be braced from the inside." I said to anyone that would listen as I rubbed my shin.

Tommy joined me up on the porch, his eyes all puffy as if from crying. He didn't say anything to me as he bent down and grabbed the key that had been strategically placed under the welcome mat, unlocked the door and walked in.

"Who still does that?" I asked him as I followed into the house.

"Talbot?" Tracy yelled from outside. I backed up and stuck my head out. "What should we do?"

"Shut off the hummer and come on in." Seemed a rational enough response. Tommy had gone in. I still had to trust his 'gift'.

A heavy dust swirled in the light. I ran my finger across an old oak table. There was an accumulated layer of the fine dirt but nothing that hinted to longevity. Maybe as much as it would take to amass say since December 7th of the previous year. Chances were that these folks, the Powells, went to their local church when the end came. I knew the family name from the sign that welcomed all guests to The Powells, Union Station.

Travis was last in as he helped his grandmother. "You want me to shut the door, Dad?"

The interior of the house was that bone-chilling cold that can only come from an untended home, and had to be at least 15 degrees cooler than outside, but cold you can suffer with. Death from unknown sources, not so much. "Yeah go ahead and shut it and we'll see if we can get a fire going."

BT was briskly rubbing his hands together. "I'll get it going Mike," he volunteered.

"Dad, what about the smoke? Won't somebody see it?" Nicole asked as she clutched her arms over her chest.

I went over to her and rubbed her shoulders in a vain attempt to generate some heat. "More concerned with freezing to death at this point. We'll deal with each life threatening event as it happens." My words did little to ease her tension. It was just the truth, really, we weren't going to have to defend ourselves if we ended up frozen to death.

I nodded to BT to get that fire going. "Alright Trace, Nicole, I hate to be sexist..."

"No, you don't, but go on," Tracy said patting my head.

"Okay smart ass, could you please check the kitchen and hopefully the pantry and see what we've got for grub. The boys and I are going to check upstairs for whatever seems useful, especially blankets," I said, as I looked over to a shivering Carol. Henry had clambered up onto the couch with her and made sure as much of his body was making contact with her as was doggily possible. She seemed to appreciate the gesture as she affectionately rubbed his back.

The house was huge with high, hard-to-heat ceilings. Never could figure out why they made such tall ceilings when people were shorter back then. The contents of the abode were Spartan to put it gently. Had the place not looked so neat, I would have thought the place had been cleaned out by raiders. Listen, we both know I'm cynical, but I really felt like the Powells had attempted to buy their way into Heaven. The clues were the bare minimum of furnishings and the multitude of crosses and pictures of Our Father Who Art in Heaven that lined almost every available space on the walls. It took closer inspection to realize that the pictures were indeed that and not some Divine Wallpaper. Yes, I know I'm going to Hell. Feel free to cut in front if it makes you feel any better.

They at least had a myriad of blankets. Apparently, God liked his children to be warm. The upstairs also yielded two flashlights and the Holy Grail, or at least a breech loading over under barrel 10-gauge shotgun with a whopping seventeen shells. I really hoped nobody came a-visitin' as I'd never shot a 10-gauge before, but with its stout wooden no-give stock, I was pretty sure it was not going to be a pleasant experience.

I sent the boys downstairs to hand out blankets to an adoring crowd. I stayed upstairs, having found old farmer Powell's closet. We were nowhere near a match, size wise, as he seemed to have been enjoying the fruits of his labors maybe a tad too much. However, his clothes weren't covered in human remains and that was good enough for me. I checked the tap hoping that the water might still be running, but no such luck. My next option was the water in the toilet bowl. Given my aversion to germs this might not seem a wise course of action, but it was still light years ahead of what was clinging to my skin. The water was frozen solid. I would have to stay a little while longer in this condition as my only other option was to find a container, get some snow and melt it.

I plodded downstairs, not happy at all. Have you ever had a runny nose and the snot gets right to the edge of your nostril and you get this insanely tickling, itching sensation that you can not immediately take care of, because maybe you're in public, possibly talking to a bank teller? Take that feeling, amp it up maybe ten or eleven times, and that's what I felt like. Every time I took a step, the drying remains of that poor soul rubbed on my legs, thighs and ass, up my butt crack and, oh fuck, on my NUTS! I wanted the feeling of how when you finally step away from the teller's window, you take the sleeve of your jacket and just go to town on that itch. That satisfying 'Ah I win' sensation and for just a few moments in time all seems right in the world. Side note, if you're female, replace sleeve with tissue.

The beginnings of a fire were being well tended by BT. Henry and Carol were swallowed up in a huge plaid comforter; both looked on the verge of a serious nap. Good for them. Tracy and Nicole were taking stuff out of a pantry that looked stocked enough to take on a complete cold Pennsylvania winter.

Tracy wiped a strand of hair out of her face. "Stuff in the fridge has mostly gone over, nothing really worth salvaging. Smells better than Henry's butt in there but not by much."

Oh, my stomach almost got queasy. The fridge was definitely off limits.

"Got a big pot in there or something?" I asked, not really all that interested in checking out the menu just yet.

"No water?" Tracy asked getting right to the root of the matter.

I shook my head as she handed me a good size container.

I went outside and stuffed that thing full. BT looked like he wanted to hit me as I started to crowd out his burgeoning fire with my giant snow-filled pot. I think the only thing that held him up was the miserable expression on my face. The snow took somewhere in the neighborhood of a half-hour to melt. I know this because I did one Mississippi, two Mississippi etc for the whole time. It was this monotonous obsessive compulsive counting that let me stay sane those last few agonizing moments.

The water had barely let go of its previous frozen state when I grabbed the pot and headed back upstairs. As it was there were still chunks of ice floating around, but it didn't matter at this point. I found what looked like lumpy homemade soap up in the master bathroom. I was so distressed I didn't even think about whose body this may have last touched. Oh, I didn't mention that small tidbit? I used to have to have my own dedicated soap bar or I'd rather forego cleansing. The motel had those small individual ones so I had been alright. Didn't matter a lick this time though. I grabbed a small towel out of the closet, soaked it in ice water, lathered it up with soap and proceeded to rub my skin to a nice shiny red rawness.

Three blood soaked towels later, I felt better, not clean mind you, but better. The bathroom floor looked like Lizzie Borden had lived here. If someone stumbled across this place after us they would have grim visions of what must have happened here. I found a belt, drilled a new fastening hole into it and cinched up my pants. I would have to go commando from here on out, I would never be 'cured' enough to put on someone else's briefs. There was a nice warm red wool plaid shirt to go along with my country-faded blue jeans, I was even able to snag a nice comfortable pair of socks. No fashion show trophies for me, but I was warm and functionality is the cornerstone of survivalism.

When I came back downstairs, BT was melting another big pot of snow, some for drinking and cooking with and some if folks wanted to clean up a bit. It must have been sometime around noon judging by the sun. BT's fire had the room not balmy but homey. Almost everyone had eaten at least one or two cans of fruit. Nearly sated belly, a warm fire and a place to rest my ass, it all spelled a recipe for some much needed shut-eye. The finished can of sweetened pears fell out of my hand as I nodded off into the netherworld.

CHAPTER 28 - JOURNAL ENTRY 22 -

The fire was a glowing ember when I awoke. The room was near to stifling, at some point I had pushed the blanket completely off of me and onto Carol. Night had descended and poetically I'd like to say so had my spirits, but in actuality they had been rising since I had been able to scrape myself clean. We were close to Maine. I could almost taste it. My previous dire predictions of what remained there now seemed ill conceived. My family was there, they were a huge factor in my Armageddon paranoia. Compared to them I was the sane one. (I know, scary thought, right!?) We would get there, bloody, beaten and bruised, but not defeated.

I headed into the kitchen to look out the window, not much good that did me. A zombie could have been on the other side of the glass looking in and I wouldn't have been able to see it on this cloudy moonless night. I shuddered and stepped back, pissed off that I was giving myself the frights. 'Shits not bad enough, Talbot, you have to go and make stuff up?' My self-chastisement over, I opened the fridge, forgetting my wife's earlier warning. The waft of stale moldy food almost knocked me on my ass. That was, of course, until I saw the telltale glint of fire embers bouncing off the glistening bottle of Pabst Blue Ribbon. Farmer Powell may have been a religious man; thank God he wasn't abstemious too. I joyfully wrapped my hand around the cold bottle, trying to figure out why the makers of PBR wasted glass on the internal contents. I didn't waste another moment dwelling on PBR's manufacturing idiosyncrasies as I twisted the cap off and drank greedily.

I could tell BT was shuffling around in the other room by his grunting and groaning. He was stoking the dying fire. A minute or two later the living room began to dance in the light of the reinvigorated blaze.

BT came into the kitchen shortly thereafter. "You found beer?" he asked, looking longingly at my bottle of beer.

"Barely." I motioned to the fridge. A good friend would have got up and got his buddy with the healing broken leg a brew, but I wanted him to experience the wonderful odor that came from the tainted appliance much like I had.

I laughed when he nearly swooned from the pungulence. (Yes I made this word up, somehow seems right.) I'll give him credit though, he hung tough and grabbed a beer before he slammed the door shut and scrambled backwards.

"You knew, right?" he asked, sitting down at the table and taking a safe breath.

I nodded as I took another gulp.

"Thanks for the warning." he said acerbically as he twisted his cap off.

"Any time. I'm going to have to get Travis up soon."

BT looked at me questioningly as he took his own pull from the beer bottle.

"I'm almost out," I said, as I shook my bottle "and I'm not opening that fridge again."

"You're not a nice man, Mike," BT said and we both laughed. His face grew more serious. "Mike, I've got to admit this is the worst I've felt since we locked those doors at Safeway a few months back."

"I think a lot had to do with losing that base. We had it pretty good for a while. Someone else was protecting us. We got to pretend we were once again living our normal lives. And now…."

"We're back in the thick of the shit," he finished solemnly.

"Yeah it's definitely much, much better being in the tapered thinner ends of the shit."

BT looked like he wanted to say something more but in the end he just nodded in agreement and drank another swig.

"Speaking of shit."

"Here we go," BT said as he shook his head.

"Why are shits tapered at the end?" I asked him.

"Please tell me this is a joke."

"So your asshole doesn't slam shut," I finished smiling.

BT had beer shooting out his nose he was laughing so violently. "You're a dick," he said, getting up to get the dishtowel hanging on the oven door handle.

Travis came into the kitchen. "Everything alright?" he asked, rubbing the sleep out of his eyes.

"Well, now that you ask. I sure could use a beer," I told him, pointing towards the fridge.

"You have no bounds, Mike," BT said as he wiped his face dry with his sleeve. "I'll get them Travis. Your dad's setting you up."

I feigned innocence, it was a pose I had adopted entirely too many times over the years. Its effectiveness had dwindled to less than zero.

"Something going to pop out?" Travis asked, intrigued.

"Something like that. Hold your breath," BT said as he slid his chair over to get a couple more brewskis.

"Dad?" Travis asked.

I nodded to BT. He grabbed an extra beer. Guy code is pretty funny. We sometimes can get a lot accomplished with very little verbiage. With one word I ascertained that my son was asking permission to drink a previously restricted beverage, and with only a head nod to BT he realized that I had answered my son's question in the affirmative and he was now fulfilling the order. I guess if someone really wants to go back to the beginning of early man, this type of communication was an evolutionary necessity. When men were hunting prey that was more dangerous than them, they had to get across as much meaning as possible without any verbal communication so as not to alert their intended dinner.

I didn't have a problem giving my underage son a beer. Societal laws were now a thing of the past. Life expectancy had gone from somewhere around 79 to most likely somewhere in the 20's. I wanted my son to enjoy as much as life still had to offer at this point, and if part of that involved a so-called 'illegal' beer, so be it. Of all the things I was going to lose sleep over, this wasn't going to be one of them. That was, of course, unless Tracy found out about it, and then she'd make sure I would.

We sat there together in blissful silence, enjoying each other's company and the beverages. Travis was halfway through with his beer when he finally spoke. "Dad, I'm scared."

I nearly choked on my beer as my heart sank somewhere down deep into the depths of despair. To protect, to shelter, to encourage, to cheer on, these are just some of the things fathers do for their kids. Now, I'm not ignorant of the situation, I knew that what was happening was far beyond my scope to control or to temper. I had been doing everything in my limited power to make everything as right as possible, but was it enough? I stood up and hugged him. I had no empty hollow words to try and assuage him, and he would have known them for what they were anyway.

BT was looking away, absently peeling the label off his beer. "How long are we staying here Mike?" he asked.

I pulled away from Travis. We both may have tried to mask an errant flow of briny water. "Tomorrow we'll check the barn and hope we get lucky with some new wheels. He should at the very least have some gas for the hummer."

"Isn't the hummer diesel though?" Travis asked.

"From the mouths of babe," I said absently. "Hadn't even thought of that."

"Diesel, gas what the hell's the difference?" BT asked.

"We put gas in that thing and we won't get a mile before the engine probably shuts down, although we couldn't get a mile with what's in that tank right now either."

"We can't stay here!" BT said, alarmed and possibly

realizing for the first time that we were in essence trapped. "Maybe we can walk to the nearest town?" he asked hopefully.

"Nothing personal BT, but between your leg, Carol's age, the frigid temperature and a short legged bulldog, we'd be in a lot of trouble. Who knows how far it is to the next anything."

"Couldn't we just go from house to house?" Travis asked.

"We got pretty lucky with this one." BT said.

"Yeah, going up to people's houses like this is sort of like playing Russian Roulette. Eventually we're going to come across an occupied place with a trigger happy, cautious owner." I said, taking another pull from my beer. I had just begun to dwell on how truly screwed we were. Out of the frying pan and into the fire, from the fire into the coals, out of the coals and into some ill placed lava, from the lava and into hell itself. "Wonderful," I said, finishing my second beer. My earlier head fog evaporated under the heat of realization.

If the night wasn't so entirely bathed in black, I would have chanced going to the barn now to see where we stood, equipment, supplies and transportation wise. This way, however, I would get to toss and turn all night guessing on what would *not* be in there.

"Anyone want another?" I asked, this time oblivious to the stink that came out of the fridge.

"Are you sure that's such a good idea?" BT asked, indicating I'd already drank two of the frothy beverages.

"I can die just as easily with three as I can with two." I stood up to see two shocked expressions looking back at me. "Sorry, just feeling a little bitter there for a sec." I stooped to unhappily put my beer back. 'I'll be back,' I whispered to it.

"We heard that." BT said.

CHAPTER 29 - JOURNAL ENTRY 23 - 

The next morning couldn't come soon enough, considering I stayed up the whole time waiting for it. The sun rose over the pine trees revealing nothing but a white expanse. I went back upstairs and rooted around until I found what I was looking for. "Thermals! Yes!" I said triumphantly. Technically these are long underwear but since I cannot wear someone else's undergarments, this was my coping mechanism. All of us are flawed. It is our responsibility to find ways around those inherent issues.

"Where are you going, Michael?" Carol asked, as I came down the stairs. Her voice was weak and thready. Stress was not doing any of us any favors but she seemed to be weathering it with more difficulty than the rest of us.

"I'm going to check the barn and see if there is something in there that will help us get out of here," I responded, patting her on the shoulder as I passed.

"We're not staying here?" she asked, gripping my arm with more strength than I thought she had left in her.

"Wow, forgot you grew up on a farm," I said rubbing my forearm. I was trying for a little grain of humor. I knew what path this conversation was going down and it looked like it was full of thorns and prickers. Carol wasn't biting on my lame attempt to diffuse her train of thought. "Carol, we can't stay here and neither can you," I said before she had the chance to bring up that very subject. She looked more than a little pissed that I had cut her off at the knees. "Listen, if you don't go, neither will Tracy and if she doesn't go, neither do the kids or me."

"Is that so bad?" Carol asked. "We have a house and at least enough food to get us through the next month or so.

Then when the weather turns we can plant everything we need to."

I truly felt bad for her. She had not been happy since she left her home in North Dakota. She wasn't looking ahead. I really tried to be gentle but it's just not in my nature. "This place would be great for about a week Carol, and then we'd be dead." Too blunt? She was taken aback at my candor. "Eliza will regroup if she hasn't already and the next time we meet she won't be so kind." I said, as I rubbed my jaw, the pain of Eliza's blow still fresh in my mind. Why I wasn't eating out of a straw right now was still a mystery to me.

"Michael, I can't keep doing this. This running, and hiding and fighting, I can't do it." She started to cry.

Tracy rounded the corner at just that moment. "Jesus, Mike what the hell did you say to her?" Tracy asked, as she wrapped her arms around her mother. "Come on Mom, let's go sit in the living room, you're freezing." She shot me a wicked glare as she turned her mother around.

I shrugged my shoulders, a victim of circumstances yet again.

"You ready?" BT asked me as he came out of the kitchen. He passed Tracy and Carol as they headed into the living room. "Jesus, Mike what the hell did you do?"

"You too? Are you kidding me? I'm going to the barn," I said indignantly.

"Do you mind if I go with you, Dad?" Nicole asked as she adjusted her gloves.

She still hadn't told me she was pregnant, and as always I was hesitant to put her in danger, especially now that she also carried the future of the Talbots. I took a long look out the side window. Everything still seemed alright and nothing smelled afoul, and I meant that literally.

"Sure, come on." I told her. I kind of had to take her. If she got to crying, Tracy would blame me for that too.

Travis was watching. He didn't look like he was in any big rush to go into the cold.

"Hey bud, could you do me a favor and go hang out

in the bedroom that overlooks the barn and just keep a watch out?" I asked Travis.

He seemed pretty relieved that his part didn't involve going outside. "No problem," he said. Tommy quickly fell into step behind him, never once looking over towards me.

"Hey Tommy, if you could keep an eye out on the other side that would be great," I shouted to his back as he headed up the stairs. I think he grunted a 'yes' in reply.

"Relax Tommy, we can't pick who we're related to," I heard Travis tell Tommy as they made it to the top of the stairs. "If we could, I would have traded Justin in years ago." Tommy laughed. It was the first time in a while. It was a welcome sound.

"I heard that little brother!" Justin shouted from the general direction of the pantry.

CHAPTER 30 - JOURNAL ENTRY 24 -

The barn was a treasure trove of trash. Broken tools lined the walls. Various sized engine blocks created a haphazard maze. In one of the far corners, debris and trash was piled so high, that any shifting of contents would cause an avalanche of refuse. I was surprised, seeing as how the house was so tidy. My guess was the house was Mrs. Powell's domain, and the barn belonged to Mr. Powell.

"Great." BT said sarcastically. "Of all the farms in Pennsylvania we have to find a hoarder's."

I shrugged my shoulders as I was climbing over a small wall of transmissions.

"Ever build a car?" I asked BT as I got to a stack of carburetors.

"Didn't I tell you?"

He said it so earnestly I had to turn and see if he was telling the truth. He wasn't. BT was still scaling the transmissions when I made it around a stack of radiators that had to be at least 10 high and 5 across. The majority of stuff here was garbage with two notable exceptions and I was staring at them. The first was a 1950's pick-up truck and the second one was an older John Deere tractor.

Nicole had come up beside me. I was apprehensive about her climbing all over the rusted metal lest she hurt something inside of her. I could tell she appreciated all the extra help I was giving her as she traversed the pile but she was also giving me a look of 'What gives?'

BT had finally mustered his way up to me, a nice looking mahogany cane in his hand. "Ah, so this isn't the only thing in here worth something," he said, holding his cane up.

One tire was flat and the bed of the truck was

exposed. All three of us had the same thought. BT voiced it first. "Gonna be pretty cold in that truck bed."

"Sure is, too bad you can't drive with that busted leg of yours."

"Nicole, have I told you lately that your dad is not a nice man?"

I shrugged my shoulders again. "Doesn't matter much if there isn't a spare," I said pointing to the flat. "On the other hand, that tractor is making me sort of gleeful."

"Gleeful?"

"Just an expression."

"Yeah, just don't stand too close," he said holding his cane up to make sure that I knew he had a weapon. "Can't really see what a tractor is going to do for us? We can't all fit and there's no cab for any of us to stay warm."

"Not the tractor itself but what it runs on."

"Diesel? That thing runs on diesel?" BT asked hopefully.

"Pretty sure and these farmers usually store it in big 55 gallon drums."

BT looked a little deflated. "This place looks like a graveyard for all things busted, you think he was even using that thing?"

"I hope so, plus it looks like we came in from the wrong side. The barn is free and clear on the other side."

"So he could drive that thing in and out."

"See, now *you* look gleeful."

"Watch it, Talbot."

"Don't worry, you're not my type."

"What, too pretty?"

"Yeah that's it." I said as I reached up and clapped his shoulder. This was the first break we'd had in a bit. I just hoped it panned out.

"Bingo!" BT yelled as he got to the other side of the tractor. He was pointing with his cane to the left hand side of the barn at four 55-gallon drums of something.

He had already found the drums, so I was going to

make sure I found the fuel. I rushed passed him. "Glory whore!" he shouted.

The first drum fell over as I pushed a little too forcefully while checking for any contents, nearly smashing Nicole's toes in the process. The second also fell away. BT was beside me as I got to the third barrel. What started off sweetly was quickly turning sour. I was getting anxious. The third barrel had a hand pump secured to the top for dispensing the fuel. It didn't move nearly as easily as the first two, but it did not hold its ground as firmly as I would have liked when I pushed against it.

"Maybe twenty gallons," I told BT. "But that's a complete guess."

"That's a start, right?"

"At 11 miles to the gallon it won't get us halfway to where we need to go."

"How many gallons does the hummer hold?"

"I think around forty, forty-two maybe."

"You going to check the fourth barrel?" he asked apprehensively.

"Why don't you, my luck isn't so good today."

BT whacked his cane against the side. The sound was resoundingly positive. The impression of fullness reverberated joyfully in our souls.

"Probably should make sure it's not cow piss before we celebrate too much." I told BT.

"Wait, what? Why would a farmer need cow piss?"

"He's messing with you BT," Nicole said with a smile.

"This is where I'd laugh my ass off if you weren't such a friggen giant." I smirked at him.

"Just check it," BT said, and I could tell by the sound of the words he wanted to add an expletive at the end.

I unscrewed the small air tap and was welcomed with the slightly metallic, bitter smell of a full drum of diesel fuel. If it was gas we'd have to take the truck and no one would relish their time in the back no matter how many blankets we could stuff back there.

"Now what?" BT asked.

"Well, first I'm ripping the upholstery out of the drivers' seat in the hummer. I don't care if I'm sitting on bare metal, there's no way I'm sitting back down on the remains of that poor bastard. Then I'm driving that thing over here, filling it up. Maybe see if there is anything worth draining out of the tractor. Then I'm going to need a little help polishing off those beers and then tomorrow we head out."

"Sounds like a plan," BT said as he headed out what was apparently the front door of the barn. With only bits of straw to impede his progress, he made good time.

"Hey, don't sweat it. I don't need any help." I shouted to his back.

"Good thing," he replied. "I'm tired and my leg hurts."

"Always with the leg, how long you gonna milk that?" BT flipped me off and then I lost him in the glare of the snow-shine as he opened the door. "Real nice, you know that hurts my feelings right?"

Nicole took this moment while we were alone to ask a question. I figured this was going to be the big reveal.

"Dad, can I talk to you?"

"Sure sweetie. What is it?" I asked as I turned away from the drums to look at her.

Two sounds took this most inopportune time to fight simultaneously for my attention, my son's shout of warning and the high-pitched whine of a small vehicle engine. Sounded like a damn mini-bike but I couldn't figure out how someone could possibly be driving one in this snow. BT was no more than two strides from the door when I caught up to him. His gaze led right to the intruder astride a snow mobile.

"Oh, that's what that is."

"He's got a rifle," BT said, squinting with his hand shielding the sunlight from his eyes.

"Doesn't necessarily mean trouble. Wouldn't you have one if you had the choice?"

"I hear your words Mike, but they're not making me

feel any better."

"Yeah, me neither. How close would I have to get to use a pitchfork?" I looked back towards the house. Travis was pointing towards the vehicle and now people were lining the windows on the first floor to get a better view. "I wish they'd be a little more inconspicuous."

"Yeah me too." BT agreed, never looking towards the house to see what I was talking about. "Umm, Mike."

"Yeah?" Just then the snowmobile revved high and shut off. The ensuing silence was not nearly as peaceful as it had been a moment before his arrival. Expectancy hung in the air.

"Good to see you're doing well, Mike." A cold calculating voice shouted across the vast white waste.

"Durgan." BT and I said simultaneously.

"He's like a cockroach," I bitched. "Can't kill him."

"Mike, we need to talk!" Durgan shouted.

"I'm a little busy right now, I've got some muffins in the oven and I really don't want them to burn!" Durgan didn't laugh. I glanced over at BT. "He really doesn't appreciate my humor."

"In this, I'm in agreement with him." BT answered.

"Let the muffins burn Mike!" Durgan shouted angrily.

"That's hilarious, he believed me." I smiled with satisfaction.

"See, that's your problem," BT said. "You have piss poor comedic timing."

"Au contraire."

BT turned to face me. "Oh come on, you throw these huge words around, I bet you don't even know what half of them mean."

"I do know what half of them mean," I lied. I had turned to face BT, neither of us looking towards Durgan. The rifle shot changed that quickly.

"I'm fucking talking here!!" Durgan screamed. I could see an arc of spittle fly from his mouth even from this distance. "I need to talk to you now Talbot, there will be no more warning shots."

"You're the one with the motorized get up, why don't you come over here?" I replied.

"Not a chance, come here now or I start taking some pot shots through the windows at your brood over there."

"Asshole," I muttered

BT and I started the trek across the field.

"Not the colored one!" Durgan shouted.

"Who?" I asked back.

"The Negroid, he is not welcome here."

"Negroid? Who's a negroid?" I asked.

Red blotches were spreading across Durgan's face.

"I think he's talking about me," BT answered loudly.

"Holy shit! You're black?!"

"Now see Talbot, that's funny!" BT said to me. Then he turned to Durgan and said words that chilled my spine and warmed my heart. "Next time I see *you,* pencil dick, I'm going to snap your cracker neck."

I absently ran my hand over my neck, thankful those words weren't directed towards me. With that said, BT went back to his spot by the barn door. Durgan looked like he might have busted a few hundred blood vessels in his face as beacon-red flushed every exposed inch of his skin.

"Into the valley of death they rode." (I wanted to finish with the pop culture phrase of 'Because I'm the biggest baddest mofo around,' but I was scared shitless.) Until you've been shot, you can't even begin to understand how much you never want to experience that sensation again. Durgan was in complete control. I had my K-Bar on me but I was sure that he wasn't going to let me get that close. I got to within twenty feet. Durgan lowered his rifle to a point directly midway on my chest.

"Stop there," he said with a sneer. I complied. "Now kneel."

"Go fuck yourself, I'm all kneeled out." Fear and pride raged within me. I watched as Durgan's trigger finger whitened under the strain of holding back. I was playing a dangerous game but I had a hunch. I usually only bet on scratch tickets with a hunch, this was a big jump for me. "Listen, we both know if you had your choice you would have already pulled that trigger, so stop preaching and do your master's bidding, messenger boy." He really was an impressive shade of red, especially from this close up. She must have had him on a short leash because he was straining every muscle in his not too shabby bulk to pull that trigger and kill me.

Could I run up there with my knife and kill him? Did he have a fail-safe switch if he were threatened that would let him defend himself. I had NO compunction whatsoever with killing this man even if he could not defend himself, *especially* if he couldn't defend himself. I took two steps closer, still not dead.

"Stop." Eliza's voice said coldly. Durgan's features slackened as Eliza took the reins. "I will let this useless piece of meat kill you. I hate him for what he is but he is still of use to me, for now. But you are almost less than useless."

"Coming from you I think I consider that a compliment."

"You dare to jest with me? Will you still seek humor as I rip the unborn fetus out of your daughter's womb as you watch?"

Her words were so cold she made sure they were laced with the imagery of her act. I dry retched into the snow.

BT yelled from the barn. "Mike, you alright?" he asked with concern.

I stood back up, dragging my sleeve across my watering mouth and with my other hand I waved back towards him.

"Are you ready to listen?" It was phrased as a question, but there were no alternate choices.

I nodded dumbly.

"I want Tomas."

I shook my head in the negative, acidic bile threatening to once again make its triumphant return.

"I do not think you understand what I am saying to you Michael. I will flay the flesh from your seed as they scream your name in vain. You will watch as I disembowel your wife and let my zombies eat her while she lives on. The last thing you will see will be your friend Lawrence as he rips your neck open to drink deeply of your blood. He will be the only thing I spare, for I think I might like to keep him as a pet for a while."

I could almost swear I saw a flicker of jealousy cross Durgan's face. Apparently this wasn't part of the original plan.

"Michael, you cannot keep running from me. Eventually your unnaturally deep well of luck will run out and I'll be there when it happens. I gave you one opportunity to be spared, but you spurned it. I am giving you and your family a chance to survive as your kind do. I will not offer you sanctuary again; even now my legion is nearing."

I looked over Durgan's shoulder to see if anything was approaching. Her words snapped me back to the fore.

"Michael, even if you run today, I know where you are going. I know where your friends Alex and Paul have gone."

She never actually mentioned places. Was Eliza bluffing? Did she need to? If our lives were divided into a standard deck of 52 cards, Eliza was holding 50 of them. I was maybe looking at the "two of Hearts" and the "four of Clubs".

"You know I can't give him up. What kind of person would that make me?"

"A live one," she replied instantly. "You have known him for two months yet you would sacrifice yourself and your family for him? That is why humans are so weak." She fairly spat out the words. "He has led you down the path of destruction like he has so many others. He cares naught for any of you!"

"You lie, Eliza!"

She laughed, but no tone of merriment accompanied

it. "You are foolish to believe that a 500-year old immortal cares at all about the fleeting lives of the humans he uses."

Her words stung deep. Being this close to her was keeping my mind clouded. I was having great difficulty distinguishing truth from lies in her venomous words. If ever a serpent spoke, it was now.

"You loved him once!" I shouted, hoping my words would knock something loose in that frozen countenance of hers.

"Michael, you misunderstand why I have let him live all these long years. Perhaps once when I was a girl I cared for him, but that is from a previous life. I now let him live merely to torment him. The look of pathetic sadness and longing on his face is what I thrive on. The pain his quest brings to others, that is all the solace I need. I forfeited my soul willingly when D'Arvain turned me. I could not now get it back even if perchance I wanted it, which I don't. I have been liberated. I am free to do as I please through this world." She spread Durgan's arms wide. "The world is mine, Michael, I have control over the largest army this planet has ever known."

I wanted to tell her that if we were talking about just sheer numbers, the army ant might protest her claims. Seemed like an inappropriate time though.

"Too bad you're dying then."

Durgan/Eliza looked pissed! If her zombies were in place, I would have been as good as dead. "Give me Tomas, Michael, and you and your kin can live out the rest of your pathetically short lives without interference from me."

Please don't misunderstand the tone of my words in this conversation; evil oozed from Eliza. She had some form of mental manipulation also and she was not afraid to place scenes of unbelievably gruesome acts of violence into my head. My knees knocked, my bladder yearned for release, my heart kept skipping beats. On occasion, I think I forgot to breathe. Still something was nagging. "Why are you even asking me? Why not just take him?"

I thought the contortions she put Durgan's face through were going to make his skin split like an overripe banana. Eliza did not do well when her authority was questioned.

"I mean if that piece of shit is here." I said motioning to her host body. "Then you must be close." The wheels in my head were threatening to spin off their axle. "It is light out though, does that whole vampire in the sun thing hold merit? At Lowe's it was daylight, but you looked way more like a zombie back then. Is there any chance I could find you before tonight and drive a stake into your shriveled black heart?"

"Enough!" she screamed. "I have listened to your ranting for entirely too long. Tomas or your family, Michael, you decide." With that she left Durgan. He fell forward a few inches as Eliza released him, then his eyes cleared and looked up at me. "I'll be back, Talbot." He started the snow mobile and gunned the engine heading straight for me. I rolled to my side and grabbed the K-Bar strapped to my ankle. As Durgan passed, I used his momentum and dragged my blade across his left calf. A small smile of satisfaction crept across my face as a crimson blossom spread out from the wound. His only acknowledgement was to open the throttle faster so he could leave quicker.

"Tommy is family," I told his/her retreating back. I dusted myself off and headed back to the barn.

"What's he want?" BT asked, as I wiped my blade off in the snow.

"He said something about making a trade for some blackberry preserves and a bushel of crab apples."

"You're not funny."

"Yeah, well neither is the alternative. They want Tommy. We need to get the hummer fueled and get the hell out of here before tonight."

"Dammit, I guess that means we aren't going to finish those beers then. Did you get hurt?" BT asked, finally noticing the blotch of red in the snow.

"Not mine, his. And no, unfortunately it wasn't a fatal blow."

"Good."

"What?" I asked incredulously.

"Because I want to do it myself."

Within an hour, we had ransacked the house for whatever might turn up as useful. It was a woefully pathetic yield. I was happy to find that the hummer actually had seat covers. I guess now that I'm thinking about it, they were designed to be removed and replaced if an occupant was to expire in there. Well that's a macabre thought. Not much, but some of the previous tenant's remains had seeped through. This was quickly fixed with a throw rug I pilfered from the upstairs bathroom.

I filled the hummer up to brimming with fuel. With the help of Tommy, Travis and Justin (I actually delegated) we put the half full remaining drum in the trunk.

"The first couple of hundred miles are going to suck," I said aloud.

Justin looked over at me, waiting for me to finish.

"The trunk isn't going to shut, gonna be as cold as Eliza's sn…." I stopped when Tracy was approaching with some boxes of food. "Uh, hi Hon."

"You've got that look of just getting caught in the cookie jar thing going on," she stared at me suspiciously. I shrugged. "Help me with these and drag your mind out of whatever gutter it's wriggling around in."

A few more back and forths and the hummer was as full as it was going to get and still hold occupants. I helped Carol into the front so she would be closest to the heat, wrapped her in a few blankets and then was halfway back to the house to get Henry when Tracy called from the front door.

"You seen Tommy?"

It was an innocent enough question, so then why did my bowels seize up? "No I…" I honestly couldn't remember the last time. Sure, he had helped with the barrel but when?

We had been bustling around so much. There had been so much activity I didn't stop to take stock. "Get Travis and Justin!" I yelled.

"What?" Tracy asked concerned. She wasn't nearly as alarmed as I was. I was halfway around the eastward side of the house looking for any tracks that led away.

Justin and Travis ran up to me, alert for signs of trouble but not seeing any. "What's up Dad?" Travis asked, checking that the shotgun was loaded.

"I want you and Justin to go completely around this house look for any foot tracks that lead away. I think Tommy left and I want to catch him before he does anything stupid."

Travis went clockwise, Justin counter. I went back to the hummer where the snow was trampled down and tried to find a fresh set of tracks away from the vehicle. BT got wind of what was going on and went up to the barn to look. When the boys and BT all came back to me and shook their heads in the negative I went up to where I met Durgan and Eliza to see if the boy had followed my steps out there and then proceeded on.

I even got Henry into the fray. I figured he might not be a bloodhound and wouldn't be able to track a person, but the dog loved food and Tommy was a walking mini-mart. My heart was racing. I had once lost sight of Travis in a Target when he was about 5. Those thirty seconds had damn near made my heart explode. I was now up to about forty-five minutes of that sensation and I did not see a cessation in the near future. "TOMMY!" I screamed. It came out a mixture of tortured bereavement and soul wrenching sadness.

"Mike," Tracy said, placing her hand on my shoulder and handing me a foil packet. "I found this on the ground behind the hummer."

Tommy had written a note with a magic marker on an empty Pop-Tart packet. 'Dear Mr. Dad. I have gone to Lizzie. Please do not try and stop me.' I turned the packet over and inside out hoping there was more to it than just that. There had to be. Lives don't just end like this.

I knew Eliza had lied. Tommy was trying to save us all, at the expense of himself. For not the last time in this saga, I dropped to my knees and cupped my face in my hands. Tears of rage and sorrow poured through my fingers. BT stood in the snow next to me with a look of confounded anguish. Tracy rested against my back, her tears soaking into my jacket. The kids were lost in their own thoughts. Even Henry felt the pain of the loss, he howled like a Bassett Hound, something he had never done before and something I hoped he never had to do again.

Time was irrelevant. I could only mark passage by the frozen tears that had fallen to the ground. Nicole, or maybe it was Justin, hell, it might even have been Tracy, helped me to my feet. For a moment or two I twisted out of the haze of loss only because of the pain my locked knees caused when I attempted to use them. Someone put me behind the wheel of the hummer and maybe even started it. For a good four hours someone else that looked like me drove on that cold desolate roadway but it wasn't me. Someone that could almost be my twin was even nice enough to refill the tank and toss the 55-gallon drum out of the trunk. I would have to send them a Thank You letter later on. Jed and Jen's deaths had hit hard. I thought it could not get worse than when Brendon was killed, but this…this was intolerable. The emotional pain had forced me out of myself. I was on autopilot. Every time I thought of his smiling face trying to hand me some ungodly disgusting flavor of Pop-Tart, I would start to cry again. Unlike previous times, I didn't care who saw me. I was living but I wasn't alive.

CHAPTER 31 - TOMMY'S DISAPPEARANCE -

Tomas had heard everything his sister had told Mr. Dad. He had no doubts that she would follow through with her threats. Lizzie was not one for idle intimidation; he had witnessed firsthand the depths her cruelty could take. Tomas could not watch another family he loved be killed merely for the sinister amusement of Lizzie.

He would stop this here and now. He would willingly give himself up to her, and before he would allow her to do to him whatever she needed to survive, he would make her promise that she would not harm the Talbots, ever. She would listen to him. She was his sister after all. With that thought in his head Tommy waited for his best chance to get away undetected. Tommy possessed more than a few of the powers his sister did and in all likelihood many more. Tommy could have walked away in plain sight and not been detected if he knew how to control it. As it was, he waited until everyone was in the house before he walked over the iced tracks the humvee had made coming up the driveway yesterday morning.

When Tommy felt he had gotten far enough away from the homestead he jumped into a small culvert. There he waited, covering his ears when he heard his dad crying his name. Tommy had been crying too. On more than one occasion he almost got up and walked back towards them, but all he could see if he walked that path were gravestones engraved with the names of the people he loved. That walkway was already long enough. He would not add to it, not this time, not ever again. He drove his fists deeper into his ears, oblivious to the pain he was causing himself. Tears pooled around him.

Tomas had been so intent on blocking out all

extraneous sensations he had missed the noise of the Talbot clan as they had passed on by. Early nightfall was threatening on the horizon when he finally looked up. "Stupid, stupid," he said to himself, rubbing the remains of his tears away from his eyes and cheeks. The farmhouse that just the night before had seemed so safe now looked oddly menacing. No residual warmth remained there, only cold, impersonal death. Tommy stood up easily, having not felt any ill effects from being in a kneeling position in the cold snow for near on 4 hours. He never wondered why he never felt pain or got sick. It was just the way it had always been for as long as he could remember. He thought maybe it was because he was 'special' like Lizzie used to tell him.

Tomas looked once to the house, once to the roadway and then headed out across the field in an easterly direction. He was walking a straight line to the psychic beacon that his sister was sending out. Within a half hour he found himself face to face with her. His need to hug and kiss her were thwarted by the indifference she flared all around her.

"Welcome brother," she intoned, without even a remote hint of love or caring.

"Hi Lizzie," Tommy, said looking down at his shoes, wishing he was anywhere but here.

"I'm so glad you could make it," she said without regard.

"You'll leave the Talbots alone?" Tommy fairly begged.

"Oh come now brother, what does the death of one more perishable family mean to you. You are immortal like I am!" she shouted.

"I am nothing like you, Lizzie," Tommy said meekly. Lizzie laughed mockingly at him. "You will leave the Talbots alone or I will leave again."

"Oh it is far too late for that, Tomas. As for the Talbots, I do not think that I am quite done yet. He has defied me twice and I do not suffer fools gladly."

Tommy was panicked. He had done no good here; he

had in fact made matters worse. If he had stayed away for a month, two at the most Lizzie would have died, no, Eliza would have died. Lizzie died 500 years ago. Tommy started to cry anew.

"Come, come brother. I will kill his family quickly if that makes you feel any better, but Michael, he will suffer in ways I have not yet dreamed." Her bitter laugh mirrored Tommy's feelings. "There is someone here that is going to help. Maybe you will recognize him."

Tommy saw the man being pushed up to Eliza's side. "Doc?" Doctor Baker looked like he had suffered greatly at the hands of his sister, and his family was nowhere to be seen.

Tommy registered Durgan's presence a fraction of a second too late. His sister had completely blocked his senses. The needle plunged far too deep, and sleep followed immediately.

CHAPTER 32 - JOURNAL ENTRY 25 -

I had felt nothing, going on ten hours. I barely registered the Maine Stateline sign hanging askew. The most conversation since we had left the Powell House revolved around a bathroom break and even that was a pinched conversation. Pardon the pun. Tommy was one of our own. He was the shining light. He was the hope of a new dawn. All of that was lost. He was lost. We were lost. Eliza wasn't going to let us go. She was too prideful and too filled with hate to let anybody that stood up to her go unpunished.

Sure we might go unnoticed for a couple of months, but as soon as Justin ran out of his shots she would be able to home back in on him and we'd be on the run again. My thoughts were as black as the night, without even a single star to light my way. Would anybody protest if I just drove on into the ocean?

So this is what my life is reduced to. I will watch as those around me fall. Maybe I will get lucky and be next, then I won't have to suffer through this anymore. I don't know how much more of this I can take, my soul is already damn near transparent. I have done everything that is within and possibly beyond my human ability and still I have come up woefully short.

The slow, steady forced march to death that all of us experience has now turned into a 4x4 relay race. Jen handed the torch to Brendon, Brendon handed it to Tommy, who will Tommy hand it to? Every time I think that my despair has bottomed out I come to realize that I was only on a false shelf, the black plummeting drop wrenching my stomach into my throat, all sense of self and awareness enshrouded in misery. Existence hardly seemed worth the effort. How much pain does one feel from a self-inflicted gunshot?

'COWARD!' Echoed off the walls of the well I was trapped in.

Alone, in the dark, huddled against a wet dank wall, I shuddered in revulsion, of my situation and more so of myself. I just wanted to be done. The burden I carried now far exceeded my limits. Something had broken inside of me. Tommy had been the crutch upon which my spirit leaned on. With him gone it had crashed to the floor, smashing into millions of pieces like littered glitter. Pretty to look at but generally just a mess of color that gets everywhere but in the trash.

The soft glow of the moon lightly lit up the interior of the hummer, and I took long moments to gaze across the faces of the ones I loved. Yes, they would be the reason I would climb out of this pit. They would be the reason I would move forward no matter how much my will resisted. For them, I would never give up.

"You keep looking at me like that and you'd better take me out to dinner," BT said with one eye half open.

"Thank you BT," I choked out.

"Yeah, you're welcome. Now I know I'm pretty and it's tough to keep from looking at all this," he said swirling his hand around his face, "but I'd much rather you keep your eyes on the road."

"Thanks BT," I reiterated.

"We will get through this, Talbot," he said reaching up from the back and placing his hands on my shoulders. My shoulders shook, my silent tears crashing through my head. I knew the big man was hurting too. Tommy was dear to all of us. Right now BT was the Cliffs of Dover and I was the tide crashing into them. In a few millennia I might wear him down but for now he was going to be my rock. I reached over my chest and gripped his left hand with my right. If ever there were a strength I could anchor to, it was within this man. "This doesn't mean we're going steady now," I quipped half-heartedly.

I propped my knee up to hold the steering wheel as I

tried to wipe away the cascading tears with my left sleeve. BT looked off to the side, letting me hold on to what little remained of my dignity. Tracy witnessed the whole scene. Maybe at a different time she would have commented that we made such a cute couple; now just didn't seem like that time.

The chain that ensnared my heart grew a little heavier that day as Tommy's death added its own links to the length. Someday I would be strong enough to carry it, but for now dragging it would have to do.

CHAPTER 33 - JOURNAL ENTRY 26 - 

Maine looked almost the same as it had before zombieism became a national pastime. It was indeed passed over from modernity. The towns we passed through seemed devoid of any type of life. Occasionally we would pass a murder of crows snacking on things better left to the imagination but that was it. Mainers were traditionally a strong stock of folks that did not much like or trust people-from-away. But hey, they were Red Sox fans, so they have that going for them. Population wise, proximity (or lack thereof) to major cities and a general distrust of all things governmental may have worked in this reclusive state's favor.

We weren't being attacked by zombies but at the same time I wasn't seeing a welcome wagon. Odds were that we had passed under more than one rifle scope as we drove on but Mainers live under the premise of 'if you don't screw with us, we won't shoot you.' (Sort of like Northeast Texas.) Some buildings had been destroyed, others ransacked. There was the occasional crashed car but for the most part this looked better than pre-zombie Detroit. Okay so that's not saying a whole hell of a lot, but we are still talking Armageddon here.

Travis looked out the window. I could tell he was starting to see things that looked familiar. "How much further?" he asked with a hint of excitement in his voice.

God, I hoped my family was okay. I needed the infusion of hope that they would offer. "Hour or so, depending on fuel." The gauge couldn't go any lower. As it was, the hummer was sucking up the rusted bits of the fuel tank. I wonder what the mpg is on diesel-soaked metal fragments? If the truck died now that hour would now become a 10-hour sojourn that Carol and possibly BT wouldn't make. I started looking around for another viable means of transportation, but any survivors had beaten me to it. Mainers typically survive some of the harshest weather conditions on the barest minimum of supplies. Anything that could help them weather this 'storm' was long gone. I'd have a better chance of getting quality dental care in England. As if on cue and to make my heart skip another beat, the hummer sputtered once, twice and then lurched forward.

Tracy looked over at me nervously. "We going to make it?"

Both variations of that question had a huge '?' at the end. I didn't say it out loud. No need to, we all felt it.

The hummer got further than I expected but less than was needed. We were a full fifteen miles short of our destination when she quit. We were on a slight downgrade and I was able to eke out another tenth of a mile. Excellent, only 14 and 9/10ths miles to go. Carol, BT, Nicole and Henry could not make this march. Hell, the way I felt, I wasn't sure if I could.

"Any ideas?" Tracy asked me. She knew the score. We were in a lot of trouble.

"I was thinking maybe Triple A." She didn't rise to the bait. It wasn't that great of a joke anyway. She scanned the roadway ahead of us. The gusts coming from the Northeast blew snow across the desolate roadway. It was somewhere in the neighborhood of noon and there was no way we were going to be at my dad's before dark. One shotgun with seventeen shots. Once they were gone then what? Deaders could catch us. Speeders would have a field day. "Shit." I said as I rubbed my hand across my face.

"Should we just stay here and wait?" Carol asked. I understood her distress.

I turned to look at her. "We can't." I could have elaborated and said that waiting was tantamount to death. Zombies, the elements or just plain old every day assholes would come across us sooner or later.

"Mike, my mom can't make it," Tracy pleaded.

"What do you suggest? Should I let someone else

die?!" I yelled.

"Oh, Mike," Tracy sobbed. She fully realized now the burden I hefted. "None of those deaths were your fault. Bad things happen to good people."

Nicole full out started to cry, her loss coming to the fore again.

"My job is to protect, them, us. It's what I do now. It's all I do now and I failed them!"

"Mike." BT shot out. "We all look out for each other. It is not just *your* (italicized) job. There was nothing you, or any one of us for that matter, could have done."

I nodded in agreement, not because I felt that was the case but rather to end the discussion.

"Can't you maybe go for help and come back for us?" Tracy asked hopefully.

"Tracy, even at a decent pace, in these conditions I won't get there for at least another three hours. I don't even know what I'll find. Absolute best case scenario, I'm back here in four hours. Since this has started, how many best case scenarios have we come across?"

"None," Tracy said, lowering her head.

"Even with the shotgun you guys are sitting ducks. We can't take that big of a chance of splitting up. I won't survive if anything happens to any of you."

Carol was first out the door. "Let's get this over with," she stated flatly.

Can't really argue with that logic, so we all piled out. The biting sting of wind-blown ice crystals against my skin was both invigorating and alarming. An hour of that and it would begin to feel like someone was dragging frozen sandpaper across my face.

"What about Henry, Dad?" Travis asked.

Henry's idea of a walk generally consisted of getting up from his comfortable pillow, going over to his dish, eating heartily, playing for 15 minutes, wandering outside, taking care of business, then going back to his comfortable pillow. Henry wouldn't make it more than a mile before he would just stubbornly lie down and wait for me to do something about it.

"Winter in Maine," I replied slowly, deep in thought.

"Folks couldn't retire to Mississippi?" BT asked as he grabbed the remainder of blankets out of the truck.

"What?" Justin asked, picking up on my earlier comment.

"Winter in Maine. We should be able to find sleds, or something that we can use." The faintest glimmer of hope flickered. The problem with Maine is there just aren't that many houses, especially where we were. We were a half mile and a full hour into our trudge through slushy snow before we came across a potential house to take respite in, maybe find some supplies and some transport.

It was a small Colonial, set off the main street by 50 feet or so. I told everyone to stay where they were while I checked it out. When I looked back to them the betting money was even on whether Carol or Henry were going to stop walking first. BT was straining but he might make it just out of meanness. I was 15 feet from the house when I heard the tell tale cocking of a pistol.

"That's far enough mister," a voice called out from a shade drawn window. One small corner was pulled up to reveal a very large caliber weapon pointed in my direction. The voice sounded feminine, or it quite possibly was a young male. That didn't help matters much; it didn't matter who pulled the trigger, I'd still be just as dead.

"We just need a little help," I said, holding my hands out in appeal, thankful and regretful at the same time that I left the shotgun behind.

"Don't care," came the reply. I definitely pegged it as female this time.

"You don't understand... ."

She cut me off. "I said I don't *care*." There was no hostility in her voice, no anger, no derision. She was merely stating a fact.

I could argue with her another ten minutes and maybe

get shot for my troubles, not really how I wanted to end my day. "Someday you'll have to atone for this," I said as I turned and walked back towards the roadway.

It was then I heard the cackling of someone who had traveled far past the line of sanity.

"Didn't go so well?" Justin asked, looking over my shoulder at the house.

"It's good to see some things never change," I told him as I walked on past.

"What's he talking about?" Justin asked Travis.

"Too bad they didn't put any brains in those shots you take." Travis replied.

"What are you talking about?" Justin queried.

"The whole Captain Obvious thing." Travis replied.

"Oh!" Slapping palm to head, Justin laughed.

"Mike, Mom needs a rest and so does BT but he'll never tell you that," Tracy said, grabbing my elbow as she came up beside me. I had not even realized it as I walked at a slow, steady pace but already Carol and BT were a good 50 yards behind.

"Shit, this isn't working out so well." I told Tracy. We were stuck. "Okay, go back and take a rest with them. There's a house a little ways up; I'm going to see what I can find." A quarter mile later I came upon a double wide that had seen better days. Nobody lived here. The snow that had piled in the open doorway was my first clue. The cold metallic stench of death was the second as I got closer. I took a big intake of air and stuck my head through the doorway. The gloom of the interior was dimmed even further with the mound of bodies that littered the floor. A small fierce battle had raged here. There were no victors. Arterial blood had cascaded down the far wall. Punctured intestine nestled in the couch like a throw pillow. Something closely resembling brain matter coated the door. I was perilously close to falling into it if I didn't get some fresh air.

I pulled my head out. There was nothing in there I wanted to retrieve. I walked around the house and was rewarded for my efforts with a small green and white striped metal Tuff Shed, its door still closed. That boded well for what I was looking for. The door slid open with only a minimal amount of effort. My eyes had nearly adjusted to the dimly lit interior when the first gunshot rang out back from the direction where I'd left my family. I grabbed what I needed to and ran full tilt back to the roadway. I had not made it even that far before another three shots rang out. At this pace they would be out of ammo before I made it another hundred yards.

I could see my family making what haste they could towards me, being followed entirely too closely by zombies. "Shit!" I started to sprint.

Travis was down to five shots when I got to them. It looked like there were maybe another dozen or so zombies left to continue on after us. Now I'm no mathematician, but even I knew that unless they lined up real nice like, with head against head so we could kill more than one per shot, we were screwed.

"Someone call a cab?" I asked as I pulled the toboggans up.

Carol looked relieved, if a little dubious. Tracy helped her down; Henry watched raptly and then, realizing what this new fangled contraption was for, plopped down in front of her, nearly asleep before Justin and Tracy grabbed the ropes.

"Let's go BT." I said. Looking at him and to our approaching party crashers.

BT's pride was taking a huge hit. I know he wanted to argue that he could do it on his own, but even he knew his limitations. He laid down heavily on the un-cushioned slab of wood with a grunt. I pulled the rope over my head and laid it against my chest. "You ready?" I asked him. "I feel like that dog that pulls the Grinch's sleigh when it's all full from stealing everybody's stuff in Whoville."

"Max," BT answered.

"Huh?" I asked turning back around.

"The dog's name was Max ... and *mush!*"

For a fleeting moment I didn't think I was going to be able to get enough traction to get this train moving. I was feeling like the little engine that could. My feet were moving faster than they had a right to but I was making damn little headway. It was the roar of Travis' shotgun that got me going. My first half-dozen steps had worn a smooth spot through the ice and snow and I took off, not like a rocket, more like a snail late for a hot date.

For an hour and a half we were in stalemate mode. We were making better time with the sleds, but not enough to outpace the zombies. We had traveled maybe three miles. Travis had taken over the other sled for his mother. Nicole intermittently got on and off depending on her fatigue level, and how bad she felt for those laboring to usher her along. My legs were screaming in protest. All higher thought had been replaced with the plodding effort of putting the next foot in front of the other and outpacing the deaders. Strain oozed into pain, pain stumbled into numbness, numbness dispersed leaving behind pain. Ever faster I cycled through those stages, stopping always longer in the depths of misery.

Night quickly descended. It seemed to happen in between steps. I was lost in a state of fugue, fatigue and torment. Occasionally Tracy would come up beside me and pull, sometimes it was Tommy, once or twice Brendon actually came to help, but he mostly pulled the other sled when Nicole was on it. I sometimes saw Jen up ahead, never speaking but always waving us forward. I would have raised my hand to wave back but the effort was beyond my capability. My chest was rubbed raw and bleeding from the contact with the old hemp rope. I heard distant gunshots but they did not hold any significance for me.

The smell of rotten meat was the only thing that kept me moving, that and the desire to be away from it. No matter how far I traversed it always seemed to be creeping right up behind me. I couldn't even tell if my legs were still moving; I had lost control of my extremities.

"Mike!" someone screamed. Cognitively, I barely

registered the fact that someone was talking to me.

The sensation of falling was capped off by my knees painfully striking the ground. My legs shook uncontrollably. I was done for and unfortunately so was the poor bastard I think that I had been pulling. I fell off to the side, my face making a loud slapping sound as it also found its way to the cold, icy surface.

The lights of God blinded my eyes. This was not the ethereal, pleasant, loving lights I had encountered previously. These were harsh and glaring. Promised Land, ready or not, here I come. My labored breathing was overshadowed by the eruption of firearms coming to life around me. 'God has a fifty cal? Fucken sweet.' That was what actually went through my mind. Something swung passed my line of sight. The bright lights illuminated a flying spider man. I would have sworn I heard a battle cry just as this figure slammed into a tree on the far side of the clearing, making my fall to the ground seem like a tender caress in comparison. The figure stood up, wobbling a bit and brought his gun to bear. My vision blurred as gore splatter from above rained down on me. Spider-man had disposed of at least four or five zombies that had come within biting distance of me.

'Spidey is an awesome shot.' I thought right before I passed out.

CHAPTER 34 - JOURNAL ENTRY 27 -

I had no idea what time it was when I finally came to. Whenever it was, it wasn't long enough. My legs were still throbbing and more irritably still, they were twitching randomly. I looked like I was trying to do River Dance. It took me moments longer for the fog to lift.

"Zombies!" I yelled, hopping out of the cot I was in, my legs giving out as fast as I tried to stand. The resulting heap I made on the floor was not a flattering sight.

BT had not left my side since I had collapsed from exhaustion. I was to later learn it was more to do with the company we were keeping than any outright concern he had for me. "Mike, Mike," BT said, standing from the chair next to my bed that I had not noticed previously.

"Zombies, BT. We gotta get out of here." My lips were pulled back in fear, my eyes so wide the whites were showing all around. "Where is everyone else?"

"Mike," BT said grabbing me by the shoulders to help me back onto my cot. "We're okay," he said, gently placing me down with no more difficulty than a child would have putting their favorite toy away. My legs were still flailing. I was more than a little self-conscious about it and placed my arms on them, trying to slow them down. "They've been doing that since we got here," BT said pointing to my legs. "Was freaken the shit out of me for the first couple of hours. Kind of used to it now, can damn near tell time to their rhythm."

"I'm glad I can be a source of entertainment for you."

BT got grave seriously quick. "Mike, I know we've been through a lot and I count you up there with some of my best friends but what you did back there…." BT sniffed. "Man, I don't know that anyone I've ever known my entire life would have done that for me except maybe my mom."

"She as big as you?"

He laughed. "No, she might have been 110 after Thanksgiving dinner but she was tough as nails. Mike, I don't know that I can ever repay you."

"BT, this isn't about keeping score. It was just my turn. Next time though it's on you." BT did something very uncharacteristic for him and leaned down and gave me a hug. I accepted mostly because I was too tired to do anything else.

"I'm gonna go get your wife," he said, standing up. My shoulder was suspiciously wet from where his cheek had rested.

"One thing, BT."

"Yeah." He stopped.

"Where the hell are we?"

"You don't know?" he laughed as he left.

I heard footfalls coming down the hallway towards my room. Unless Tracy had gained 100 pounds and now had combat boots on, this wasn't her. I was apprehensive, even if BT had given me no reason to be. Paranoia was the foundation from which I had survived thus far. I did not see a reason to deviate from the norm, distorted as it might be.

I could see nothing as the figure stopped in the doorway and was now silhouetted in the light from beyond him.

"Happy Birthday little brother, what took you so long?"

"Ron? Ron!" I jumped out of the bed to only be met with the previous fate. Isn't that the definition of insanity, to repeat the same action over and over, expecting different results?

"The one and only," he said, picking me up and placing me back on the cot.

"Getting a little sick of that."

"Eh, stop trying to stand and it won't happen."

"That's what the world needs…a pragmatist."

He gave me a hug to rival BT's. "Didn't think you

were going to make your own party."

"Wasn't so sure myself." I told him.

"I've heard."

"Yeah?"

"Nicole has been telling us your story from the day it started. She's damn near a tape machine the way she plays it back."

"I know. Where are you up to?" I asked him.

"When Paul and Alex left to go down South." Two more souls I missed. "Are you up for joining us?" His affirmative nod left unspoken that the extended Talbot clan was in good shape, if not whole.

"I don't think I'm ready, Ron." That had more to do with listening to Nicole's retelling of our story than anything else. I could not go through those losses again, not now, not ever.

Ron, as intuitive as ever, picked up on my mood. "We need a break anyway, Mike, Nicole can finish the story later on. I've had to keep Dad on a leash from busting in here every twenty seconds."

"Alright, but I can't walk and I'm sure as hell not going to let you carry me in there."

"Got that figured out," he said, leaving the room and coming back quickly with a wheeled office chair.

"That'll do, I guess."

"One more thing, Mike," Ron started, as he got me into the chair. I looked up at him. We've been over this ground, nobody prefaces anything good with 'One more thing…' and ends it with 'you've won a million bucks!!!!' It's always more along the lines of 'One more thing…I ran over your cat.' "Naw, maybe I'll just let you see for yourself," he said as he began to wheel me out of the room and down the hallway.

"Is it about Dad?" I asked nervously. We had lost Mom not so long ago and I was concerned that it might have been too much for him.

"Dad? Hell no. This zombie stuff has been the best

thing for him."

"Really? How the hell is a zombie apocalypse the best thing for anyone?"

"He's been doing what you have been doing Mike, protecting his own. It's brought a spark to his eye that I thought Mom's death had permanently extinguished. Come Spring he was planning on making a trek out to get you."

"Are you kidding me?" I asked incredulously.

Ron shook his head. "He's been worried sick about you guys. If the weather hadn't been so crappy he would have left a month ago. I've been barely holding onto him telling him that if you were alive you'd be trying to get back here."

"If?"

Ron shrugged his shoulders.

I shrugged my shoulders too. Hell, the Colorado Talbots almost bought the farm on Day One and it hadn't gotten much easier since then.

"So what then?"

We were turning into the kitchen. My eyes immediately teared up. The kitchen was packed way past fire code. Besides Tracy, Carol, Nicole, Justin, Travis, BT and Henry, there was also my Dad, my sister Lyndsey, her husband Steve and their son Jesse. Ron's wife Nancy stood to the side with their kids Meredith, Melissa and Mark. Standing somewhat at the position of attention, seemingly guarding the gathering was something that used to pass as my brother Gary.

His head was wrapped in what once was a red bandanna. It had been washed one too many times and now suspiciously resembled what one might buy for their eight year old daughter. His outfit was a hunter camouflage arrangement. On his camo clad pants was tied the largest bowie knife I had ever seen, and his mismatched combat boots were quite literally the kicker.

"What gives?" I whispered to Ron.

"He thinks he's Rambo."

"More like Gambo," I said without thinking. For all

the extended Talbot clan that was in presence there were some notable absences. Ron's oldest daughter Melanie was not here and neither was my brother Glenn, along with his wife and three kids.

"Have you heard anything?" I asked Ron as I scanned the room.

A look of sorrow and worry crossed his face. His tight lipped stare made me think an answer was not forthcoming. Finally he said, "Melanie called from Massachusetts the night it started, said her boyfriend had beat her up, even bit her a few times."

My heart sank.

Ron pressed on. "At the time I just figured he had been an asshole whose ass I was going to have to kick eventually, I just wanted my baby home and I told her that." He paused to wipe his hand over his eyes. "We haven't heard from her since then. I've driven the route down to Mass a couple of times since then, just trying to find her car. More for some closure I guess, than anything else. Then sometimes I think that maybe her boyfriend wasn't infected and had just drank too much and she needs my help." We both knew that was a lie. Melanie's boyfriend Dan was a born again Christian. I don't think he even listened to music unless it was of the Gospel variety.

"I can't get the picture of her cold and hurt huddled in some alleyway out of my head."

I reached my hand up and grabbed his. The pain wasn't lessened but mutual comfort was increased.

"What about Glenn?"

"Nothing."

Glenn was Gary's twin brother, he lived in NC and for a fleeting second I thought of calling Paul on my cell and seeing if he would stop in and check on him. A small sigh for all that had been lost escaped me. Luckily the room was noisy enough to cover up my transgression. I was spared any further insight as my dad got sight of me. He started to full on cry with relief when he saw me. My cheeks flamed but then I realized how would I feel if one of my kids was missing and there was no way to tell what had happened to them. My tear ducts matched him drop for drop. All in all it was an incredible night. I was home! Gambo was going to take some getting used to. I would learn later from Ron that something in Gary had broken when he lost the connection to Glen. He shook my hand once and then took up his vigil again by the front door.

I noticed a large red scrape on the side of his face, my spider man was revealed. Occasionally he would reach up and touch it only to pull back with a wince when he got near it.

"You should put some Neosporin on that," I told him later that night. I also thanked him for saving our lives.

I kid you not, he deepened his voice to tell me that he was alright and saving lives was his business.

"Mike, I thought you were the nutty one," BT said coming up to my side when there was a lull around my chair. "You whip these people up in a blender and you could make peanut butter."

"BT, I didn't just come into existence like this. I was carefully molded and sculpted."

"Apparently crafted by crazy artisans and they did a fine job," BT said looking around the cacophony that was the Talbot's. "Are we planning on staying here?"

I didn't realize that he was serious when I answered, "You're hilarious, man." Had I looked to see his response to my words, I would have seen him mouth the word 'Great' and it would have been used sarcastically.

My sister came up carrying a tray of what at one time may or may not have been some sort of edible food product. Right now it resembled something more along the lines of what Henry would evacuate after a particularly bad bout of bloody diarrhea.

"I made your favorite," she said, sticking the plate of something under my nose. It even smelled like the aforementioned waste product.

"My favorite what?" I asked seriously.

My sister laughed, thinking that I had just made a joke. Lyndsey had on occasion been known to burn water. She had once made raspberry jello that was green and nearly as hard as a brick. Her husband Steve, unbeknownst to my sister even though everyone else knew, had paid a substantial amount of money for a doctor to write up papers that he suffered from some rare genetic stomach disorder that only allowed him to eat take-out. Her son Jesse while growing up had found multiple sympathetic parents that would feed 'the starving boy' dinner. He had actually worked out a calendar of where he would eat on any given night.

Lyndsey and Steve's dog, Baxter, had suffered for all the discarded meals. He died young and not happy.

BT grabbed a cookie thinking it was the socially acceptable thing to do, and my sister beamed at him. I shook my head frenetically side to side at him, waving my arms over my head, telling him 'no.' It was too late; he brought the thing up to his mouth. My sister was nodding in the affirmative, silently willing him onward. I couldn't watch. I turned away as he nearly chipped a tooth biting down on what might have been a pebble chip. Maybe it was only Formica, that made more sense.

BT shifted it to his stronger back teeth, trying to get some leverage.

I'd had enough. "Lyndsey, I think Steve needs something."

As soon as Lyndsey turned away, BT flung that thing with a flick of his wrist like a skipping stone. It smashed into the wall behind Gambo, who thought we were now under attack as he dropped and rolled. He came back up with his knife at the ready. I put my face in my hands. 'Oh no, what have I got us into.'

Eventually the room quieted down once Gambo realized we weren't under attack and something akin to order was restored. The room quieted as all eyes once again turned to Nicole. She was an adept storyteller and she had left her audience wanting more.

"You want to stay for this?" Ron asked me. "How about a beer?"

Tracy pulled up a chair from the kitchen table and sat next to me so she could grab my hand.

"Any chance you have some Molson?"

Ron looked at me with that 'What do you think? face'. He was a self-made millionaire who lived a frugal life. I wouldn't be surprised if he pulled out a white can that had the word 'Beer' in stark black letters.

He handed me a can of Busch. "I see you're moving up," I told him sarcastically.

"Yeah, when I knew something was really wrong we went to Tozier's (the local grocery store) and damn near emptied it out."

"The end of the world and you couldn't splurge on something a little better?"

"What's wrong with Busch? It cost almost $4.50 a twelve pack."

"Is this a joke? Are you hiding the good stuff?" But I saw the futility in that tactic. Ron wouldn't needlessly spend money on a joke.

"What?" he asked.

I choked four of those things down as Nicole picked up her narrative from the Motel 6 to the Red Neck encounter. She had to stop on more than one occasion as she recounted what had occurred at Carol's homestead. The entire room was wrapped up in her story. This was the direction life was going, when families gathered around for storytelling. No more television or video games. The families that survived would be strengthened by the closeness of doing things the way they had been done in bygone eras.

Nicole had pushed on. In her story we now were at Camp Custer and it was looking like humanity had gained a toe hold; unfortunately it was all a lie. Nicole told of our escape from the camp and then of our time at the Powell farm. I wept silently as she told of Tommy's leaving. Tracy's hand pressed mine more firmly. I was in the grips of a burgeoning buzz as the story wrapped up. There was a collective inhalation as she finished, almost like everyone had forgotten to breathe.

Ron turned to me, not one to ever miss much. "How much time do we have until Eliza finds us?" he asked me directly.

"She's done with us, isn't she?" Carol asked anxiously. "What more could she want? She has her brother."

"That might have been the original intent," Ron answered her. "But she doesn't seem the type to let a transgression slide."

I nodded in assent. "I figure a month and half," I said, alluding to the amount of shots Justin possessed.

"That'll give us plenty of time to shore up some weak spots," my dad added.

"We'll have to get the electric fence up before Spring then," Ron said, thinking more out loud than telling anyone.

"Wait!" I said, standing on my wobbly legs. "You guys don't get it, we can't stay here."

Gary started to protest. "I've already lost one brother, I won't lose another."

"You can't know that," my dad said angrily to Gary. He then turned my way and looked like he was going to ground me. Ron gave me that condescending look that only an older brother can pull off.

"Guys, did you hear Nicole's story? Were you listening? Eliza took out a military base in less than a day, what do you think she'll do here?"

"What are you going to do Mike?" Ron asked. "Keep running? For the rest of your lives? Seems to me Eliza will be able to outlast you if she is what you say she is. No, you'll stay and we'll see this through to the end."

"That's easy for you to say now Ron. But when your family is in peril, what then?"

Ron looked more than a little pissed that I was questioning his authority or his ability to protect us all. "You know, you little pissant, it hasn't been all tea and roses before you got here, we've had our own trials and battles."

"How many Ron? A couple dozen maybe? Any speeders? Did they have a distinct, directed purpose? Were they being single mindedly ordered to end your lives?"

Ron's rage came to the surface. His fists clenched at his sides. He shook his head slowly in the negative. "None of those things, Mike. So what do you propose? Should we just let you, all of you, just walk out of our lives?"

"I will not risk your lives, any of you," I said sweeping my arm across the room, "for ours."

"You already did Mike," my sister said. "The second you walked up that road, we all became involved."

I sat back down defeated, but not beaten. A direct confrontation would not work, but Tommy had shown me how I could take care of this. We would leave when the opportunity presented itself.

CHAPTER THIRTY-FIVE - 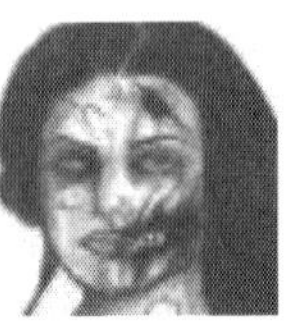

"Where is he, Tomas?" Eliza asked as she walked around the gurney Tommy was strapped to. Rivulets of blood poured from a half dozen lacerations on his chest and stomach. Tears of pain and fear cascaded down his face. "Come, come, Tomas I will find them soon enough. Once the boy runs out of his poison that blocks me." She spat.

"What did you do to Doc?" Tommy cried.

"Don't concern yourself with him. He has paid for what he has done to me as Michael must," she said as she dragged a fingernail through a particularly deep wound. Tommy screamed. "Now you can save us all some trouble, Tomas. Tell me where he is and I will end his worthless existence. I know you can see him."

Tommy shook his head violently from side to side. "NO!" he screamed in rage.

"Again." Eliza said almost sweetly to Durgan.

The crack of the bullwhip as it sliced through the air at supersonic speed crucified Tommy's flesh as it split it deeply. Blood welled in the newly formed crevice. Tommy's screams pierced the air.

Durgan had worked up a lather of sweat by the time Tommy had finally given Eliza something. Tommy hadn't meant to give her anything, and it wasn't exactly what she had hoped for, but it was a start and it might turn out to be better than what she had originally planned.

"You've done well, brother. You might be able to keep me from linking with Michael but I can pick through your thoughts as easily as I can my own," Eliza said as she licked a runnel of blood from his cheek.

Tommy sobbed inconsolably as she left him, tied to the bed and alone in the dark. "I'm sorry Auntie Marta," he wailed.

CHAPTER 36 - JOURNAL ENTRY 28 -

I came out of sleep violently. I could have sworn I heard Tommy and he didn't sound good at all. Trying to go back to bed now was beyond useless. I became fully awake as my feet hit the near freezing floor boards. In the best of times Ron kept his home a balmy 48 degrees in the winter. Now, as I watched my breath, I thought to grab an extra sweater, blanket, thermal underwear and electric socks. I was headed towards the pellet stove. I was going to stoke that stove so high it was going to turn cherry red. Then I laughed at myself. 'Who am I kidding? Ron probably has each individual pellet counted. That or he has the door to the stove padlocked. That would be just like him,' I thought, as I headed into the living room.

It was even worse. He was guarding the damn thing. I had to get closer before I realized my mistake. It was my father. He turned to look as I approached. The look of joy as I got closer warmed my heart enough to almost make me forget that the mucous in my nostrils was hardening from the frigidness.

"You look cold, come closer to the fire. Your brother would rather put on 4 jackets instead of burning fuel. He'd get away with it too, if it weren't for Nancy putting her foot down."

I dragged a chair close to my dad's. We sat there for long moments staring at the fire, neither of us saying anything. He broke the ice, almost literally.

"It sounds like you've had it rough, Mike."

I shrugged my shoulders.

"As much as I miss your mother, I'm glad she isn't here for this. This is no way for anybody to live. I was worried sick about you, Tracy and the kids. I felt helpless."

I nodded in agreement. "Been there a few times myself," I said commiserating with him.

"I suppose you have," he said, glancing over towards me. "We don't have much here, but we have each other." My dad turned back towards the fire, his eyes glistening.

Did he know I was planning on leaving? It sure seemed like it. "Dad, you don't understand."

"Michael, what don't I understand?" He turned back to me. "Do you think that you would do something for your family that I would not do for mine? Would you not stand with your brothers and sister as they would stand with you? Didn't the Marines teach you anything? We do not retreat."

"Yeah, but we withdraw strategically."

"Point taken," my dad said with a slight bow of his head. "Still, we are stronger together. We need to meet this threat head on."

"Dad, don't take me wrong. If I thought we had any chance of success I would gladly stay and fight but Eliza is unlike anyone any of us have ever encountered." My dad listened as I recounted my brushings with the Queen of the Dead. I'll give him this. He didn't ground me for lying.

"What are you planning on doing then?" my father asked. He would patiently hear me out. Whether or not he would let me act was still open for debate.

"Justin's shots have bought us some time. But none of that matters, I still have to go back and get Tommy."

"Sounds to me, son, like that boy was leading you along and into a trap the whole time."

"Dad, you might be right, maybe it did even start out like that. I don't know. If you met the kid you'd know there isn't a deceitful bone in him. He radiates love and warmth. He was like traveling with our own personal saint." My dad still looked skeptical. "Dad, I know what you must be thinking, but I loved the kid enough to adopt him. It wasn't a fluke. He wasn't tricking me into caring for him. Hell Dad, I don't know if I can even count how many times he saved our lives. I think now it's time to start evening the score."

"From what you said, can't you sit and wait for them to come here?"

"Possibly, in a month and half, the link with Justin and Eliza will be re-established. I don't want Justin to have to go through that again. If I can somehow bring some resolution before then, so much the better. For good or bad I never told Tommy exactly where we were going. I mean, I know he knew we were coming to Maine but other than that... ." I shrugged my shoulders. I kept my grim thoughts to myself, that at least she wouldn't be able to beat that information out of him. My soul took another dent thinking of that. "I haven't heard anything from him since he left."

"I hate to ask this Michael, but do you think he is still alive?"

I took an involuntary large gasp of air. I had thought of that possibility but hearing it verbalized struck heavily. "Dad, he has to be," I almost cried. "I'd know." But would I? All I had received from our connection was black nothingness, sort of like death.

"You can't put your family through that. You've got a pregnant daughter."

"Wait, you know?"

"Yeah, she told me."

"She hasn't even told *me*."

"Well that's probably because I'm infinitely more likable."

"Wonderful."

"But that's beside the point."

"May be beside your point, but I'm the one being poked with it."

"Michael, I'm trying to be serious."

"So am I."

"You're lucky your mother loved you, I would have made the stork fly on by if I saw you coming. Listen, you've got a pregnant daughter, a sick son and your youngest is barely hitting manhood. Are those the people you want to expose to danger?"

"Come on Dad, obviously not. I wish I could round up my old platoon and teach that bitch what a fire team is all about, but I don't have that luxury." I might be 45 but I can't even begin to convey the feelings of safety and warmth that flooded through me as my dad wrapped me in his arms. I almost wanted to suck my thumb.

"Will Nicole stay behind?"

"I'll ask her, Dad. I'll even try to convince her and her mother that they should stay here. I already know the answer I'm going to get."

"Can't you make them stay?"

"You're hilarious, have you met Tracy?"

My dad laughed. "How long, Michael?"

"Well not tonight for sure." My father looked sternly at me. He'd known me long enough to realize that getting a straight answer out of me could be damn near infuriating. "A couple of weeks," I told him.

"How are you planning on finding her?"

"That's never really been much of a problem. To tell you the truth, I'll just venture out and I can almost guarantee she'll take care of the rest."

He squeezed my knee and got up painfully. "I'm going to bed Michael. I love you."

"I love you too, Dad." I stayed another hour staring into the fire, trying to make some sort of contact with Tommy. My only reward was a blossoming headache.

CHAPTER 37 - JOURNAL ENTRY 29 -

The dismality of my mood did not lighten with the breaking of dawn. The shingles that my sister was going to try to pass off as French toast were not going to make matters any better. She somehow made them smell like steaming broccoli mixed with liver. I had to get out. I went into the garage, thankful that my father had kept my skates hanging up where I had left them. The peacefulness of being out on the ice was exactly what my soul needed. I grabbed my hockey stick and a couple of pucks and headed out to the pond, a mere 50 yards away.

It was cold but not nearly as frigid as Ron's house had been the night before. I was halfway to the edge of the ice, my head down checking my footing, when Gary scared the hell out of me.

"Going to do some skating, little brother?" I did a complete 360 looking for him. "Up here."

I looked up. He was about 15 feet high in a tree with a deluxe model hunter's stand. It was actually a pretty neat set up. It had a chair, a canopy roof, wind break walls all around and it must have even had a small heater in there too because he looked pretty toasty. I think I even saw a curing sleeve of meat, maybe salami. It was more a small tree house than a stand.

"Nice set up. You got heat in there?"

"Sort of, the Coleman lamp I've got running keeps it nice in here. Better than the house, that's for sure."

We both said "cheap bastard" at the same time. Who it was directed at was common knowledge.

"There enough room to sleep up there?" I asked him. He laughed, but I was serious.

"Have fun Mike, haven't seen anything around here

you need to be worried about. There's some deer on the other side of the pond but I haven't been able to get a clear shot at them."

"You don't mind if I skate? I don't want to scare them away."

"No, enjoy yourself, a couple of days ago I shoveled off a hockey rink."

"Sweet, thanks." I trudged on through the snow. My fingers froze as I laced up my skates. "Why has no one ever created Velcro laces for skates? Another million dollar idea I'll never be able to bring to fruition now." I said sourly.

"You say something?" my brother shouted. I had forgot how easily sound could travel over the pond. I shook my head in the negative.

The weather was crisp and had a bite to it, not like a grizzly bear mind you, more like a pissed off weasel. It was invigorating. Pulling the cold air deep into my lungs was somehow refreshing. I'll say this for the apocalypse, the air had gotten a lot cleaner since man's machinations no longer wheeled and spun. I could feel Gary's gaze on me for a while. Really wasn't a whole bunch else to look at, and then even I must have become boring because he started to belt out his rendition of 'Sister Christian' while listening to what appeared to be an ancient Walkman by the bulky look of it.

"Might as well get an old reel to reel," I muttered to myself as I finally finished lacing my skates. I dropped the puck on the ice, grabbed my stick and just flat out enjoyed the feeling of cool air sliding across my face as I glided on the ice. The sound of my blades cutting across the frozen water was interrupted only by my occasional less than stellar slap shots and Gary's high-pitched tone deaf crooning. It sounded like he was halfway through 'Welcome to the Jungle' by Guns and Roses, but I wouldn't attest to that fact in court. When I said aloud "Good thing American Idol can't hear this," I immediately wished I hadn't. That one malignant thought spiraled into thoughts about the host, Ryan Seacrest, and then right back to Tommy.

The thought of the kid missing and most likely with Eliza brought me to a complete halt. It also saved my life. I had been concentrating so hard on my skating and puck control I had not even checked my surroundings. Four zombies dressed like hunters were almost halfway across the pond. They had entered from across the other side. Their pace was hampered somewhat by the snow but they were now less than 25 feet away.

They had come upwind from me so that I could not smell them. My hope was that it was an unintentional coincidence, not that I had come across many of those lately. I quickly patted down my pockets. No gun. I absolutely could not believe my stupidity. It was just that I had come home, I should be safe, I shouldn't have to wear a gun constantly. Having a gun in the outside world had been such a necessity not having one was akin to a mother going to a grocery store with her infant and not bringing a diaper bag, who does that? "Only the ill prepared," I said aloud. "Yeah but without a diaper bag you only have a fussy smelly baby, without a gun you have death. Talbot, stop talking to yourself." Yep, I said that aloud.

Plan B: Get Gary's attention, he had a 30-30 and from this range it should be pretty easy pickings. I shouted until my throat felt like I had swallowed fish bones, but Gary was looking in the complete opposite direction down the access road and now singing some horrible nightmare equivalent of 'Every Rose Has a Thorn'. I made a snowball but unless I had a slingshot or Dwight Evan's arm (the star outfielder for the Red Sox in the 70's) I was never going to be able to hit him. The lead zombie had just entered onto the rink from the opposite corner. He immediately slipped and fell on his head. Somehow I didn't think a concussion was going to stop him.

"GARY!!!" I reached way down for that and put everything into it from my Marine Corps years. I would be sucking down Sucrets for three days to pay for that scream but it was worth it.

There must have been a lull on Gary's mix cassette

(yes it was a cassette) because he turned to see where the offending noise had come from.

"Zombies!" he screamed, his headphones still on.

"You think?"

"What?" he screamed again.

I motioned for him to take off the headphones.

"Oh sorry!" he screamed again. "Zombies," he said in a much more conversational tone with the ear gear off.

All four zombies had made it onto the shoveled ice. Their progress was greatly impeded but it would only be a matter of time. Gary lifted his rifle up, from this angle the barrel looked like a cannon.

"Umm, I'd rather you waited until I moved," I yelled, a little too late. His first round blew one of my pucks up.

"Was that your puck?"

"Are you kidding me!" I yelled at him.

"Bet I couldn't do that again if I tried."

"I really wish you wouldn't."

The sound of the shot reverberating through the woods brought some reinforcements from the Talbot clan. I had begun to punch holes through the snow with my skate laden feet. The zombies were halfway across the rink by this time. I was in no immediate danger of being caught but I honestly didn't want to dull my blades by walking on the ground. Trivial matter, sure I know that, but when's the next time I'm going to be able to take them down to the hardware store to get them sharpened?

Gary's next shot splintered the lead zombie's head in two. "Hell of a shot!" I yelled, getting away from the killing rink.

"Can't stand zombies, Mike!" he yelled back.

"I got that," I said, giving him the thumbs up.

My dad was on the porch watching, a look of concern on his face; the illusion of peace had been shattered.

My nephew Mark asked his dad, my brother Ron, something and then headed down to the edge of the pond with his gun. Looked like a .22 long rifle caliber. It's a relatively high velocity round but it is used mostly for small game. Now I'm not saying I'd want to get shot with one, I was just wondering how effective it would be against men. Travis and Justin immediately followed with much heavier calibers.

Mark's first shot skidded off the lead hunter zombie's head, a three inch swath of skin pulled back to reveal a gleaming shiny white skull. I thanked God I had not eaten Lyn's breakfast because I could not imagine that it would taste any better coming up than it had going down. Mark's next shot, much like Gary's puck crusher, could not be duplicated on a bet. It skidded to the left this time nearly making an equal skin flap. It looked like the zombie was trying to sprout a head visor. The whole front of his forehead was exposed in all its horrid glory. The small window of quiet was only broken by Gary's splashing vomit as it rained down from on high.

He, unlike the hunters was downhill; the smell of his tossed up salami would take that magically delicious deli meat off my menu for the remainder of my life.

"Sorry," he gurgled. There is something disturbingly fascinating about watching half digested round meat slices swirl through the air in a haze of brownish bile. My reverie was short lived as much larger rounds punched through the air. The Flapper fell in a puddle of his own making. Mark took a few more shots, actually felling one of the smaller zombies. Travis' shotgun ended the minor threat that had unveiled itself.

My dad had come down to the edge of the pond to see if he knew any of the men, but the gory nature of zombie killing can make even the most basic of identification damn near impossible.

"The big guy with the peeled back scalp looks like a guy I'd seen a few times in the post office. The other three, can't really tell." My dad looked more than a little upset. "Haven't had any this close to the house in over a week."

"We tend to have that effect," I said absently.

Gary's dry retching filled the air.

"You alright?" Ron asked him.

Something along the lines of "fine" was Gary's only response. A perimeter of brown now encircled the tree he was perched in.

Ronnie's youngest daughter Melissa ran out of the house to see what all the 'to do' was about. Like a typical teenage girl, she was way late to the party. All she got to witness was Gary's fragile constitution expressing itself.

"Oh my God, why is everyone out here watching Uncle Gary puke. Eww, that is so gross! It's way too cold out here. Why does Mark have a rifle? Do I smell gunpowder or is that Uncle Gary? Dad, are you going to get Aunt Lyndsey away from the stove, she's making the house smell like dead mice again! Mom says Mark has to clean his room. Can't you make my cell phone work again? I haven't heard from my friends in Massachusetts in forever. Do you think I could turn on the second generator, I really want to use a hair dryer. Are there dead guys over there? Oh gross, I'm so not cleaning that up." The whirlwind that was Missy immediately turned and fled back into the house. The scene was once again quiet, broken only by Gary's gurgling geyser.

Ron came down to inspect the situation, then looked over at me. "You had nothing to do with this little brother."

"Can you be so sure? Ron, she took down a fully fortified military base in a few hours."

"This is just a coincidence."

I wasn't nearly as convinced as he was. She couldn't have found us this quickly, could she? She had Tommy and if she could follow his link to us then that was really the answer, wasn't it? That's why I hadn't heard anything from the kid. He knew that too. "Oh Tommy." My gut was beginning to feel a lot like Gary's.

My sister poked her head out the door. "Breakfast!" she yelled. Gary threw up again. Now I don't know if it was in response to my sister's threat but his timing was impeccable.

CHAPTER 38 - JOURNAL ENTRY 30 - 

"You can't be serious, Mike?" Tracy asked. I stopped packing to look over at her. "You don't honestly think those zombies were from Eliza?"

"They probably weren't, at least not this time, but it really is only a matter of time. Eventually Justin's shots will run out or Tommy is going to cave and the mind highway is going to open at that point. Eliza will just waltz on down the yellow brick road."

"Nicole won't stay behind, and are you going to be the one to tell BT he's staying here?"

"It's for the best, and I really wish you'd stay here too," I said grabbing her shoulders tenderly.

She shrugged my hands off. "Not a chance. Tommy has as much access to me as he does to you, and I don't trust you not to get into trouble."

"But I've been doing it for so long, why stop now," I asked facetiously.

"Yeah, I just wish you weren't in such a rush to hook up with it again."

"This is my ... our family I cannot bring her to them. She's already taken Tommy away. I will not let her do us more harm."

"Do you think you can get him back?"

"I have to try." Which loosely translated to, 'I doubt it, but I'll die trying.' Now the hard part of the equation was, was I willing to sacrifice my two sons in a vain attempt?

"If Nicole stays behind, can't Tommy link to her?" Tracy asked.

It was a valid question. Tommy was so completely enamored with her, he could barely say 'hi.' Making that intimate linkage through the mind would probably shut him down. I smiled wryly at that thought. I missed that kid. So much so that I would be willing to try one of his cherry frosted sausage Pop-Tarts.

"I'll tell Nicole, but you get the pleasure of telling BT."

"I'd rather eat Lyndsey's cooking!" I groused.

"Come on, be realistic. BT will only kick your ass. Your sister's cooking can kill you."

"True. What about your mom?"

"I think she'll be thrilled to stay here. She'll be able to watch over Nicole, and truth be told I think she might be a little smitten with your dad."

"Really?"

"Why not? You had to get your good looks from somewhere."

Man, that woman knew how to stroke my ego. I was the violin and she was the world-class musician. The real damned problem was that I knew I was being played. I just couldn't do anything about it. "Wouldn't that make us brother and sister if they hooked up?"

"First off I don't think they'd use the term 'hooking up' and second, ewww, what is wrong with you?"

I grew serious. "You know, Tracy, I'd prefer you stay here also."

"I know you would,." she said, stroking my cheek. She turned to go downstairs and talk to her daughter.

That was the end of that discussion. How the hell was I going to tell BT and survive? I did the long march down the hallway. Nicole was on the couch wrapped up in her grandmother's arms, both had tears streaking down their faces. BT was sitting across watching the entire scene unfold. He looked over at me suspiciously. "Don't you even think it, Talbot." He fairly thundered. "I can't eat any more of your sister's food," he added in a conspiratorial tone.

Melissa had been standing at the entry to the living room. "It'll be alright, Nicole, this way I can brush your hair and then Dad will have to let us turn on the extra generator for the hair dryers and then we can give each other pedicures and manicures, it will be amazing! So what do you think of Justin Bieber? I always thought he was a little too pretty, but I'd still go out with him. Did you watch the Twilight movies? Oh, why couldn't we have had vampires or werewolves instead of stinky zombies and then there was this one time when this boy Matt kissed me and my whole face felt hot. He was super cute and he was going out with Cathy Jacobsen, I can't stand her but I would have kissed him anyway." As Melissa rambled on, Nicole cried harder.

"Mike, my man. Come on," BT said pleadingly.

"BT, I can't think of anyplace I'd rather have you than by my side, but you need to heal."

"Then wait."

"We don't have that kind of time my friend. She'll find us long before then. It has to be this way. She won't be expecting me to come for her."

"Said the mouse to the eagle," BT said dejectedly.

"Appreciate the sentiment," I retorted sarcastically.

"You know what I meant."

"Yeah, unfortunately it's a fitting analogy."

"I'm going with you," I heard from behind me. I didn't turn around, I knew who the artificially deep voice belonged to.

"Thanks, Gary," I said, looking squarely at BT. I was going to add that this was a family thing, but hell if BT wasn't family.

"You dead set on this expedition?" Ron asked. I merely nodded. I didn't want to do it. I had to do it. "I've got something for you then," he said as he quickly left the room.

My hope was for a cloak of invincibility, the shortwave radio transmitter he gave me was the next best thing.

My dad steered clear of me for the next two days leading up to our departure. For as much as he stayed away, BT made up for it, damn near crawling up my ass. My dad's avoidance hurt. Every time I walked into a room he was in, he would walk out. I don't even think he was doing it intentionally. Maybe it was his subconscious way of reconciling my upcoming departure. Nicole was disconsolate. Her hormones were already out of whack because of the pregnancy and her family leaving her behind was not sitting well. The only thing that kept her from constantly barraging me with her pleas was a morning sickness that thankfully lasted all day. More times than not she was relegated to the bathroom.

Carol was fast becoming a favorite within the Talbot household. She had gently but forcibly pushed my sister out of the kitchen. Much silent cheering ensued.

I had no idea what day it was when I awoke on the morning of our departure. It was cold but the sun was shining and the sky was a brilliant blue. Still, I couldn't shake the darkness around my heart. Old words haunted me and I wasn't listening to them. 'The sacrifice of the one for the many.' I was endangering five lives for Tommy. How would God transcribe this in his vast bookkeeping ledgers? Folly or wisdom?

The entire clan was in the kitchen patiently awaiting whatever divine concoction Carol was preparing for breakfast.

"You always were late to rise," my dad said, the first words he had spoken to me in days.

"It can't be 6:30," I said in my defense.

"6:48," Gary threw in for good measure. The face paint he had smeared on his face and lips were getting all over the breakfast roll he was trying to eat.

"That can't be good for you." Lyndsey told him.

I wanted to tell her it was probably better for him than what she had been feeding him but I couldn't get the words to come out.

BT looked miserable, and the distant retching noises from the bathroom told me Nicole felt like he looked.

"I wish you weren't going little brother," Ron said, getting up from the table. His wife Nancy came up behind him, placing her head on his shoulder as I wrapped my arms around them both. There were no words that could sufficiently express how I felt. My emotions were raggedly torn in two. I was stuck between duty and a hard place.

One by one we said our goodbyes. The sun was climbing higher into the sky, my misgivings digging deeper, until it finally became my father's turn. I had seen the man cry twice in his life. First when my mom had died and now. I did not like what that implied.

"You come back here, all of you. Do you understand me?" he said through his tears. "Make sure you bring your brother back too."

I silently nodded my head up and down. Words would have been intertwined with sobs and then it would have just been a blubbery mess. This was harder than fighting zombies. Heartache loss and homesickness hurt more than war. There was no time to feel emotions in the heat of battle. You merely survived longer than your enemy. I had lived to die another day and that's really the best any of us can do. We were leaving home…again. Some of us, probably all of us, wouldn't make it back.

CHAPTER THIRTY-NINE - 

Eliza strode into the room. She could smell the fear pheromones exude off of the men as they stood patiently waiting for her arrival. She did not acknowledge any of them as she laid down her order. "Prepare your men, we leave in ten minutes."

"Eliza… mistress," one of the bolder men started. "I, um, that is some of the men are concerned over your hold on the zombies after what happened at the base."

Eliza crossed the length of the room in less than a blink, her left hand on the top of the man's scalp as she bent his neck far beyond God's original design. Her teeth sank deeply into his neck as the snap of vertebrae echoed off the walls. Nobody stirred as she drank her fill. When she was done, she allowed the empty carcass to fall hollowly to the floor. As she exited the room, the remaining men scrambled to be ready by her deadline.

Fifty military troop transport trucks, laden with zombies, rolled away from the military base that was up until recently, the largest humanity hold-out in the United States. What little remained was burning uncontrollably. Twenty or so human stock had been rounded up as prisoners. Sort of like a meals on wheels for Eliza.

Durgan drove the lead humvee. Along with him were Eliza and Tommy. The malevolence that was Eliza was unaffected by the underlying current of virtue that issued forth from Tommy. Those first few days, Tommy had pleaded with the being that looked like his sister. He had learned the hard way, the thing that possessed her body now wanted nothing more to do with him unless it furthered her quest. Tommy had dozens of slashes that were weeping puss and blood and they stung every time he moved. His pain and discomfort seemed about the only thing that brought any emotion from his sister, and it wasn't the kind he was hoping for.

She turned back to look at him, her eyes blazing with fury. "You know little brother, when I am finally healed, I have decided I will fully turn you."

Tommy's eyes snapped wide open. He shook his head furiously from side to side.

"Oh yes," she said, dragging a nail across his cheek bringing up an angry red welt. "We'll be able to have all those fun times that we missed out on all these years." Her throat mimicked a laugh. Her eyes never moved from his. "I think when I finally catch up with Michael Talbot, it would be fascinating for me to watch you drain him of his life." Eliza grasped his face in her hand. His struggles ceased as he realized the futility. "We will rule this new world, little brother, you and I. No more hiding in the shadows."

Durgan couldn't help but notice she did not mention him in that equation. To question Eliza, however, invoked death.

CHAPTER 40 - PAUL AND ALEX - 

For the first three hours since Alex had driven away from the Talbots, he was completely convinced he had made the singular biggest epic mistake of his life. This wasn't about losing money on a sporting bet or picking up the wrong brand of tampons at the store (both of which could land you in a lot of hot water). No, this was about lives, his, his wife's and most importantly, his two small children.

"Marta, this doesn't feel right,." He said over the rumble of the 500 hp diesel engine. The further they got away from the comforting sphere of Tommy's presence, the more the harsh reality of the world drew closer.

"I, too, wish that Tommy had come with us," she said, staring straight through the windshield.

Alex worried that she might be regressing into that near catatonic state she had been in before they got to Little Turtle. Everything had started to turn for the better for the Carbonaras when they arrived there and met Mike and Tommy. Now all that was gained was lost.

"Should I turn around?" he asked Marta.

"I still do not think he would come with us, that Michael Talbot has some sort of hold over him," she said, Michael's name coming out more like a swear word than a means of identification.

Alex didn't think that was the case at all, more like the polar opposite, but he was not going to fight with his wife. The last time he had won she wasn't even there. It had been more of a moral victory. "I meant more along the lines of going with them."

Marta did not answer for a few ticks longer than was expected in the situation. He held out hope that she might be considering his request. That was a short lived dream. She turned to look at him, dark ringed eyes narrowed to half their normal size, her nostrils flared open, her mouth pinched down to a line. It was not an attractive pose, it was no 'Magnum' from Zoolander. Alex had seen it twice before. Once when the youngest had just been born and he told her that he and a bunch of friends were going to a strip joint, and the second time had been when he told Marta the day before, his mother came to visit for two weeks. Those two transgressions had cost him dearly in kowtowing and flowers. And right now he wouldn't be able to make amends because he hadn't seen a florist in months.

"Michael Talbot is the devil," she spat. "Death has gotten fat and lazy merely following in Michael's wake. Is it not bad enough he has taken my nephew into the depths of el infierno with him. You do not think that is payment enough?! You think he needs to have our two pequenos also?" She was fairly crying now. "El es el Diablo," she muttered, making the sign of the Trinity on her chest.

Marta only reverted to her native tongue under times of great distress. The three days after the zombie invasion were laden with a steady stream of the Rosary Prayer's, Our Father's and Hail Mary's. He even thought he recognized some paganism mixed in and they were all in Spanish. No, going back to find Mike was not going to be an option, unless of course he could come across an industrial sized bottle of Ambien. He could slip a few in her water every day, what she didn't know... 'Yeah and when she finally woke up and realized what was happening she'd slip a nail file through the small of my back,' he thought. It still seemed like the right thing to do, even if he could almost feel the grooved surface of the small metal utensil dragging against the jagged edges of his lacerated vertebrae.

After another hour of uncomfortable silence Alex pulled the truck over. Marta merely looked over at him. "Bathroom break," he said as he slid out of the truck.

They had no sooner come to a complete stop then Paul rolled open the big door in the back. He jumped down and began popping and stretching his back and legs, his gun left forgotten within the confines of the trailer. Alex couldn't help but remember that Mike's first priority every time they stopped was to check the integrity of their perimeter. Paul could have been eaten twice before he finished his routine.

"Hey Alex," Paul said, bending at the waist to stretch out his hamstrings.

"Just what I wanted to see… your ass," Mrs. Devereaux said as she reached the edge of the trailer. "Are you going to keep pretending you're a 25 year old athlete or are you going to help me down off this truck?"

Paul stood up, looking straight at Alex. "She hasn't quit bitching for the last three hours."

Alex was extremely thankful he was the only one that knew how to drive the truck. The punishment he took steering the big rig was paltry compared to being stuck in the back with that witch.

"I wish that BT fellow were still here," she started. "Those blacks know how to drive. Mexicans on the other hand…" she finished off by looking straight at Alex.

"You're welcome," Alex said, walking away. Alex wished she *had* gone with Mike, because Mike would have definitely turned around if only to be rid of her wicked tongue.

Erin, Paul's wife, ultimately helped Mrs. Devereaux off the truck. "You could have done better, my dear," Mrs. Devereaux said to her.

"You're welcome," Erin replied exasperatedly.

Joann, then Jodi, the young mother with three kids, came next. April, whose last amorous affair ended in the death of her latest fling, only came out when she was absolutely sure no one was getting eaten. April hadn't slept well in days; her eyes looked like she had already ended up as the trailer trash she was destined to become, and her abusive husband with the wife beater t-shirt had once again shown her the business end of his knuckles.

Alex couldn't help but feel that he was on the end of a practical joke gone completely awry. He had willingly left a trained Marine, his two crack shot sons, the largest man he had ever seen in his life and a boy who might have a direct connection to Dios, for this rag tag group. He shook his head. He had to go back, this was a death sentence. Marta would have to listen to him and she may have, if what happened next never transpired. The next few moments, ultimately made him forget to even bring it up.

Alex rounded the truck to find Jodi and her three kids, Eddy who was 8, his younger sister Renee 4 and their infant sister Penelope, but something wasn't quite right. Her kids were up against the truck and she was a few feet away sobbing uncontrollably. The revelation struck Alex immediately but still ultimately too late. It was a firing squad, composed of a deranged mother and her unsuspecting children. She had grabbed a pistol from the small arsenal they possessed in the trailer and was waving it around violently.

"God has forsaken us," she said to Alex.

"Wait Jodi there's still…"

"Hope?" she laughed. "Not for us. We're dead already. We just haven't realized our true potential yet. I will not allow my children to become those demons," she said, referring to the zombies.

Alex wondered if that was what they truly were. "Jodi, don't do this. They're your children. For the love of God..."

"You don't understand, Alex, I'm doing it FOR the love of God."

Paul rounded the corner to see what was happening. "Holy shit!"

Her eyes barely glanced over towards him. Her attention swung back to her children, who were becoming increasingly distraught over the amount of emotions being issued forth, even if they didn't understand what was truly happening.

"Mom, I'm scared," Jodi's oldest son Eddy said. "Can we come with you?" he said, referring to bridging the physical gap between them now.

"Oh honey, we are all gonna be going together," she said, referring to something much vaster and catastrophic.

"Jodi wait!" Alex shouted, fearful that the conclusion to this macabre scene was rapidly approaching.

"Don't you dare come any closer!" she yelled shrilly.

By now all of the occupants of the truck were behind Paul watching in grisly fascination. Even Mrs. Devereaux, who always found a way to interject the wrong word at the wrong moment, was silent.

Erin came to the forefront. "Jodi, those are your children and you're scaring them." By now all three of the children were crying inconsolably.

"This is for their own good, Erin," Jodi said clearly.

"What is for their own good?" Erin asked with alarm in her voice.

Jodi never answered directly, she let the roar of her gun finish her statement. Alex didn't know whether to turn and run away or run forward to stop the travesty as it was taking place. One second a gurgling crying rotund bundle of joy disintegrated into a burst form of human parts and down feathers as the sleeping bag he was swaddled in ruptured. Jodi's gun did not stop as she swung it slightly to the left and drove a bullet into the awaiting mouth of her daughter. The look of betrayal was immediately wiped clean from Renee's face as the back of her head erupted onto the trailer bed. The gun roared again as Eddy ducked under the truck, the bullet coming dangerously close to his leg.

It was April that reacted the quickest, knocking Jodi off of her feet. The gun went off one more time. April rolled over covered in blood, none of which was hers. Jodi lay still, a fatal wound pumping out her life, one heartbeat at a time.

Her eyes shifted over to April's. "Do you smell rotten eggs?" and said no more.

"Brimstone," Mrs. Devereaux said, her eyes as large as saucers.

Eddy had buried himself deep into Joann's midriff.

They were both shaking.

Paul's face nearly matched the color of the snow. "Do we bury them? Do we have shovels?" Then he threw up.

"We will place them in the snow and say a prayer. It is the best we can offer them right now," Alex said.

Paul managed to nod in agreement, even with his head between his legs. Alex held it in as he dragged Jodi over to the embankment and still held a tight grip as he picked up the small girl. It was when he got to the infant that all his composure ran in floods out of his system. He fell to his knees as he placed the remains of the infant boy in the snow bank. "God, I don't understand!" he shouted. "Why would you save them, for this!" His shoulders quaked. Paul gently helped him up.

It was long moments before any of them could speak. It was finally Paul that managed. "God, I know that I have my doubts about your existence but if you are there, please allow these two children to enter into Heaven's Gate and show your mercy unto their mother. She thought she was doing what was right. Amen." He wouldn't swear that his prayers were answered, but he felt better for saying it.

Marta was sitting in the passenger seat when Alex finally got in. She kept her gaze straight ahead and did not even acknowledge his presence.

'Three hours in,' Alex thought, 'and we've already lost three people and my wife is on the verge of a nervous breakdown.' The red stain of death faded in his rearview mirror as he put the truck into gear and sped down south and away from this tragedy. All thoughts of Mike were pushed far back into the linings of his brain. It would be far too late to turn around by the time that thought came up again.

That first night they stayed in an old gas station. The glass building was not what Alex would consider an optimum place to hole up, but fueling the truck's tanks with a hand pump had taken almost an hour and he was exhausted. Eddy, and April for that matter, cried for most of the night. This was one of the old school service facilities that hadn't yet figured out that the real money lay in selling tacquitos and slushees. This place smelled stale, like old motor oil and sweat. The Slim Jim beef snacks display looked long empty.

It was cold and the few emergency blankets on the shelves would have a hard time keeping a cat warm. At a time when the travelers should have been huddling for warmth, they were all lost in their own thoughts. Each of them marked out their individual nooks, putting as much distance as they could between themselves. Alex offered to take first watch. Mrs. Devereaux, who had never taken a watch before, told him that he looked exhausted and that she was willing to do it.

Alex couldn't help himself and he didn't mean to be as harsh in his thoughts as he was, but it came out all the same. 'Bitch has a soul.'

Mrs. Devereaux knew that not many people liked her, and to be quite honest that was alright with her because she wanted very little to do with humanity. Her bastard husband had become a cliché, having run off with his twenty-something secretary. 'I knew he was full of shit when he said that Viagra prescription was for us,' she thought bitterly. The last time they had sex, George Senior had been in office. Not only had her husband run off, he had managed to hide all their assets beforehand. She had barely been able to scrape together enough to buy the run-down little town home in Little Turtle. She wouldn't be eating cat food anytime soon but her days of caviar and pearls were long over.

She had never been able to reconcile to the fact that she was now living in the type of housing that her servants had. This wasn't her station; she was above this. She had grabbed as many of her possessions out of her mansion as she could before the sheriff threw her out. Her townhome was crammed full of mink stoles, rare paintings, statues of varying sizes and antique furniture. If she had sold half, she would have wanted for nothing but she had already lost so much she could not fathom parting with any more.

Mrs. Devereaux had no time for religion. Much like

Karl Marx, she felt it was the opiate of the masses. It was for the poor fools who had nothing in this lifetime and could only hope for the promise of a better afterlife. She knew better. There was only *now*. Take what was needed now. There is no judgment at the end. Your actions are not balanced and weighed. You have one run through. This wasn't practice for a higher purpose. She had lived her entire life under that premise. She knew others thought her a bitch and worse. She really did not care. More times than not she got what she wanted; it did not matter who got upset. It was dominion over others, that was how the animal world was set up. You ran the machine or the machine ran you, and she much preferred the role of decision maker. That, of course was up until today when she had witnessed a young mother murder two out of her three children. The burnt egg smell could only refer to sulphur, and sulphur meant brimstone. Everything she believed had immediately come into question. Were there now consequences for one's actions? Was this a new development or had it always been like this?

"Should have stayed with Michael," she cackled softly. "He might be a prickly S.O.B. but he'd keep me alive a lot longer than these buffoons." That was her last thought before she fell asleep, her head pressed up against the cold glass.

The sunshine was diffused through the grime streaked windows and was further hindered by the bodies that pressed against the outside windows. Mrs. Devereaux let out an involuntary scream as she opened her eyes only to be facing an opaque, rheumy puss leaking eye. Alex was the first to react, Paul was close behind him.

Alex scrambled out of his foil blanket. Ten to fifteen zombies were in a small cluster around the spot Mrs. Devereaux had previously been occupying. "Oh mi madre," he said worriedly.

"Whoa, shit," Paul said, no more alarmed than if someone had burnt his English muffin.

They had learned their lesson in Vona. The truck was

parked right up against the store. Anything wider than 5 inches was going to have a hell of a time getting through. With so few travelers now, fitting them all in the cab for emergency purposes would not be a problem. Eddy began to scream uncontrollably, either from waking and realizing his family was no more or because zombies were at the window. The noise seemed to agitate the zombies, who began to bounce again and again off of the windows. The small store began to vibrate from the effect.

"We should go," Erin said to Paul.

"You're right, this frozen indecision is going to get us killed," Paul replied.

"What?" Alex asked him.

"This shit. We're sitting here watching zombies trying to break in and we might as well be sitting on our hands. Mike would have someone posted to watch them while the rest of us grabbed anything that was useful and we made our hasty escape. Mike would have stopped yesterday from happening."

Marta made the sign of the trinity on her chest.

"You can't know that, Paul," Alex said defensively.

"What were we thinking?" Paul replied, a look of frustration etched across his face.

"We were thinking we wanted to get to our families as much as he wanted to get to his own. We still do."

"Will we?" Joann asked.

A spider thin crack developed in the pane of glass directly opposite them. "I think maybe we should discuss this later, Alex said hurriedly. "Everyone in the truck."

The service station was now in the hands of the zombies. The small loss should have meant nothing to Alex but it rankled him all the same. He wanted to draw a line in the sand but the tide had already shifted and the beach was covered.

They drove for a couple of miles with the nine of them in the front and the sleeping quarters. Even Mrs. Devereaux somehow found this tangle of humanity comforting. The cold of the night was quickly replaced with the heat of the living.

"I've been thinking," Alex said. "Maybe it's time we found something a little smaller to drive. Something a little easier on the kidneys, something we can all take turns driving."

"Yeah, I won't miss sitting in the back bouncing around like a super ball," Erin added.

"I wish I had a super ball," Eddy sniffed.

Erin hugged him tight. "I'll get you one the next time we stop."

"Will we still be together?" Eddy asked.

Alex hadn't thought about it much but the kid's question made sense. They would be splitting up again in the next couple of days.

"Are we still planning on once again halving our numbers?" Mrs. Devereaux asked incredulously.

"That's been the plan all along. I don't see why we should change it now," Paul answered her.

"What of myself, Joann, April and Eddy?" she asked.

"You can choose who to stay with, or obviously you can keep going on."

Mrs. Devereaux looked over dubiously at Paul. "Just how long do you think any of us would survive on our own?"

Paul had reached his limit. His stress meter had always ridden a little higher than the national average and these extraordinary circumstances certainly had not helped matters. He red-lined. "You know what!? I've been making mistakes since this all started. Mike told me that if there was ever a national emergency, I was supposed to get Erin and Rebel and get to his house as fast as I could. Well what did I do? I got my family trapped in our attic. I got our dog killed. I damn near killed Mike's son when they came to rescue us, and what does Mike do for me? He saves Erin and me. He gives us a relatively safe place to stay and makes sure we have food to eat. Then when everything goes to hell, what does he do? He saves us all, all of us! Then what do we do?

We leave him. We leave the most capable person who could get us through all of this. I watched a woman damn near kill her entire family yesterday. Now I'm not saying Mike could have prevented it. That woman had lost hope, hope that there was a better future for her children. But Mike brings us that hope. Maybe she would have felt that hope long enough at least to push on to the next day and the next. Let's not forget last night. Mrs. Devereaux takes first watch and nobody thought to relieve her. We were lucky it was only a dozen zombies, what happens next time?"

"Eliza is following him though," April said meekly. "Or at least his son."

"That's really the reason we all left, isn't it," he said, stating a fact. "We were afraid, we were cowards. We took what we thought was going to be the easier path."

"Now see here," Mrs. Devereaux started. "We are not cowards because we want to survive."

"You *would* think that." Paul shot back. Mrs. Devereaux was more stung by the words than she thought she would be. "It's Mike's hour of need and we abandoned him. I can guarantee he would not have done that to anyone of us, including you, Mrs. Devereaux. I consider him my brother and I walked away." Erin hugged him tightly but he gently pushed her away. He felt disgusted with himself.

"It's too late to turn around now Paul," Alex said practically.

"Survival is a powerful motivator," Joann told the group.

"Yes, but did we increase or decrease our odds when we left?" Paul asked.

The group drove on another fifteen minutes in utter silence before Alex started to gently apply the brakes.

Paul saw a white panel van up ahead on the side of the road. Alex pulled up alongside it. Paul hopped down from the truck and quickly realized his mistake. The van was still running. Paul put one foot on the running board, prepared to regain the safety of the cab if things went wrong.

"Stop right there, mister!" a voice shouted from the tree line.

Paul could almost feel the steel sights of a rifle press against the small of his back. Paul turned back around with his hands in the air.

"Put your arms down. I didn't say this was a stick up. Don't go reaching for anything though, this thing's liable to go off."

"What's going on?" April asked, unrolling the window.

A whistle of approval issued once again from the tree line. "Whoowee, you're traveling in some fine company," the disembodied voice shouted. The truck window immediately rolled up. "I haven't seen a live woman in weeks! Although some of the dead ones have been alright, bad manners though, always wanting to eat before dinner." A loud laugh ensued. "What are you doing in these parts? You weren't planning on taking my ride where you, because rudeness can get you killed."

Alex came around the front of the truck, rifle in hand.

"Not sure who invited you to the party," came the voice. "You're completely overdressed. Now put down the party favor before someone gets hurt."

"I'd rather not," Alex answered back shakily.

"Now I understand your hesitation, I really do, especially in these times. Nary a person you can trust, least of all some crazy bastard hiding in the woods. Seeing as I have a fully automatic machine pistol in my possession and that looks like a bolt action 30-30, I figure I can get off a good hundred or so rounds before you can do two. You don't really know where I am and you two are as clear as cable TV, so what say we start over?"

Alex laid his rifle on the ground and proceeded to put his hands over his head.

The laughing ensued. "Now like I told your friend. This isn't a stick up. I just want to make sure nobody gets hurt, 'specially me, if you get my meaning. Now first things first, is that girl you have with you of a legal age?"

"What?" Alex asked confused.

"The one that looked out the window, is she of an age to be legally wooed?"

"What?" Alex again. "What the hell is wooed?"

"Do I have to spell it out to you man! Some considered me a very dapper chap until of course they tried to eat all my vitals."

"This guy is nuts," Paul whispered to Alex.

"Yeah, and he has a directional microphone," came the voice from the woods.

"Wonderful," Paul sighed.

"I know, isn't it? Now seeing as it appears that you two wanted to pilfer my ride and that I am basically the law unto myself, I have two options."

There was a long pause.

"Umm, this is where you two are supposed to ask what the options are."

"Okay, I'll play," Paul said. "What are these options?"

"I can kill you where you stand." Paul and Alex tensed. "Damn near made you both piss your pants didn't I?" he cackled again.

"Fucking hilarious!" Paul yelled hoping that the increased volume hurt their captor's ears.

"Or you can let me come with you."

"Well, let's see." Alex said. "You kill us or we let you come with us. Hmm, let me think."

"Ah, not really funny Alex," Paul said, putting his hands back up in the air.

"Who are you?" Alex asked.

"Answer me first."

"Fine, you can come with us," Alex said.

"Great, I was starting to get a little lonely." It was tough to describe the man that walked out of the woods being that he was fully clothed in a gilly suit. (A specially designed camouflage for elite snipers.) "They call me Mad Jack. Well actually I call myself Mad Jack. I was going to go with Mad

Max but that Mel fellow already used it and I wanted something unique."

"Is that a toy?" Paul asked, pointing at the red tipped 'machine pistol' Mad Jack was holding.

"It is most certainly not a toy!" Mad Jack said indignantly. "It shoots air soft pellets at 325 feet per second at the cyclical rate of 125 rounds per minute. It can cause quite the stinger if it hits a vital area."

"Crazy Jack might have been a better name," Alex said, grabbing his rifle off the ground.

"What are you doing out here Cra...I mean Mad Jack?" Paul asked.

"Had to take a piss, been drinking since the sun came up."

"With a directional microphone?" Alex asked.

"Oh yeah, let me get that." Mad Jack turned back around and went into the woods.

"He's friggen crazy, Paul. We should just get out of here."

"Still have my ear piece on!" Mad Jack yelled back from the woods.

"Just kidding," Alex replied.

Mad Jack came out of the woods with an impressive array of equipment. "I was a techie nerd. Worked for the State Department before the biters came. Been ransacking Radio Shacks ever since."

Now that the threat was over, Paul walked over to look in the van to see what wares Mad Jack might possess. "Holy shit!" Paul exclaimed.

Mad Jack looked down at the ground. "Yeah, I really like Schlitz."

"Must be twenty or thirty cases of the stuff."

"Thirty-two." Mad Jack answered.

"I'll ride with MJ," Paul said happily.

Alex walked up to Mad Jack just as he pulled off his headgear. He looked to be somewhere in his late twenties and as far as men go would be considered on the plus side of the good looking column. Not Brad Pitt but definitely better than Quasimodo. The relief in MJ's eyes was evident. He had been alone for a long time. They shook hands.

"What brings you out this way, Mad Jack?" Alex asked.

"Had an apartment in Kansas City before the city burned to the ground. Been on the road ever since. Seen some things that I can't unsee," he answered vacantly.

"That's the way of the world now," Paul answered, coming up to the duo. "Is that the only weapon you've been using?" Paul asked, pointing to the pellet gun.

"This thing is bad assed," Mad Jack said, plowing some rounds into the side of the tractor trailer. They bounced off hollowly. "See!" he said proudly.

"How?" Paul asked, shaking his head, meaning how had MJ survived so long.

After a few moments when the occupants of the truck realized that there was no immediate threat, they took the opportunity to stretch their legs and to meet the stranger.

Mad Jack could not keep his eyes off of April. She didn't seem to mind all that much but she remained guarded all the same.

"Oh, get a room." Mrs. Devereaux said, lighting a cigarette.

Mad Jack blushed.

"We really should get going," Marta said to Alex. Alex was inclined to agree. Standing in the open was an invitation for trouble.

"I'm glad you're letting me come with you," Mad Jack blurted out.

"Yeah, it's a good thing we said yes," Paul stated sarcastically. "It would have been a bitch treating all those red welts if you had opened fire."

"Which direction you headed?" Joann asked.

"Whichever way you are. I've only been wandering since I left home," MJ told her.

"Oh great, another mouth to feed for nothing," Mrs.

Devereaux said.

"As opposed to all you bring to the table," April said sharply.

Paul would argue that they were both dead weight but he was not going to get in the middle of a catfight.

Mad Jack spoke up before things got really heated. "I know how to stop the zombies."

"That settles that. Let's get going," Alex said.

THE END...FOR NOW

BEFORE THE AFTERWORD - MIKE & RON -

It was a typical fall night in New England, mid-40's and cool. Mike was enjoying the start of his sophomore year at the University of Massachusetts, which typically involved entirely too much partying and entirely too little studying. His roommate and best friend Paul was at a social function for his girlfriend Amy's Sorority house. Mike's girlfriend at the time, Jamie, had gone back home to North Attleboro for the weekend. As was typical, Mike's dorm room door was open and The Who was singing loudly about Joining the Band over the stereo.

"Mike! Mike! Turn that down."

Mike's face was buried in a Sports Illustrated and had not heard Peter Cables from the room two doors down. Pete actually had to grab Mike's shoulder before he realized that someone else was in the room.

"Hey Pete!" Mike yelled.

"You mind?" Pete asked heading to the stereo.

"No, go ahead," Mike said putting his magazine down.

With the volume down to a dull roar, a somewhat normal conversational tone could be taken. "Hey Mike what you got going on tonight?" Pete asked.

"Whole bunch of nothing. Paul's at some dance and my girl's gone home."

"Me, Brian and Dean are going to get an ounce of 'shrooms;' you want to go in on it?"

"I'm in!" Mike got up, closed up his room and went on over to Pete's room.

"Hey Mike," Dean said. "Want a beer?" he asked, opening up a mini fridge stuffed to the gills with Budweiser.

At that time, Mike wasn't nearly the beer snob then

that he would grow up to be. "Sure, thanks."

After a few minutes, Pete returned with a baggie half full of mushrooms.

"Threw in a few for free." Pete said proudly.

"Sweet." Brian said.

Pete divided the piles into four somewhat even, lumpy approximations of each other. "Bon appétit," he said, grabbing his pile and shoving the whole mass into his mouth.

The grimace he made as he chewed them down attested to the fact of why people generally cook these in brownies. Considering they were living in a dorm and didn't have access to an oven, this would have to do.

Mike grabbed his pile and took a more manageable amount, chewing and swigging beer as he tried to wash the foul taste from his mouth. A little card playing and a beer or two later and the full effects of the psychedelics began to kick in. Mike began to feel that surreal detachment from reality. A ring of light pressure formed around his eyes. This was Mike's tell-tale sign he had crossed over into the realm of transcendentalism. The images on the playing cards began to take on mystic proportions and had no meaning whatsoever in the world of the sane.

"What game are we playing?" Mike asked Brian, who had completely broken out into riotous laughter.

"He doesn't even know what game we're playing," Brian said, grabbing his gut, tears streaking down his face. "Oh no!" Brian said alarmed. "Neither do I!" That got the whole room in stitches. Breathing was becoming difficult due to the excessive laughing.

For the next two hours Mike fluctuated between great introspection into the workings of the mind to pre-pubescent humor revolving around flatulence. Now that Mike contemplated the whole process, he thought tripping should actually be called 'skipping,' because that is what you did, you skipped from thought to thought.

Pete, in addition to being the person you should go to whenever you needed to get 'hooked up' drug wise, was also a fairly responsible young adult. He was one of three people on the entire floor who had not had his phone turned off yet. Thus, the knock on his door was not unexpected. Pete was a businessman and visitors were frequent. What was the surprise was who was at the door: Jenny Murphy. She was fodder for just about every wet dream in the building. That she lived on this floor was just bonus points. She was easily on every guy's short list for most attractive girl on campus. Sure, there were other beauties but she ranked high among them. At 5'7", jet black hair and riveting deep blue eyes, she was a vision.

The room which had been near raucous a moment before was now as silent as a convent at midnight.

"Hi Pete, can I use your phone?"

"Sure, come on in," the ever affable Pete told her.

She scanned the room looking at all of the occupants. As her gaze swept past Mike, he hoped that she couldn't read his mind full of all the lascivious fantasies that he had ever thought regarding her. The more he dwelled on it, the more convinced he was that she could do just that. Like his head was an open porno magazine and she was the centerfold looking out at him.

Jenny sat down on the couch next to Mike, the phone on the table next to her. Four guys tried their best to pretend not only that they weren't four and a half sheets to the wind but also that they weren't looking at her. It did not go very well.

Jenny got on the phone with her mother. "Hi Mom, yeah, everything is fine. I went down to WBCK today. Yeah, of course I applied for the internship." Jenny was now becoming self conscious that there was no other conversation going on in the room.

Mike, meanwhile, not having an outlet for his tripping mind, began to dive deeper and deeper into the hidden recesses of his mind, much like Alice down the rabbit hole. It was so dark and lonely in there. This was the point at which Mike realized that he had taken too strong a dose. That was the problem with mushrooms. There was no viable way to tell just how much one had taken. Sometimes one mushroom could send someone half way into orbit; at other times it could take half a bag for the same results. This seemed to be more of the former. Mike was concentrating so hard on not making an ass of himself in front of this goddess, he slipped. Holding his racing mind in check was like trying to hold a charging buffalo back with thread.

Jenny looked over at Mike. A look of horror and disgust appeared on her face as she spoke into the handset. "Mom, I've got to go," she said, hanging the phone up abruptly and quickly thanking Pete before she exited the room.

A foot long thread of drool hung from Mike's mouth and was pooling in his lap. The laughter from Pete, Brian and Dean as she left was good-natured, but it was way too late for Mike. His trip had soured. He made some excuse about going to the bathroom and never looked back. Mike was in a panic and he didn't know where to turn. He thought about going back to his room but was fearful that Pete would find him there. Mike hit the elevator button, praying to a God he didn't believe in to please make sure nobody else was in there. Having to share that tiny confined space with another human could send him over the precarious edge he was already barely holding onto.

For not being real, God really came through, the twenty-one story ride was externally completely uneventful. That all changed of course when you entered into the hyper-active over-imaginative super speed neuron firing brain of Michael Talbot. Sounds began to echo. Every time Mike moved his head, tracers formed in his vision. His sneakers sounded like tap shoes on the hard slate tiled lobby floor of his dorm.

"Outside, outside," he whispered to himself. Two co-eds walked past him giggling. Mike knew they knew he was messed up. It was easy to tell when someone was tripping. Their pupils were generally the size of small saucers. The laughs bounced around the edges of his mind. As he stepped outside the bracing breeze helped to reel his awareness in, but only temporarily. The tree-lined street he was on usually gave him comfort, reminding him of his boyhood home, but now the trees loomed ominously, their branches seeking to snatch and tear at the unsuspecting. The hallucinatory doubling of all imagery only added to the illusion.

Mike was damn near in a panic by the time he got to the massive student parking lot off of the south fields. Even in this state, Mike knew that he had had entirely too much to drink (and eat for that matter) to drive but the comfort of getting to his car could be just what he needed to turn this bad ride around. His 1976 Plymouth Fury looked like heaven, all in white resplendent with a red roof and red trim. He almost kissed the seat as he got in. Mike, however, was fearful to put the key in the ignition in case some extremely bad timing brought the campus police out to this deserted location. Mike would get a DUI for merely sitting there with the ignition on. If he went to jail in this state he'd never get his mind back.

"So much for putting music on," Mike said with a shiver.

For a minute all was well within, but like a mouse that burrows a hole through the sidewall of a house, stray thoughts began to first leak out and then chip through the wall Mike had erected. Structural damage ensued. Mike's meager defenses crashed in around him, and just as fast as he got in he got out. Mike took long breaths, believing that he had not been able to get enough air inside the car.

Mike found himself in a huge parking lot surrounded by cars, any one of which could be hiding a 7-foot clown with white face paint and a machete. The gravel he walked on was so loud he could barely think. He didn't realize, that was a good thing. Mike's heart was racing as he kept his head down, fearful to look at the trees. They were moving but it had more to do with the wind than Mike's bad perception. That mattered little at this point.

Back onto the slate tile of the lobby, thank God for muscle memory. He pulled his student ID out of his pocket and showed it to the security guard who took a cursory glance. Security was composed of students who would much rather be having a good time than any type of officiating, but money is money.

Mike got to the elevators where three other students waited. "Can't do it," he muttered, and immediately went into the stairwell. He soon realized the error of his ways as the echoes his psychosis was producing in that enclosed cement area now had their own echoes. Twenty-one flights up he went. The smell of sweaty fear pervaded his entire being. He poked his head out the door hoping nobody would be in the hallway. He rushed to his door and fumbled with the keys, happy to be back in his room without getting caught.

"Okay, its midnight now, when will Paul be back, he can get me down." The reality was that Paul wouldn't be coming home tonight, he was already in bed with his girlfriend and wouldn't be leaving those confines until sometime around lunch the next day.

Mike waited three minutes, almost an eternity when your brain was racing forty-two times its normal pace. "Okay, so how mad would Jamie's parents get if I called right now?" Mike had met Jamie's parents a few times already. They were alright, maybe a little stuck up but for the most part decent. The reality was they couldn't stand Mike. They were of the Blue Blood variety, old New England money, and could not see what their daughter saw in this working class man, a common laborer at that. Mike would have called Jamie's home but he didn't think he could handle the 20-second conversation with her parents it would take to get her on the phone.

Mike huddled up in the corner of his bed, arms wrapped around his legs, one dim light on. "I don't know how long I can do this," he told himself as he rocked back and forth.

THE PAST

Put quite simply because Mike's mother had told him so, he was a mistake. Mike had three older brothers and an older sister. His brother Ron, who was fifteen years his senior, was almost a generation past Mike. Not too many teenage boys want anything at all to do with a gurgling smelly infant, and with a sister as a buffer, Ron never found himself in the position of babysitter. The years went past, and Mike's early remembrances of his brother were few. He was basically some guy that stopped by to do his laundry while he attended college. Now there was no physical distance in the relationship, just the distance caused by the difference in age. They loved each other as brothers do, but there also was no closeness, no bond, beyond the normal family ties. That gap only seemed to widen as Mike came into his formative teenage years, and Ron was already married and fast tracking in the corporate world. They were brothers and nothing more. That would all change in Mike's sophomore year.

BACK TO THE PRESENT

Mike was quickly running out of options and sanity. He picked up his phone, hopeful that no one was on the other line, more specifically the girl that lived in the dorm below him. Mike and Paul were not part of the trio of responsible students on that floor that had paid their phone bill. Mike knew just enough to be dangerous; he had unscrewed the phone jack and spliced into another set of phone wires until he had found a pair that worked. It wasn't the optimum scenario and they had nearly gotten busted a couple of times, but they always informed whoever they were calling that they might need to hang up abruptly and to not talk to the 'crazy chick' that got on the other line. Mike's parents were a little dubious but they let it go. Ma Bell would catch on eventually but tonight they still had service.

"Hello." A groggy, just woken up voice responded.

"Uh…uh…hi, Nancy, is Ron there?"

"He's sleeping Mike, it's late."

"So he's there?" Mike asked desperately. The lifeline had been thrown overboard, now he had to hope someone grabbed it or he might be adrift for a long time. Mike heard some fumbling with the phone being handed over and then someone, probably Nancy, getting out of bed.

"Mike?" Ron started it as a question. The last time Mike had called Ron, scratch that, Mike never called Ron. They just weren't on each other's life radar except around the holidays and Christmas was still two months away.

Mike was going to start with some chitchat but he didn't think he could pull it off, not this incapacitated. "Ron, I'm in some trouble."

Mike could hear Ron sit up, his cobwebs of sleep quickly dusted away. "I'm listening," Ron said.

For the next forty-five minutes Mike proceeded to tell him everything that had happened that night, from the mushrooms to the hot girl, to the drool, to the evil trees and the walk up the stairwell, finishing up with his now hiding out in his room. Ron patiently listened to his baby brother rattle off a tale of a bad trip, offering words of encouragement along the way. "Just stay in your room, Mike. It will be over in a few hours."

"Will I be the same? Will I be sane?"

Ron laughed. Mike instantly felt at ease. "You'll be fine and even a little wiser for the wear."

"Ron, thank you," Mike was nearly in tears. "I didn't think I was going to make it there for a while."

"You weren't planning on doing anything stupid, were you?" Ron asked with concern.

"No, nothing like that, I just, I've just never felt this way. I am completely fucked up."

"Good night, Mike."

"Good night Ron, thank you."

"Any time."

'Any time' ended up being twenty-eight and a half

minutes later. "Hello," came Nancy's voice again. To her credit there was not a hint of menace.

"Uh hi, Nancy, is Ron there?"

"Ron..." Nancy said, handing the phone to him.

"Hey Mike," Ron said. "What's up?"

"Still fucked up," Mike told him.

This time it only took a half hour to get Mike away from the abyss of despair.

"You alright this time?"

"Yeah, I think I'm over the hard part."

"You call me if you need anything, you understand?"

"I'm okay now, I think."

"Alright then, good night again Mike."

"Good night, Ron." Mike did feel better. It only took one more call before Mike was back onto fairly even ground. He would not sleep at all that night and when Paul showed up the next afternoon he found Mike sitting on the mattress, his back up against the wall.

"Holy crap, roomie, you look like shit!' Paul exclaimed.

"Yeah, but I feel much better than I look."

And that was it. It was that act of kindness alone that pushed Ron from distant brother to trusted friend. The bond had only intensified as the years went past. Mike could think of no place he would rather be when the walls of Little Turtle fell than at his brother's side.

AFTERWORD (OR AFTERTHOUGHT) -

JOURNAL ENTRY 31 -

Almost decided not to put this in my journal but once I figured I was going to I had no room so I put it here at the end.

So when I was sitting in the hospital at Camp Custer (obviously before Eliza came a calling) doing my best to not go insane, strapped to a bed because apparently I'm a bad patient, this assh..., I mean guy comes up to me, says he found my first journal. I almost shit myself, which given the circumstances wouldn't have been a memory worthy incident. I'll relate how the encounter went.

Just so you know, I was almost asleep at the time when the guy grabbed my foot.

"Hey are you Mitchell Tulbert?"

"What?" I asked coming out of a drug induced stupor.

"Mitchell Tulbert, are you him?"

Now normally I won't give my name to anyone who didn't know me, it's that whole paranoia thing. But I was pretty heavily morphined up and I didn't have all my faculties. "I'm Michael Talbot."

"Yeah that's what I meant. I've been looking for you."

Now it's never good news when someone you don't know is looking for you, it usually revolves around a warrant.

"Are you from the IRS? Fast Tax said that I could claim any kids under the age of 18 living in my household and Henry is as much one of my kids as any of them. I mean he never talks back, hardly ever complains. Sure, he smells like wet garbage sometimes but that's sort of his appeal."

Assh... I mean Guy says, "No, I'm not from the IRS. You have a kid that smells like wet garbage?"

"Long story," I told him and would have waved an

arm to disperse my words if I wasn't restrained.

"No, I was foraging for some food out in Colorado, in a place called Little Turtle. Not much left except one row of housing and the sign to the complex."

My heart at this point is thudding in my chest.

"Gotta admit man, coming across your place saved my life. We were running out of everything, food, clothes you name it. So I'm rummaging around in what I guess was your office."

Why do I feel violated?

"Sure did have a lot of Red Sox stuff, was a Philly fan myself."

"Of course you were," I said, urging him to keep talking.

He looked at me sideways and then kept going. "Man, you had more MRE's than we could carry. Sat there for a week fattening up on them. I looked over your books too. You had a lot of zombie fiction, wasn't really in the mood to read any more about them."

Couldn't blame him there at all.

"Then I come across your journal. That was some informative stuff. You sure did have a lot of grammatical errors and what not."

"You do realize it was a journal right?" I asked him, and he nodded in reply.

"Yeah but it even looked like you made up some words."

"I'm sorry Ass… I mean Guy. I was struggling to survive at the time. I was just trying to get a point across anyway I could. Didn't really have access to a dictionary or a thesaurus."

"Yeah, but couldn't you have cleaned it up a bit?"

"Dude, what are you, an English professor? Don't read it if it upsets your delicate constitution. Just give me the damn thing will you!"

He looked down at his feet. "Sorry, I can't."

I was boring holes through his head with my eyes.

"We used it for kindling somewhere outside of Kansas."

"So how the hell did you track me down and for what fucking reason? To let me know I might have used 'there' instead of 'their' or I used one too many commas? Do you see a tweed sweater with leather patches on my elbows?" I was pretty much screaming at this point.

BT moved his privacy curtain over and eyed the man. "Talbot, you want me to kick his ass?" he said menacingly.

Douche…, I mean Assh ..., I mean Guy backed up, having got a full look at BT.

"No, he's fine. As soon as he clarifies a couple of things he's leaving on his own."

Guy again looked over nervously at BT. Even in traction the big dude could impose fear in a badger.

"Well…well, um your journal said you would be going back east and when I ran into this place (meaning the base) I thought that maybe you might also be here, so I started asking around."

"Wow, now isn't that just my luck. Tracked down by a critic," I said, and BT laughed.

"He's giving you shit about what you wrote in a private journal? What an ass," BT echoed.

"You'd think I was charging him," I said. BT and I both started laughing like loons. The guy left in a huff sometime during our outburst.

If you find this journal could you please not use it for kindling I would greatly appreciate it.

Check out these other titles by Mark Tufo

Zombie Fallout

It was a flu season like no other. With fears of contracting the H1N1 virus running rampant through the country, people lined up in droves to try and obtain one of the coveted vaccines. What was not known, was the effect this largely untested, rushed to market, inoculation was to have on the unsuspecting throngs.

Within days, feverish folk throughout the country, convulsed, collapsed and died, only to be re-born. With a taste for brains, blood and bodies, these modern day zombies scoured the lands for their next meal. Overnight the country became a killing ground for the hordes of zombies that ravaged the land. This is the story of Michael Talbot, his family and his friends. When disaster strikes, Mike a self-proclaimed survivalist, does his best to ensure the safety and security of those he cares for. Can brains beat brain eaters? It's a battle for survival, winner take all!

Zombie Fallout 2: A Plague Upon Your Family

Zombies have destroyed Little Turtle, the Talbot's find themselves on the run from a ruthless enemy that will stop at nothing to end their lineage. Here are the journal entries of Michael Talbot, his wife Tracy, their three kids Nicole, Justin and Travis. With them are Brendon, Nicole's fiancée and Tommy previously a Wal-Mart door greeter who may be more than he seems. Together they struggle against a relentless enemy that has singled them out above all others. As they travel across the war-torn country side they soon learn that there are more than just zombies to be fearful of, with law and order a long distant memory some humans have decided to take any and all matters into their own hands. Can the Talbots come through unscathed or will they suffer the fate of so many countless millions before them. It's not just brains versus brain-eaters anymore. And the stakes may be higher than merely life and death with eternal souls on the line.

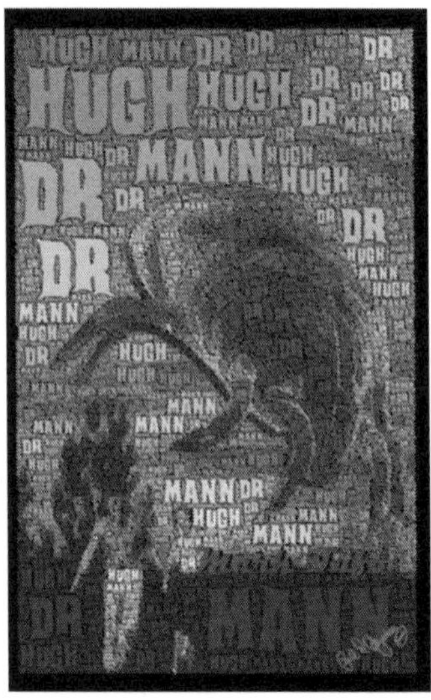

Dr. Hugh Mann – A Zombie Fallout Prequel 3.5

Dr Hugh Mann delves deeper into what caused the zombie invasion. Early in the 1900's Dr. Mann discovers a parasite that brings man to the brink of an early extinction. Come along on the journey with Jonathan Talbot is bride to be Marissa and the occasional visitations from the boy with the incredible baklava. Could there be a cure somewhere here and what part does the blood locket play?

Zombie Fallout IV: The End…Has Come and Gone

The End…has come and gone. This is the new beginning, the new world order and it sucks. The end for humanity came the moment the U.S. government sent out the infected flu shots. My name is Michael Talbot and this is my journal. I'm writing this because no one's tomorrow is guaranteed, and I have to leave something behind to those who may follow.

So continues Mike's journey, will he give up all that he is in a desperate bid to save his family and friends? Eliza is coming, can anyone be prepared?

Indian Hill

This first story is about an ordinary boy, who grows up in relatively normal times to find himself thrust into an extra-ordinary position. Growing up in suburban Boston he enjoys the trials and tribulations that all adolescents go through. From the seemingly tyrannical mother, to girl problems to run-ins with the law. From there he escapes to college out in Colorado with his best friend, Paul, where they begin to forge new relationships with those around them. It is one girl in particular that has caught the eye of Michael and he alternately pines for her and then laments ever meeting her.

It is on their true 'first' date that things go strangely askew. Mike soon finds himself captive aboard an alien vessel, fighting for his very survival. The aliens have devised gladiator type games. The games are of two-fold importance for the aliens. One reason, being for the entertainment value, the other reason being that they want to see how combative humans are, what our weaknesses and strengths are.

Follow Mike as he battles for his life and Paul as he battles to try and keep main stream US safe.

Timothy

Timothy was not a good man in life being undead did little to improve his disposition. Find out what a man trapped in his own mind will do to survive when he wakes up to find himself a zombie controlled by a self-aware virus.

Please look also for:
the story ‘**My Name is Riley**’ published in the Undead Tales Anthology by Rymfire books!

Follow Riley an American Bulldog as she struggles to keep what remains of her pack/family safe from a zombie invasion.

Made in the USA
San Bernardino, CA
12 December 2012